W9-DAV-547

BACK FROM CHAOS

Book One of

EARTH'S PENDULUM

*For Brooke & Michael
Good Friends
Forever
Love*

iUniverse, Inc.
New York   Bloomington

Back From Chaos

Book One of Earth's Pendulum

Copyright © 2009 by Yvonne Hertzberger

All rights reserved. No part of this book may be used or reproduced by any means, graphic, electronic, or mechanical, including photocopying, recording, taping or by any information storage retrieval system without the written permission of the publisher except in the case of brief quotations embodied in critical articles and reviews.

iUniverse books may be ordered through booksellers or by contacting:

iUniverse
1663 Liberty Drive
Bloomington, IN 47403
www.iuniverse.com
1-800-Authors (1-800-288-4677)

Because of the dynamic nature of the Internet, any Web addresses or links contained in this book may have changed since publication and may no longer be valid. The views expressed in this work are solely those of the author and do not necessarily reflect the views of the publisher, and the publisher hereby disclaims any responsibility for them.

ISBN: 978-1-4401-5290-0 (pbk)
ISBN: 978-1-4401-5292-4 (cloth)
ISBN: 978-1-4401-5291-7 (ebk)

Printed in the United States of America

iUniverse rev. date: 7/17/2009

BACK FROM CHAOS

Book One of
EARTH'S PENDULUM

Yvonne Hertzberger

ACKNOWLEDGEMENTS

This endeavour would not have been possible without the support and assistance from a number of special people. I would like to thank each of them.

During the writing process I relied heavily on support and feedback from my spouse, Mark, and friend Thomas. They believed in me when my confidence flagged.

My readers also deserve special thanks: Angie, Grace, Janet, Kathleen, Lyrra, Noah, Pretty, Ruth and Tish. You are all the best.

Contents

LIST OF CHARACTERS:

Earth: source of all life, sentient

CATANIA (cat-**an**-yah):
Cataniast (cat-**an**-yast), defeated lord
Marja (**mar**-yah), only surviving member of his line
Brensa (**bren**-sah), her lady in waiting
Nellis (**nell**-is), second lady in waiting, expecting first child soon
Mikost (**mee**-kost), Nellis' husband, stable hand
Keisha (**kay**-shah), Marja's mare
Wilnor (**wil**-nor), aristocrat, plotter

BARGIA (**Bar**-geeah):
Gaelen (**gay**-len), second son of Lord Bargest, now lord of both
    Catania and Bargia
Lionn (**lee**-on), Gaelen's elder brother, now dead
Klast (klast), trusted spy for Bargia (also uses name Mirral when
    under cover)
Argost (**ar**-gost), advisor to Gaelen
Janest (**ja**-nest), advisor to Gaelen
Sinnath (**sinn**-ath), advisor to Gaelen
Grenth (grenth), advisor to Gaelen, head of military
Marlis (**mar**-liss), Sinnath's wife
Wendan (**wen**-dun), Janest's wife
Naila (**nay**-lah), Grenth's wife
Messalia (mess-**al**-yah), schemer, believed to be seer
Liethis (**lee**-thiss), true seer
Kerrissa (cair-**iss**-ah), Sinnath's mistress
Grinth (grinth), justice
Gorn (gorn), spy
Rellin (**rell**-in), mercenary, ringleader
Gurth (gurth), Farl (farl), Rellin's men

Lotha (**loath**-ah), midwife
Simna (**sim**-nah), prostitute and friend to Klast
Ornan (**or**-nan), traitor
Norlain (**nor**-lain), innkeeper's wife
Haslin (**haz**-lin), innkeeper
Liannis (lee-**an**-iss), unborn seer

LIETH (leeth), Demesne to west
Wernost (**wer**-nost), lord of Lieth
Merlost (**mer**-lost), his son and heir

GHARN (garn), Demesne to east of Catania and north of Bargia
Rand (rand), Klast's abuser as a boy

1: VICTORY AND CAPTURE

Marja clutched her small jewelled dagger with white-knuckled fingers. She crouched in the corner, pressed tightly behind the door of the privy, willing herself invisible. The rough wood at her back pricked her through the light linen of her gown, and the muscles in her legs threatened to cramp from holding herself rigid. Her heart raced with terror. She knew if they found her she was dead, or even worse. She had heard what soldiers did to women, especially young, comely ones. Her beauty would not serve her now, nor would her rank as daughter of the ruling house. She gripped the dagger tighter. *They will not take me. I will not suffer that. I cannot.*

She suppressed the impulse to gag from the reek of burnt buildings and charred flesh. Even the usual stench of the privy was preferable to this. She tried in vain to blink away the smoke that filled every space and burned her eyes. Her nose tickled, and she fought the urge to sneeze or cough. Any noise might give her away.

Mercifully, she no longer heard the screams of the women and children. The last span or so had gone quiet except for the muffled sounds of men putting out fires. She could make out only the occasional shouted order from a soldier. She hoped to Earth that meant it was over. Perhaps she would escape after all … if she could stay hidden until dark. She knew a back way out but could not safely get to it. They might see her crossing the hall if she left her hiding place now. Too many enemy soldiers still moved about. *Keep still. Do not give yourself away. Wait,* she repeated to herself, over and over, like a hypnotic chant.

Marja's body jerked in a spasmodic shudder as she recalled again the chaos that had wakened her at dawn. The Bargian army was well-trained and well-armed. They had successfully taken her father's army by surprise, by hiding in the forest only half a day's

1

ride away and slipping close under cover of darkness. Had her father not scorned the advice of his advisors to guard the city more vigilantly, his people might not now be paying the price of his madness. The thought filled Marja with a moment of fury. Why had he not listened?

Marja wondered how Cataniast's informants had convinced him that the rumours of a planned invasion were false. Somehow they had persuaded the suspicious autocrat that the Bargians wanted to finish spring planting before coming to take Catania. Who had managed this clever misdirection? Had the Bargians bought off her father's informants?

Marja knew that many in Catania would be pleased to see the House of Cataniast fall. A pall of fear, suspicion and secrecy had hung over his court for years. She had watched many merchants and shopkeepers flee Catania, and she could not blame them. Some had gone to Bargia, the enemy who now bore responsibility for their defeat.

Only spans earlier, a servant had come running to Marja, crying, "Flee, my Lady. We must go now!" Marja had refused. At the girl's tearful request for permission to go, Marja had given it freely. She saw no purpose in keeping the terrified maid with her.

How could things have come to this so quickly? She had heard Northgate fall before midday. The sounds of clashing swords, the shouting of soldiers and the cries of men dying had reached her even where she hid deep within the castle.

Marja knew that her father had fought at Northgate and had heard from the frantic shouts of the retreating men that he had been slain. After that, the invaders soon breached Eastgate and Southgate and overran the city. Those who had not been killed had fled. Now she waited alone for the death that surely awaited her.

When she could remain still no longer, Marja decided to venture into the main hall. If she could make her way to the hidden passage across the balcony it could lead her to freedom. She had just emerged from her hiding place when she heard the trudge of boots on stone and froze again.

"Looks clear. Klast, you take that side and I will check this one."

The words drifted up to where Marja stood rooted to the floor. Heart pounding, she found her feet and quickly shrank back into her corner. *Here they come,* she thought. *I waited too long.*

Marja made herself as small as she could as she listened to the man climb the stairs and check the room beside hers. Then his steps became louder as he entered her chamber. She held her breath as the steps went silent for a moment, then resumed in the direction of her privy. Her eyes went to the dagger still clenched in white-knuckled fingers. She could not have pried her hand open even if she had wanted to. Her fingers seemed welded shut. *Do I have the courage to do it? I must! I will not let them use me. I cannot.*

Suddenly, the door swung out, and he stood before her.

Marja froze and caught a look of surprise crossing the soldier's face as he halted. She took in his air of authority, his broad shoulders and the wavy, straw-coloured hair, now lank with sweat and tied out of the way. He wore well-cut breeches, a tunic in the blue and yellow of Bargia, now stained with blood, and he carried a fine sword. Marja recognized her assailant. Here stood the son of Lord Bargest, the spawn of the enemy who had brought this upon them.

He raised his sword for the killing blow. It felt like she watched from a distance, the motion slow and dreamlike, as if time had stopped. He halted, arm in midair, seeming to assess the woman before him.

What did he see, she wondered? Could he see her determination, her terror? Could he see past the dirt and smoke to her expensive clothing, the heavy gold chain still about her throat, the jewelled earrings and the hands unused to rough work? Would he understand that she was someone of rank? Would her russet hair tell him he beheld someone from Cataniast's family? Would it make any difference?

Slowly, he lowered his sword's point to the ground. Time resumed its normal pace. His face showed no signs of battle frenzy, but his eyes remained alert, and she knew he would not hesitate to use the sword if he needed to. Marja remained crouched, unwavering, dagger ready, defiance now faltering as confusion pierced her mental armour.

"I am Lord Gaelen of Bargia." He spoke formally, but she did not miss the weariness in his face and tone. "There is no point in resisting. My army has defeated you, and this demesne is now mine. Give me the knife. I will offer you my protection, at least until I decide how to proceed with the governance of this land. You will not be harmed. Surrender your weapon. Enough have died today."

This could not be true. He could not let her live. Marja smelled deception. "A daughter of the House of Cataniast will not be allowed to live!" she spat back. "You cannot take that risk. My people will rally behind me and continue to fight." Marja remained where she stood, knife just below her left breast, poised for the killing thrust. "I will not be taken to be used as a gaming piece and disposed of later."

She watched Gaelen raise one eyebrow slightly at her declaration. Then he rubbed his free hand across his eyes and pinched the bridge of his nose. "Lady, you mistake me for someone without honour. I have given my word that you will not be harmed, and I am a man of my word. Surrender your weapon." He hesitated. "I cannot assure you will not be injured if you force me to take it from you. But I have seen enough blood today and have no wish to spill yours. We will speak later on your fate. Unlike your lord father, I am not a man who acts in haste."

Marja did not miss the fleeting expression of anger at his mention of her father.

When she did not move, he added, "I gain nothing from spilling more blood. I swear, you and your people will be treated justly. Now give me the knife."

Something in his weary tone and the unwavering stance, feet planted apart, broke through Marja's defiance. What had he said? Honour? Justice? Her people? Could she trust him even so far? Could she yet effect some good for her people? A small flicker of hope ignited. With it, the iron will that had sustained her crumbled. Her arm lowered, and the dagger fell out of her hand to the floor.

Just as her knees buckled, he caught and steadied her, kicking the knife away in the same fluid motion.

Her legs responded woodenly as she let herself be led through the castle, his hand firmly holding her arm. His grip told her escape was out of the question. Marja's mind ran in useless circles, no longer able to hold a coherent thought.

As they emerged from the castle, she waited numbly in his grasp. Some part of her heard him hail one of his men.

"Argost, secure that dwelling to use as headquarters. And find two men you trust and have them report to me immediately." Marja felt more than saw him jerk his head in her direction. "We have a hostage, Cataniast's daughter. She must be closely guarded. She speaks with no one. No one must be told we have her. Have the guards find a defendable room upstairs out of sight. Take her there, and find her something to eat and drink. Find Sinnath and Janest. Set up a table and chairs in the front room. We will meet as soon as everyone can get there. Order must be established here without delay."

Later, she would remember and wonder at the ease with which Gaelen assumed the role of lord. It appeared as though he had been born to it, though she knew his older brother, Lionn, should have inherited. Gaelen was the second son.

Marja listened with only one ear. Then she remembered who she was and that her people were watching her. She forced her head proudly erect, squared her shoulders and took in the destruction around her. Anything made of wood looked burned or charred. Only stone remained unmarred, though it, too, had been blackened by soot. Windows stared empty-eyed, their glass and oiled skins broken or burned. Doors swung from broken hinges. Torn rags and broken crockery littered the near-empty square.

Struck by the devastation, her resolve faltered. She stumbled, momentarily overcome, when he marched her past a large group of women, children and old men standing silent. They waited, packed shoulder to shoulder like sheep, guarded by soldiers who held swords ready. She recognized defeat, fear and despair in the bowed heads and slumped shoulders. Eyes stared at her with the blankness of those who had seen more horror than they could comprehend.

Her people, or what was left of them. Earth, what would happen to them now? And what of her family? Her brother, sister-in-law and their three little ones? Had any survived? The questions screamed in her head, but her tongue remained silent. Now was not the time. She must assess her situation, must think carefully about her next move. Everything depended on it. Everything!

Marja put up no resistance. She let them march her into the mansion, up the stairs and usher her into a small bedroom. Though she saw signs of scorching, the furniture here had not burned. She took in the sliced featherbed, empty of linens. No doubt they had been stolen. But a chair still sat intact, and with the last shred of dignity she could muster, she allowed herself to be lowered into it.

She watched dully as the guards checked the window and privy, determining that escape was impossible. They stationed themselves, one outside the door, the other inside, to watch her. In spite of their weariness, they appeared alert and ready to act.

Neither spoke a word to her before or after the door closed. She eyed the guard who remained inside. He avoided her gaze, and she concluded that information from that quarter was unlikely.

After some time, a young soldier with a bandaged arm entered and set a tray on the small table beside her. Marja stared absently at the tray of stale bread and cheese and ewer of water, knowing she should at least drink but could not find the energy to reach for the mug.

The sound of voices raised in anger seeped through the door, and she realized she ought to try to make out what they were saying. That, too, was too much effort. It occurred to her that she ought to be forming a strategy to deal with her captors, seeking a way to escape. Those thoughts warred with the desire to know what had become of her family, what the future would hold for her people.

Finally thirst won out. She put aside suspicions of poison and made herself drink. The water tasted fresh and cool and revived her somewhat. She forced herself to gnaw at some bread and cheese and take another swallow of water.

The enormity of her situation threatened to overwhelm her, but she knew her survival depended on staying focused. She recalled how she had recognized Gaelen. Just over a year ago an offer had come from his father, the now late Lord Bargest. He had sent a proposal of alliance. Part of the bargain had been a request for Marja to be joined with his second son, Gaelen. Gaelen himself had delivered the offer, and she had watched him from a curtained balcony. Her father had ordered her to stay out of sight, so Gaelen had not been aware of her scrutiny. Marja felt a moment of anger as she remembered that Cataniast had refused the offer. He had regarded it as a ploy, a way for Bargia to gain a foothold in Catania and subvert his authority. It had cost him his life and his demesne. A wave of rage washed over her, then as quickly ebbed. She had not the energy to sustain it.

Marja wondered if that information could be used to her

benefit. So far Gaelen had kept his word. She remained unharmed and relatively comfortable. What plans could he have for her? Now that he had successfully taken Catania, would he see any advantage in keeping her alive? How could she convince him it would be prudent to court her goodwill? Could that be parlayed into concessions for her people? She knew letting her live would fly in the face of traditional thinking, which called for the deaths of all members of conquered ruling families. How would her position be affected if other members of her family still lived? If so, what difference would it make if they were still at large, or if they too had been taken prisoner? So many questions. So little information.

The spans passed, and eventually her exhaustion, coupled with the rise and fall of the voices below, lulled her into a fitful doze. Her chin dropped to her chest, and her hands fell lax in her lap.

2: LIETHIS

Far away, Liethis, true seer to the court of Bargia, most powerful seer on the One Isle, bent double in pain. She sensed Earth's sending, and in her trance understood that Her essential Balance had been disrupted, that Earth was in pain. She sank to the ground and rocked back and forth, moaning, her hands clasped tightly over her temples, eyes squeezed shut.

Earth's sending filled Liethis with a deep foreboding. She could not block the pain from the fire and blood searing Earth's crust. She understood that all the peoples on the One Isle would face hardships until those wounds healed; until Her people had atoned for Her wounds.

Whenever Earth convulsed in pain, Her people inevitably suffered with Her. Famines, plagues, crop failures, harsh winters or greater strife between the demesnes would follow, until Balance was re-established. Peace and prosperity depended on restoring Earth's Balance. Seers such as Liethis saw, in the cycles of destruction and healing, evidence of the symbiosis between Earth, source of life, and Her people. When the people lived in harmony, Earth supplied them with what they needed. But when they acted with violence and destruction, such as in times of war, She had not the power to sustain Her support. Each needed the other. Thus swung the pendulum of Balance.

Liethis wept, and as her tears watered the soil in empathy, Earth withdrew Her sending. Liethis could again raise herself up, the pain now a shadow of its former force.

Liethis sent her awareness out in the direction of Catania, where she knew Lord Bargest had taken his army. Where the energies of Lord Bargest and his heir, Lionn, should have been she could sense only a void, and she knew they had not survived. But Gaelen's orange light burned strong. She could sense that Bargia had prevailed, and that Gaelen had assumed power. Now both Bargia and Catania would look to him as Lord. It gave her some hope.

Another presence came into her awareness. A young woman. Ah! Cataniast's daughter. Her aura burned a calming blue. Liethis' spirit lifted. This woman would be good for Earth, her blue a complement to Gaelen's orange. She would be one to keep an eye on. She, too, would have a role to play in Earth's recovery.

Liethis became aware of yet a third aura. This one she recognized as Lord Bargest's most trusted spy and assassin, though she did not recall his name. His colour was green shot with red. Over it hung the grey film of a spirit hiding from itself. Its loneliness made Liethis sigh. His quest would be hardest of all ... and the most important. But try as she might, Liethis could not see if he would succeed. She suspected even Earth did not know.

She sent her awareness further, in search of the members of the council. Janest's aura remained a steady, bright blue. Argost's also still burned blue, but his was deeper, almost indigo. Good, they both lived. Gaelen would need them. Then she searched for Sinnath's glow. She always had difficulty reading him, as he seemed to keep his aura shrouded. Now she could barely detect him. A murkiness covered his dark green; that worried her. Liethis sighed as she wondered at this. Why did he need to keep himself hidden?

"Oh, Earth, let me see what must be done. How can the Balance be restored?" Liethis was unaware that she whispered her plea aloud.

Bone weary, as such sendings always left her, she stumbled into her bed and fell into a restless sleep.

3: A BEGINNING

Gaelen strode briskly through the city to take stock of the wounded and assess the damage. He stopped beside an injured soldier being tended to one side of the square. "What is your name?"

From long habit, Klast followed close behind, his keen eyes missing little. Over years of practice, Klast had honed his powers of observation. He had mastered reading the subtle signs that gave away others' attitudes better than anyone else on the One Isle. He had also developed the tricks of posture and dress that allowed him to blend so well that people often did not notice his presence or forgot he was there. These skills had made him invaluable to the late Lord Bargest in his duties as spy and assassin. Now he transferred his loyalty to Gaelen, as Lord Bargest's rightful successor. As Gaelen passed among the people, Klast took note of their reactions to relay them later to Gaelen.

The soldier's pinched face managed a flash of gratitude. "Garent, my lord."

"Garent, we will have you moved to a cot as soon as may be. I thank you for your service to Bargia today. Your efforts have helped secure our victory. You will receive whatever care you require." Gaelen pressed the man's shoulder and went on.

Gaelen commended several more for their bravery and loyalty, touching each one briefly. He made a quick survey of the prisoners, then proceeded to the new temporary headquarters to meet with his advisors.

When he reached the meeting room, Klast saw that Argost and Sinnath had scavenged a table and four chairs. They met Janest at the door. Gaelen paused to look at the makeshift meeting room.

"Jonath," he called to the young soldier who had brought the food for Marja, "Find us some bread and cheese, and some decent wine. And fetch Rhiall and Gheal to guard the door. Allow no one in."

"Yes, my lord."

Gaelen smiled when the lad returned with four goblets and a knife as well. "Well done. Now get some rest. We will be long before you are needed again."

Klast watched Jonath square his shoulders at the praise and leave with a quick, tired grin and more spring in his step.

From his post at the door, Klast admired the way Gaelen took command. He had the makings of a strong leader.

Gaelen looked around the room before starting. "My friends." He paused again.

Klast watched the trio's eyes turn to Gaelen and Gaelen meet each one in turn. His composure remained strong and steady. Klast knew the best son had come to power. Lionn would not have been an effective leader. Klast observed the others surreptitiously as Gaelen spoke.

"We have achieved a great victory today. All of you have my gratitude. Now, bring me up to date on our losses and our current situation. We must act quickly to assert our dominion. Argost, report on the North quarter. I hear there was heavy fighting at that gate."

Argost was a tall, spare man, ramrod straight in spite of his late middle years, with a full head of iron grey hair and a beard which he kept trimmed short.

Klast felt relieved that Argost had not been killed or wounded. The man had a reputation for solid decisions, and Klast expected Gaelen would rely on his steady presence. Of all the advisors, Argost could be relied on most for keeping his head when emotions ran high. Lord Bargest had often taken his advice when the others had disagreed. Those decisions had never failed him.

Klast watched Argost stroke his beard with one hand, a familiar gesture when deep in thought, somehow calming.

When Argost looked up again, he answered Gaelen with firm

confidence. "As you say, my lord, fighting at that end was heavy. We lost some good men." He looked away a moment as he passed his hand across his mouth and stroked his beard, looking once more at the table. Then he raised his head and met Gaelen's gaze again. "My lord, I regret to report that your lord father was among the last to fall. We were fighting at close quarters, and they cut him down before we could reach him. He fought courageously, four at once at the end." Argost's voice caught. "None live to tell of it. We made certain of that."

He cleared his throat and went on. "The area is secure. Fires have been put out, and all surviving locals wait in the city square, under guard with the other prisoners. Our men fought bravely and with discipline. I am pleased to report I saw very little looting and no killing of women or children, except those who used weapons to resist."

"Thank you, Argost. You have served my father bravely and loyally." Gaelen turned to Sinnath. "Sinnath, you had Eastgate."

As the traditionalist of the group, Sinnath had always provided the word of caution in council. Gaelen's father had considered him a personal friend. But Klast thought he lacked vision. He would have made a great advisor to Lionn, but Gaelen liked to find fresh solutions to problems. Sinnath's resistance to change might prove a thorn in Gaelen's side.

Sinnath was even taller than Argost, thin to the point of austerity. He kept himself meticulously groomed, and usually managed to look fresh even after a long day in the saddle. Even now, with no opportunity to refresh himself, Sinnath's tunic bore only a few small blood stains.

Klast considered his own poor appearance and Gaelen's blood stained tunic, and wondered how Sinnath managed it. Such tight control spoke of compulsiveness.

"Yes, my lord." Klast noted the studied way Sinnath steepled his long fingers and leaned forward as he spoke, seeming relaxed, but Klast saw tension behind the pose.

Sinnath spoke with the smooth, resonant timbre of an orator. "We were led, as you know, by your brother Lionn. His horse threw him early in the battle, and he was severely trampled in the melee. We did reach him and tended him off the field, but he died of his injuries only spans later. I am sorry."

Gaelen nodded acknowledgement at the thin smile of regret Sinnath gave him.

Sinnath continued. "The battle grew more disorganized after that, and we lost too many men. But the area is now secure, and the prisoners rest with the ones taken at Northgate." He leaned back, and Klast noted that his eyes went to the table. They no longer met Gaelen's as he went on.

"I am ashamed to say the men grew overzealous in their revenge. Discipline faltered after your brother was taken from the field. I have the names of those who failed to restrain themselves. They will be dealt with according to your wishes." His eyes came up to meet Gaelen's again. "Order has been restored and fires put out."

"Thank you, Sinnath. We will speak of this later." Klast could tell that this news disturbed Gaelen by the sudden tightening in his mouth and the deepening furrow between his brows. He understood why. Bargia had strict laws forbidding rape or kill-ing those not engaged in fighting. He watched Gaelen regain his composure as he turned to Janest.

"Janest, what news of the south and west? I understand they were poorly defended."

Janest, although a man of middle years, was the youngest of the group. He had the distracted appearance of someone who always had some worry on his mind. But when it came down to it, Klast knew, his observations and insights always showed that he had missed nothing. He had a habit of running his hands over his hair when he tried to gather his thoughts. Klast smiled inwardly as he saw the familiar gesture, before Janest raised his eyes to Gaelen and began to speak.

"That is correct, my lord. The west is bordered by the ravine and deep woods beyond. It is of little use to travellers and so has no gate. The wall is defence enough. Southgate was poorly defended. Most of the resistance came from the citizens. Once they realized they had no hope of rescue, they took it upon themselves to destroy as much as they could. Fire damage there is heavy, but most fires are now under control. If we get the rain that threatens, it will put out those remaining." He shook his head in regret. "The deliberate firing of the buildings caused a great deal of confusion. Some citizens escaped over the wall. I have been informed by one of my best men, Brean, that the wife of Cataniast's heir had hidden in one of the warehouses with their three young children. None came out alive. Her husband also fell in the fighting there. Those citizens remaining alive wait with the other prisoners."

"Thank you, Janest. Do any of you know what became of Cataniast himself? I heard rumours he met his death outside Eastgate. Can you confirm this?" Gaelen looked about the room.

"My lord." Gaelen turned as Sinnath spoke up. "I did not see how he died, but his body lies with the others of the family, on display in the market square. That leaves only one member unaccounted for. His daughter. She must be apprehended to prevent her from rallying resistance."

Gaelen smiled. "She will not cause trouble my friends. I have her upstairs under guard. That is one of the situations we must discuss before we leave this room."

Klast saw Janest raise his brows in surprise and Sinnath furrow his in concern. Argost looked interested but showed no surprise, as he had known of her arrest

Gaelen sobered and went on. "The other urgent business concerns how we will handle the prisoners and what steps we need to take to restore order and to establish Bargia's dominion."

"Gentlemen," Gaelen continued, "the events of today have

placed both demesnes in greater chaos than anticipated. As second son, everyone assumed that I would never rule. Some will attempt to undermine my position, saying that I have not the skills, that I am not trained to take command. This is false." He scanned the room as if to make sure he detected no disagreement.

As Gaelen's strategy and arms tutor, Klast felt a moment of pride, hearing the firm voice and confident manner with which Gaelen kept command of the room. These men were all many years his senior. Yet Gaelen left no doubt who was in charge.

"Yet, my enemies will use it to portray me as unprepared for leadership. If any of you have questions about my right or ability to rule, I wish to hear them now so they may be discussed openly. To govern effectively, I need the pulse, not only of the people, but especially of you, the members of my advisory council. I am confident I will allay your fears so that we move forward with one mind. I need to know I can depend on your allegiance." He paused and met each man's eyes again. "I expect you may have concerns about my leadership. Speak freely, here and now. We have not the freedom to delay this. Too much demands immediate action. There will be no reprisals for your candour."

Janest spoke first, with the other two nodding immediate agreement. "My lord, we have all known you many years, I from your earliest childhood. You have my full allegiance as rightful lord, both of Bargia, and now of Catania. If we have any concerns in the future, I hope that we may speak with you as they arise."

"Argost? Sinnath? You are in agreement with Janest?"

"I am, my lord," each asserted earnestly.

Gaelen's shoulders relaxed slightly, and his tone became lighter. "Then I know I am well served. Let us proceed."

"I have thought hard on our situation here. With no male of my family remaining to act as lord's representative in Catania, it will be necessary to take measures that may not be popular or understood. Some might regard them as weak or ill advised."

Klast noted that each man watched Gaelen with rapt attention.

"I have decided to allow all prisoners and citizens who will swear allegiance to me to return to their homes and their duties, even in the castle."

Argost nodded immediately. Janest looked surprised, then resumed his usual eager expression. Sinnath frowned as if deep in thought but made no move to respond. Klast watched closely as Gaelen went on. This was the important part of the meeting. Gaelen would want to hear how each man reacted to his decisions.

"They will be permitted to pick up the pieces of their lives as best they can with no fear of settling scores." As Sinnath started to shake his head Gaelen added smoothly, "I realize some cannot be trusted. That is a risk we must take."

"Your duties will be to make sure those of influence, both in my forces and among the surviving Catanian merchants, advisory council, traders and others, understand and support this. They must be led to see that it will be to their benefit, both politically and financially. I suggest this may be accomplished by moving among the people and listening, ready with convincing arguments. We must appear to be in all places at all times. And we must demonstrate that loyalty will be rewarded."

Gaelen paused and let his words sink in before he continued. "I command all looters to return stolen booty back where they found it. They will receive full amnesty for three days to do so. We especially need to restore the castle, as it will be the centre of government. After three days, anyone found in possession of stolen goods will be dealt with as a thief, in accordance with the law. Any who dispute that they have rightfully earned these goods may bring their arguments to you, Argost. I appoint you governor and justice of Catania."

Argost's eyebrows rose and fell back again, as he nodded his acceptance.

Gaelen continued. "Those who argue that they deserve compensation due to losses suffered may take their case to you as well. You will decide if compensation is warranted and what form that will take. I have no time to deal with individual grievances."

Gaelen hesitated, and for the first time, Klast heard a hint of uncertainty creep into his voice. "These decisions will establish me as honourable, resolute and even-handed. You will report to me in two days, and we will see if changes need to be made. Do you all understand thus far?" Gaelen paused as he watched each man take in what he had proposed.

When Argost smiled with apparent satisfaction, Klast noticed that Gaelen took a deep breath, and his shoulders relaxed again. He wondered if any of the others noticed. If they did, they did not show it.

Klast applauded Gaelen's choice of Argost for governor. The man's sound judgment and even-handed manner would go far to instil confidence and trust among the Catanians.

"My lord," Argost declared, "I will do so with pleasure. This plan shows good judgment. It shows both strength and decisive action at the same time. It tells the people that you may not be trifled with but that you will be just." His voice rang with confidence, and he nodded vigorously in agreement.

The replies of the other two were less enthusiastic. Klast watched Janest take his time, run his fingers through his hair, then nod slowly. "I understand what you are trying to accomplish, my lord. It may work. I have no better suggestions, so I will stand behind it for the time being. Time will give us the answers. If I see this begin to undermine your authority, I will speak with you again."

Sinnath looked concerned. "My lord, I recommend a stronger stance. Perhaps this idea will work with our own soldiers, but I fear it may send the Catanians a message that you are too lenient and can be bent to their own ends. To let them return to their homes at no further cost may suggest rebellion has no consequences."

"Thank you Janest, Argost … Sinnath, I appreciate your opinion. However, this was not a decision made carelessly. The Catanians are not rebels who committed treason. They are families who were going about their normal lives, until we invaded them. I believe that, given the opportunity, they will gladly return to the lives they knew. I trust they know the difference between the actions of armed men and those of regular citizens. They will see this as recognition that we understand it as well. It will make them more compliant to my rule. Are you willing to support me on this until we see results?"

"Of course, my lord. Have I not just sworn allegiance?" Irony crept into Sinnath's voice as he added, "Did you not say we were to express our concerns openly?"

Gaelen laughed wryly, shaking his head. "You are correct, Sinnath. Thank you for reminding me. I will need such reminders again I am certain. One does not step into the position of lord knowing all one needs to know."

They all relaxed, and Klast knew Gaelen had passed his first test.

"My next decision may please you less," Gaelen began again, studying each of them carefully before continuing. "Be assured I came to this plan after carefully considering all possible outcomes. I will not be swayed on this and will need your full support, until I satisfy you that it is sound."

Klast came even more alert. Gaelen had not had time to inform him of what was coming. The amnesty was already making the council sit up and take notice. From the look on Gaelen's face, he was aware that they might have a hard time swallowing the next announcement.

4: A RISKY CHOICE

The wary faces around the table told Klast that this test might be a more difficult one. He could see that Gaelen knew it too. But Gaelen went ahead as though he expected full support.

"The prisoner we hold upstairs is Cataniast's daughter, Marja. You will recall that, just over a year ago, I was sent by my lord father to Lord Cataniast to negotiate an offer of alliance. You also know that a section of that agreement stated that his daughter would be sent to join with me, to become my wife. The joining would add strength to the alliance. You will recall that Cataniast refused. I intend to extend that offer again."

Klast watched shock and concern flash on both Sinnath's and Janest's faces. Argost showed little surprise.

Gaelen paused before continuing. "Not only is she most comely," he flashed a quick, mischievous grin, then sobered again, "she has shown remarkable courage and intelligence. If I can persuade her to agree, I am of the opinion that it will help convince the Catanians they will be treated fairly. And so they will be less likely to plot rebellion."

All three looked ready to speak at once. Gaelen forestalled them, raising his hands. "My friends, let me anticipate your concerns. The woman is beautiful and intelligent. Some will claim I have been bespelled, that she holds me in thrall."

Sinnath nodded.

Gaelen forged on. "Only time will allay those superstitions. Some will say I am merely swayed by the wiles of a beautiful woman, and these, too, will choose to see her hand in my decisions. The doubters will need to wait and see. The challenge lies in keeping her safe long enough to convince them. Objections will be most prevalent among our own people. The Catanians will be slower to see ill in this."

Gaelen grew even more solemn. "I charge all of you with

convincing the superstitious that there is no spell at work. While I do not deny that I find her desirable, you know me well enough to understand I will not be swayed from what is best for Bargia."

"Consider the alternatives." Gaelen gave them no time to interrupt. "We could keep her as a political hostage. That may have some small impact on the response of Catanians to my authority. Some of our own will also see it as a means to bend the Catanians to our will. Yet she is a woman, and so cannot inherit power. There is no male child for whom she could act as regent. That makes her value as a hostage unconvincing. As well, we need to consider the costs and efforts required to keep her comfortable and under constant guard."

Gaelen searched the three silent faces, each intent with concentration. Klast knew this development would challenge each one. Gaelen turned, as Argost leaned forward and placed his elbows on the table, hands loosely linked ahead of him, his expression thoughtful but unreadable. Janest, too, had leaned forward, eyes wide and eager, like a child about to be handed a fascinating new toy. Sinnath, in contrast, leaned back against his chair, his arms crossed, his expression masked.

"We could execute her." Gaelen tossed his hand in the air dismissively, indicating this would not be considered seriously.

Klast watched Sinnath's expression become even grimmer, and he leaned further away from the table, as if to distance himself from this discussion, as Gaelen continued.

"That would satisfy the traditional thinkers, unable to adapt to change. It will also antagonize her people and make them less inclined to comply with my authority. Besides," now Gaelen grinned a little sheepishly, "I have given her my word she will come to no harm."

As Gaelen paused to gauge their reactions, Klast saw Sinnath grimace. Janest still seemed to be waiting for more, and Argost looked even more thoughtful, if such a thing were possible.

Gaelen took a deep breath. "On the other hand, what do we gain if she becomes my wife? First, it courts the goodwill of her people. They may take a wait-and-see attitude to Bargia's rule. We gain time to establish order and dominion. We earn a reputation for sound leadership that can be trusted and for myself as a man of honour. Secondly, it gives her people hope of an heir with Catanian blood. That will appease some."

All three faces had become unreadable. No one seemed ready to interrupt now. They listened intently.

"Since we do not have a male member of my family to take up governance in Catania, it is important to avoid plots against Bargia for as long as possible. I have considered that the lady may use her position to plot against the House of Bargest for vengeance or power. We will need to be vigilant. Yet it is a risk we must take. I am convinced she is astute enough to see that her agreement will be in her people's interests as well as her own. It will rest with me to convince her to my proposal and to have her swear allegiance to me publicly. I am aware that guiding our own people to see the merits of this plan may prove difficult. Thus it is of the utmost importance that you three stand behind it and convince others to do so as well." Gaelen stopped. "Now I am ready to hear what you have to say."

"My lord, this is madness!" sputtered Sinnath. "She will surely betray you. You will wake one night with a knife in your heart! To take the enemy to wife! I beg you to reconsider!"

Janest's answer was more circumspect. "Do you have a plan if she refuses? And a way to make sure she does not betray you if she does agree? This is a dangerous path you tread, my lord."

This time it was Argost who appeared more hesitant. "It could be beneficial, as you say, my lord, but I, too, am concerned for your safety. Even if she produces an heir, she could still find a way to rid herself of you and act as regent for your son. Have you thought on how to ascertain her intentions and secure her allegiance?"

"You know that I cannot do so. But I am well-versed in reading the signs in speech and body that will give clues to her state of mind. And I will have Klast with me when the agreement is presented." He looked at Klast, who acknowledged him with a short bow. "You all know Klast's reputation for smelling deceit. I will proceed as carefully as I may.

"There are risks, serious ones, but I am convinced they are worth taking ... and necessary." Gaelen smiled grimly. "I will also make sure there are no knives in the bedchamber ... at least until I am more confident of her compliance." He rose from his chair. "I leave you now to present her with my offer. Talk among yourselves, but only in this room. Sleep on it tonight. We will speak of it again tomorrow. Until then it remains with you alone. No one must hear of it. Good night, my friends."

Gaelen took the tray with some of the remaining bread and cheese and the pitcher of wine with him. He beckoned to Klast waiting by the door. "Come with me."

Klast heard the clamour of the men's voices as soon as he closed the door. As they headed for the stairs he heard Gaelen sigh. This would make a thorny hurdle for them. Yet he believed Gaelen was right. It was the best way ... if she would agree. They trudged together up the stairs to the room where Marja waited.

When he reached the top of the stairs, Gaelen turned to Klast. "My friend, I will not be swayed from this. I will need you to be my eyes and ears. I wish to present the proposal to Lady Marja immediately. Come. Watch and listen."

Klast nodded, keeping his face inscrutable. "As you wish, my lord."

At the door Gaelen told the young guard to wait at the bottom of the stairs. "We must not be disturbed. This may be a long interrogation." He repeated this to the guard sitting in the room.

5: CAT AND MOUSE

Marja woke from fitful dreams to the sound of Gaelen's instructions to the guards. By the time he entered the room, she had remembered where she was and come fully awake and alert. *Here it comes. This is where it will be decided.*

As she straightened herself up, she became aware of how stiff and sore she felt. The day's privations, and sleeping upright, had taken their toll. While she listened to Gaelen giving orders to the second guard, she took the opportunity to take a long drink of water and a bite of cheese. She needed her strength. Who knew when the next meal would come?

She studied Gaelen as he turned and barred the door with his free hand. He looked grey with weariness and appeared to hold himself erect with a sheer effort of will, feet planted firmly apart. He wore the same clothes as when he had taken her captive, spattered with dried blood, covered with dust and reeking of smoke. His hair hung in lank, greasy laces, escaping their thong. Even so, she thought, he made an impressive figure, with a natural air of confidence and authority.

And who was the coarse man with him? she thought as Klast placed himself with his back to the door. He looked vaguely familiar. Why?

Marja had a small advantage. At least she had rested. And this was not the elder Lord Bargest, nor even Lionn, the heir intended, but the second son, one who had never thought to come to power. Perhaps she could use that knowledge to her advantage. She watched as he set the tray on the table beside her. Then he pulled the second chair over and set it down facing her.

He studied her silently for a moment, then scanned the room, letting his gaze rest on the empty bed. "My apologies, lady; I had thought the bed ready with blankets and pillow. I regret you were unable to rest more comfortably."

"That would certainly have made what you intend more comfortable for you," she replied acidly, to test his reaction.

Gaelen sighed deeply, shaking his head, and lowered himself into the second chair. "Lady, I know not what you expected my intentions to be, but I assure you I find rape distasteful. I gave you my word that you would not be harmed."

She remained still as he poured wine into the goblets, then raised his eyes to meet hers evenly. "You may choose," he said, "so you will know it is not poisoned," and waited for her to take one. "It is passably good wine, one of your own. Please, it will fortify us for our negotiations. They could take some time."

Marja took a sip. It was good. Somehow they had found a cask of Catania's second best. She took another swallow, watching him silently, gauging him, searching for signs of weakness. So far the only one that struck her was his exhaustion. It was now well into the night. The battle had begun at dawn, and he clearly had not rested at all. Yet his eyes looked alert and purposeful, and he had himself well under control. There would be no hasty actions taken. She was safe, at least for the moment. She needed to take care not to drink too much … and to watch to see if he did. In his current state it would not take a lot to affect his judgment. That could work either for or against her. She shook her head as he offered her the platter of food.

Marja remained silent, watching him cut a slice from the cheese and tear off a chunk of bread, taking the time to chew it before he began to speak.

"What I am about to say will not be what you apparently expected. Let me recall you to last spring. At that time, my lord father sent a delegation to negotiate an alliance with your father, Lord Cataniast. I was part of that delegation. We hoped to strengthen trade and, of course, to be able to call on the forces of Catania for assistance in the event that we were invaded from the west by the Handosh. Included in that offer was the request that you become my wife, to strengthen our ties. Those negotiations fell through, and no alliance was formed. Tell me, did you know of the offer?"

"Yes, I did."

"If your father had agreed, would you have come willingly?"

"That is of no consequence now. The alliance was never formed."

He grew thoughtful for a moment. When he answered, his voice betrayed his anger at that decision. "True. Yet we acted in good faith. It was unfortunate that Lord Cataniast did not trust our intentions. I hope that you do not share his penchant for seeing plots where there are none. Forgive me if this offends you. I am too weary to play games. The outcome of this discussion will have consequences for both our peoples, and we have but little time."

Against her better judgment, she had to ask. She could not wait any longer. "You speak of my father. I know he was killed. What do you know of the rest of my family?"

Gaelen shook his head regretfully. "I am sorry, lady. None survived. My men have seen the bodies."

Marja's voice broke. "Even the children?"

"Yes, lady. They hid in a building that our soldiers fired and were overcome by smoke, along with their mother. Your brother was cut down in the fighting. You are the last of your line. I regret being the bearer of such grave news."

"I see," she whispered, lowering her head and squeezing her eyes shut to stop the tears. Alone. Just as she had suspected. It was up to her now. She looked away, fighting to regain her composure. She must not break down. She would have time to mourn later.

When she finally turned to face him again, he ventured, "Lady, I know something of what you feel. I, too, lost a father and brother today and am the last of my line. While I believe it was none of your doing, I also lost my mother, a sister, a brother's wife and his infant son to assassins a year ago. Your father sent those assassins after our failed negotiations. That was the reason for our attack today. All this is the fruit of Cataniast's faithlessness and suspicion. While I feel sympathy for your losses, you must understand the necessity of our retaliation. Such an act of aggression could not go unanswered."

Marja heard this with stoic silence. She had known of the assassinations. It had been her father's misguided attempt to prove his supremacy. Those of his family and inner circle had grown increasingly aware of the madness that drove him to such extreme measures, and which precluded any attempts by others to form alliances. He had also executed two close advisors who had the temerity to point out that such actions were unwise, accusing them of treason. In the last few years, any who wished to live learned to tread carefully.

Marja had been willing to join Gaelen when the offer came. She had seen it as a way to escape the air of wary mistrust surrounding all who lived under Cataniast's scrutiny. Or those who used his suspiciousness to manipulate him to their own advantage. Her father's madness had increased over the last years, fuelled by whisperings from those who recognized they could use it to increase their own influence and power. The castle had become a bleak place where no one smiled. Celebrations had ceased, and visitors avoided coming. Cataniast's reputation had spread, in spite of efforts to conceal it. Marja knew that many had feared knowledge of it would incite others to invade. When the attack from Bargest finally came, it had not surprised her.

Yet Marja held her peace. To admit that her father had been mad would put her at a disadvantage. She must bluff it out. "Since you obviously feel justified, it leaves me wondering why I yet live? Would it not be more prudent to rid yourself of all members of Cataniast's family?" As an afterthought, she added scornfully, "My lord …" She paused, then asked, "What could you possibly gain by letting me live?"

Gaelen sighed again and passed his hand over his eyes,

pinching the bridge of his nose, just as she had seen him do when he arrested her. Marja felt a moment of triumph over his obvious discouragement. This was not going well for him.

Gaelen raised his head and met her gaze. "My lady, you are not alone in these thoughts. Even as we speak, my advisors argue this very point. Yet, I believe my reasons are sound. I will set them before you. Please hear me out, and think carefully before you answer. The futures of both our peoples may depend on your response. Your own may also be determined by how you answer. If my bluntness offends you, be kind enough to attribute it to fatigue. I have been a full day without rest and with very little food. Were it not so critical, I would have waited until tomorrow.

"Even as we speak, my men are setting a secure room to rights in the castle. You will be moved there, to wait in comfort and greater safety. I do not require your answer today. I will lay my plan before you as fully as possible and also explain my reasoning. Then I will leave to rest. You have until tomorrow to think over what I propose. We will speak again at that time, when I will require your answer."

And so, Marja listened, resisting the urge to ask for clarification or to interrupt with a caustic retort. She wanted to remember every word, to etch every nuance of tone and expression into her mind. She tried to memorize changes in his posture and face, however subtle. Gaelen's voice was low and flat as he laid out his proposal and reasoning. When he finished, after what seemed like a long silence, he rose and called the guards. As though unwilling to leave anything to chance, he and Klast both accompanied her as they escorted her to the castle. Marja experienced an instance of shock as she realized she had forgotten Klast had been present the whole time. How could she have done that? What kind of man could make himself invisible like that? The thought made her skin crawl. She vowed be more careful.

6: KLAST

In his usual fashion, Klast remained silent when they left Marja's new chamber, waiting for Gaelen to ask his opinion of her. Gaelen made him wait longer than he expected. When the question finally came, it showed just how much his new lord needed his support. He knew that Gaelen trusted him to be strictly frank. Gaelen had never wanted approval unless it could be given sincerely.

"Well?" Gaelen turned to him as they walked together and let the question hang.

Klast chose his words carefully. "She is strong and intelligent, not someone who can be swayed by pretty words. Your strategy is a good one, though not traditional, which will prick some. If the lady can be persuaded to your plan and agrees to join with you, you will have a useful ally. If she cannot be persuaded to your plan, she could prove a formidable opponent."

Gaelen nodded thoughtfully. "Thank you, my friend. Then we are of the same mind."

Klast studied Gaelen as he walked away. It seemed his young lord had aged ten years in the last day. The unexpected burden of lordship sat heavy on his shoulders. Yet Klast believed the best son had achieved that title. Lionn, Gaelen's elder brother and heir, while popular, had shown no vision. He had been unable to think beyond what tradition dictated. Gaelen, on the other hand, had always found original and clever solutions for traditional situations.

Klast gave his head an imperceptible shake as he recalled how he had come to serve Bargia over fifteen years ago. Now, his loyalty to the House of Bargia would never fail. He owed them his life.

7: KLAST'S STORY

Klast had entered the service of the house of Bargia in a very roundabout way. Born in neighbouring Gharn, his father, Nathis, owned a small tack shop close to the border of Lieth. Until the age of four, Klast enjoyed the love of family and the security of a quiet, if humble, home. All that changed when his mother died in childbirth, along with his stillborn sister. No relatives lived close by to look after Klast, and as the shop bordered the road out of the village, he did not have access to other children. He had to learn very quickly how to amuse himself.

While his father did his best, his work demanded almost all his attention. Klast soon knew to stay out of his way and not distract him with questions. Klast learned, mostly by trial and error, how to make porridge, feed their six chickens and gather and cook their eggs. Before he turned six, his father could trust him with errands in the village. By age seven Klast had the responsibility for the home, such as it was.

Young Klast spent much of his time silently observing. He began to pick up on nuances in a customer's tone, posture and facial expressions that his father missed. On more than one occasion Klast alerted his father to an unscrupulous customer. When his father came to realize this talent in his son, they developed a secret signal. Klast would scuffle his feet while he sat on the floor and hum a familiar tune as he pretended to play.

It was a lonely, hard life, but not an altogether unhappy one. That all changed when Klast was nine.

On this day, four youths looking for trouble crossed the border into Gharn, where they chanced upon Nathis' shop. Laughing, they pushed him around and ransacked his wares, sliced tack, defecated on new saddles and burned his tools in the fire pit. When Klast's father drew a knife to defend himself, they handily took it from him and killed him with it.

Klast came upon the murder just as he returned from the village with bread and meat. Hearing the laughter and clamour, he ran the last of the way home as quickly as he could. His father's last words to him were a hoarse, "Run, boy, run!" through the red foam between his lips.

Too late. Before he could turn away, one of the hooligans grabbed him by the tunic and held him aloft in a vice-like grip. He shook Klast, laughing, "Look what I found. A scrawny cockerel who thinks he is a rooster! What shall we do with this one? He can't be left to tell. Do we gut him? Or can he still prove profitable?"

They trussed him, threw him in front of the leader's saddle and returned across the border into Lieth. There they sold him to a man named Rand, known to have uses for young, pretty boys.

Klast hated his new owner. Rand was a tall man, slack from inactivity and doughy from self-indulgence. His skin always bore a sheen of sweat and grease, his cheeks and jowls shook when he spoke and his lips pursed wetly even when at rest. He proved to be a sadist who considered it a point of pride that he could make any man, boy, woman or girl weep. Fear aroused him.

It was for this reason that he soon lost interest in Klast. The boy quickly recognized what increased his captor's enjoyment and schooled himself not to react.

He observed the same arousal with others in Rand's menagerie, boys, girls and young men alike. He felt certain, too, that not all who disappeared from the place left alive. So he schooled himself to stony indifference. The less he reacted, the less Rand took interest in him.

When Rand realized that Klast could not be broken like the others, he hobbled him with ankle chains and made him his house boy. Klast became part of the furniture. All the while, he watched, learned and waited for the chance to escape. That opportunity did not come for more than two years.

During the nights, when Klast found himself alone in the

dark, he worked at his chain, until he wore one link so thin he was sure a good blow would sever it and he would be able to run.

Rand employed a cook named Klee, almost as twisted as he was, who entrusted him with the keys to the cells at feeding time.

Klast promised himself that, if and when the opportunity came to escape, he would somehow manage to leave the cells unlocked. He could not save anyone else, but perhaps some might still have enough courage to run.

On a midwinter evening Rand had a visitor. This Drell eyed Klast several times and eventually made an offer for him.

One last time, Klee called Klast to feed the others and handed him the keys. Here was the opportunity he had waited for. He left all the cells unlocked and calmly returned the keys.

Rand called him into the study and passed Klast a ragged, grey blanket and a pair of low boots two sizes too large and shoved him over to Drell with a cruel laugh. "He be a silent one."

Drell ordered Klast to lie down in the back of the open carriage and cover up with the blanket so he would not be seen. Klast scrambled in awkwardly, doing his best to appear spiritless. Drell fell for the ruse and did not bother to tie him but hauled himself up onto the driver's seat and took the reins.

When Klast deemed he had waited long enough, he managed to roll out the back of the carriage, the blanket still wrapped around him. He stifled a grunt of pain as he hit the road, and he made himself roll over in the snow until he bumped against the trunk of a tree. Only then did he lower the blanket from his head. The carriage had not stopped. Good. He took stock. The trees thickened to his right. He crawled deeper into the thicket and stopped under another tree to think. Darkness and the blanket of snow lent a stillness to the woods that Klast found comforting.

While he pondered his next move, he found a small rock, and with three sharp blows severed the chain that hobbled his stride.

The snow could prove a problem. His tracks would be easy to follow. Klast's only hope lay in finding a settlement. The presence of other people could be the only deterrent either man might heed. He tried to imagine what would happen when he did find others. Each scenario grew more terrifying than the previous one. It had been so long since he had been among ordinary folk. He was no longer a small boy. And he was wearing leg chains. Would they believe him, if he told the truth? Even if they believed him, would they want a wild youth with no apparent skills around? Or would they chase him out to fend for himself, alone in the cold? With each new thought Klast's fear grew.

The first rosy hint of dawn had begun to light the eastern horizon when Klast spotted a grey plume of smoke. Klast's stomach growled. People meant food ... but people also meant danger.

A cock crowed its wake-up call. Klast chose a shed at the outer edge that looked like it might be a smokehouse and made a dash for it. As soon as he slipped inside, he knew he had made a grave mistake. The shed also served as a winter storeroom for root vegetables, cheeses, milk, and hung meats. He had no sooner tucked himself into the darkest corner when he heard the voices of a woman and a man approaching. He could hear the last of the conversation clearly.

"Saevin, I hev some good sausages left to trade. You may hev those, and a quarter o' the old cheese fer the eggs and that big sack o' flour yer da' sent." The door opened and light limned the two in the entrance. Klast froze. His corner no longer hid him.

As soon as she spotted him the woman shouted, "Thief!" and made to grab him. Klast ducked away under her arm, but the young man with her still stood in the doorway and nabbed him before she could turn around. Klast struggled in vain. Saevin was twice his size and strong as an ox. Klast deflated and lowered his eyes in submission.

"What will we do with 'im, Missus?" Saevin asked.

Missus Larn poked him in the ribs, eyed him thoughtfully a moment and said, "Boy, ye hev not taken anything, hev ye?"

Klast shook his head, doing his best to look helpless and forlorn.

Missus Larn turned to Saevin. "Take 'im into the house. He looks near starved. I will feed 'im some while I think on what to do. Dinna let 'im get away, mind."

Missus Larn looked a woman in late-middle years, heavy set, with a round face and an underchin that jiggled as she spoke. Under heavy eyebrows her pale blue eyes sparked with keen intelligence, and her lips pursed as though whistling silently as she worked. She moved with the efficiency of long practice. A few wisps escaped the severe knot at the nape of her neck. She absently brushed them away with the back of her hand as she worked. Now she bustled about as though fussing for company. She placed a bowl of thick, hot porridge and a wooden spoon in front of Klast and bade him eat. Then she cut a generous slice from a round of cheese, placing it and a clay mug of hot cider beside the porridge.

The heat from the stove after the bitter cold he had endured all night, the failure of his bid for freedom, the food and drink and, most of all, the rough kindness of the matron was too much for Klast. His shoulders started shaking, and soon his whole body wracked with bitter tears. Even his gnawing hunger was no match for his misery.

Missus Larn shook her head slowly, studying Klast.

One of his boots had come off in the skirmish, and her gaze fell on his bare ankle. Klast heard her gasp at the manacle still there. Finally, she murmured, "Eat, boy. Ye can tell us who ye be after. Ye look ill used. There be a story here, I warrant. But it can wait 'til yer fed." She seemed to make up her mind.

"Saevin, go fetch the justice. He be needin' to hear the lad's story."

Klast started at that, spoon halfway to his mouth.

"Dinna fear, boy. I dinna aim to hand ye to a monster. The justice be a fair man. He be knowin' what be right." She nodded to Saevin to go.

Saevin brought the justice a span later. Klast had eaten his fill and sat with his feet soaking in a bucket of warm, salted water. Missus Larn had managed to remove his manacles. She had clucked over the raw, weeping sores there from Klast's winter walk and at the ropey web of scars from previous injuries. The water had stung at first, but by now the pain had melted into bliss. Klast wanted to stay in this woman's care forever and allowed himself a few moments to dream about it as sleep threatened to overtake him. The knock on the door brought him swiftly back to reality.

While Klast had no idea of it, this was his lucky day. He had wandered into Bargia, into the village of Ilonja, under the jurisdiction of Justice Grinth, a fair man who could not be bought.

The good missus put a mug of hot cider into Justice Grinth's hand and bade him take the chair Saevin had vacated. Then she recounted in great detail the events of the morning. When she finished, Grinth thanked her and turned his full attention to Klast.

"Now, boy, this is your chance. You have, no doubt, a revealing tale to tell. Tell it truthfully, and fully, and you may save yourself. Do not lie. I will surely know it. Then we will speak of what your fate may be."

Klast had assessed Grinth while he had spoken with Missus Larn. He could not mistake the keen mind that dwelt behind those grey eyes. Grinth was not a man to be trifled with.

Klast told his story tersely, leaving out many sordid details. But he did not lie. There seemed no point. These people would surely treat him no worse than Rand had.

While Klast spoke, he saw that Justice Grinth watched him closely.

Grinth seemed to be able to tell when Klast held something back. Finally, he looked at Missus Larn.

"Missus, what do you think? Will he slit our throats in our sleep? Rob us? Take up with criminals?"

Klast kept his face inscrutable.

"Or will he obey orders if given a chance?"

Klast held himself rigid and waited.

"I warrant 'e be no killer, Master Grinth. As for the rest ..." she trailed off with a small shrug.

Grinth made up his mind.

He gave Klast a hard look. "You will accompany me to Bargia Castle to be trained as a soldier. I will leave it to you what you wish to divulge of yourself. The only story the commander will hear from me is that I found you living by your wits and offered you this opportunity. Only Lord Bargest will hear your true past. He needs to know the risk he is taking."

The next came almost as an afterthought, but Klast was not fooled.

"I will have your information about Rand and his cronies checked." Grinth regarded Klast through lidded eyes.

Klast gave him no reaction. He kept the skills he had learned firmly in place, the same skills that would serve him so well in his role as spy. It would not be until much later that he would learn to kill.

Klast took to military training with a fierce intensity. Yet he never fit into the social life of the barracks but kept determinedly apart. His reputation as a strange loner without feeling grew.

Eventually, Klast was given individual assignments that required his particular skills. His unique abilities, coupled with his immaculate record, led to missions of greater importance.

Lord Bargest began to include him in private strategy discussions with his advisory council. It was one such meeting that led to his first killing. Lord Bargest had received intelligence about a traitor in their upper circles, a man of status who had the trust of the most influential members of the court. To prove his treason would be extremely difficult and would lead to rifts that could damage the security of Bargia. Lord Bargest charged Klast with bringing back proof of treason, and if treason was proven, to dispose of the traitor in such a way that no suspicion would come to Lord Bargest or his advisors. He fulfilled his duty and removed the threat.

Klast hated killing, but in each such assignment he clearly understood the need. Thankfully, the need did not arise often. He had learned very young to get by on little sleep. It was the only way to keep the nightmares at bay.

In time, Klast had earned the position of trust that placed him at the right hand of the lord of Bargia. His loyalty remained unassailable.

*   *   *

Now, he watched Gaelen assume the mantle of power as though born to it. Gaelen's actions had been decisive and well thought out, if somewhat unusual. Klast wondered how many of his advisors understood what it cost Gaelen to hide his uncertainty and keep up his appearance of strength. Klast understood. He had known Gaelen almost all his life. They had spent many pleasant hours discussing strategy, sparring in weapons practice, hunting and on lesser missions together as Gaelen came of age.

Klast could see through Gaelen's mask of confidence. Gaelen had desperately needed to hear that he approved of his current plan. If Klast had not supported it, Gaelen might have succumbed to the pressure from Sinnath and Janest. The council might have become divided, and Gaelen's control might have crumbled. But Klast had seen the value of Gaelen's strategy and approved it. His response to Gaelen had held nothing back. Gaelen needed a truthful supporter, and Klast felt honoured to provide it. He knew he would do whatever it took to keep Gaelen safe and in power. Bargia needed Gaelen. And Gaelen needed Klast.

So Klast slipped unnoticed through Catania, eyes and ears open, senses alert.

8: WHAT NOW?

The door had barely closed behind Klast and Gaelen before Argost, Janest, and Sinnath all began talking over each other. All three stopped at the same time, looked at each other and laughed at their own lack of discipline. A fine way for the most influential men of the land to conduct themselves!

Argost leaned toward the others, placing his hands on the table in front of him, and took the lead. "Friends, this has been a day of great changes. We have lost and gained a lord, won a battle and lost many good soldiers, many of them friends who leave behind families. We have added a demesne, passed tests and survived to talk about it. Our new lord is proving to be his own man. Given time and experience, it is my opinion that he will be a strong and able leader. Yet he is young and untried. He will need us sorely in the next months if he is to come into his birthright with his lands and authority intact, especially if he is to avoid rebellion in Catania. We have, all three, sworn to support him and to uphold his sovereignty. We must show unity before the people. It is critical we keep any questions and disagreements within our closed council. Can we agree on that much?"

Argost looked first to Janest, who nodded solemnly, apparently having come to the same conclusion.

"To withhold support for Lord Gaelen at this juncture would throw Bargest into chaos. He is the legitimate heir. That alone will buy time from those loyal to his father. They will wait to see what kind of leader he is before they consider treason. I have known Gaelen all of his life. I was his history tutor and taught him diplomacy. He has often sought unorthodox solutions, but they were always well thought out. He is a man of reason who will hear arguments from all quarters before making decisions. I also know him to be honourable. This scheme to take Cataniast's daughter to wife worries me. Yet, that alone is not reason enough to withhold support. I say we do as he requests. We owe him the chance to prove himself. And there is always the problem of who would succeed him. The alternatives strike me as most undesirable."

Sinnath sat back in his seat with arms crossed and a frown on his face. He had remained silent while Argost spoke. Now he leaned forward with the deliberate posture of a man about to make a formal speech.

"Friends." He paused and met the eyes of first Janest and then Argost. "You know me to be a traditional man. I am the one who advises caution, who argues for the known ways ahead of the untried. What you both say has merit. Gaelen is our right-ful lord. Therefore we owe him our allegiance. That is the way it ought to be, the way it has worked for hundreds of years. And so I pledge to obey my liege lord. If, at some time in the future, that is shown to be dangerous to our people, I might be persuaded to reconsider. At the current time, to disobey my liege lord would make me traitor, a decision I am unwilling to even consider. Yet this proposal to wed Cataniast's daughter does not sit well with me in the least. It goes against proven wisdom, and I fear it may be our undoing."

"We are agreed then to support Gaelen for now?" Argost drew the meeting to a close. When the others nodded agree-ment, he suggested they return to their encampment to sleep. "Tomorrow will be another long day, my friends," he said as he stood to leave.

9: HONOURED PRISONER

As luck would have it, the room chosen for her had been her own … was it only yesterday? Then she had been free to move about as she pleased. No one would have dared question where she went or what she did. She had been the lord's daughter. Yesterday, Marja had been the one giving orders. She had had ladies to wait on her.

She wondered how young, innocent Brensa, and cheerful Nellis who expected her first child, had fared. Had they escaped? Had they been raped or killed … or both? She shuddered suddenly at that thought. Was Nellis' man alive and still able to care for her? She could only hope they had found safety and remained well.

Now, she entered her own chamber as a captive. The irony was not lost on Marja. It almost made her weep. No fine clothes, no bath, no one to dress her hair or exclaim over her gown. No one to keep her company, laugh at her jokes or serve her tea and cakes. A prisoner behind a locked door. Forbidden to speak to anyone. Alone.

When the door shut behind her and the bar slid into the lock, Marja took stock. She could find not so much as a needle to use for embroidery to pass the time. Gaelen had scoured the room before he left to make sure there were no sharp objects and no possible means of escape. She recognized the bed as her own, but the pillows and blankets had been cobbled together from various sources. They smelled of smoke and were smeared with soot and grime, but they would serve their purpose. The mattress was straw, not the featherbed she was accustomed to. No hangings remained on the walls or draperies over the window slit. But a comfortable chair had been found, and a table stood in one corner. On it waited a tray holding a pitcher of fresh water and more bread and cheese, also a handful of dried apple slices and some butter and honey.

On a stand in the other corner a wash basin held a ewer of tepid water. There was even a sliver of soap. She picked it up idly to smell it … rosemary. She also found a brush for her hair but no polished silver disc to view herself in. Two cloths hung on a hook on the wall beside the basin, a small one for washing and a larger for drying off with. They had even laid a fairly clean night-shift across the foot of the bed. Someone had gone to a good deal of trouble under difficult circumstances to see to her comfort. She hoped to Earth it was a good omen.

When she opened her old chest at the foot of the bed, she was surprised to see that the looters had missed one of her old gowns. It lay crumpled in the bottom corner. While it smelled of smoke, like everything else, it looked clean. She would be able to make herself presentable tomorrow. That would help her appear stronger when Gaelen returned for her decision.

Suddenly the events of the day caught up with her. She felt weary beyond thinking. The bed seemed to call out to her. She knew she should be considering what Gaelen had told her, but her mind could not hold a coherent thought. To be able to think clearly, she needed at least a few spans sleep. She tried to remember … had he said he would return this afternoon or not until tomorrow? After all, it had been almost dawn when he brought her here. Surely he meant tomorrow. He had said he needed to rest, too. Yes, that must be what he meant. She could afford a few spans sleep.

She forced herself to strip down, wash, put on the nightdress and brush as much of the grime and dust from her hair as possible. It was a small attempt at control, to stave off complete despair. Then she lay down on the bed and fell quickly into a restless sleep. Her dreams were filled with blood, screams and fire. And of Gaelen trying to kiss her, then turning into a demon with hungry, leering eyes, attempting to devour her.

10: ROUGH JUSTICE

Sinnath faced the distasteful duty of punishing those soldiers who had raped or injured women and young girls. Discipline had broken, and now it fell to him to decide who would be punished and what form that would take. The most difficult part would be determining who was guilty. Men would be loath to inform on their mates. Victims would hesitate to come forward with what they would consider their ultimate shame and degradation. Mothers would cover their daughter's reputations as much as possible. Or go to the opposite extreme of making false accusations, especially if their loved one had been killed or maimed. Sinnath knew that disciplinary action needed to be swift and decisive, both to reinforce the laws within the army and to demonstrate to Catanians they would be treated fairly.

He decided that each soldier found guilty of rape would receive five lashes in the public square. One captain argued for leniency, claiming battle frenzy as an explanation. Sinnath quickly silenced him with the reply that others had not succumbed to battle frenzy, and that he had failed in his duty to maintain discipline in his men. He informed captains that they must round up the accused and advise them of their sentences. A captain's non-compliance meant demotion to regular foot soldier ... or dismissal.

"First, request that victims come forward and point out the guilty." He looked at Mesor, the captain who had protested, and gave him the names of the two men he had himself witnessed raping a young woman. "You will take these men, strip them to the waist, and tie the first to the post. The other will await his turn under guard. All soldiers not on patrol must gather in the square to watch. I want no further incidents of this nature."

Mesor stiffened with anger but said nothing.

"Now, Mesor!"

Sinnath eyed the other two as a scowling Mesor strode off. "If either of you know of others who are guilty, tell me now. Failure to do so will show me you are unfit to command. You will be demoted and take the lashes yourselves when it is found out … and it will be found out. These acts shame Bargia; they shame us all."

Both men shuffled from one foot to the other.

Larn cleared his throat. "There was one Glash in my company, sir. I have already dismissed him without pay. He is no longer here."

"I see." Sinnath waited a moment longer. "Since you have no further names, go among the Catanians and see if you can find any willing to come forward. Understand that I do not intend to believe every accusation. When we have gathered all the accused in the square, I will make it plain that each accuser must convince me of their claim. If I discover a soldier has been lashed on the basis of a false accusation, that soldier will be given the right to mete out the same punishment to his accuser."

He stood and regarded the two men again thoughtfully. "I find this as distasteful as you. But discipline must be upheld … I will see you in the square in two spans." He turned on his heels and strode away before they could protest. Inwardly, he sighed. Leadership could be a heavy burden.

When he returned to the square two spans later, a small crowd had gathered, Catanians on one side, soldiers on the other. Next to the post stood a group of eight guarded men, stripped to the waist, eyes on the one already tied to it.

Sinnath approached, lash in hand. Its grip was two hands long and made of tightly woven leather. From it sprouted five thongs the length of a man with knots tied into them at random spaces. Each stroke would both gash the skin and leave deep bruises.

The waiting miscreants eyed it, then quickly looked away and back at the first in line, no doubt imagining the lash on their own backs.

Sinnath considered. Who would he choose to administer it? He found Mesor, the captain who had protested, now studiously avoiding his gaze. "Mesor, take the lash from me."

Mesor took it, eyes blazing with suppressed fury. Sinnath added in a voice only Mesor could hear, "You will use proper force if you wish to retain your position. I will not tolerate disobedience, from you or any other soldier of Bargia." Then he looked out over the crowd, as Mesor, still glowering, took his place next to the whipping post.

"Hear me, people of Catania and Bargia. Your new lord, Lord Gaelen, like his father before him, has no taste for wanton cruelty. Even in times of war, Bargian law forbids misusing women and children. To those of you who have been ill used, Lord Gaelen sends his most sincere regrets. I am here to represent him in seeing justice done."

Sinnath went on to explain what he had told the captains, then continued, "These nine men you see before you stand accused of rape. Two I myself witnessed in the act. They will be the first to feel the lash. Seven have been accused by you. Is there anyone among you who wishes to retract their accusation? You know the punishment for lying. Speak now and no more will be said of it."

He watched one man shuffle forward fearfully. "Sir, my daughter knows not if ye got the right 'un. But she be used and still canna' walk. She lies abed. She be ruined." His voice rose as he became emboldened. "How can she be avenged if she canna' name the beast? Where be her justice, and mine?" Loud murmurs of agreement rose from the crowd.

Sinnath had his words ready. "People, I have offered all the opportunity to come forward. I am certain that no act went unwitnessed. If any man remains free who should stand among these accused, you must look to yourselves for that failure."

That brought more murmurs, more subdued this time.

He turned to the man and asked, "Do you wish to retract your accusation?"

The man blanched, let his chin fall to his chest, nodded his head, and mumbled 'no bloody justice' as he backed away into the crowd.

Sinnath nodded to Mesor to begin. The crowd remained uncharacteristically subdued for such a spectacle. Only two of the accused cried out. One had adamantly maintained his innocence, even after he had finished. Sinnath ordered his accuser to come forward. The older woman broke from the crowd and started to run away. She was quickly brought back and made to stand before Sinnath, facing the man who claimed he had done no wrong.

Sinnath turned to the woman. "You have accused this man of rape. He has received the lash based on your words. Convince me that justice has been done."

The woman apparently decided to brazen it out, seeing that there was no escape. She turned to Sinnath defiantly and shouted, "Yer soldiers be all the same. They all look the same. How can I tell? My daughter took 'er own life. She be attacked by three men. How can I tell if he be one of 'em? My daughter be dead and someone mus' pay. I got no one left. What do you care fer an old woman? What did yer men care fer my girl? Whip me if ye like. It willna bring her back. I care not anymore." With that, she spat at Sinnath before the guard could grab her.

The crowd seemed to hold its breath as Sinnath wiped off the spittle. He eyed the woman. After careful consideration he turned to the man who had suffered the lash. "Kars. You have been unjustly accused and punished. It is now your right to take from this woman what she took from you. The decision is yours. What is your wish?"

The woman continued to glare at Kars as he considered his decision.

Finally, Kars spoke. "Missus, I am truly sorry for the loss of your daughter." He turned to Sinnath. "Sir, I will not die of my injuries. This woman has suffered more than I. I give up my right to restitution." Then he squared his shoulders, failing to hide a wince, and once more faced the woman, who stood gaping in astonishment.

Sinnath smiled to himself. This ordinary soldier had done much to repair trust among the Catanians. He turned to the woman. "You may go. But if I hear you speak ill of my men I will mete out the punishment myself."

The woman's head bobbed convulsively in agreement as she hurried away into the crowd.

Sinnath turned back to the soldier. "You will receive an extra eightday's pay and may rest two days to heal your back. You have acted with wisdom and compassion. I will commend you to your captain."

11: MY LADY LIVES!

Marja had been escorted to the castle in darkness. Despite this, a few saw and recognized her. News that she lived spread like floodwaters and, as rumours will, grew to ridiculous proportions. Some had her in heavy chains, some near death from injuries. Others thought she was being tortured to get information and wanted to rescue her. A few even accused her of having plotted with Bargia to set up the invasion. When she did not reappear it was said she had been secretly killed. The tales grew with each span.

Brensa heard some of these rumours almost as soon as she and Nellis arrived at the castle. She was elated. It appeared their lady and friend lived! When Brensa had settled Nellis on her cot and could leave her for a few moments, she determined to find out what she could. Familiar with the layout of the castle, it did not take long to figure out that someone important was being held in Marja's old chamber. Two formidable looking soldiers guarded the door. They refused to answer any questions. So Brensa explained her relationship to Marja and begged the guards to tell Lord Gaelen. Just as she started to turn away in frustration at their stubborn silence, she spied Gaelen striding toward the room with three other men. Brensa gathered all her courage and fell to her knees in front of him. The guards immediately grabbed her from behind and pulled her roughly away.

Brensa cried out in panic. "My lord. Does my lady live? Please, I must know. I was her lady's maid. If she lives she needs me. Please, my lord, I beg you."

Gaelen held up a hand to forestall the guards. "What is your name, miss?"

"It is Brensa, my lord … and her other maid, Nellis, is also here," she blurted as an afterthought.

"Brensa, your loyalty and courage do you credit." Nodding

to the guards, he said, "Let her go. She will not harm me." He turned back to Brensa and studied her silently for a moment as if to make up his mind. "Brensa, your lady does indeed live and is unharmed. You have my leave to share that news."

As Brensa watched him turn to the door she curtsied deeply, relief almost buckling her knees. "Thank you, my lord. Will you tell my lady that Nellis and her husband also live?"

But Gaelen had already entered the room. The guards once more took up their positions. The three who had accompanied Gaelen waited outside the door.

Brensa turned and hurried to share the wonderful news with Nellis. Then, as Nellis urged her to do, she went back and waited in the hall several paces away for Gaelen to re-emerge. Frightened though she was, nothing would stop her from begging to see Marja. The wait felt interminable. But she would not fail her lady. Marja needed her.

At first the guards watched her closely. As time passed and she had not moved or spoken they relaxed and finally ignored her altogether. Eventually, the men who had arrived with Gaelen were invited into the room.

After two spans, but what felt like much longer, the three men emerged and marched off, one soldier holding a rolled leather document. The one who did not wear Bargia's colours looked decidedly forbidding. Brensa's worry increased at this. Had something gone wrong? What was happening to her lady? But the men did not even acknowledge her and strode in the opposite direction toward the castle entrance.

Waiting even longer for Gaelen to emerge was agony for Brensa. As time passed without any sign of him, she imagined all sorts of scenarios in which Marja was in danger, each one more dire than the last. The guards continued to ignore her. Then, just as she was trying to decide if she had the courage to approach the door, it opened, and Gaelen stepped out. Brensa almost fainted with tension.

Gaelen immediately noticed her still there. His mouth gave a small quirk, and he said, "Your lady waits inside. She has need of the services of an attendant. Go to her."

Brensa stammered, totally unprepared for this good fortune. She remembered Nellis also needed her and would not know what had happened. Why she blurted out her question she would never know. It was outrageous, unthinkable even, to press Gaelen's good will even further. It just popped out.

"My lord, what of Nellis? She is near her time and needs me too. May I go tell her first?" When she realized what she had done, her hands flew over her mouth in terror. He would think her disloyal. He would take back his invitation. Oh Earth, what had she done?

Gaelen turned back to her with a stern look. "Brensa, your duty is to your lady. If you are unable to perform your duty, I will find someone else." Then he saw the consternation on her face and relented. "Brensa, Nellis will be told of events. Is she having pains at present?"

"No, my lord." Brensa sobbed uncontrollably now. "Forgive me."

"Go to your lady. I will send word to Nellis. Loyalty to a friend is commendable, but remember in the future that your first allegiance is to your lord and your lady." Then, as Brensa nodded vigorously through tears of relief, he dropped the stern facade and broke into a grin. She thought it the most beautiful vision she had ever seen. In that instant, he gained her loyalty for life.

Before she rushed in to see her lady, she caught a glimpse of Gaelen as he turned and strode away with a smile on his lips.

12: SINNATH FACES A DILEMMA

Sinnath had already left for Bargia, with Janest and two companies of men, to prepare for Gaelen's return and for the transfer of power. Their task lay largely in persuading Bargians to accept Gaelen's strategies for Catania, his joining to Marja and the reforms that both would bring. A tall order indeed.

As they travelled through the forest that led back home they rode quickly, mostly single file. They had little opportunity for conversation. When not on horseback, Sinnath and the men ate cold meals and spent the short spans until morning rolled up in their blankets. But this gave Sinnath a lot of time to think. Those thoughts trod a dark path.

Sinnath left Catania a deeply troubled man. He felt caught between two incompatible traditions. The first was loyalty to his rightful lord. Until now, nothing could have induced him to even consider breaking his vows of allegiance. The second held that all members of a conquered ruling family must be eliminated so that they could not organize resistance. Gaelen had broken the second tradition.

Sinnath's reservations about Gaelen's marriage to Marja ran deep. Her father, Lord Cataniast, had been treacherous and suspicious. Sinnath found it hard to accept that any offspring would be different. As the adage went, an apple does not fall far from the branch.

He hoped he would find evidence of Marja's treachery before it undid Gaelen. He believed Gaelen's youth and inexperience blinded him to the woman's beauty. She must not find an opportunity to subvert the supremacy of the House of Bargia. For now, Sinnath decided he would be vigilant. Evidence would no doubt present itself, if he just kept his eyes open. Perhaps Gaelen could still be made to see reason.

So Sinnath kept his counsel and did not voice his misgivings to anyone along the way, not even to Janest. Janest had been a mentor to Gaelen for many years and could see no fault in him. He would not understand.

But Sinnath did understand the implications of his line of thinking. His loyalty to Gaelen's father had never wavered. He did not even think himself capable of treason ... yet, here it was. If he acted on his doubts that is exactly what it would be.

13: A WARY TRUCE

Marja had wakened to sun streaming directly onto her face. With no drapes to cover the window slit there was nothing to dim its effect.

The room faced south, so she reckoned the time to be just before midday. As soon as she realised that she had slept longer than she had intended, she roused herself quickly. Knowing that the crucial interview with Gaelen was almost upon her, she took care to dress and groom herself. With no silvered disc to see into, she had to rely on touch to style her hair, so she kept it in a simple knot. It was really too dirty to do more anyway. After drinking some water she made herself eat the stale bread and cheese that was left. The honey and butter softened the bread a little. Washing it down with more water took the edge off her hunger so she felt more revived and ready to face what was to come.

While she waited, Marja went over the conversation of the day before. Trust had been rare in Cataniast's household. She had learned to be wary of promises and appeals for her understanding. Now her situation demanded she make a choice … to accept on trust that Gaelen's offer was genuine … or to disbelieve him and see treachery in his strategy. Her training and experience told her she would be a fool to believe. Yet Gaelen's direct manner and detailed reasoning had an air of sincerity that she found hard to ignore. Today she must choose. The choice would affect not only her own life, but those of the peoples of both Catania and Bargia. Making political decisions had not been part of her training. Her education and upbringing had focused on needlework, music and managing a household. As a woman of rank, she had expected to be sent off to an arranged marriage. She would not have been consulted.

These thoughts turned over in her mind as she paced, wishing it were finished and at the same time wanting to flee from facing it. Part of her, the part that related to her old life, just wanted a bath, clean hair and her ladies to share romantic dreams with. Much as she tried to banish that ghost from her mind, she could not completely extinguish the childish longing for everything to be back the way it was. She felt like she was two people: the girl she could barely remember and the woman she had not yet become. And now, circumstance required that she make that leap on her own, with no one to guide her and no time to learn. Her heart raced with both terror and excitement.

After what felt like an eternity but was actually only a short span, the door opened, and the guards admitted a servant carrying a tray with ale, a bowl of hot stew and fresh bread. The aroma of meat and vegetables tantalized her nostrils. Marja's stomach growled in anticipation, reminding her how hungry she was. She made herself stop pacing and sat down. In very short order, she had emptied the bowl. Well, at least they did not intend to starve her. It tasted delicious.

When the servant returned to retrieve the tray she told Marja, "Lord Gaelen sends word that he will meet with you anon."

So … he was coming, and she had made no progress with her decision. Panic set her heart pounding. Her hands prickled for a moment with the rush. *How can I make such a decision without more information?* With a mental shake she chided herself. *Do you really believe you have a choice, silly girl? What you need to do is stay calm, listen, watch, and wait. Don't let him see how confused you feel. A way to salvage something will present itself. He said he would demand an answer, but surely there would be time for some discussion first, something that would give her the clues she needed.* She breathed deeply and forced herself to sit in the chair facing the door to wait, hands folded demurely in her lap.

One of the guards knocked and quickly opened the door to admit Gaelen. It closed immediately again behind him. Marja rose, ready to face him, as she heard the bar slide back.

Neither said a word for a long moment. She found herself

appraising him. How different he looked today from the weary soldier who had presented his plan to her. He made an imposing figure, standing half a head taller than most. He had bathed and shaved. His hair, which had been tied out of the way yesterday, now gleamed in soft, wheaten waves almost to his shoulders. He had donned civilian dress: woollen breaches of dark brown, a linen shirt covering his broad shoulders and over that a belted tunic of soft, tawny suede that matched the colour of his hair and brought out his amber eyes. His boots and belt shone. Around his throat lay his torque of office, his only adornment. The simplicity of it suited him perfectly. For a moment, Marja felt again the shiver of excitement she had experienced when she had first seen him over the balcony so long ago. Then she caught herself. That dream belonged to another life. This was the man who had helped to destroy everything she had loved. She must not act like a romantic young girl.

"My lady, I am pleased to see you looking much recovered from the privations of the last days. I hope you have rested and eaten well."

Marja took an aloof tone. "I have, my lord, though a bath would have been most welcome."

"I will have that remedied as soon as I leave. May I sit?" Gaelen asked.

"It is not for a prisoner to deny a lord a chair. You will do as you wish." She put more coolness into her voice than she felt and hoped it hid her nervousness.

Gaelen sighed. "Think of yourself more as an honoured guest, lady."

Marja resumed her seat, and Gaelen followed suit. She continued to regard him coolly as he continued.

"I have with me a document detailing my proposal. I hope you will agree to it." Gaelen indicated the sheaf of scraped leather he held in his hand. "Shall I read it to you? My scribe and two of my men wait outside to act as witnesses, should you agree to the terms."

"I am quite capable of reading it myself. All the women in my father's house were taught to read and cipher. We were not kept ignorant." Effrontery added to the ice in her voice. She hesitated before putting deliberate emphasis on, "My lord."

"Forgive me, lady. It seems I underestimated Lord Cataniast," he apologized smoothly, handing her the document.

"Indeed." Her hands remained steady as she took it, the last traces of tremor stilled by anger. She began to read silently. Gaelen made no attempt to interrupt, neither moving to explain, nor soliciting questions. She could feel his eyes on her, but this was her turn. She knew he could afford to be patient. He did have the upper hand after all. Soon she forgot him as she burned the conditions of his proposal into her mind.

"This seems just as you presented it to me. I am required to swear allegiance to you, to recognize you as rightful lord of both Bargia and Catania and to swear to uphold that right. In your turn, you offer me the position of wife and consort, and all the privileges that implies. Our children will become the heirs of both demesnes. As well, all citizens of Catania willing to swear allegiance to you may return to their lands and livelihoods with no penalties. Young men will be required to take training in your army and to serve in any campaigns you undertake. You swear to treat them no differently from the conscripts from Bargia ... This appears a generous offer, my lord, but I have some questions." Marja looked Gaelen in the eye.

"Speak. I will do my best to answer them."

"It strikes me that any agreement signed by a woman, who cannot, by law, hold power except as regent for an heir, may be deemed to have no legal value. Why are we playing this game when you may have what you want merely by commanding it? It strikes me that the choice you offer is really no choice at all, but merely a formality to gain my compliance."

Gaelen raised his eyebrows at this, then nodded, understanding dawning on his face. She could almost see him reassessing his opinion of her. Good. She wanted him to realize that she was no fool. She hoped he was learning not to underestimate her.

"Secondly, I need to know more about your intentions regarding the people of Catania," Marja went on. "You are our conqueror. That puts us at your mercy."

"My third question concerns my own position. At this time I am locked in a solitary room. I have no contact with anyone, no access to information about how my people fare and no one to keep me company or tend to my needs. If I agree to your plan, how soon, and in what ways, may I expect that to change? What is meant in your agreement by 'the privileges of wife and consort,' and how soon may I see those?" She waited with rigid poise as he considered his response.

"It is true, lady, that there are some, possibly many, who will say our pact carries no formal weight. But I swear to uphold it. As lord, no one may gainsay me. Time will bear out my wisdom in this. The naysayers will be won over. I am confident of this. Yet I cannot offer you more than my word to convince you." He paused to let her take this in before continuing.

"I intend to offer the people of Catania all the same privileges and responsibilities that I afford those of Bargia and rule them by the same laws, provided they swear allegiance to me. I will place some of my trusted men here, along with a contingent of soldiers, to see those commands carried out. Argost will head that group. I trust him completely to carry out his duties with wisdom and loyalty."

Marja kept her cool silence and let him finish.

"As to your personal situation, I must be candid. To give you full freedom at this time would put your life at grave risk, something I am not willing to do. I assume you understand the wisdom in this. Eventually, you will have all the freedoms and privileges a lord's wife may expect. I hope we may reach a level of trust that will enable me to discuss matters of state with you as a partner and advisor. I have already come to admire your astute grasp of politics. But that is for the future. For now you must remain under heavy, protective guard. We leave in a matter of days for Bargia. Before we do so, I hope to find two ladies to attend you. I have already made inquiries to that end."

When he was through he sat back and regarded her silently, appearing relaxed and confident. Marja wondered if that took as much effort as it did for her.

She considered her reply carefully. "I do understand the need for caution. For the rest I must rely on your word. So I have no choice but to agree to your plan. However, my continued allegiance will, in some measure, depend upon how you make good on your promises. I am not a fool, and I will not be your game piece, now or ever. Betray me at your peril." Her heart raced at her own audacity. To challenge a lord, especially one who could take your life with a mere word, was not prudent.

A look of profound relief came over Gaelen's face. He rose, saying, "I am pleased that you agree. With your leave then, lady, I will have my men enter to witness the signing."

Marja nodded, suddenly very tired.

Gaelen admitted the three others, who took their places behind him. The scribe, Erland, set ink and quill on the table, stood behind her and made to show her how to make her mark.

She waved him off, bristling with indignation. "I have no need of your assistance. I am quite capable of finding where I must place my signature."

Gaelen actually gave a low chuckle at this. "I think you will find the Lady Marja well educated, Erland."

Erland remained standing to one side as she took up the quill, dipped it in the ink and affixed her signature. Then she rose, and Gaelen sat to add his own.

A clever move, she thought. *It adds legitimacy to the document.*

Marja watched as Erland handed Gaelen his seal and held a candle flame to the yellow wax. They all witnessed him place his official stamp on it. It was done. No ceremony had taken place. No official had spoken words over them. Yet they were joined, at least formally.

"Thank you, gentlemen." Gaelen rose. "Proclaim this to the people. See to it that all hear. They have a new lady." Gaelen smiled, exuding confidence and power, as he handed the scroll to one of the guards. "Take this immediately to Argost for safe-keeping."

When the door closed, he turned to face Marja. He reached over to touch her face and ran his thumb lightly down her cheek until it met the pulse at her throat.

His touch sent a shock through her. Would he take her here and now? Is this what he intended? She forced herself not to react and stood stock still.

When her racing pulse could not hide her fear, he withdrew abruptly, with a look of dismay and some irritation. "What is this? What do you fear so? Is my touch so abhorrent?" Then, his expression softening, he took both her hands in his.

Marja jerked back, filled with a mix of fear and sudden fury.

He took a step back and looked at her questioningly.

Marja stammered, and she felt herself tremble slightly. "I had hoped for a little more time to prepare … my lord." The words came out with effort. It was all she could do not to retreat behind the bed.

His face grew dark. "What do you think me? That I am so filled with lust? Have I not told you I find rape distasteful? I have sworn not to harm you. Have you not believed a word?"

"I have agreed to be your wife. That makes it rape no longer … my lord." Unable to hold her rigid self-control any longer she began to shudder violently, staring at him with wide-eyed wretchedness, her knees threatening to buckle.

Marja saw a look of surprise and sudden understanding cross

Gaelen's face, as if he knew what this was, had seen it before. His anger evaporated. "My lady," he murmured, gently taking her shaking hands again, "I am no monster, to treat you thus. I could never do so. Nor am I your enemy. My intention was merely to show you a new beginning. I swore I would never harm you. Surely to force you to lie with me would do so. Wife you may be, but I swear to you that I will never force myself upon you … however much I desire you … and I do desire you." The last was almost a caress, a soft, throaty whisper.

Marja shuddered so violently that she felt about to fall. As her fear ebbed with the understanding that he had never intended to rape her, so did her strength. Suddenly she needed to sit down. He let her go, and she sank into the empty chair.

After several moments her shaking subsided. When she once more had herself under control, Gaelen spoke again. "Lady, it distresses me to see you so. If you will permit, perhaps I may see you in private tonight, and we may make a better beginning."

Marja sensed something had profoundly changed between them. Somehow she understood, though she could not have explained why, that he was not her enemy. The cold core that had kept her strong melted, replaced by a softer feeling that she was not sure she understood, except that it was much lighter than before. Perhaps it was hope … confusion? … desire? She could not make sense of it.

Gaelen once more reached out to lift her chin so that he looked into her eyes. "May I visit you tonight, my lady?"

Still unable to speak, Marja managed a small nod. He bent to brush his lips against her hair. When he withdrew, she felt she had lost something important but did not know what.

"There is much that needs my attention before we leave for Bargia. I can stay no longer than a few days. But I will return tonight if I can. It may be very late, so please do not wait for me. I can see you are exhausted from the events of the last days. When I return … if you waken … perhaps … with your leave," he seemed suddenly shy, and his voice fell to a low murmur, "we may make a better beginning."

When she gave no indication that she objected, a slightly teasing smile crept into his eyes and over his lips. "I have earned a reputation as a skilled lover. There have been no complaints."

Marja managed a wan smile. "What if I request more time … my lord?"

He sobered instantly. "I shall not press you, my lady. But the people will wish to see the staining on our sheets before we leave for Bargia." He must have read the dismay in her expression because he grew thoughtful and added, "There are other ways of providing proof. I will bring the blood of a fowl to use if it should be necessary. I should very much like to have you completely willing. You have lost much. I can be patient."

Marja's relieved smile was more heartfelt this time. "Thank you, my lord. I shall not ask more patience of you than I need."

Gaelen headed for the door, and as his hand fell on the latch he turned back with a conspiratorial smile. "Oh, I almost forgot. You have a visitor who is most anxious to see you."

Before she could question him, he was gone, leaving the door open. Within moments a wonderfully familiar figure appeared in it.

14: REUNION

They both exclaimed at once.

"Brensa!"

"My lady!" and flew into each others arms, hugging tightly.

"Thank Earth you are well, my lady. As soon as I heard we might come back to our positions, I tried to find out if you yet lived. I had seen the bodies …" Brensa stopped abruptly. Her hand flew over her mouth in consternation, and she drew back.

"It is all right, Brensa. I know they are all dead." Marja gave her another quick squeeze. "But I cannot tell you what joy it brings me to see you well. What of Nellis? How fares she, the babe, Mikost? Oh, it is good to see a familiar face. Give me all the news, quickly. They have told me almost nothing." The questions tumbled out in rapid succession.

Within moments, servants appeared with a copper tub, buckets of hot water, scented soap and oils, and cloths for drying. Gaelen had been true to his word. As soon as the door closed again, Marja let Brensa help her out of her gown.

"I will tell you all I know, my lady, but you must have your bath as we speak or it will grow cold. Let me help you. It will be as it was before."

Marja listened as Brensa began her tale. "Nellis escaped outside the wall with me. She breathed in some smoke and coughed a lot, but recovered and seems fine … the babe too. We thought it might come early, but then the pains stopped, and all is well now. Mikost had a burning beam fall on his arm. It is badly burned, but as long as it heals clean he should recover … though his arm may never move so well again. Until it heals he can do little work. But he lives and they are well."

By now Marja had sunk into the deliciously warm water. Brensa poured some over her hair and began to lather in the scented soap with practiced fingers. Through it all, she kept up her stream of chatter. So Marja just listened, enjoying the cadences of her familiar voice and taking in the news as it poured out. There would be time for questions later. She smiled to herself. Brensa had always been a talkative girl who knew all the latest gossip. If she just let her go on, most of what she wished to hear would come of its own accord.

15: BRENSA'S TALE

As Brensa spoke, she relived the horror of those spans in her mind: the women's headlong flight over the wall, Nellis' terror at not knowing where Mikost was.

"We hid among the trees and watched the black smoke pouring over the wall. We could hear women and children screaming … horses, too, my lady. That is a terrible sound. We could hear soldiers shouting orders, too, and were glad to be over the wall."

They watched as more and more people climbed the wall, grasping tree branches to hold as they jumped, or found crevices to squeeze through, faces glazed with fear. With a stroke of pure luck, they had spotted Mikost jump from the wall and roll to the ground, clutching his arm.

"Nellis screamed and rushed to him, not thinking of the danger it put us all in if we were seen. We dragged him back into the cover of the trees, away from the noise and smoke. His arm was badly burned, my lady, and he was in a lot of pain. Nellis coughed for a long time and began to have birth pains again."

Eventually, both the coughing and pains subsided, to everyone's great relief. For a long while they huddled there, afraid to show themselves. Slowly, the noise grew less, and the smoke ebbed. They were hungry and cold as night set in. By morning they knew they must chance returning. Nellis needed food. They stole back, keeping under cover. When they reached the point where they could see the wall, they met two women who told them about Gaelen's offer of amnesty.

"Mikost asked us, 'Do you believe this may be trusted? It could be a trap to get us inside.'

"When we heard everyone could return to their homes we did not believe it at first. So we hid a while longer inside the edge of the forest. But there was nothing to eat in the woods. Nellis was faint with hunger, and Mikost was still bleeding through the shirt he had wrapped around his burn. He needed to have his arm properly bandaged."

Realizing they had no choice, they ventured back inside. Terrible destruction greeted their eyes. The houses and shops almost all showed fire damage. Dead bodies lay piled in the central square, perhaps because that was the only safe place to burn them. Two huge pyres sent up columns of choking black smoke. The stench of burning flesh nearly felled them.

Brensa's voice caught with suppressed horror. "So many bodies, my lady."

On the other side of the square, the invaders had made a separate pyre for their own fallen. She had turned away in horror, unable to watch.

Soldiers accosted them as soon as they were spotted. Mikost tried to keep Nellis behind him, but the men, acting very stern and official, commanded she show herself. They took in her advanced pregnancy and demanded to know who they all were and what they were doing.

After Mikost explained their need for food and care, the soldiers advised them that if they wished to return they must first swear allegiance to Lord Gaelen.

'Swear allegiance and you are free to go about your lives,' they told us. 'Refuse and you will be taken to a holding camp outside the walls.'

"They also wanted to know if we had taken anything." The amnesty included all those who returned stolen property immediately.

Brensa's voice shook as she continued her tale. "We had nothing. We fled with just our lives!"

Mikost had not trusted the soldiers at first, but Nellis needed food. So, when he saw so many familiar people walking freely about, he told the women they really had no choice. They agreed to swear allegiance. There seemed no harm in it for now.

When they had sworn their oaths, the soldiers pointed them

in the direction of a large tent, where they were told they would find a meal and could have Mikost's arm looked at. While Brensa walked to the tent she looked around.

"I saw so many people returning to their shops. Some were already trying to repair damage from the fires. They were fixing broken doors and covering up the windows. People looked afraid. They kept their heads down and did not speak to each other, but the soldiers left them alone as long as they just acted normal."

Brensa poured fresh water over Marja's hair as the account spilled out and began to rub a small amount of oil, scented with lavender, into it, running her fingers through it to remove some of the tangles. Then, as Marja soaked in the warm water, Brensa proceeded to carefully comb out the knots. Suddenly, she burst into tears. "Oh, my lady! I thought never to see you again."

Marja reached a hand up to her, saying, "Hush, Brensa. You have been very brave, and you bring me much good news. We are safe together for now. The worst is over, I am certain."

Brensa continued to sob quietly as she finished combing. By the time Marja was ready to dry off, Brensa's tears had also dried, and she resumed her tale.

"When we got to the tent, Nellis was almost fainting, and we had to hold her up. Mikost called for help, and someone, an older woman I think, found us a spot where Nellis could sit down on a mat. Then she showed me where to get three bowls of stew and a jug of water. She told Mikost to wait with Nellis and went to find someone to dress his arm. By the time I got back with the stew, he was already being tended."

Brensa recalled the crowded tent. People milled about, elbow to elbow, some looking lost, others with bowls and cups in their hands. The table with the food and water stood at the far end, and she had to jostle her way through the crowd. She had never seen so many people in such a small space before and feared she would not be able to find Nellis and Mikost again. When she finally reached the food table, it took some persuasion before the servers agreed to give her enough for three. They had not believed her at first, and she had begun to weep. Since she did not know how she could carry three bowls, as well as a jug of water and cups, they found a large crock and put a goodly amount in it. She tied the cups and spoons in her apron and hugged the bowl and jug close under each arm as she wormed her way back to the others.

"I was so relieved to find them again, my lady!" By the time she reached them, Nellis was shaking so badly Brensa had to hold the cup for her and to feed her the first several bites. By then Mikost's arm had been bandaged, and he fed himself. Brensa ate what was left. Mikost had learned that the burn on his arm was very bad, and that it was likely the scarring would cause permanent stiffness. But he was grateful that as long as it healed clean, he would not lose it.

"Someone in the tent had found a cup of watered wine and brought it to Nellis. It revived her quite a bit. They said there was not much wine or ale, so Mikost and I had to make do with water."

While Brensa and Nellis rested, Mikost left to find out what they should do and where they could go. The news he brought back was both good and bad. The rooms that Mikost and Nellis had shared had no roof. They had been burned. But, since both Nellis and Brensa had worked at the castle as ladies to Marja, they could return there and would be put up in temporary quarters. They might have to share a room with other women, but at least they would be safe and dry. Soldiers at the castle would ask them what their duties had been and find something for them to do until permanent positions could be found. But it meant that Nellis and Mikost could not be together, a worry when she was so near her time.

As Mikost would not be allowed past the castle gate, he and Nellis clung to each other for long moments, until Brensa convinced him that she would look after Nellis. Mikost made Brensa swear, over and over, that at the first sign of danger she would get Nellis out.

"I swore to him I would look after her, else I think he might never have left."

Finally, Nellis had bid Mikost a tearful farewell. Nellis made him swear, in his turn, that he would take care of his arm. He reassured her that he would find shelter and promised to come back the next midday to check on them. When she looked back as they entered the castle, Brensa saw Mikost still watching them.

Once inside the castle, more soldiers directed Brensa and Nellis to a line of citizens waiting to speak with yet another soldier, seated at a small table at the far end of the great hall. She watched the line snake forward. After they spoke with this guard, he would send some people further into the castle. Soldiers escorted others out again, and she heard them direct these people elsewhere.

Brensa hoped that she and Nellis would not be sent away. They squeezed each other's hands as they approached the table. When they advanced close enough to overhear, she learned that those allowed to stay needed some skill that could be used in the castle. And they had to have held positions there before the invasion.

Still others had left under guarded escort. This often led to shouting and angry outbursts. But the guards remained firm. Only once had someone completely refused to obey them. This man pulled a knife from his boot and attacked a soldier. The response was swift. The guard ran him through and ordered two of Catania's own citizens to carry his body out to the pyre that still burned in the square.

"We were so frightened, my lady."

When it came their turn to explain themselves to the official it concluded very quickly. They had no positions at the moment for ladies in waiting.

"My heart sank, then. I felt certain you must be dead."

They gave Brensa work in the laundry, and in helping restore the rooms, to make them habitable. Nellis was told to rest for two days, then light work would be found for her. They assigned the women two cots in a narrow room down the hall from where the late lord's family had slept. The other four cots were already occupied.

"You remember Narga and Meera from the kitchen, my lady? They are here. Narga told us we would have fresh bread come morning, as the kitchen would be running again."

By the time they had settled in, darkness had fallen. All the women were called to a large meeting room where they were given cheese, bread, dried apple slices, and ale.

Back in their room, Brensa had lain on Nellis' cot with her until she fell asleep before climbing into her own. There had been little conversation among the women. Fatigue claimed them as soon as their heads hit their pillows.

Brensa brought herself back to the present. "How shall I dress your hair, my lady?" The question came after Brensa helped Marja get her gown back on, and she had seated herself in one of the chairs. "The knots are all combed out now."

"Just a simple braid, Brensa. It is soon time for bed. Thank you. I feel so much better, and your news is most encouraging ..." Marja looked suddenly apprehensive. "I expect Lord Gaelen may come back tonight. You may share my bed until then."

16: NEW ORDER

"Come in and be seated, my friend." Gaelen could not help noting that Argost looked grey with exhaustion and that he had lost weight. No doubt he, himself, had done so as well. They had had little time to sleep and less for eating. Yet, Argost held himself as erect as ever, and his eyes remained clear and alert. Thank Earth he had not been killed. No one else could be trusted to govern Catania with his wisdom and heart. Gaelen would be lost without him.

"Tell me how Catania fares." Gaelen pushed a mug of ale and a platter of meat and bread toward Argost. "What is the mood among the people? How are they responding to my amnesty?"

"I think you will be pleased, my lord." Argost's face creased into a weary smile, and he sank into the chair across from Gaelen. Gaelen noted with approval that he took a good swig of ale and began to slice meat before he spoke. Formality here would only stilt the frankness Gaelen needed from Argost. He had so little time before he must return to Bargia, and he needed as much information as possible.

As Gaelen listened to Argost's report he said very little, interrupting only when he needed clarification. What Argost related confirmed Gaelen's own observations. His plan appeared to be bearing fruit.

At first, people had straggled in fearfully in ones and twos, distrusting Gaelen's promise of amnesty. When it became apparent that he was indeed sincere, they returned in larger groups and more quickly. By the end of the first day, long lines of people formed, awaiting their turn to make the oath of allegiance to the new lord.

"Maybe this one will have more honour than Cataniast," the talk went.

"Look, that shop is open."

"He said we could go home!"

Furtive whispers had given way to open astonishment. Slowly, an element of hope crept into the conversations Gaelen's men overheard. As soon as the people realized no soldiers would stop them, many returned to their homes and set to work making repairs. Men who had come back alone, fearing for the safety of their families, went to retrieve them. Slowly, the city showed signs of behaving like a community again.

The bakeries reopened the second day, as did the cheese stands, the ale shops and the wine sellers. They had customers to feed and coin to make. Those who had secretly stowed provisions when the invasion began retrieved them to sell or to use themselves. Butchers set out the cured meats they had stored and began carving fresh carcasses.

"This is only the third day, my lord, and but for the signs of fire a stranger might think Catania has always been this way. Already many windows and doors have been replaced. Most roofs have at least temporary covers."

Gaelen noted the pride in Argost's voice and nodded, smiling. "I am very pleased with what I see. There has been so little unrest that I no longer fear returning to Bargia. I am confident that I have placed Catania in good hands. I am in your debt, Argost."

"Your plan is sound, my lord. I, too, am confident it is working." He went on with his report.

Even soldiers need to eat. When the shops reopened, they were among the first to demand fresh provisions. To their credit, or rather by Argost's orders, they did not steal what they needed, something Catanians might have expected. Instead, they paid what they would have in Bargia, not trusting the people to charge a fair price. Though food remained scarce, everyone ate, and few complained. Most agreed this was fair.

Argost had also sent several men among the citizens to gather information. "Find out who might incite false rumours, create unrest. Who wishes to profit from the chaos? And who among the wealthy and powerful had schemed behind Cataniast's back?" He wanted to let Gaelen know who might attempt to use the present disorder for their own ends.

Argost's spies had been carefully selected to blend in, so they appeared virtually invisible. They had skills in gaining trust, in getting people to take them into their confidence. A handful were also trained assassins. These were men who could get rid of influential enemies quietly and efficiently, in ways that brought no blame to their lord. During times of peace, assassins were rarely used. Argost regretted they were necessary now.

"I took this decision upon myself, my lord. There have been only three deaths. We apprehended two planning your assassination. The other carried a message from an informant, with details about the castle, and where you and your lady have your chambers."

Gaelen grimaced before he replied. "Argost, you well know that I dislike such clandestine executions. But I chose you to govern Catania precisely because I trust you to make such difficult decisions. I have no doubt that these deaths were necessary."

"Indeed, my lord." Argost bowed his head slightly in acknowledgement.

Gaelen preferred to think that most people could be reasoned with, but he had learned that some men never gave up plotting. They thrived on just such disorder as they now lived in. There was only one way to control that kind. It had been Klast who had convinced him several years earlier that such decisions could not always be avoided.

It was to Klast that Argost had given the special assignment of infiltrating the wealthy merchants and traders guild, where rumour had it many of the old conspirators met. Argost explained that it was Klast who had taken care of the first two.

Gaelen decided to talk to Klast about this. He knew that Klast loathed that part of his duties and that he would suffer from nightmares. He might welcome hearing that Gaelen under-stood that this had been necessary at this time.

One of the first things Argost had done, after giving orders to his senior officers, was to commandeer the castle and prepare an apartment there for Gaelen, next to the guarded room Marja occupied. The great hall now served as an assessment area for returnees.

"My lord, you asked me to stay alert for possible attendants for the Lady Marja. It seems two of those who previously attended her have returned to the castle. I will have them brought to you if you wish."

Gaelen laughed. "Would they be named Brensa and Nellis, perchance?"

Argost's eyebrows rose in surprise. Then he, too, smiled broadly. "It seems you are ahead of me, my lord. Those are indeed the names of the young women. Have you met them?"

"Brensa is with my lady now. I daresay theirs was a most happy reunion." Gaelen chuckled at the memory of his encoun-ter with Brensa. Seeing the questioning look Argost gave him Gaelen related how he had met Marja's maid.

"Well played, my lord." Argost chuckled at the tale.

Gaelen felt relieved to see his friend relax. Another test passed. He started to rise, but another idea came to him, and he sank back into his chair. "One more thing, my friend. It strikes me that you will need men to fill positions, both in the guard and to run the castle. You will need servants, stable hands, blacksmiths, horsemen. Speak with Lady Marja. Take Klast and another spy to observe and Erland to write down the names of those she thinks may be trusted and those she suspects cannot be. The informa-tion may prove invaluable. I will remain away, so that she may be less guarded in her speech." Gaelen stopped a moment to think. "And did you not tell me that Nellis has a man? Perhaps he should be present as well as the two women. If her man can be trained as an informant, perhaps he and Nellis should stay behind when I leave."

"Yes, my lord. Her man's name is Mikost. His arm received a bad burn during the attack. I will order him to come." Argost stopped, and Gaelen saw him hesitate. "What shall I tell Lady Marja when I see her? She will expect you to be present."

Gaelen took off his seal ring and handed it to Argost. "Tell her I had not the time to prepare her. You will know what to say." He gave Argost a confident smile. "Lady Marja is astute enough to understand the value of cooperation."

He rose again, this time opening the door and leaving the chamber, Argost at his heels. As they strode out together, Gaelen added, "I will delay my departure a few more days, so that we can interrogate those Lady Marja suggests may be useful together. I want Klast there as well. I must take him with me when I leave. His opinions will be helpful in placing the men and their families."

As Argost strode in the direction of the barracks, Gaelen returned to the castle. He wondered what they would learn from Marja. He expected she would be angry that he had not told her Argost was coming.

17: INTERROGATION

Marja rose abruptly, with a rush of fear, when her door opened, and Argost and three men filed in. Her heart continued to pound as she watched Erland seat himself at the small table with his writing materials and the two spies take up positions in the corners facing her chair.

With more courage than she felt, she demanded, "What is the meaning of this intrusion?"

"My lady," Argost handed her Gaelen's seal ring, "Lord Gaelen regrets he did not have the opportunity to prepare you."

Before he could finish, Marja spied Mikost following the others in, holding Nellis by the hand. As soon as Nellis spotted her lady, she broke away and rushed to her. Marja fought tears as they embraced. Mikost hurried to stand protectively beside them. Marja quickly got herself under control and saw that Argost remained standing, waiting to take back the ring.

She gestured to Mikost that he and Nellis should stand behind her. With more confidence than she felt, she said, "It is all right, Mikost. These men will not harm me." She turned back to Argost. Examining the ring, she handed it back.

"Explain, sir," she ordered, hoping her voice did not betray her fear.

"Lord Gaelen has need of information, my lady. He regrets that he cannot be present and trusts that you will tell us what you can." Argost had given her a small bow as he spoke. Now she watched him scan the room until his eyes fell on Nellis. "This will take some time, lady. If you will permit, I will send for another chair for Nellis."

Marja nodded coolly, waiting. Something important was about to happen. At the last, her eyes moved to the tall man standing relaxed and apparently indifferent in the far left corner. This one she recognized. He had been present with Gaelen when

75

his offer had been presented. Now she remembered why he had seemed so familiar. He had spent time in her father's court, a hanger-on, the kind who curried favour with those most likely to benefit him in some way. The kind who did not work for their bread and who slunk around to take advantage of court intrigue for personal gain.

Marja bristled, then caught herself and walked over to stand purposefully in front of him. As he moved his hand casually toward his sword, Mikost made to stand between them. She held out her hand to deter him, eyes never leaving the man's face, and said calmly, "It is all right, Mikost. He will not harm me. He knows I am unarmed." Her eyes never left the man's face.

"I have seen you at my father's court," she challenged him icily.

He gave a small nod of acknowledgement, and Marja thought she detected a ghost of admiration cross his face. Then she decided she must have imagined it, as he looked as impassive as before.

"You went by the name … Terban, I believe."

He nodded slightly again, and this time Marja knew she had not mistaken the momentary quirk of approval.

"What is your true name?" she demanded, holding his gaze levelly.

Terban kept silent until she heard Argost say, "Tell her. We are allies now. We must show some trust."

"My name is Klast, my lady," the man replied evenly, eyes never leaving hers, expression still inscrutable.

"And where were your loyalties when you sat at my father's table and enjoyed his hospitality?" She could barely control the cold fury in her voice as she realized just how easily she and her father had overlooked him as inconsequential. He had been there to spy all along.

"My allegiance has always been to Bargia, my lady," he replied, still expressionless, still meeting her gaze steadily.

As Marja's anger mounted, Argost broke in, his voice smooth

and calm. "My lady, Klast has been one of only a handful of informants that has the complete trust of the House of Bargest. Distressing as it must be for you to hear, his information was instrumental in our successful attack on Catania. His loyalty is beyond question. Sometimes it is necessary, in affairs of state, to do things that are objectionable. The House of Cataniast is no more. It is time to set aside old loyalties. We have all sworn allegiance to the House of Bargest now." He spoke bluntly.

She recognized the ploy. He hoped to shock her back to her weaker position. She determined he would not see her back down. She, too, could play that game. She could refuse to speak at all, but that, too, would tell him something. She must tread carefully.

Marja bridled. "So I must show trust for this spy. What will you do, in your turn, that shows trust in me? I am your lady now … and his." She put as much disdain into her voice as she could, and jerked her head back in Klast's direction.

"My lady, Klast has earned our trust over many years of loyal service. Our purpose today is to listen to you. For now that must be enough. Please be seated, so we can begin our discussion. This posturing achieves nothing. We all want what is best for Catania. The information you can give will help make that possible."

"I trust this not. Why did Lord Gaelen not inform me of this interrogation?" Marja practically spat it out, holding her chin high.

"My lady, I am here at the suggestion of Lord Gaelen. He gave me his seal as proof." Argost gestured to the ring again. "He had no time to tell you personally. We decided only this morning, and we have much to do before Lord Gaelen returns to Bargia. The information we desire from you is of the utmost importance for restoring order here in Catania."

He paused, then added, "Perhaps I have been remiss in not explaining our purpose more thoroughly. The information you provide will allow us to place men of Catania in key positions, men who are familiar with the land and the people, men who may be trusted not to betray yourself or Lord Gaelen. Lord Gaelen is well aware that he has not enough men to rule here without the assistance of the people of Catania. He has great admiration for your political acumen and hopes that you will be willing to assist us." Then he waited, silent.

"And what is the purpose of having your spies here? It reeks of mistrust." Marja was not about to drop her show of anger yet. Argost would have to do better than that.

"A good question, my lady."

Marja heard admiration creep into his tone, and allowed herself a moment of satisfaction. She would show him she could not be trifled with.

Argost continued. "They act as my ears and eyes. They leave me free to concentrate on the questions, while they remember the details, names, and stories that Erland has not enough time to record. They have done this work long, lady, and are very good at seeing what is not apparent. Their impressions will assist us in understanding the information you provide. I assure you it shows no lack of trust in yourself, or indeed your companions, who have shown themselves above reproach."

"I see. It seems I have no choice then, if I may also be considered above reproach. This is a test. So be it. Ask your questions. But do not delude yourself into thinking you have gained my trust. Lord Gaelen will hear of this. I will not submit to such treatment again."

Argost ignored the bait. "Thank you, my lady. May we begin?"

Marja sat down and nodded curtly. "You may."

For the next three spans, Marja, with the help of Nellis and Mikost, told them all she could remember of the people connected to Cataniast's court, the guilds, the army officers, as well as any other person or group of any consequence who had lived in Catania prior to the invasion. To Marja's dismay, she discovered that many of those she had considered loyal were among the slain. Those she had not trusted had fared less badly.

She was not the only one disappointed. Argost's brow seemed to crease more deeply every time they discovered that a good man had been killed. She understood that his job would be more difficult with this imbalance. Throughout the entire procedure the two spies spoke not a word.

By the end, Marja developed a grudging respect for Argost, and he seemed to have relaxed somewhat with her as well. Marja had demanded that food and drink be brought about halfway through, noting that Nellis needed to eat.

When they were finished, Argost addressed Marja a last time. "I thank you, my lady. The information you have provided will prove most valuable to Catania and to Lord Gaelen. Now, if you wish it, Lord Gaelen has agreed it will be safe for you to tour the castle. He wishes you to satisfy yourself that all is as he has told you, and to see if it jogs any other pertinent memories. But, he insists that one guard remain at your door to make sure no one gains entry, and that the other, as well as these two men, stay with you. Your friends may accompany you, if you wish."

Marja was elated but answered formally, "Thank you, Argost. I do indeed wish to see the castle." Then, seeing how tired Nellis looked, she added, "But Nellis will stay behind to rest."

Argost nodded agreement. "When you have finished, my lady, please send Mikost to me. I wish to offer him a position."

Marja simply nodded assent. She must ask Mikost what he had seen and heard and caution him not to trust too quickly.

18: THE TOUR

While Nellis rested, Marja led Brensa and Mikost through the castle. There were so many people Marja wished to hear news of. Who had lost husbands, sons, suitors? Who had been injured, and who had lost others of their families or their homes? It greatly relieved Marja to see many familiar faces among those in the kitchen, the laundry and bustling about the large halls, putting things back to rights as best they could. She greeted each familiar person warmly. She listened to their stories, offered condolences and did her best to make them feel like things had returned to normal again.

One woman she recognized from her work in the kitchen wept. "Oh my lady, I fear what may become of us. My man lost an arm in the attack, and me with a babe on the way. How will we survive? What work can he do now?"

Marja promised to speak to Gaelen. Surely work could be found for him when he recovered, even with only one arm.

Almost without exception, people greeted her with joy at her survival. Unlike her late father, Marja had always enjoyed the respect of the people. She took careful note of those who greeted her less warmly. The information might prove useful later.

When Marja entered the kitchen, Cook, her favourite member of the castle's servants, crowed her delight. "My lady! You are well!"

Marja's eyes pricked as they embraced. Cook had never married and so had no children of her own. Perhaps that made the bond between them stronger.

They had always been close. After Marja's mother died of a fever when she was just nine, Marja had found a welcome refuge in the kitchen. Cook had always listened to her woes and kept treats for her favourite member of the lord's family. The kitchen had become a haven where Marja could escape the suspicion and scheming that was such a prominent aspect of court life under Lord Cataniast. Even now, the familiar aromas of bread, onions and venison calmed her. She could almost believe things remained as they had been. Only the missing faces reminded her what she had lost ... that, and the hovering guards.

Cook revealed with some pride that Lord Gaelen had spoken to her personally when she had come to resume her position. It seemed she was quite taken with him and thrilled that he and Marja were now joined. Cook had been one of the few who had known of the previous request for Marja's hand. Marja had confided it to her, as well as her disappointment when Cataniast had declined.

"It is a match meant to be," Cook enthused.

Marja had to smile at her ebullience, secretly hoping to Earth she was right.

All through her reconnaissance, the guard stayed by her side, and the two spies moved about silently, observing but seemingly not part of the retinue. Marja wondered how many actually noticed their presence, they blended in so well. As bodyguards they were certainly more effective than the one who hovered so obviously at her shoulder. Marja's appreciation of their usefulness grew as she watched how skilfully they went about their work. She vowed to be more vigilant of them in the future.

Marja felt elated to be out of her chamber and to reconnect with the people she had known. It relieved her to find that the death toll appeared much lower than she had expected. Since everyone who knew her wanted a moment of her time, it took about three spans before she had toured all her old haunts. By then darkness had fallen, and it was time for the evening meal. She and Brensa went back to her chamber, tired but more content.

19: WHO IS GAELEN?

After the rigors of the day, fatigue dictated that they retire early, Nellis back to her shared room, and Brensa with Marja, to share her bed until Gaelen returned. Brensa drifted off quickly, but it took some time before Marja succumbed. When she finally slipped into a fitful doze she had come no closer to resolving her dilemma.

Marja knew that, as Gaelen's new wife, she would be expected to lie with him when he returned. He had not come to her the first night, possibly because it had been so late he had decided to let her sleep. She tried to sort out her feelings about him. On the one hand, he had been part of the family responsible for invading and conquering her homeland and killing her family. Yet Lord Bargest's motivation for the invasion appeared justified in the wake of her own father's treachery. That was how imbalances in power were resolved. It was the traditional way of things.

And Gaelen himself had spared her own life without hesitation. More, he had offered her an honourable union, with higher status than she would have received had she wed him at the time of the original offer. She somehow felt she ought to be grateful.

He had treated her people with fairness thus far, though with an iron hand that brooked no dispute. This, too, she understood as necessary under the circumstances. He would lose control if he showed weakness. As it was, his amnesty brought suspicions of poor judgment. Yet many of her people had come back to their homes and occupations, free to take up the threads of their lives. This had imbued an air of optimism rarely heard of in a conquered people. The mood tended to be much in Lord Gaelen's favour, at least among the Catanians.

In his contacts with her, too, he had been most circumspect, firm yet unambiguous. He had been honest with her and had kept his word, both to her and regarding her people. He had restored her attendants to her and had increased her freedom as much as he deemed possible … though she wished to challenge him more on that score. Just as important, and now she smiled to herself, Cook liked him. And Cook had always been a good judge of character. And he was handsome, she had to admit, and charming when he softened.

Marja found herself wanting to believe all would come out well. Since Gaelen was to be her husband, she wanted to let the relationship develop freely into the kind of bond all women dream of. What was stopping her? Partly, a sense of duty to her slain family, she realized. It felt wrong to fall into the arms of the enemy.

Second, and perhaps more important, was that she still did not quite believe Gaelen could be trusted. There had been so little time for her to ascertain his character. Would he remain true to his word? Would he continue to rule with the good of her people in mind? Her experience of her own father, turning into a suspicious autocrat who grew completely out of touch with the needs of his people, made her cautious of bestowing trust too soon. She remembered his promise to wait until she was ready, the offer of fowl's blood. That had been most unexpected and showed a willingness to compromise.

Marja felt completely unable to think her way out of her muddle. It kept her mind running in circles, like a dog chasing its tail.

When Gaelen came to her chamber in the middle of the night, Marja pretended not to wake. After watching a moment, he slipped noiselessly out again to sleep in his own room. Relieved at this reprieve, Marja relaxed and settled into a dreamless sleep for the remainder of the night.

20: A SCHEMER

What Cook had not told Marja was that Gaelen had sworn her to secrecy. He had something special planned for their joining night and had requested Cook's assistance. Now, well after midnight on the third night, he slipped into her room carrying an odd bundle wrapped in snowy linen.

Marja woke instantly at the click of the lock. Brensa roused more slowly, stared out owlishly, then bolted upright as she recognized Gaelen.

He laughed, the sound warm and rich to Marja's ears. "Brensa, you may rejoin Nellis until you are summoned in the morning."

Brensa scurried to put on her shoes and grab her gown, whispering, "Yes, my lord." She dipped a brief curtsey as she scuttled out the door.

Marja made to rise, but Gaelen motioned her to stay seated on the bed. With a conspiratorial grin he placed his bundle between them. Then he removed his boots and tunic, and sat in just his breeches and shirt, cross legged on the bed, facing her. Once seated, he opened the bundle to reveal two small honey cakes and a wide mouthed clay jar of honey on a tray. To one side stood two silver goblets and a small flagon of mead.

Seeing the cakes Marja gasped in delight. "My favourite! How did you get these?"

"I have an informant in the kitchen," he quipped, looking pleased with himself, "and it seems she knows how to keep a secret."

He gave her a boyish, mischievous grin. "I thought that, as this is our joining night, it would be fitting to share a tradition from Bargia with you." He gave Marja a teasing, sideways glance.

She could not help but smile back. Marja had thought herself quite familiar with the traditions of both demesnes. They were not so different. She had studied them when she thought she might be sent to Bargia as a bride.

She kept her voice light. "I am not aware of a tradition involving cakes in bed."

The grin broadened, lighting up his face. "I just invented it … but I am certain it will catch on when it is discovered." With that, he broke off a piece of cake, dipped it into the honey, and held it to her lips, explaining as she accepted the bite, "The rules are that only the bride's fingers may touch the groom's lips, and only the groom's fingers may touch the bride's. They must feed each other with their fingers until the cakes are gone." He waited expectantly, still grinning. "Well …?"

This was a side of Gaelen Marja had not seen, a playful, youthful side she found hard to resist. She smiled back. Suddenly shy, she took a deep breath, broke off a piece of cake, dipped it in honey, and held it to his lips.

"That must make all the joining beds in Bargia very sticky."

"The more pleasure, then, to find all the sweetness there." He fed her another bite.

Marja asked if it was permitted for the bride to pour mead. It was, he told her, but they must help each other drink. So Marja poured and lifted her goblet to Gaelen's mouth, as he did to hers.

When the cakes were about half gone, he stopped her hand as she fed him, and, holding her wrist lightly, brought the tips of her fingers into his mouth, where he teased them with his tongue, checking for her reaction. Marja felt herself blush and looked away quickly, though she let her fingers remain in his hand. The sensation sent shivers through her, and she felt her whole body must be blushing. Gaelen let go and raised another bite to her, letting his fingers stroke her lips, and finally, gently inserting their tips into her mouth. His expression had become more earnest now, liquid and soft.

Marja allowed her teeth to part and found she liked the taste of his honey-coated finger. They fell silent as the ritual continued with the few remaining bites.

When the last had been eaten, he looked at her and murmured, "There is honey on your mouth." He bent toward her and kissed her, softly at first, as if to make sure the honey was gone, then more deeply, sending a shiver through her.

As he let her go, he stood and quickly removed the tray from the bed. In the next deft motion, he pulled his shirt off over his head and stood before her in just his breeches.

The sight made her hold her breath. He was even more well made than she had imagined. The firelight glinted copper off the hair on his chest and turned his skin pale gold. He had very broad shoulders and a firm, well muscled chest and arms. Here and there, she could see scars and wondered how he had acquired them. She wanted to touch each one and ask about it in turn.

He wasn't smiling now but gazed at her with an intensity that seemed to see into her inner being. It awoke new sensations that confused and excited her at the same time. She could not take her eyes away, needing to etch the image into her memory, lest it never be the same again.

By the time she let go the breath she had not known she was holding, he had again seated himself across from her, drawing her into his arms and kissing her mouth. This time there was no tray in the way. Her thin night shift was the only barrier between them.

"Sweet lady," he breathed in her ear, "I would see you as well," and reached for the ribbon that held up her shift. "Will you permit me?" He looked to see if she agreed.

She gave a tiny, shy nod.

He pulled the ribbon loose and helped the shift slide slowly from her shoulders to the bed, where it puddled around her waist. Then he bent to kiss her neck and shoulders, taking care not to let his body touch hers yet.

When she shivered and leaned toward him, he finally pulled

her close and held her, both of them silent and motionless. With the next kiss, he lay her gently down and arranged himself beside her, watching her with his head on his elbow. The caress of his free hand on her skin felt like the whisper of a butterfly's wing.

She finally reached up to put her hand behind his head and pulled him toward her for the first kiss initiated by her. She felt his desire against her thigh as he leaned into her, and her own body responded with heat deep inside her belly. When she shivered, he drew her closer in response.

Very tentatively, she let her hand slide over the skin on his back and pause at the scars there. Now it was his turn to shiver, and Marja discovered that she could cause him to react, too. It was a heady awakening. She had to stop a moment to wonder at the significance of that. Did this mean that he felt some of the same things she was experiencing? She could tell she was affecting him deeply. Did she really want to do that?

"Do not stop, my love." His voice was raw, as though with pain.

Marja tentatively resumed her exploration until her fingers touched the biggest scar.

"Tell me how you came by this?" She lifted her eyes questioningly to his.

He placed his hand over hers. "No great battle wound, I'm afraid," he chuckled. "I fell off my horse, attempting a movement I had not trained enough for, and my own sword caught my side as I fell. Not a moment I am proud of," he added with a wry face.

He seemed in no hurry, allowing her to touch each scar, telling her the tale of each one as she asked. He caressed her skin in turn, and slowly moved to more sensitive parts with both fingers and lips, as he slipped her shift off. It felt like a delicious, new dance, to which she was just learning the steps.

Then he asked if he might remove his breeches. They were causing discomfort, he explained. At her nod, they came off swiftly, and he lay beside her again. Marja found she had to look away a moment. Shyness overcame curiosity. He pretended not to notice.

When she sensed he could no longer wait, she did not hold back but gave herself to the moment. He had called her his love, and she had heard truth in it. With those words her confusion had dissolved. She knew that she trusted him. This felt right.

21: THE MORNING AFTER

They slept entwined. Marja woke first. Sun streamed in the window slit and danced on the pillows. It surprised her to see Gaelen still abed. He had told her he must be up at dawn. Perhaps the rigors of the last days had finally caught up with him. His arm still lay draped over her, and when she moved, his grip tightened as if to hold her there, but he did not waken. Marja observed him in sleep. He looked younger without the pressures of his new responsibilities on his face. He was only twenty, two years older than she, so young to have such a heavy burden placed upon him.

She recalled the events of the night before. He had gone to great lengths to make her feel cherished, from enlisting Cook to make the cakes to the effort he had shown to make sure he did not rush her, in spite of the intensity of his desire.

He was, indeed, a good lover, as he had said. And lover he was. Had he not said so? Named her his love?

She watched his slow, steady breathing and recalled his tenderness, his concern that she was all right. These thoughts filled her with a softness, a protectiveness. She discovered she wanted him to always sleep with this contentment. She noticed that a lock of his hair had fallen across his eyes. Not wanting to wake him, she reached over and brushed it back with feathered fingers. It was wonderful to see him thus, unburdened, in peaceful repose.

The sun crossed until it began to shine on Gaelen's face. She tried to shield it with her hand, but he noticed the movement and woke. As soon as he realized where he was and how late, he bolted upright and made to rise. "My man was told to wake me at dawn." He looked thunderous. "He will hear of this."

Marja placed a hand to his chest to stop him. "Gaelen, you

have had almost no sleep for these many nights. Perhaps your man knew better than you that you needed this."

Gaelen stopped, but his look remained dark.

Marja went on. "I warrant the world will not end because its new lord is absent for a few spans. Perhaps your man felt it was meet that your joining night should not be cut short. And I am quite certain that your men have their orders and are doing your bidding in your absence. Perhaps you might reconsider your ire."

Gaelen's posture relaxed somewhat, and he regarded her steadily. "Perhaps you are right. They have enough to do that does not require my presence." Then he fell silent, still watching her. "I see that there may be another reason to have you by me. You will remind me that I am but a man ruling other men." He gifted her with an ironic smile.

Marja relaxed and released the breath she had been holding. She had been waiting for his reaction to her boldness. He could have seen it as overstepping her authority and become even more angry. That he had listened and taken her words seriously boded well. "You are a good man and will make a fine leader, of that I have no doubt." She smiled at him.

He relaxed more and bent to draw her to him to kiss her. When he let her go, she watched him don his breeches and head for the door, demanding breakfast be brought immediately.

His man had anticipated him and handed him a tray already filled with tea, dark bread, butter, soft cheese and honey. He ate as he dressed, stuffing food into his mouth between donning articles of clothing, washing it down with gulps of lukewarm tea and a large goblet of water from the pitcher, left over from the night before.

Marja gathered more courage and said, "Gaelen, it was wonderful yesterday to walk about the castle and see so many old faces. I know we must leave for Bargia. Before I go, I would see the rest of the grounds and the city. I wish to see how the people are faring, and look at the damage." She paused, gauging his reaction before going on. "I think it would be good for the people to see me. It will reassure them that your intentions are, indeed, as you claim, that I am truly their lady." She gave a short laugh. "Besides, I need air."

Gaelen stopped, his second boot midway up his calf. His expression turned grave as he pulled it the rest of the way before facing her. "My lady ... Marja ... you are not a prisoner. But I am most concerned for your safety. I fear there are those who would use the opportunity to undo what I have accomplished here by harming you. The area is not yet stable or secure."

She waited, silent, not conceding, as he thought it over.

Finally, he relented. "You cannot go unguarded. I will have men sent to accompany you. Do not leave this chamber until they present themselves to the guards at the door. They will have a password. Please obey them if they caution your movements. Can you promise me that?"

She smiled again, satisfied. "I can and I will, my lord. Thank you."

She received a distracted smile as he made for the door, his mind apparently already on the duties of the day. As his hand reached the latch, she called softly, "Gaelen?" He turned. "I think we may be well together."

The smile he gave her filled the chamber with light. Then he turned and was gone.

22: MESSALIA

On the way home to Bargia, Sinnath listened to the speculative murmurings of the men. What he heard fuelled his misgivings regarding Gaelen's union with Marja. The more he ruminated, the more convinced he became that the joining was a suicidal mistake for his new lord. Only one course of action could solve the problem. Marja must be removed. He determined to seek out Messalia, a professed seer with a reputation for astute predictions. Maybe she could enlighten him as to the best course of action.

Sinnath had had little use for seers in the past, but now he needed one to assuage his guilt around the direction his thoughts were taking. He needed someone behind him who shared his views and had the influence to support them. Sinnath knew of Messalia from others in his circle. Many had been pleased with her insights and had benefited from them, particularly with regards to political power brokering. Sinnath had strong doubts that she was a true seer. But he did not need a true seer. He needed someone with political influence.

*　　*　　*

When Sinnath requested to see her in the middle of the night, his choice of time gave her clues to his attitude. Messalia was no fool. She had not reached her position of prominence by luck. Before agreeing to see Sinnath, Messalia had quietly inquired how other persons of influence leaned. She found there was no agreement among them. Most were taking a wait-and-see attitude. Messalia knew she must tread very carefully if she wished use this meeting to her own benefit. One false step, anything that would implicate her, could topple her little empire, and she might find her head in a basket.

Messalia never took any detail for granted. She had located

her large, well-appointed home just behind those of the most prominent and influential. Not beside, for that would lead her betters to believe she aspired to equal status. No, Messalia knew her place, and kept to it.

Her attire made the same statement. She dressed herself just as richly as the elite, but kept it ever so slightly understated, showing a preference for darker colours so as not to compete with the more richly hued court ladies. A woman in her late thirties, rather tall, with a slim yet mature figure, she carried herself with cool dignity. She kept her jewels and hairstyles similarly rich, yet understated. Everything was of the finest quality but kept just shy of ostentation.

No one could say that she overstepped her position, yet her actual influence far outweighed that of her more highly placed neighbours. She knew not to draw too much attention to herself. Someone might notice just how far her reach extended. If her clients began to complain that she was rising too high, the advisory council might take too close an interest in her.

Messalia owned a walled stone house with a large double entrance at the front and two smaller ones at the back and side. These last remained hidden to all but those who had been made privy to their location. It was by one of these that she personally admitted Sinnath and led him through a private hall to a small, windowless chamber.

"Welcome, Sinnath. My servant woman still sleeps. She does make better tea, but I sense that you prefer our meeting remain confidential." She smiled as she closed the door.

"Thank you, Messalia. You have indeed anticipated me."

Her wealthiest visitors were afforded the utmost privacy. Many secrets had been revealed within these walls, never to leave the room. Many had sought Messalia's advice. Until now Sinnath had not been one of them. Indeed, Messalia had been somewhat surprised by his request to consult her, so she had taken extra care to get her facts in order. She smelled high intrigue.

She followed Sinnath silently into the room and, indicating a comfortable carved chair for him, set about pouring tea. He had worn dark clothing and kept his face covered by a wide-brimmed hat and high collar. He entered furtively and did not raise his head until the door closed.

Interesting, a man with a guilty conscience ... hmmm ... Messalia observed Sinnath covertly as she poured. Rigid posture, on the edge of the seat, hands twisting, eyes darting about as though waiting to be discovered. She made sure Sinnath remained unaware of her appraisal.

"We are quite safe here, Sinnath. No one will know you have come. I am proud of my record of privacy."

Sinnath relaxed somewhat at this announcement and exhaled the breath he had been holding. He took the tea she handed him and with shaking hands added milk and sugar, which he stirred with absent-minded vigour.

"Won't you try one of these pastries? They are excellent. My cook is very good."

Sinnath shook his head. "Thank you, Messalia. Perhaps later."

Messalia set the tray back on the small, ornate table and sat opposite him in a matching chair. A small fire burned in the hearth. This inner room never quite lost its chill.

When Sinnath made no move to speak and did not meet her eyes, Messalia took the lead. This might require all her skill. She must get him to betray his real need without seeming to press him, so she started with the obvious.

"There are many changes facing Bargia of late. I do not see any difficulties in your family that would bring you to me, so I must assume it is these changes that have prompted you to seek me out." She observed him through the steam over her teacup as she waited.

Sinnath cleared his throat, glanced at her and lowered his eyes again. "Yes." He groped for words. "Bargia has succeeded thus far, I believe, in large part due to the traditions we have honoured. Circumstances have brought these traditions into serious peril. I need to know whether the breaking of them will lead to the downfall of the demesne and of the ruling house." He let out his breath again and leaned back into the chair, apparently relieved.

"I see. Do you merely wish to know the future? Or are you asking if different paths may lead to different outcomes? You must ask specific questions before I consult Earth. Only one question at a time, but I will need them all before I start. A misleading line of questions will lead to confusing answers."

Messalia waited again, observing Sinnath closely. He knotted his hands again and cleared his throat twice more before continuing. Messalia smiled inwardly. It amused her to see powerful men squirm. They took their power for granted, while she had had to work so hard for hers. So many came to her as Sinnath did now, unknown to each other, but all known to her. If they even guessed at the webs she wove with the knowledge they inadvertently supplied, they would see to it that she met a swift end.

Messalia let Sinnath lead where he wanted to go. She could see no personal stake in the outcome. Her position was secure. But she enjoyed intrigue, and it amused her to see where men's minds led them. This new twist might prove very interesting.

As always, she made sure that her predictions could not be held to close scrutiny.

23: TREASON

In the end, Sinnath left Messalia's house no more confident. However, he had become even more entrenched in his line of thinking. There are times when the way someone speaks about a thing affects the way others receive it. Sinnath could not hide his misgivings about Gaelen's decision to join with Marja. His opinion carried considerable weight. So the responses he received to his inquiries tended to support what he wanted to hear, both from Messalia and from others.

The more Sinnath tried to get a sense of the mood of the people of Bargia, the surer he became that Gaelen had erred gravely in joining with Marja. And the more confident he became, the more his bias showed. It became a self-fulfilling prophecy. Sinnath reached the painful conclusion that Marja must be removed. He crossed the line.

Even before his meeting with Messalia, Sinnath had secretly contacted a man, who knew a man, who could be counted on to do certain things for a fee. Sinnath's plan required speed and must be carried out before Gaelen returned to Bargia. Sinnath had arrangements to meet with this Rellin that very morning, before first light. Until now, Sinnath had left himself the option of backing out. This meeting would commit him to his course of action.

Instead of going home to his wife, Sinnath made another visit, still under cover of darkness. After he left Messalia, he sent a street urchin with a message to Rellin to confirm their meeting. Then, keeping to the shadows, he made his way to a small but well-kept stone house in the merchants quarter, discreetly set back among similar ones. Its outer wall had a narrow iron gate. A small private courtyard garden sat in the back.

This was Sinnath's home away from home, where he kept his mistress, Kerissa, along with their seven-year-old son. In return for a comfortable life, support and tutelage for their son, she played hostess to Sinnath's night time visitors and kept quiet about what took place there. Until now, Sinnath had given her no reasons to worry about these clandestine meetings. They had served Bargia and its ruling family loyally. Tonight would be different.

"I expect company this night. Get dressed," Sinnath told her when she came to the door. "He goes by Rellin. Show him into my meeting room as soon as he arrives. Leave the lamp covered when you answer the door. He wishes to remain unknown." When he saw the worried question in her eyes he told her, "There is nothing to fear."

When she showed Rellin in, Sinnath had Kerissa bring wine, cold fowl, bread and sweets, then told her to go to bed as he would not need her again.

"I will see the man out," Sinnath told her. He had noticed Rellin leering at Kerrissa and her look of fear as she hurried out of the room. Sinnath heard her check in on their son, Merist, on her way to bed.

Rellin left about a half span later. Once he had disappeared, Sinnath waited a few moments and slipped out himself unnoticed.

He had given Rellin a small sack of coin and hoped, not for the first time, that he had not made a grave mistake. Rellin had placed the sack in his breeches and grinned knowingly at Sinnath as he made it jingle. Sinnath also could not forget the leer on Rellin's face when Kerrissa had shown him in and how he licked his lips when she had hurried out of the room. He would have to see to it that further meetings took place away from this house.

24: THE CITY

Marja's heart ached as she toured the city with Brensa and Nellis. The fires had left so much damage. The two oily black spots on the cobblestones where the pyres had burned made her shudder with revulsion, but she forced herself to take it all in.

Yet, pride buoyed her spirits at the way her people had rallied, making the best of things. She saw repairs underway all over the city. Businesses offered their wares, even while roofs and windows underwent repairs. Her people showed determination and purpose. Their spirit had not been defeated, even if their lord had been.

Everywhere, citizens greeted Marja with deference, pleasure and pride. They extended the optimism generated by Gaelen's amnesty to her new status as lady. Most spoke to her of new beginnings rather than of anger or loss. Marja could see them brighten when she showed them she had the freedom to speak with them. She hoped her words and presence reassured them.

"Lady, are you well?"

"You see, we have reopened the shop. We have bread again."

"He has truly joined with you?"

The last was impertinent, and the guards made to interrupt, but Marja stopped them with a gesture and answered, "He has, indeed. I am again your lady. I have faith he may be trusted. You may tell the people that for me."

At her last words she saw the guards relax. Perhaps they could finally grasp that she, too, could be trusted. She hoped they would spread the word to the other Bargians. It might help them accept a Catanian lady.

"That is good, my lady." The concern in the man's face gave way to relief, which she saw mirrored in the faces of the others who had stopped their work to gather around her.

Her guards had difficulty staying near enough to protect her.

People pressed close to speak with her, and many wished to touch her. Marja did not miss the fact that Klast hovered near in his "I am not here" guise. She could tell that he knew she was aware of him, from the tiny nod of recognition he had given her. What an insufferable man. How could Gaelen show such complete trust in him? She must challenge him again on that when she got the chance.

25: GOOD-BYES

Two mornings later, the party, carefully chosen by Gaelen and Argost, left for Bargia. Argost, of course, stayed behind to govern Catania. For the present, the demesne appeared stable and recovering. The bulk of the armed men remained behind with Argost. In two eightdays' time, if things continued according to plan, two more companies would follow Gaelen home to Bargia.

Marja mounted her mare in front of the stables across from the castle and took a last look at her home, willing the images into her memory. Earth only knew when she would see it again. The square had been cleared of debris, and only the two scorched circles, one for each people, still bore mute witness to the pyres that had turned so many to ashes and bones. Eventually, the rains would erase even this reminder.

Repairs had proceeded apace, and the other reminders of the battle had dwindled. Most homes and shops bore at least temporary roofs. Windows either gleamed with new glass or were covered with oiled leather that could be lifted to admit more daylight. Most shops had reopened, with the exception of a few too badly damaged or whose owners had been killed. Business as usual seemed the order of the day, albeit somewhat subdued. Small groups of soldiers patrolled the streets, but the people ignored them, seemingly by tacit agreement. The air no longer held the aura of fear or suspicion.

Marja's eyes lingered on a large two-level building nestled between the stables and the castle that had mercifully escaped major damage. It housed many of the stable hands, gardeners and their families, most of whom had returned. Nellis had told her that Argost had found two small rooms there for her and Mikost, as their previous ones still remained uninhabitable. Though she would miss Nellis sorely, Marja felt grateful that she and Mikost would live among friends, and that Nellis would receive the care she needed. Nellis was very near her time now and needed a place to prepare for the child. Marja had bid her a tearful farewell earlier. Nellis had declined to see her off, saying she could not bear it. Marja had fought back her own tears watching Brensa weep quietly as she took her final leave from Nellis.

Marja had learned from Gaelen that he and Argost deemed Mikost trustworthy and well enough recovered for a position in the stables again. His more important duty would be to bring to Argost all he learned from people coming and going.

Marja saw the efficiency and sound judgment with which Argost took charge and felt a growing gratitude for Gaelen's choice of governor. Catania could depend on steady, fair-minded leadership. It made leaving easier.

She let her gaze roam further out.

The city of Catania itself was the oldest on the One Isle, smaller than those built later and more densely packed inside its protecting wall. Unlike other cities, which tended to form a square grid of streets, Catania City lay in the shape of a spoked wheel, with one narrow street forming a circle midway from the centre hub, intersecting the spokes, and another most of the way out, close to the wall. Some shops and the homes of wealthier merchants and guildsmen nestled close to the castle. Most of these homes had their own walled yard, the front of which framed the entrance to the house. Inside the walls, in rear courtyards, owners grew small gardens; herbs, some vegetables and flowers and usually a tree for shade if the yard had enough space. Here and there, close to homes and shops, where fire had not done too much damage, new spring green peeked out amid the spaces between the stones and in beds around buildings. Trees showed the first haze of pale green, full of promise. What did the gardens in Bargia look like, Marja wondered?

Further from the central area the buildings became smaller and poorer, as befitted the status and wealth of their inhabitants. Areas on the outskirts intermittently showed swaths blackened by fire and larger areas that remained untouched, indicating where fighting had been lighter. Marja saw again, with pride, the resilience and strength of her people. So much had been done in such a short time. Everywhere, people worked on repairs and cleanup. Even young children helped where they could, carrying wood, fetching tools and holding pieces of oiled leather in place while parents nailed them over windows. Most wore soot and grime as testimony to their labours. She watched a moment as a father directed his young son.

"That is right, Visk. Hold it even at the top so I can drive in the pegs. Good." He withdrew his hands from the new window covering. "See how straight it hangs? Now hold this one for me. Then we will work on the door." Visk beamed at his father's praise, chest out, full of self-importance.

Marja noted that the armed troops had evolved into a cooperative unit with the people. They showed none of the bristling arrogance of conquerors. Instead, many could be seen working alongside citizens, especially in areas where repairs required strong bodies. It appeared Gaelen's strategy was bearing fruit.

Just as Gaelen lifted his hand to give the order to ride, Marja spied Cook running out. She tearfully pressed a cloth bundle into Marja's hands. The honey cakes were still warm.

"Oh, lady, we will miss you. Please stay safe."

Marja's throat closed with emotion, and she squeezed Cook's hands in silent farewell. She would miss Cook most of all. Then, as stubborn tears forced silent tracks down her cheeks, she turned resolutely away and followed Gaelen out the gate.

As they rode out, many citizens stopped to watch, hand on chest in obeisance, or hat in front, faces solemn.

Marja looked over their retinue. Gaelen had explained he would take only twenty soldiers with him. The group also included Klast and two other spies, to serve as eyes and ears, and as bodyguards for Gaelen and the two women.

Marja and Brensa both rode well-mannered mares. Marja sat

her own beloved Keisha, a dappled grey, and Brensa, her small pied. Only one narrow wagon, pulled by a sturdy gelding, accompanied the party. All their food supplies, two small tents and the women's meagre belongings rode on its narrow bed between two waist-high side planks. The forest trails were too tight for anything wider. No space for gowns. But, thought Marja with some sadness, those had been destroyed or burned anyway.

Marja agreed with Gaelen's choice of Northgate to leave by. It was the largest and gave the clearest view all the way from the square, allowing as many as possible to watch them leave. It also gave the widest access to the route they would take to Bargia, although not the most direct. Gaelen had deemed it important that people see him riding out in state, a symbol of his status as their new lord. It also provided an opportunity for Catanians to see the respect Marja received as his lady. A double message. So, hoping no one could see her tears, Marja held her head erect and her shoulders back. She waved at the people she passed. Would she ever see any of them again? She tried without success to swallow the lump in her throat.

26: AWAY

In the distant past, the walled city of Catania had lain closer to the centre of the demesne, but previous invasions had wrested much of the area to the south away. Now it lay only a short distance from the southern border. Northgate retained its status as official entry to the city even though it faced away from the direction of most incoming traffic. It opened onto the widest road and continued north only a short distance before it curved sharply to the east and forked to the south.

The interior consisted of mostly low rolling hills ideal for growing crops and grazing sheep or cattle. As far as the eye could see, small steadings raised plumes of smoke from hearth fires. Here and there, orchards showed branches blushing with the promise of spring green.

The party took the southern fork in the direction of Bargia. Within only a span, the edge of the forest in which the Bargians had hidden the night before the invasion came into view. The road narrowed as it entered between the trees. The sun had grown hot as they had ridden out, so they welcomed the relative coolness of the forest canopy over their heads, even though the trees had not yet leafed out. Once within the woods, Marja could no longer keep her home in sight.

The trees at the edge consisted mostly of oak, sycamore and beech. As they progressed further, these gave way to tall conifers, whose needles muffled the sounds of the horses' hooves and swallowed the creak of the wagon. This had an almost hypnotic effect on the riders, and they conducted the little conversation that was necessary in soft murmurs. Both Marja and Brensa drank in as much of the scenery as they could store in their memories, against the times of homesickness ahead.

Marja noticed that only Gaelen and the three spies remained completely alert, not allowing the peace of the forest to lull them into inattention. Gaelen had told her that ambush was not only possible but expected. He had sent scouts ahead to check for sites where the party might be vulnerable, and they reported back with two likely locations. The largest and least defensible lay a day's ride ahead. Another lay close to the border of Bargia four days ride hence. The scouts gave detailed descriptions of the land and its features. Marja listened intently while Gaelen briefed his men and admired the ease with which he took command. *He is a natural leader*, she thought.

Marja had spied Klast before they left Catania and tried to keep track of where he was, as she still did not trust him in spite of Gaelen's assurances. But Klast blended so well, she could not keep him in sight. Often, he took off ahead, disappearing into the forest, only to show up, ghost-like, beside or behind them. At Gaelen's orders, one of the two remaining bodyguards stayed close to the women at all times. The women rode in the centre of the party. Gaelen told her he was taking no chances with their safety.

Both women were accomplished riders, so they made good progress.

They stopped at noon a short way into the forest for a quick meal of bread, meat, cheese and ale, stretched their legs and remounted. By early evening the forest thinned out again to deciduous trees and scrub, which eventually opened into a large clearing by the bank of a shallow river. They set up camp there and erected the two tents near the central fire, the larger for Gaelen and Marja and the smaller next to it for Brensa. Some discussion ensued as to whether Brensa should share Marja's tent, rather than Gaelen, but Gaelen decided that Marja would be safer if it were known she was with him. Brensa made a less likely target. Marja heard some of the men snicker about that decision and make some off-colour jokes, which Gaelen bore with good humour.

The remaining men unrolled their blankets in a protective

circle around the tents. They hobbled the horses nearby and set two guards to watch them. Two other soldiers stayed awake in shifts to guard the camp. Each shift included one of the spies. Marja noticed that Klast took first shift, positioning himself close to the tents. This made Marja uncomfortable, though she held her peace.

The camp fire made a hot meal possible. Marja felt a pang of homesickness when she discovered that Cook had sent a large pot of stew along, which everyone wolfed down along with the last of the fresh bread. Their next dinners would be poorer fare made from dried meats, beans and root vegetables. Journey bread, gruel, hard cheese and jerked meat would have to do for the rest of their meals until they reached Bargia.

This journey was not a processional or a progress. Gaelen had told her he wished to complete it unannounced and as swiftly as possible. The sooner they reached Bargia, the less opportunity for ambush. He had driven them hard today. By the time they made camp, even the hardened soldiers were looking forward to their blankets.

Both Marja and Brensa, unaccustomed to such long periods on horseback, were saddle sore and needed assistance to dismount. They had to pace about for several moments to loosen tight muscles. Brensa dutifully tried to give Marja her arm, but Marja shrugged her off with a laugh. "That is like the legless leading the lame. You can walk no better than I."

Marja felt awkward about the tent arrangement. Not only was she unaccustomed to sleeping in close proximity to others, but the fact that those others were Gaelen's men, and they would know she was sleeping with him, made her intensely uncomfortable. She sincerely hoped Gaelen would not expect anything, because the men would be sure to hear and know. She shuddered to think what the looks and comments would be next morning. Even though Gaelen made her feel safe, and she understood his reasoning, she would have preferred to share her tent with Brensa, and hang the danger.

The second day they made camp by late afternoon. With no one ready to bed down yet, after dinner they sat around the campfire sharing stories and jokes. To Marja's delight, one of the men pulled out a small wooden flute and played a sprightly tune, his heel keeping the beat on the ground. Then he accompanied another, who sang a heroic ballad in a fair tenor. Each successive song grew bawdier than the last. And, Marja noted with a smile, more off-key, as the ale flowed to wet parched throats. But she noticed that in spite of the merriment, the guards who were scheduled for the next watch stopped drinking well before they were due to work. And Klast drank only water.

After the third song Marja piped up, "Brensa will sing for us. She has a sweet voice." She looked at Brensa, who agreed shyly. She performed a melancholy hero's tale with many verses. At each chorus Marja chimed in with the harmony. When the last note faded away, the rapt men sat in silence for a moment, then broke into loud applause, with great huzzahs and much stomping of feet. By then the moon rode high, and Gaelen ordered the party to break for the night.

Once again, Marja watched Klast take the first shift. She knew he would be awake before first light as well. Did the man ever sleep? He was like a ghost.

27: AMBUSH

The first three nights passed without mishap. As the other men relaxed more with each uneventful day. They talked excitedly about getting home, Klast became more restive and spent more time scouting. Gaelen seemed to find this contagious and grew wary as they approached the last camp area.

Klast had private orders from Gaelen that, in the event of an attack, his first duty was to see to Marja's safety. Klast knew the men would protect Gaelen, but he agreed they would not be so careful of Marja. He understood how important her role was to the future of Bargia and a united Catania, and knew Gaelen relied on him not to be swayed from his orders in the event that Gaelen found himself in danger.

Klast observed Marja trying unsuccessfully to soothe Gaelen's unrest. Eventually, she gave up and stayed close to Brensa, who chatted animatedly with her. His respect for Marja, and even Brensa, grew as neither woman complained throughout the journey. They remained cheerful and cooperative.

Their final encampment lay just south of the forest where it had thinned again to scrub. To the rear rose the woods they had just traversed, its dark pines rising high up a steep slope, the brighter new green of the oaks further down.

Progress had been slow that day. They descended carefully down a narrow gorge covered with loose rocks that could turn an ankle or disable a horse. They had to make this part of the journey on foot, as it was not safe to ride, and led the horses by hand until the forest floor levelled enough for the party to remount.

At the top, the trail had been only a short distance from a deep ravine. Klast heard the rush of water in spots but could not see it. The path ran several paces inside, so the view was blocked by a thin layer of trees. Rumour held that caves existed above, which bandits used to hide in and to cache their booty until it was safe to retrieve it. Klast knew those rumours were true. He mentioned it to Gaelen. They both stayed alert for ambush.

Where the ground levelled off enough to make camp the river widened to a cold current. It provided welcome fresh water for both men and horses. Unfortunately, it lay too far away to provide protection from attack. Yet, the ground was too uneven to camp closer. The other two sides had no cover, and only the north side had trees at its back. The trees made Klast uneasy, as they provided good cover for potential enemies. At Klast's suggestion, Gaelen doubled the guard that night.

Gaelen waited until Klast returned from a last look around before entering his tent, and then only at Klast's urging. Klast assured him that he would remain awake.

Klast was about to wake the next guards for their shift when he saw a flaming arrow arc towards the tents.

"Attack!"

"Fire!"

The two shouts came almost simultaneously.

Gaelen had Marja up and out the tent flap just as the first flaming arrow hit and ignited the oiled canvas. The second arrow missed the other tent and landed between them, where it was immediately extinguished. By now the larger tent was engulfed in flame. It provided a lurid illumination to the fighting. Klast kept Marja between himself and Gaelen. For a split second he saw Marja pointing frantically.

"Brensa!" she screamed and gesticulated wildly in the direction of the trees.

When he looked where Marja pointed he was just in time to see a heavy sack pulled over Brensa's head and watch her disappear into the darkness of the forest. There was nothing he could do. His orders were to protect Marja.

"Klast! Behind you!"

At Gaelen's shout of warning, Klast's sword barely parried a sudden thrust from one of the attackers. He had been careless to let himself be distracted.

The melee ended almost as soon as it began. The men doused the fire. When Gaelen took stock, four enemies lay slain on the ground, as well as two of his own men. Two more men had minor injuries. One attacker still breathed but died before they could question him. Brensa had vanished without a trace. And it was still spans until daylight.

Klast knew he was the only man with the ability to track in the dark. Only he could remain silent and undetected while doing so. So he was not surprised when Gaelen beckoned him to him at the edge of the camp, out of hearing of the others.

"Klast, find her and bring her back."

"As you wish, my lord."

Klast melted away into the darkness.

28: KIDNAPPED

Brensa found it hard to breathe within the heavy canvas bag. She soon grasped that if she did not stop struggling and kicking her feet, she would not have enough air and could suffocate. So she mustered what courage she had left to arrest her panic and tried to adjust to slow shallow breaths. That seemed to work. She tried to distract herself by concentrating on the smells and sounds around her. The bag must have held root vegetables as it had an earthy odour. She could tell her captor was taking her uphill by the grunts of effort and heavy breathing. And even through the sack she detected the smell of sour wine and stale sweat. Her efforts to stay calm were not entirely successful, but the distractions helped stave off complete panic.

Part way up the path, her captor handed her to another, who hoisted her for the next lap. This handover happened three more times before they reached their destination near the top of the mountain. It took about three spans. Once there, they dumped her unceremoniously on the ground and yanked the bag off her head.

As her eyes adjusted to the dim light of the fire, Brensa found herself in a large cave. The back wall remained obscured by darkness. A fire burned near the mouth. Wild hopes of escape died when she made out four savage looking men wearing ragged, filthy clothes. Their hair and beards looked equally unkempt, except for the youngest, who showed only a thin scrag of facial hair.

Before she could take in more, the smallest man erupted in a roar of rage.

"Fools! Ye got the wrong one! This one be dark. Ye were told to bring back the red fox!"

He kicked Brensa viciously in her side so that she fell over with a yelp, doubled in pain. Two of the others cowered and looked at the ground. The third, who looked alike enough to be brother to one of them, stared dumbly as if he did not understand what was wrong.

Rellin, for that was the small man's name, kicked her again. When she curled up tighter to ward off the blows, she saw a sly, hungry look come over him, his leer unveiling blackened teeth. He rocked gleefully back on his heels and fumbled with his breeches. "Well, if she be no use to Sinnath, mayhap she be sport for us, eh? Gurth, Farl, hold 'er down."

Brensa made a mad, futile scramble to get away, which only made the men laugh. The two grabbed her ankles, and she twisted frantically as the horror of what they were about to do overtook her.

Grinning in anticipation, Rellin licked his lips and lowered his breeches. Then he reached down and tore her bodice to reveal her breasts. Brensa bucked and screamed, but to no avail. He pulled her skirts up and was on her. In her nightmares she would always relive the cruel leer and the foul reek of his breath. Terror threatened to banish sanity.

With the two holding her arms and legs, she could barely move. And when she tried to resist, it only excited Rellin more. When he entered her, she gave a long, keening scream. The searing pain seemed to go on forever. She screamed again when Gurn took his turn. By the time Farl was on her she only whimpered, like an animal in a leg trap that sees the trapper coming to collect his trophy. When she saw Hanish, the youngest and last, lower his stinking bulk onto her she went limp, her eyes blank.

Brensa had left. She had gone to a place beyond pain and fear, to the top of the cave, in the dark, where they could not see her. She looked on in a daze, disconnected, as Hanish heaved and thrust until he was sated. She watched him climb clumsily off her, panting, and relace his breeches, tongue lolling like a satisfied dog.

When they all returned to the fire, their lust abated for now,

Brensa slowly came to awareness of her body again and the burning pain that filled her. She saw the blood on her skirts, and noted with odd detachment that it was fresh and that she was still bleeding. Slowly she lowered her skirts, absently pulled her blouse together and crab-walked her way backwards to the rear of the cave. There she curled into a tight ball pressed against the rock and tried in vain to ignore the burning throbbing between her legs and in her ribs. She wondered distantly if she was dying and how long that would take. She hoped it would not be too long. Somewhere in the recesses of her mind, it occurred to her that her death meant that at least Marja was safe ... she hoped ... but it was a thought that belonged to another time and place.

29: TOO LATE

The sound of that first, piercing scream told Klast he was too late. He had failed. That scream tore open memories tightly locked away for many years. He had schooled himself for so long to feel nothing. Feeling left a man open to weakness and deceit. An assassin could not afford to feel.

But that scream reverberated down into his past and opened a crack in the crypt in which he had sealed away his heart. Two unwanted, dangerous emotions woke in him. First was his rage against Rand and against his own impotence to save himself or any of the others. He heard again, in his mind, those same screams from the young girls and boys that Rand had used. Klast burned for revenge against the men who were doing those same bestial things to Brensa. And against the beasts that had murdered his father without a second thought. He wanted to kill them all. In Klast's fury, Brensa's captors became everyone who had ever done him ill.

The second feeling, even more threatening to his hard held control, was compassion. He wanted to save young, innocent Brensa in spite of, or perhaps because of, knowing she would never be the same girl again. Somehow, if he could save her, some of the rage he held against himself, the blame and guilt, might be atoned. These were not conscious thoughts. They happened without Klast recognizing their importance. The feelings seemed part of another world.

In spite of his fury, Klast's training held. He did not rush in swinging his sword.

Those men had to die. That was certain. He needed to remain in control. That was also certain. So he calmed himself with several slow, deep breaths until the red haze ebbed and he could think clearly again. Then he resumed his careful ascent to the cave. He could see the glow from their fire now.

Fools! Did they not know Lord Gaelen would stop at nothing to find them?

The second scream told him Brensa lived, though he knew she would wish she did not. He had seen more than one suicide after such an attack. But he was determined that Brensa would not be another, unaware that he needed it as much for himself as for her.

Klast did not know how many waited in the cave, but he had heard voices and believed it to be at least three. For the time being, patience was his only tool. He would have to pick them off one by one. The men did not keep him waiting long. The first came out to relieve himself over the edge of the ravine behind the cave. Klast broke his neck with a practiced twist and tossed him over the cliff before the fool could even register that he had been attacked. The knowledge that he now had one less enemy improved Klast's focus.

He crept closer and heard a second say he was leaving to join the first, laughing, "Maybe he got lost. Not too much upstairs there."

Klast waited until the man had moved several paces from the mouth of the cave and looked about to call out to his missing companion. A knife across the throat cut him short before a sound escaped his lips. Klast lowered him silently to the ground and melted back into the trees beside the mouth of the cave to listen.

"I could use some sleep. We need to guard 'er ye think?"

Another voice answered. "Nah. She be goin' nowhere. Just fall off the cliff. No loss if she did." The man's laugh became suggestive. "Unless ye fancy another go? Willna even need to hold 'er down. No fight left." Another laugh, then Klast heard him grunt as he rolled into his blanket. "Dinna reckon we be needin' to tell Sinnath we got the wrong one. Reckon he be knowin' soon enough. Wasted five men … and fer what?"

Klast heard him fall silent a moment. Then, aware that the

other two had not returned, he added, "Say, they be takin' their bloody time."

But the other already snored loudly and did not answer. Klast heard the man rise and come to the mouth of the cave, where he stood silhouetted in front of the fire. There he yelled out the names of the other two. When they did not answer, he returned to his companion.

Klast crept close and saw him give the other a hard kick.

"Hey, get up. Get yer sword. Somethin's amiss." Then he bent for his own sword, which lay on the floor of the cave beside his blanket. He did not reach it.

Klast ran him through the back and had his sword out again, ready to take the other before he was fully awake. He had time to yell only once before he was cut down. Klast felt a surge of disgust. The man had not even the skills of a raw recruit.

Klast looked hastily around for more, his back against the wall ... silence .... He had killed them all. The fire had died to a dull glow, and its light no longer lit the recesses of the cave. Klast had not lived this long by being a fool. He waited until his eyes adjusted to the dim light and listened for breathing or any noise that would indicate another enemy. When no sound reached him, he risked throwing one of the branches, piled ready, onto the fire to increase the light. Nothing moved. No more enemies lurked in the shadows.

With the danger past, Klast turned his attention to Brensa. Where was she? He scanned the cave and spotted a bundle at the back. As he approached slowly, it moved, and he heard a low, mewling, "Nooooo," as Brensa tried to shrink further into the stone at her back.

Good. She was alive then. He stopped and turned to the side, so that the fire would illuminate him, hoping she would recognize him and understand that he was Gaelen's man.

"Lady, I am Klast. The men who took you are all dead. You are safe now. Lord Gaelen sent me to rescue you." He kept his voice in a low croon, the voice a mother uses to soothe a frightened child or a trainer to tame a wild animal.

Brensa neither moved nor made a sound. Klast had expected this. He had seen the same lack of response in other victims. It would take much more than soothing words to gain Brensa's trust.

Klast busied himself about the cave, gathering the men's blankets in a pile near the fire, keeping all his movements slow and obvious. He faced a dilemma. Gaelen expected him to return with Brensa immediately. He would become concerned in a matter of days if Klast did not arrive. Yet experience told him just how small his chances were of bringing Brensa back with any sanity left. If he touched her without her permission she might retreat into herself so far that no one would be able to reach her. He needed time ... a lot of it ... to coax Brensa to the point where she would allow him to touch her. Yet he had no time. Brensa was injured. He needed to examine her to ascertain just how badly. And he needed to tend to those wounds before they festered.

There was an additional urgency. He had overheard Sinnath's name and understood that he was the one behind the attack. His loyalty to Gaelen demanded that he bring that knowledge to him with all haste. He knew that the Lady Marja was still in danger from Sinnath, because the attack on Gaelen's party had failed. They had captured the wrong woman.

Yet Brensa was in no condition to move, and Klast knew that it was absolutely necessary that he take whatever time it required to gain her trust. Trust was essential to Brensa's healing ... for her to her hold on to her mind. This was also part of his mission as he understood it. If Brensa lost her sanity she might as well be dead, and he would have failed Gaelen.

For the first time in many years, Klast knew the agony of indecision. In the past, he would simply have bundled Brensa up and carried her bodily to Bargia castle. Now, for the first time since Rand had taken him, he faced choices, neither of which satisfied his duty. For the first time, he understood that choices could not always be solved by logic alone. He had rediscovered part of what it meant to be human. It proved a most unwelcome sensation.

The conscious part of his awareness focused on Brensa and the need to tend her. He moved slowly around the fire, always trying to remain in sight, explaining everything in a steady, calming monotone.

"Brensa, I am making you a medicinal tea. It contains willow bark for pain and fever, valerian to help you sleep and goldenseal for healing. The valerian will make it taste and smell terrible, but I hope you will drink it all, as you need to sleep in order to recover. I would sorely like to examine your wounds, but I think that may have to wait until you are calmer."

Klast always carried a small leather pouch on his belt containing a variety of medicinals. He had studied the uses of many herbs and had found that skill beneficial on several occasions, both for himself and for others when they had been ill or wounded. Herbalists and healers tended to be unavailable when one travelled by stealth.

Brensa merely eyed him as he worked. Her wary expression never wavered. She did not move.

When the pot boiled, Klast spread the men's dirty blankets on top of each other near the fire for a bed. He left his own on the ground beside them and looked at Brensa.

"Brensa, it is much warmer by the fire. You will be more comfortable on these blankets. They are not clean, but at least they are softer and warmer." He indicated his own. "You may wrap up in mine on top. Can you make it to the fire? I will leave to fetch more fresh water while you move, so you will not be watched. When I get back, I will heat it in the cook pot for you to clean yourself with if you can manage it, especially where you are bleeding. This is important to avoid sickness."

When she showed no sign that she would come closer, he grew more concerned. He added, very softly, "Brensa, let me help you. You need not fear me. You are safe now." He watched her a moment longer, looking for the slightest response that might show she understood. Seeing none, he slipped quietly out of the cave, hoping she would find the courage to do as he bade her. If she could not, Klast feared she would be beyond his abilities to save her. It was imperative that she understand.

30: TEA

Brensa watched him go. She had seen sadness in his eyes as he spoke. It was the first time he had shown any emotion in all the times she had met him. She waited a while, then painfully crabbed her way on her backside to the blankets. If he meant to harm her, what difference did it make where she died? She wrapped his blanket around her and lay down on the others. It was more comfortable and definitely warmer. The back of the cave had felt so cold and unyielding.

His blanket smelled of smoke, and horse and male sweat. She made sure a corner of it was under her face. The others reeked of rancid grease, stale bodies, spilled ale and sour wine.

She was still in so much pain that she curled up again in a tight ball against it. She thought over what Klast had said. Warm water to clean herself? But that would mean uncovering. She did not think she could reach between her thighs. The pain from her ribs made movement difficult. And she did not feel ready to confront what she would find there … the evidence of her shame and ruin. No, she would just drink the tea and wait to die.

When Klast returned with the water and noticed that she had made it to the blankets, she saw him nod, apparently relieved. She watched him set the water for washing on to heat, pour the now steeped tea into one of the chipped, clay mugs and set it in front of her.

Then he backed away, urging softly, "Please drink the tea, Brensa. It will help."

While the larger pot heated, he sliced meat and vegetables into the smaller kettle to boil a stew. The meat smelled a little high even from where she lay, and the vegetables looked shrivelled, but they were all the cave held. When he had finished, he turned back to her and checked to see if she had drunk the tea. It still sat in front of her, untouched.

He squatted between her and the fire and indicated the cup. "I urge you to drink this draught. Its taste will not be to your liking, but I must insist that you drink it all." His voice held a calm authority that cut through her apathy. "I can help you sit and hold it, if you cannot."

"No!" She shrank from him, clutching the blanket tightly under her chin.

Klast smiled benignly at her, an expression that looked somehow out of place on his face, though she could not have said why she felt that way. "Then you must drink it, Brensa, or I shall find it necessary to assist you."

She shrank further back. He pushed the mug closer, so she could reach it without getting up, sat back on his haunches again, and waited as though he expected her to obey.

The threat that he would touch her, even if only to help, was too much. Slowly, painfully, Brensa sat up, the blanket still clutched tightly around her with one hand. With the other, she reached for the cup and dragged it toward herself. The mug was still warm but not hot. She ventured a sip. The taste was so bad she almost choked.

He gave her a rueful, understanding look. "Terrible isn't it? It works best if you hold your breath and drink it in one draught."

She took a deep breath, downed it as instructed, then gagged, but the tea stayed down.

He handed her another cup. "Mint," he explained, "for the taste."

The shock of the taste blocked her fear long enough that she took the next cup reflexively from his hand. She gulped half of that and stopped for breath. The rest went down more slowly. Klast reached for the empty cup. She hesitated, looked at his hand, thrust the cup convulsively into it and quickly withdrew.

"The water is warm now, Brensa. I will bring it and leave so you can wash."

She jerked her head and whispered, "I cannot," then lay

carefully down again, pulled his blanket back under her cheek and shut her eyes against him. She heard him wait a moment, sigh, and quietly withdraw from the cave. Alone now, she allowed herself to release the breath she had been holding.

31: SELF-DOUBT

The tea had the desired effect. Brensa slept for several spans. Klast used that time to think through the situation, not the least of which was his own reaction. He became uncomfortably aware that something had changed in him. Something had opened that he might never be able to seal again. That knowledge unsettled him immensely. He had depended for so long on his ability to repress emotion. His missions had depended on it.

He worried, too, about what might be taking place at court. Were Gaelen and Marja safe? Had Sinnath devised another scheme to thwart their union? Would what Klast had learned have changed anything, even if he had been able to inform Gaelen? Would Gaelen even believe him? Sinnath had been one of the elder Lord Bargest's closest and most trusted advisors. The only evidence Klast had was one overheard sentence. He knew Marja distrusted him. Would she convince Gaelen that he had made up the story as a way to get rid of him? Klast chafed at this forced constraint. Too many questions. No answers. As a man of action, it ate at him.

Klast watched Brensa as she slept. She looked so small and fragile, so like those Rand had used. It encouraged him that she had shown some progress. Just speaking and taking the cup were significant tokens of trust. Physically, too, she seemed stronger than he had feared. He wondered how soon she would be able to manage the trail down to the ravine and into Bargia. And would she come with him? That still concerned him greatly, as he knew she would never allow him to carry her. She would choose to walk on her own, no matter how difficult. He hoped she would wash and eat when she woke. Her wounds needed tending, and he was afraid that forcing her would erode the tenuous trust he was building.

Klast had never watched a woman sleep before. He eschewed

the company of most men and avoided women even more. He had had several offers from the whores at the inns and taverns his duties took him to but had not felt the desire to accept, not even from the clean, comely ones. He preferred to keep to himself. Besides, pillow talk could be deadly for a spy.

So now it felt oddly fascinating to see the rhythmic rise and fall of Brensa's chest. She still lay half on her side, but he could see her breathing, the way her chestnut curls, though matted, spilled over the blankets, the small hand under her cheek holding his blanket in her clenched fist. Covered as she was, he could not see blood on her skirts, so she looked unhurt except for the tight, pained expression on her face and the occasional spasm that drew a tiny moan from her lips.

Klast tried to decide if she was attractive and came to the conclusion that she must be. He remembered her as she had been: petite, lively, with a bright smile on her gamine face, her high, clear voice. He could not remember the colour of her eyes. Fool, he berated himself, you were lax in your duty because she was just a girl. You did not observe her as you would had she been a man. Was that why their attackers had been able to take her, because he had considered her insignificant and watched her less vigilantly? Could he have avoided her abduction?

She mewled in her sleep again, and he checked her to see that she was all right. No change. How would he convince her to wash and let him attend to her wounds? He knew how to be very persuasive with any number of difficult sorts but felt at a loss with this young woman. This was new territory. Perhaps his uncertainty stemmed from the unwelcome awareness that this had become more than just another mission. This had importance for himself. Now it had become imperative not to use deception, a technique he would have used without hesitation on previous missions. Somehow, he knew he had to be honest with Brensa. Klast had never felt so unsure of himself. His confidence had evaporated.

32: TRUST ME

Once Klast felt confident Brensa would not wake, he took advantage of the time to set snares for rabbits, so they would have fresh meat. As he did so, he mulled over his options. He needed to assess the extent of her injuries in order to plan how soon they could leave for Bargia. He had already made the difficult decision that his first duty was to keep her safe rather than rush her beyond her capacity. Gaelen would have to wait.

As he set his snares he kept his eyes open for any herbs and wild vegetables he could bring back. He had formed that habit years ago, so it took little attention from his thoughts. When he made his way back to the cave he had wild garlic, onions, fiddlehead ferns and chamomile. The chamomile would make a soothing addition to the water for washing.

On his return a span or so later, he found her still asleep in the same curled position. He put the water back on the fire, added the chamomile to steep, and decided he must risk pressing the issue of washing and seeing to her hurts. His efforts would come to nought if she died from festering fever. Meanwhile he added his fresh items to the stew and kept it simmering. He would also need to convince her to eat.

He had discovered a hive while he was out and set about making a balm: honey from the hive to prevent festering, goldenseal from his pouch to promote healing, and chamomile to soothe the pain. He had no pieces of cloth available, so he would have to use one of Brensa's undershifts, torn into strips and cleaned by boiling. He would use them to bathe her and if necessary to bandage her. He doubted it would take much to convince her to give it up, stained as it was with the reminders of her rape.

As he finished stirring the salve he felt eyes on him and turned to see that she had wakened. Her position had not changed. Only her eyes followed him. He had expected her to sleep longer.

Her eyes widened slightly as he approached her, but she remained rigid. Klast squatted in front of her, set down the bowl of balm and let his hands rest loosely between his knees to show he meant no threat.

"Brensa, there is something we must do. We must clean your wounds. I also need to take your skirts, to wash them in the stream below. And one of your shifts is needed for cloths and bandages. Do you understand?"

Brensa shrank in on herself. Not a good sign. Klast lowered his voice to almost a whisper.

"Brensa, I must do this. I swear I will be as gentle as I can and will touch you no more than necessary. I have no wish to harm you. Please believe me." He opened his hands wide in supplication. "It must be done now. I will turn away so you may remove your skirts and cover back up. Then I will take them to wash. I cannot bathe you until we have clean cloths. If you cannot manage, I will need to do it for you."

Klast watched her for a moment more, then stood, turned away and tended to the stew, hoping fiercely that she would act. After a moment or two he heard furtive movements. She gasped in pain a couple of times but did not stop. Finally he heard her settle, and her breathing slowed. "Are you ready?" he asked.

"Yes." Her whisper was barely audible.

Klast turned slowly and found her once again wrapped tightly in his blanket, atop the others. He set camomile tea in front of her, gathered her skirts, told her he would return after washing them and left the cave.

When Klast returned he spread her skirts around the fire to dry. He tore one undershift into large squares and some long strips. Darker spots still showed where the blood had been, but they were faint. He placed the cloths into the pot with the boiled water and chamomile and set the pot next to her pallet.

"Would you like more tea before we begin?" She nodded. He refilled her cup and poured himself one as well, hoping the gesture would help calm her fear. The water needed to cool anyway. Then, the tea drunk in silence, he regarded her a moment longer and said simply, "It is time."

Klast's movements were deft and gentle. He had tended men's wounds many times and had learned how to be quick without causing undue pain. At first Brensa submitted rigidly, but when he touched her thighs, she whimpered. He felt her go limp and watched her retreat into that inner world that admits no pain or shame. She would feel nothing now until she chose to return. He fervently hoped she would make that choice.

Klast was relieved to see only minor tearing. She was badly bruised and swollen, but the bleeding had slowed to spotting. She would heal. He cleaned the area and applied the honey balm, then quickly covered her again with the blanket. He had also noticed a purple bruise deepening just above her waist and probed carefully to see if any ribs were broken. Thankfully they appeared intact, but the ribs would cause considerable pain when she moved. He carefully raised her up again and lifted her arms to wrap the bandages around her chest. She cooperated as if in a trance, showing no response. He worked quickly, lowered her gently back onto the blankets, covered her again with his own and retreated to let her come back to herself.

Klast left Brensa alone again and went out to check his snares. When he came back with three hares, he found her awake. She sat on the blankets, arms wrapped tightly around her knees, rocking rhythmically back and forth, keening. How Klast knew what to do he could never have explained. Instinct took over. He sat beside her, scooped her onto his lap, and cradled her head in his huge hand, against his chest.

She, too, responded from old memory, and curled up against him, still keening softly. He rocked her, crooning the refrain of a melody long forgotten, a lullaby. Before long he felt a wetness coming through Brensa's skirts. His first thought was that she had begun bleeding again. Then he realized there was no colour, so it could not be blood. She had lost control of her bladder. For Klast this was good news. It meant the swelling had gone down, making it possible to pass the tea he had served her. But he understood that to Brensa, it meant further humiliation.

"It is all right. Your skirts can be washed again," he murmured softly, rocking her all the while. "It is my fault. I should have left you something to use."

Brensa's sobbing continued for a time, then slowly subsided into intermittent sniffles and hiccups. She gave no indication that she had heard or understood him. Klast noticed that his blanket, the one she had used to wrap herself in, lay aside on the ground. She had managed to shrug it off before she lost control.

He relaxed his hold and reached for it, "Here, if you can, take off your skirts again, and wrap up in the blanket. I will take the wet things down to wash them." Then he turned away again and waited for her to comply. She did so, still sniffling and taking broken, shuddering breaths. When she became still once more, he took the wet things and left, assuring her again that it was not her fault. She did not meet his eyes but kept hers resolutely shut to hide her shame.

When he returned he found her sitting close to the fire wrapped in his blanket. She watched him, wary still but much calmer, the beginnings of trust in her posture.

33: HOME

Gaelen's party got no more sleep that night. By the time they
had buried the dead and discussed the events of the night, dawn
heralded the new day. They made a hasty breakfast, packed up
and moved on. By evening, Bargia castle would welcome them
with hot food, soft beds and old friends.

The events of the night would make their homecoming bit-
tersweet, not the victory celebration they had hoped for. Two
families would receive the grim news of their loved one's death.

Gaelen was anxious to meet with Sinnath and Janest to see
if they knew anything of who attacked them and why. He had
been away too long and needed information on events in Bargia
since his departure. His people would be eager to see their new
lord, and they would look for assurances that their lives would
go on much as before. A period of mourning needed to be set for
the elder Lord Bargest and Gaelen's brother, Lionn. And Gaelen
wanted to firmly establish Marja as his wife and lady in the eyes
of the people, a duty he believed essential to consolidating peace
and order.

He could not understand that Marja did not accept his judgment regarding Klast. She simply would not believe Klast could
be trusted, and it had become a sore point between them. All
Gaelen could do was to assure her. "Klast is the man most skilled
and most likely to bring Brensa back alive. Is that not what you
wish? He has been loyal to my father and to Bargia for many
years. There is no man I trust more." But he could not hide his
frustration.

Marja remained unconvinced. "He has dead eyes and no feeling. How can such a man be trusted? He will treat Brensa coldly
when she most needs kindness."

Gaelen merely sighed and let it go. Only time would change
her mind.

They rode mostly in silence, every man alert for further treachery. Marja retreated inside herself and sat stiff in the saddle, answering in single words only when spoken to directly. Gaelen understood her anguished thoughts were on Brensa. The difference of opinion over Klast hung between them like a black cloud. To make matters worse, Gaelen had no time for her and could not give the attention to her worry and grief over Brensa that he wished to. He could not help her. He had other matters that demanded his attention.

They crossed into Bargia by late morning. A patrolling scout had spotted them and had warned his captain of their imminent arrival. By midday, a full cadre of twenty armed men in official blue and yellow tunics came to escort Gaelen into the city. Danger of attack was all but past.

Gaelen sent a soldier ahead to arrange an immediate meeting with Janest and Sinnath, as well as Grenth, the commanding officer and council member who had remained in Bargia. It could not wait until after dinner.

34: BARGIA

Gaelen's spirits lifted at the sight of his home. With the safety of the castle in view, and the added armed escort, he could finally relax enough to enjoy the remainder of the ride.

Bargia lay at the bottom of a wide valley, its northern border the shallow river the party had just forded. Earlier in spring the water would have been high enough that the horses would have needed to swim. By now, they were able to walk across. The party could stay astride, with their feet lifted high, as the water reached the horses' underbellies.

The walled city lay nestled at the bottom of the dale, the castle at its centre, with small crofts and villages dotted randomly around it. The land here was more fertile than the craggier Catania to the north, and it showed in the level of prosperity of its inhabitants. This, coupled with the lack of obvious characteristics that could be used for defence, made it a prime target for invasion. But Bargia had managed to remain independent for several generations by establishing strong alliances with its neighbours and trading for grains and other local products in shorter supply outside its boundaries. It was just such an alliance that Lord Cataniast had refused.

Gaelen raised his hand in greeting to the crofters along the way. They stopped their work in the fields and bowed as his party passed. He saw them wait until they rode past, arms leaning on scythes and hoes, with bags of seed for the more tender crops, such as beans, set down at their feet. The peaceful, pastoral scene calmed Gaelen's frayed nerves.

The low mountain behind them stood at the end of a small range of alps. From its peak flowed the ravine that fed the river. The rolling hills at the bottom gradually levelled around the eastern and northern sides of the dale, where Bargia City stood.

As Gaelen approached the city, the first barrier he had to

cross was a low berm, intersected by the four roads leading to the outer gates. The berm had been formed at the time the city had first been built, from the earth dug to create the moat around the castle and from the stones and dirt removed to make the many cellars and canals. Originally, it had been intended as a first line of defence against invasion, but it had not served that purpose for as long as anyone could remember. Now, it offered grazing for the many sheep and cattle that provided meat and dairy products to the city. Only when scouts or spies announced that the city was in danger of attack were any soldiers sent to patrol the perimeter around the berm.

Gaelen remarked to Marja and to Klast, riding beside him, "It is good to be home and to see that the planting has not suffered from our absence."

As with most cities, Bargia could be entered through four main gates, one facing roughly each of the four directions. Gaelen's party rode in at the main gate, which stood on the east side.

"There is so much more space here." Marja brightened slightly as she took in her new home. It was the first time she had spoken since their argument about Klast, other than to answer direct questions. "The buildings are farther apart. It feels less crowded."

Gaelen smiled proudly and nodded.

Bargia castle itself was unusual in that it had an extra fortification wall, with a wide moat at its feet, outside its exterior walls. To enter one had to pass through one of only two gates. The early rulers had added this extra fortification as a fall back for the people in case of attack, due to the lack of natural defences. It had two deep wells within its walls, one inside the castle itself.

On the berm and between it and the outer wall, a motley mix of businesses had sprouted and flourished. As they crossed the berm Gaelen noted the respect its inhabitants showed him. They, too, stopped working and touched hands to chests as he passed. He made a point of meeting as many eyes as he could and nodded or waved in acknowledgement. He could see curiosity on the faces of those close enough to spy Marja riding beside him. Well, they would have their questions answered soon enough. He hoped they would take her presence as good news.

35: ARRIVAL

As soon as they entered the gates of Bargia City and approached the castle, Gaelen hurried ahead to his meeting. A guard escorted Marja to the lord's chambers. As their new lady, the choice of chambers was automatic. Two ladies, who had previously attended Gaelen's mother, already waited for her with a hot bath scented with rosemary, soap for her hair and scented oil for her skin. Marja learned they had been called into service when news reached the castle that she had no ladies to attend to her. Several gowns and undergarments in a variety of colours and sizes lay arranged on the bed.

Marja welcomed the bath but wished she had been left to take it alone. With Brensa gone, the stresses from the events of the past eightdays and the privations of travel, she craved solitude. What she really wanted was her own soft bed back home, with Brensa and Nellis by her side to share songs, needlework and romantic dreams. Those days were gone forever, and Marja resented that.

She understood how critical it was that she make a good first impression in Bargia, but she could muster only a brusque politeness. She finished with the bath, was helped into one of the makeshift gowns, and had her hair simply dressed. As soon as they were done, she excused her attendants, bidding them to summon her when it was time to go to dinner. She needed rest.

Her attitude must have been formidable, because the two women left hastily, backing out the door with much curtsying and assurances that they would remain close at hand, in case she needed anything. Apparently she had not made the desired impression. Well, so be it. They would not be friendly and cheerful either, if they had endured what she had been through. That thought made her even grumpier. She wondered what they would say if she did not attend dinner. Gaelen would certainly expect her to be there. He wanted his people to see her and to accept her. And this gown was ugly and didn't fit properly. Why had she ever agreed to this? Maybe she could say she did not feel well … not so far from the truth. Marja paced the room as she fretted, trying to decide if she could manage the formal dinner.

Suddenly, she laughed out loud. She was acting like a spoiled child! She gave herself a shake and took a long draught of the good wine that sat on the round table in the corner. Then she made herself lie down and dozed off quickly.

36: COUNCIL

Gaelen proceeded at once to meet with his council.

The large, rectangular council chamber, located at the centre of the castle, had no windows, to insure privacy. The two longest stone walls each bore a large tapestry depicting scenes of battle. One of these showed Gaelen's great-grandfather winning an important victory against Gharn. The rest of the room wore no decoration. In the centre stood a long carved table lined with twenty heavy wooden chairs. The table was covered with a coarse linen cloth woven in the yellow and blue of Bargia. The chairs had cushions of the same cloth. Everything here was ancient, used by generations of lords and their advisors.

The only visible way in or out was one door at the end. This could be locked from the inside with a heavy, sliding, wooden bolt and would take a battering ram to break down. A small door hidden behind a tapestry afforded a means of escape in the event of attack. This door was known only to the lord and his top three advisors.

Gaelen reached the council chamber before the others and stood beside the chair at the head of the table for the few moments before they arrived to gather his thoughts. He remembered his father presiding from this chair and wished that he were here to guide him. He ran his hand over his eyes and pinched the bridge of his nose. Standing in his father's place made the changes of the last days finally real. It did not seem right to take his place. But he had no time to mourn. Janest had arrived.

"Welcome home, my lord. I am eager to hear your news. Here in Bargia we have little to report."

Gaelen made himself sit in the lord's seat. He poured himself a goblet of wine, which a young maid had just delivered along with bread and meat. The guard posted outside the door had admitted her on Gaelen's orders. The others members filed in almost as soon as she had left.

At the last moment, Gaelen sent two guards to Marja's door and posted two more at each end of the hall outside their chambers. Being home had almost made him forget the danger they were all in. He must not let his attention fail again. He gave the guards orders to let Marja move about freely but to stay with her at all times. Gaelen also sent for Liethis, the true seer that his father had relied on and trusted. She refused to live within the walls of the city and so would not arrive until tomorrow. By then, Gaelen hoped to have the right questions for her.

When Grenth, the last member, entered, Gaelen bade him bar the door. He wasted no time. "Friends, we were attacked on our journey home. My lady's maid has been kidnapped." Then he brought everyone up to date. When the meeting finally ended, he was grey with exhaustion.

37: BANQUET

When a timid knock on her door woke Marja, she roused immediately and got off the bed. "Enter."

The door opened, and one of the waiting women poked her head in. "My lady, if you permit, I will escort you to the great hall for the banquet. Lord Gaelen has sent word that he will be there anon." She stood in the doorway, twisting her fingers nervously.

My, thought Marja with chagrin, *I must really have made an impression.* Aloud, she answered, "Thank you, Parna, I am ready," and gave what she hoped was a reassuring smile. As she followed Parna, the two guards took their positions and kept pace.

Marja looked around as she entered the great hall. The hall was huge, much larger than its counterpart in Catania. The ceiling was hung with numerous pennants and banners, all in variations of the blue and yellow of Bargia. Tapestries showing scenes of the hunt and heroic deeds covered most of the walls between the four glowing hearths. Candles burned in profusion from chandeliers and sconces. More were set on the tables. The effect was of light and celebration, as if the whole room sparkled in anticipation. She knew that on other days, only the necessary candles and fires would be lit. Tonight it had been arrayed for a victory banquet.

But for me this is no victory, she thought. *Oh, Brensa, where are you? How can I smile and act the lady without you by my side? Do you live? What is that horrid man doing to you?* She pushed the thoughts aside, squared her shoulders and followed Parna in.

Marja saw Gaelen stride in just as she was being seated. He looked haggard and had taken time only to change his tunic. Her brief rest made her more charitable, and she felt a stab of concern for him. He needed to sleep, too. Marja marvelled that he was able to carry on at all. She resolved to put aside her worries for

Brensa for now and do her best to make a better impression, for Gaelen's sake.

Marja sat on Gaelen's right at the head table, which stood on a low dais at one end of the great hall. The floor of the hall was filled with simple trestle tables and benches. Around these sat the heads of all the important families, their wives and their children past the age of twelve.

Beside them at the head table sat Sinnath, his wife, Marlis; Janest, his wife, Wendan; Grenth, Gaelen's chief of the military, and his wife, Naila. Marja greeted each with a nod as Gaelen introduced them to her. The chair that Argost usually occupied remained empty.

Marja noticed that protocol here was similar to that in Catania. When Gaelen entered, everyone stood and waited until he was seated to resume their seats. First, wine was brought out and poured, then huge platters of meats: venison, wild boar, roast goose and stewed hare. Then came bowls of boiled onions and carrots, pitchers of gravies, fresh bread and cheeses. Fresh greens in oil, wine vinegar and herbs added a seasonal treat available only in early summer. Already on the tables sat salt cellars, butter and bowls of preserves sweetened with honey.

Marja's anxiety rose when she watched Gaelen rise to address his guests as the last platters were placed on the tables. She hoped to Earth his speech would be well received. Not only was this his first official banquet and his first speech as lord, but she knew he would officially introduce her. How effectively he managed would determine how easily the people accepted her. She listened intently as he held up his hand for silence.

"My people, we come together tonight both to celebrate our victory over Catania and to mourn our losses ... my father, Lord Bargest, and my brother, Lionn, as well as those brave soldiers who gave their lives so that we might be here today. I am sure my trusted friends and advisors, Sinnath and Janest here, have told you how hard won that victory came."

Marja warmed to his voice. It came through strong and confident. He did not hide his sadness or regret over their losses, but he showed his pride in their victory. She smiled at him as he paused a moment, then looked around the room, meeting as many eyes as possible before continuing. Her admiration of his skill grew as she heard him speak.

"I did not expect to occupy this chair. My lord father was a great man, a good ruler and a wonderful teacher to my brother and myself. We all keenly feel his loss. But I pledge to you that I am ready to rule. We will recover from our losses and prosper. We will work together to hold Catania and rule there with the same strong and able governance you may expect from me here in Bargia."

When Gaelen raised his goblet high and in a voice that carried to the far corners of the hall cheered, "To Bargia!" Marja felt as taken up in the fervour as the rest of the citizens. She raised her goblet and joined in the toast, as the room erupted in cheers. *He is born to lead,* she thought, watching how he played the crowd with another well-placed pause before he raised his wine again with, "To Catania, may we prosper together," which brought another round of cheers.

Gaelen held up his hands for silence and indicated to Marja that she should stand beside him. She rose, holding his gaze with a proud smile, and let him take her hand in both of his.

"Good people," Gaelen began.

Marja shivered a moment as she realized that this was what she had waited for, what she had feared.

"I have here the greatest prize of all. Please welcome your new lady, my wife and consort, Lady Marja. She has willingly agreed to do what she can to strengthen our union with Catania."

The room remained silent for a moment, and Marja knew a second of panic. Then she heard Janest begin to cheer, "To the Lady Marja!"

At this, first Sinnath, then the others at the head table, joined in. To Marja's relief the room once again filled with cheers. She saw Gaelen give Janest and Sinnath grateful nods before turning back to his guests. Someone on the floor started to thump his knife on the table chanting, "Kiss ... kiss ... kiss." Soon the entire hall joined him.

Gaelen's face split into a grin, and first giving Marja an apologetic shrug, he put his arms around her and kissed her soundly. The room erupted even more loudly than before. In spite of her embarrassment, Marja knew that this was just what Gaelen needed. She sent a silent thank you to the man who had started the chant.

She kept her wits about her. Not missing a beat, with a broad smile of her own, she addressed the floor. "Good people of Bargia, do you agree that one good kiss deserves another?" Without waiting for a reply, she took Gaelen's face between her hands and firmly returned his kiss.

After his initial surprise, he beamed proudly at her amid raucous yells, whistles and much pounding of knives on tables and thundering of boots on the stone floor. Marja had passed another test.

38: LIETHIS

Liethis shunned court whenever possible. She found it draining to block the sendings that assaulted her mind among so many people. She preferred to live quietly in a small cabin, sparsely but cosily furnished, a half-day's ride from the city. The sod roof kept out the elements. Her herb and vegetable garden supplied her with fresh produce. Those who visited to request her services paid her with the other items she needed: meat, eggs, flour and enough coin to purchase clothing and other necessities. This allowed her to avoid going into the city more than a few times per year. Those times almost always came at the behest of the Lord or one of his advisors.

She knew what had transpired in recent times. She had sensed the deaths of Lord Bargest and Lionn and Gaelen's ascent to lordship. The terror and turmoil of the party's return trip had filled her with unease. She knew, too, that treachery had been involved, although she had no name to put to it. No one needed to tell her these things. Earth's sendings pressed so insistently she could not ignore them.

Liethis' power as a seer was renowned. She intuited that Gaelen's man would come for her. When she saw him riding up the path, she met him already mounted on her old roan mare, saddlebags packed. She handed the awed rider half a loaf of fresh dark bread, a slice of fragrant cheese and a skin of watered wine.

"I know Lord Gaelen wishes to see me as soon as may be. These will refresh you on our way." With that she led the way back to Bargia castle, leaving the dumbstruck messenger to catch up.

Liethis kept her senses open along the way, collecting as many impressions as she could. Once she reached the castle it would be harder to sort out the tumult that would assault her mind.

She knew Gaelen was aware how hard it would be for her

at court. His father had always kept a private room prepared for her, deep within the walls of the castle. There the thickness of the stone filtered out at least some of the press of information. This is where she would meet with Gaelen as soon as she arrived. Her presence would be kept as quiet as possible, though she knew that would not last long.

Liethis enjoyed the ride to court in spite of the reason for it. This was late spring, almost summer. On the way through the low, rolling hills they passed several crofter's steads.

Liethis lifted her eyes to meet those of a passing crow. The crow agreed to share his view, and through his eyes, Liethis beheld a varicoloured patchwork of greens interspersed with the occasional brown of a field not yet grown or a patch of an orchard in bloom. She saw pinpoints of colour where flowers grew amid the green and on the thatched roofs of the crofters' cottages. When she had enjoyed the view she thanked the crow, and he flew on.

Bargia glowed verdant in its quilt of many shades of new growth: the blue-green of oats, the darker green of barley and the bright, vibrant green of new spelt. Meadows showed patches of white, yellow and lavender where wildflowers had not yet been cropped by sheep, cattle or the occasional mule or horse. Here and there, a willow waved its yellow-green withes in welcome, and evergreens stretched out new tips of fresh needles. Oak and maple still had not reached full leaf, and the sun played between their branches, leaving dappled patterns on the earth below. The paths to the crofters' cottages were lined with bright patchworks of yellow, pink, purple and white, their doors framed in ivies or rambling rose vines, still vibrant with the newness of the season.

Soon the heat of high summer would mute the colours. The soil would dry, and roots would reach deeper for the moisture that gave them their strength. Dust would cover the fields with its dun haze, and the world would settle into a slow buzz. But for now, Earth revelled in Her new life and danced in Her best clothes.

Liethis took all this in with quiet contentment. Her special sight allowed her to commune with Earth and feel Her joy at being reawakened. Another cycle begun.

Summer solstice was only days away, the time for Summer Festival. With crops planted and growing, the people had time for gathering together and celebrating the new season with dancing and music. They celebrated Festival with feasting, with fresh roasted meats, new greens, honey cakes and other small, sweet pastries made with hazelnuts and walnuts, with new ale and old wine. A prized treat was the tiny lumps of sugar boiled down from the sap of the maples.

The cheerful activities of the birds and wild animals were mirrored in those of the people, especially the women and girls busy preparing for the festivities. Hearths held bubbling stews and roasting meats, ovens filled with baking; and perfumes wafted from the garlands decorating doors and windows. The air filled with inviting aromas. Optimism and anticipation kept smiles on faces normally more dour.

Liethis felt buoyed by the new life around her. It helped her forget, for a while, the darker signs she knew Earth would expect her to understand and respond to.

In spite of her modest gown of unbleached linen, customary for seers, and her unremarkable mount, Liethis made an imposing figure. She was uncommonly tall for a woman, spare of build, with thick, chestnut hair that she kept in a single braid down her back. Though she did nothing to draw attention, she had an aura about her that caused those in her path to stop what they were doing and stare. To those who managed to catch her eye, she gave a simple wave and smile, which they returned with small bows of respect.

Liethis dismissed her guide as soon as she had made arrangements for him to stable and care for her horse. Only a handful of people knew the location of her chamber, and she preferred to keep it that way. She made her way there as quickly and unobtrusively as possible. At the door she paused, letting her senses flow into the room, checking for signs of occupation. While the door could be barred from the inside, the lock on the outside was a simple one that could be easily breached. Sensing no signs of life, she entered the room and barred the door.

She smiled as she saw that the bed had been made with fresh linens, and a bouquet of wild flowers adorned the small chest at the foot of the bed. A small fire glowed in the hearth to take off the chill that never quite left this inner room. The square table in the centre had been set with dried fruit, fresh dark bread, a wedge of soft, new cheese and a small crock of ale. Gaelen had remembered that she preferred it to wine. In the far corner stood a stand with a basin and a pitcher filled with cool water to refresh herself. If it were not for the constant noise of the sendings she could not block, she might almost feel at home.

Liethis had time only to wash her hands and face before a rap announced Gaelen's arrival. His smile of welcome was both genuine and relieved, as she unbarred the door to admit him. He entered swiftly. Liethis pulled the bar back across the door behind him, motioning him into one of the two comfortable chairs beside the table.

She eyed him with a teasing, mischievous smile, and before he could speak, said, "The child your lady carries is a son, your heir." Gaelen's stunned reaction told her that Marja had not yet informed him of her condition. Perhaps she herself did not know, as it was very early yet. "I am eager to meet this woman who has stolen your heart. She must be special, indeed."

"Liethis," Gaelen stammered, flustered for a moment, until he retrieved his self-control, "this is news to me. Wonderful news to be sure, but I did not know it."

Liethis laughed, a rich warm sound. "It is possible that Lady Marja herself is not aware yet. You have been together such a short time. She was not prepared for it. I suggest you let her tell you when she is ready. She faces enough without taking that joy from her."

Liethis poured ale as she spoke and offered a goblet to Gaelen, gesturing to the food. "Please, eat with me while we speak of more serious matters. I will tell you what I can. However, you know that my gift is not always certain. Sometimes events change Earth's rhythms. I can tell you only what is now and what appears likely to come."

Gaelen nodded and remained silent, waiting respectfully for Liethis to continue as he accepted the ale from her.

Liethis closed her eyes and opened her senses. There was much she already knew, but here, closer to the centre of activity, there might be more to glean that could prove important. "Someone you trust has betrayed you. It is he who arranged the attempt on your lady's life that led to the abduction of her maid. The treason causes him conflict, but he has convinced himself he does this for the good of Bargia. I cannot see where this will lead. Events may bring about a change of heart, or may lead to further treason. If so, they will require decisions from you that may shake your position as lord."

Liethis became still a moment before continuing. "You must keep your lady and her maid safe. They are bound together, and one cannot continue long without the other. Her maid returns even now with the rescuer, though her experience will leave her much changed. Catania remains stable, and your position there will continue to strengthen ... I sense a threat from the east. This may be linked to the treason I spoke of. Beware of news from that direction."

Liethis opened her eyes and looked directly at Gaelen. "Your greatest weakness is not your attachment to your lady. It is your desire to seek justice in all situations. It causes you to doubt yourself. You cannot afford the luxury of doubt. Your lordship is too young. Leniency will make you appear weak. You will be required to make decisions that will cause you sleepless nights, but you must make them swiftly and with confidence. Your advisors cannot be allowed to see your doubts." Then she smiled. "Perhaps you may earn the luxury of indecision in your dotage."

Gaelen gave her a brief, distracted smile in return, but said nothing for several moments. Liethis could sense that he had many questions but wanted to choose the right ones. After some time, Gaelen sighed and raised his head.

"Liethis, this news of a traitor close to me troubles me greatly. What can you tell me that will allow him to be identified and brought to justice? I have inherited the men who sit on my advisory council from my father. There is not one he did not trust completely. My spies and war leaders, too, have earned trust. I am at a loss where to begin to find the traitor out. I have spies in the east. Do you sense his presence there?"

Liethis let her senses flow for a moment before responding. "The traitor is here at court, close to you. His disloyalty is to yourself and your lady. He gave your father no reason to doubt him. Use the rescuer to unmask him. The rescuer will play a greater role than expected in your future ... and that of your lady. He can be trusted, though he is not a native of Bargia. His decisions, too, will prove thorny, as will those of the maid he restores to your lady."

With that, she gave a weary smile and added, "I can tell you no more. I must rest. I will remain at court a few days, until after Summer Festival, and will meet with you again before I return home." Then she brightened a moment, as if struck with a new sending that pleased her. "I can tell you that your lady is loyal, as is her maid. Do not look for deceit there."

Liethis knew Gaelen had not dared to ask that question, and his relief was almost palpable. He smiled his gratitude as he rose to leave. "Liethis, I know you are not comfortable at court. I am most grateful for your presence and your advice."

She nodded her understanding as he opened the door and turned to go. When he had left she barred the door and lay wearily on the bed. Though she longed to spend the Summer Festival at her own home, she resigned herself to being at court for the festivities. She did not look forward to the barrage of impressions and sendings that would assail her at that time, even more than usual.

39: KLAST AND BRENSA

Klast waited two more days to give Brensa time to gain back some strength. He had to coax her to eat, the first time even spoon feeding her. She obeyed his requests listlessly and made no moves on her own. Klast had found a spot close to the entrance of the cave where Brensa could relieve herself without being seen, but where he would know if anyone else approached. After the second day of inactivity he assessed that Brensa could walk, albeit slowly. Movement would speed her healing and help her regain strength.

Klast's sense of urgency had not left him. He still needed to reach Gaelen as soon as possible. Perhaps it was already too late. But the journey would take several days more, as the pace had to be adjusted to what Brensa could manage.

The first day they made very poor progress. Brensa moved with painful slowness, and Klast had to support her much of the time, something she accepted with wary reluctance.

Nights were still cold on the mountain so late in spring, but Klast risked only a small, smokeless cook fire each day before dark, which he put out as soon as he had prepared their supper. Even though Klast gave Brensa all the blankets, he could tell the first night that the cold was preventing her from falling asleep. And she needed sleep or she would not have the strength to walk. He decided to test her trust.

"Brensa, I know you cannot sleep due to the cold. If you do not sleep you will not be rested enough to go on tomorrow. We will need to share our body heat. Will you to permit me to lie behind you under the blankets, to warm you? I swear I will do no more. Can you allow this?"

Brensa remained silent for a long time, showing no sign that she had heard. Then need overcame suspicion, and she jerked a tiny nod. Klast spooned himself behind her and rewrapped them both in the blankets. It took some time before her shivering subsided, and her rigid body relaxed against him into a fitful sleep. To his surprise, in her sleep she took the arm that Klast had wrapped around her and tucked his hand under her chin, as though it were his blanket.

Klast only dozed, holding himself still so Brensa would not wake and become afraid. He had never lain touching a woman before. Her hair pressed against his face. Even after all this time, he detected a hint of lavender there, a feminine scent. That, and her slight body against his, stirred him in spite of himself. The fear that she would wake and notice spurred him to regain control. It would be disastrous to have her think he wanted her. His arousal troubled Klast, too. He had always successfully denied he had any feelings for women.

The pattern became familiar, with Brensa growing stronger each day and less rigid every night. Yet, in all this time, Brensa gave only one word answers to his questions. Her silence was convenient, but it concerned Klast. He hoped that reuniting with Lady Marja would induce her to speak again.

It took them six days to reach the ford in the stream that bordered Bargia. Klast became even more alert as they approached it. He took a hidden, though more difficult, route. They could not afford to be seen. He knew this territory well, so he had no trouble keeping them out of sight.

When Bargia came into view, they dismounted and waited in a nearby copse of oaks for the light to dim. As the shadows lengthened to cover their approach they crept up to the wall.

Klast led her through a hidden, seldom used passage inside the stone wall to a tiny, cell-like room, unfurnished except for two rickety, wooden chairs. This was one of several hidden meeting and interrogation rooms. Besides Klast, only Gaelen and Argost were privy to their existence. The cell had no window and no fireplace. Its walls were thick stone. No sound could escape to attract attention.

Klast looked at Brensa, making sure he had her full attention. "Brensa, I must leave you alone while I fetch Lady Marja to you. You will be safe here until I return. No one knows of this place." He lit a small oil lamp that he had taken from behind a loose stone in the wall outside the cell and set it on the floor. It threw shadows against the walls with a thin, wavering light.

Brensa quailed. "How long?" she whispered, shrinking into herself.

"No more than two spans. If I cannot bring Lady Marja back, I will return myself to see you to safety."

"I ... she ..." Brensa's voice trailed off in indecision. "I cannot go back to her. She will not want me ... not now." Her face crumpled, and she sat dejectedly on the chair, her eyes brimming with unshed tears. "I am ruined."

"No, Brensa. Your lady has great need of you. You are her only friend."

Brensa merely hung her head, shaking it sadly.

"Brensa, your lady is with child. Do not ask me how I know. Trust that I am certain it is so. She needs you by her more than ever now. Who else will she confide in?"

Klast knew that what he said was true. It did not occur often, but very occasionally he just knew things. He had never told anyone of his gift. It was not something he could control, not even something he wanted, but when it came it was always true. Seers were always women, but occasionally a boy would be born with a shadow of the gift. If others had known this about him, his life would have been very different in ways he could not have controlled. It was best kept secret.

"I will return as soon as I may." He turned and left, closing the door tightly behind him, and waited until he heard her slide the bar into place as he had instructed. Then he hurried as quickly as he could, aware how frightening that dark cell must be to Brensa, all alone.

40: REUNION

Klast found Marja in the courtyard garden outside her quarters, cutting flowers for the table in their chambers. The guard announced him as he entered.

So. She was still under protective guard. Good. Klast was relieved to see that she was unharmed though clearly not happy from her posture and expression.

Marja straightened immediately and was about to speak when Klast raised his hand to forestall her, saying immediately, "She lives, my lady. If you will come I will take you to her straightaway."

Marja put down the flowers and called to the guards to follow. Klast intervened. "My lady, Brensa is in a safe place that is known only to Lord Gaelen and myself. We must keep it so. The guards cannot come."

"That is impossible!" Marja sputtered in indignation. "They have strict orders from Lord Gaelen himself not to leave me for any reason. And how do I know I can trust you?"

Klast had anticipated her reluctance. "My lady, Brensa is alone and very frightened. If you cannot come I must go back to her without you. She has been through an ordeal you cannot imagine. If I inform her that you have refused to come, I fear for her sanity. Yet, I cannot reveal the location of this place to anyone without compromising the safety of Bargia and Lord Gaelen, to whom I am sworn. If you come, it must be alone. I have kept Brensa safe. I will do the same for you. It is your choice. Trust me, or see me leave without you. I must see Lord Gaelen with all haste as well. I have news that cannot wait. You must choose now, my lady." With that he turned and headed for the entrance. He paused there, turning to see if Marja would follow. She stood rigid, plainly unable to decide.

As Klast turned once more to leave, she called, "Wait." Marja turned to the guards, hoping they would obey her. "Felson, I will leave with Klast. Go immediately to Lord Gaelen and tell him what has occurred." She looked at Klast. "Is there a sign you can give the guard that will inform Lord Gaelen where we are?"

Klast took a small, nondescript copper ring from a hidden pocket in his breeches and gave it to Felson. "Lord Gaelen will understand if you give him this. Tell him I will come to him by dusk."

Felson took the ring, yet hesitated. His orders were to stay with Marja. Klast made up his mind for him by knocking him on the temple just hard enough to render him unconscious for a short time. Marja gasped.

The second guard had his sword out, ready to defend her, but backed off when he saw that Klast was ready for him. Klast had a formidable reputation and a fierce expression to match it. The guard sheathed his sword.

Marja had already reached the gate and followed Klast out. "Tell me all," she demanded.

Klast shook his head. "My lady, I will tell you as soon as we are safely away," and strode swiftly ahead of her. He looked back, nodded for her to follow and slipped into a narrow passage that Marja had not known was there even though she had passed that way several times. Klast saw her hesitate before she followed him into it. He understood her reluctance. Now, no one could see or hear them.

Klast led her though a series of narrow passages with many twists and turns. Klast knew his job well. She would never be able to remember her way back.

When they were well away, Klast turned to look over his shoulder. "You may ask your questions now, my lady. We will not be heard here." Then he turned back and kept walking. She would have to talk to his back. He wasted no time.

"Tell me what happened. Is Brensa all right?"

"You will find her much changed, my lady. She has endured

what no woman should suffer. It will take a long time for her to recover. Bodily she is as well as may be expected ... but ..." Klast gave her a brief sketch of the events since Brensa's kidnapping, but told her very little of the role he had played in her rescue. He finished his report with, "She is very frightened, my lady. It will take time."

With that he held up his hand for silence as they approached the door behind which Brensa waited. He stopped before it and knocked firmly. Then he called in a firm voice, face close to the door, "Brensa, it is I, Klast. I have brought Lady Marja. Please open the door," and waited.

When Brensa unbarred the door, Klast entered first to find her backed against the far corner of the cell, trembling in fear. Klast held the door for Marja and barred it immediately behind her again.

Marja entered swiftly, then stopped short with a gasp. "Brensa! What has happened to you!?"

She whirled on Klast, who stood to the side, thumbs hooked into his belt, feet apart. He chose that studied pose, meant to look relaxed and non-threatening, but, out of habit, one hand rested close to his sword. The stance kept him ready to fight in an instant if necessary.

Marja's shock at the sight of the ragged, bone-thin scarecrow that confronted her expressed itself in fury. Klast remained implacable as she rounded on him.

"What have you done to her? I will have you hanged! Lord Gaelen should never have trusted you! I will have you ..."

She did not have time to finish. Brensa stepped between them. "Stop, my lady!"

Brensa's anguish cut through Marja's rage. She stopped abruptly, mouth still open, eyes widening in surprise.

Klast stood stock still as Brensa moved in front of him and placed the tips of the fingers of her right hand on his left wrist in a protective gesture.

He was astonished. Brensa, so frightened, had found the courage to intervene on his behalf. All the time they had spent together she had spoken not a word voluntarily.

Now she went on in a rush. "Klast saved me. He took care of me." She hesitated a moment, then added in a whisper, her courage used up, "He is a good man."

Klast hardly dared to breathe. He wanted to keep that touch on him, tenuous as it was. It was the first time any person had done so since the Missus had bathed his ankles years ago. He could feel Brensa tremble and understood what it cost her to defend him against her lady.

Marja stayed silent for a long time, studying each of them in turn.

Brensa dropped her hand but stayed where she was.

Finally, Marja broke the silence. "I think I see." She turned to Klast and met his eyes. "It seems I have misjudged you."

Klast could see the effort it cost her to admit she had been wrong in not trusting him. She would never like him. He knew that. But he hoped she could no longer doubt his loyalty. He waited for her to continue.

"I am deeply grateful to you for bringing Brensa back safely. Now, Brensa needs care. Please see us back to our quarters so that I may tend to her. Then I am certain Lord Gaelen will wish to meet with you. He needs to hear what you have learned." Her manner became more curt again.

"As you wish, my lady." Klast heard the chill in Marja's voice. He understood that it had bruised her pride to admit she had been wrong. At least she would no longer speak against him. He had hoped for no more than that.

Brensa spoke up then, holding back before following Klast out, and looked at Marja through lowered lids, head down, as if afraid. "My lady? ... Am I still? ... Do you still? ... I don't wish to ..."

Klast finished for her, as it became clear that she could not voice what she feared. "My lady, Brensa fears she is no longer welcome at court after what has happened to her. She does not wish to cause you shame or embarrassment." His voice cut like ice, and he eyed Marja closely to see her reaction, prepared to take Brensa away again if necessary.

Marja looked as though she had been sluiced with cold water and just come to her senses. "Oh, Brensa! Forgive me." She stepped up and tried to embrace her. Brensa stiffened, then relaxed slightly, as Marja backed away again.

Marja soothed, "Of course I still need you with me. How could you imagine that I would no longer want you by me?" With that she finally broke down and drew Brensa close as they wept together. "My dear friend, I have been frantic for you. I have missed you so much. I am so glad you are here again. Come home where I can look after you."

Brensa's shoulders lost their rigidity, and a flicker of hope came into her eyes.

Klast opened the door and held it for the two women. No one spoke on the way back.

Felson, the guard who had gone to tell Gaelen of Klast's return, looked greatly relieved when the trio appeared at the garden gate. He hurried to meet them. "Lord Gaelen waits for you at the appointed place."

"Thank you."

With that, Klast was gone as though he had never been there.

41: A BATH

Marja wasted no time in ordering a bath, clean clothes and food. Sensing that Brensa needed time away from curious eyes, she dismissed her waiting women.

As soon as they were alone, she coaxed a reluctant Brensa into the bath.

"I do not want you to see, my lady." Brensa's head hung, and she avoided meeting Marja's eyes. "I am ruined … I do not wish you to see what they did … and I am so dirty."

"Nonsense, Brensa. I am not so fine that I cannot help my dearest friend. A little dirt will not hurt me. Please, let me help you take off those rags. The water will be cold."

Brensa obeyed hesitantly, her eyes on the floor.

The hot water and the calming scent of lavender soon achieved their desired effect, and Brensa began to relax. Marja did not ply her for information, though it was hard to stop herself. She gently sponged off the dirt, washed Brensa's hair, and spent the next span detangling it. Marja hoped she would not need to deal with lice or fleas later, but pushed that thought aside.

Instead of asking Brensa to tell her what happened to her, she brought her up to date on events in Bargia, as though this were the most normal conversation in the world.

In between, she urged Brensa to eat bites of the fresh bread, honey and the mild new cheese that sat on a tray beside them. She was careful to water the wine lest Brensa fall asleep before she could get her out of the tub. Marja cringed when she saw Brensa's injured ribs, but did not let her notice and did not remark on them. All that could wait until later, when Brensa had slept. Her heart ached to see how thin her friend had become. That would need to be remedied quickly.

42: A TRAITOR

Klast found Gaelen waiting on a rickety grey chair in a cell similar to the one where he had hidden Brensa. It held another stool and a small, crude table. Klast saw with gratitude that Gaelen had anticipated he would be hungry. On the table sat fresh spelt bread, cold venison and cheese, along with a crock of cool ale and two clay cups. Gaelen had brought these from the castle kitchen on his way. When he admitted him upon hearing the coded rap, Klast stepped in and barred the door again behind himself.

"Welcome, my friend," Gaelen began. "It is good to see you again. I understand Brensa is restored to us. I am sure you have much to report."

"Indeed I do, my lord." Klast tore into the bread and cut a large slice of cheese. "Some you will not wish to hear." He swallowed a large bite and took a gulp of the ale Gaelen had poured before continuing. "You have a traitor among your most trusted. Your lady is in grave danger. I was much relieved to see her safe on my return."

Klast went on to report on finding and rescuing Brensa, leaving out the details of her care, but letting Gaelen know how badly affected she was.

Gaelen waited patiently throughout, his expression growing more grave. He stopped Klast only twice for more details. When Klast revealed that he had heard the brigands mention Sinnath's name, Gaelen became very sombre and looked at the table.

"I regret that I must be the bearer of such dire news, my lord. And I understand that his treason may be impossible to prove."

Klast kept silent as he waited for Gaelen to take in this disturbing revelation. Klast knew that Lord Bargest had trusted Sinnath for as long as either of them could remember. To hear that that same man now plotted to kill his lady hit him hard.

Finally, Gaelen ran his hand across his eyes and pinched the bridge of his nose. He looked up at Klast. "Thank you, my friend. Once again you have done Bargia and myself an invaluable service. I do not doubt that you heard correctly. As you may imagine, this news distresses me. Sinnath has been highly regarded at court for my entire life. So he cannot be openly accused. Without proof, an accusation of treason would split the court and weaken Bargia. And you are correct in saying it will be difficult to prove. That leaves me with only one choice. Once again, my friend, I must call on your services. You are the only one who knows of this? Do you think Brensa overheard?"

"No, my lord. I do not believe Brensa knows. Even if she does, she is unlikely to speak of it to any, excepting, perhaps, to Lady Marja. She speaks very little since her ordeal," Klast ended softly as he put down his knife and drained the last of the ale, replete.

"Then you know what must be done. No one must hear of this. I rely on you to find the proof we need. It must be such that no one can doubt it. Meanwhile, we must carry on as if all is well. Sinnath must not suspect. I had thought to send you back to Catania and inquire of Argost what is needed there. However, I see that you are needed more here. I will send Gorn to Catania." Gaelen slumped wearily on his chair, again rubbing his hand over his eyes in the familiar gesture.

It struck Klast that Gaelen had aged ten years since inheriting the title. The sudden responsibility showed its effects. This was no longer the cheerful, enthusiastic young man he had sparred with in weapons training or argued strategy with.

Klast had expected Gaelen would assign him to spy on Sinnath. He was the only one with the skill to succeed undetected. In a way, it pleased him to remain in Bargia. It gave him a chance to check on Brensa. It occurred to him to wonder for a moment why that mattered.

Gaelen handed Klast the copper ring back. The interview

over, they both rose, Gaelen gathering the pitcher and goblets to take back to the kitchen.

It did not occur to Klast that his lord need not perform such a mundane task. When alone together, formalities were forgotten.

As Klast locked the door, Gaelen said, "I must see how my lady fares now that Brensa is restored to her … and find out how Brensa is." Then he turned back to Klast and asked, "How did Lady Marja appear when she saw her friend?"

Klast understood the unspoken question behind the obvious one. "We have reached an understanding, my lord." He gave Gaelen a tight smile and walked away in the opposite direction. He pretended not to see the relief Gaelen had been unable to hide.

43: BAIT

Klast trudged his way to the Black Bull, a third-rate inn in the western quarter, where he knew he could get both a bath and a decent meal. He might also get a feel for the latest gossip and the mood of the common folk. Weary as he felt, he did not allow himself the luxury of rest. He had inured himself long ago to getting by on little sleep. A bath and food would revive him. His understanding of the urgency of his mission to the stability of Bargia's future and Gaelen's rule of it pressed him to push the limits of his endurance. Gaelen needed proof against Sinnath quickly.

On entering the inn, Klast donned his "I am nobody you want to notice" mien and approached the bar. He showed his coin to prove he could pay and requested a hot tub in the men's common bathing room and a large jug of ale. Many of the less expensive inns in Bargia had a room set aside where men who had no coin for single rooms could bathe. Usually this also involved a good deal of cheap local ale or wine. The warm water and the drink loosened men's tongues, making these inns good places to gather information.

As he lowered himself into the hot water, he feigned drunkenness and settled clumsily down to soak, occasionally coming up for more ale.

The three men in the other tubs barely glanced in his direction. They had more interest in the maids bringing hot water, engaging them in bawdy talk, and making lewd suggestions. As in most such establishments, the maids were experienced with this kind of behaviour and skilled at deflecting all but the most persistent. Those tended to end up with cold water, until they got the message.

After making a show of interest in the maid who brought his water, Klast settled down to listen. When he deemed the wait long enough, he steered the conversation into his desired direction. "Canna count on anythin' stayin' the same. Come back from tradin' in the north, and there be all kinds o' soldiers stoppin' me, snoopin' into all my goods, askin' stupid questions. Guess the new lord be scared of his own shadow. Hear he brought back a wife from Catania. Seems our own isna good enough fer 'im." He took another long pull of nothing from the jug and waited for a response.

He heard a snort from the tub behind him, where he remembered the one with the full red beard soaked.

"Word is, she seduced 'im with a spell."

Klast responded, "Way I hear, he keeps 'er locked up tight … s'posed to be a beauty."

The room remained silent for a long moment. Then the second man, the big one with the dark curly hair, spoke up cautiously. "Dinna know about that. Heard somebody wants 'er gone, though. Heard they got the wrong one on the mountain."

"Mayhap they couldna tell the lady from the maid," red beard chortled.

Klast huffed his acknowledgement of the jibe but remained silent. This was the talk he had been hoping for. That the man was so quick to bring it up showed that Sinnath had been busy, indeed. The doubts he had planted had already circulated. Klast waited to see what the other might say. A natural break came when the maids returned with more hot water.

Klast asked, "They really got the wrong one?" He feigned another pull from the jug and wiped his arm across his mouth, "Mayhap they sent fools to do a man's job," and gave another derisive snort.

Red beard piped up. "You lookin' for the job? Think yer better'n them? Me, I want to keep my head on my neck. 'Sides, who cares if she isna one of our own. Long as she keeps him busy so's he dinna look too close at us poor folk. Got enough taxes 'n laws now."

"Nah," Klast demurred. "I dinna need trouble. 'Sides, like I said, he keeps her locked up. Couldna get close enough anyhow." He paused as if thinking, then mused, "Still, might be gold in it fer the right man." He paused again. "Too risky fer me, though. Dinna think it would pay enough."

The dark man remained silent, and Klast knew he had heard all from him he was willing to say in public. If he was involved, Klast knew the fellow would be in touch with him. He took another long pull from the jug and sank further into his tub. He could feel the man's eyes on him, assessing him, making sure he would remember him. *So far, so good,* Klast thought.

The dark man waited only a short time longer, then shouted for the maid to bring him a cloth to dry off with. When he was dry and dressed, he nodded briefly at Klast before leaving. Klast understood it as a signal and waited only a moment before ending his own bath. He dressed quickly and took a corner table in the common room. He ordered stew and dark bread, having brought his jug with him. However, he was soon disappointed. He finished his stew and ordered more bread. When the man did not appear, it told Klast that he would need to tread carefully. This one would not give himself away easily.

44: BAD NEWS

Gaelen hailed the nearest soldier he met and had him call together the council members for an emergency meeting. He needed to flush Sinnath out before he did more damage. As long as Sinnath remained unsuspected he would be free to further his schemes. Marja would remain in danger … and his son. A smile softened his face for a moment at that thought … a son, an heir. Then he pulled his attention back to the business at hand.

Liethis had not been able to guarantee his future. He needed to take action, yet she had warned that he must tread cautiously. Somehow he must appear to be unaware of Sinnath's duplicity while leading him to reveal himself. Gaelen's frown deepened as he realized he had no idea how he might accomplish this. He wondered briefly if Klast might be wrong, then shook his head. No, Klast had always been frank whenever he had any doubts, and he had been very certain this time.

On his way to the conference chamber he decided how he might make Sinnath squirm. He would let the council know he had met with Liethis. But he would need to take great care just how he presented what she had revealed, and how much. As the others filed in and took their places, he still had not decided exactly what he would say.

When they had all taken their seats, Gaelen rose to get their attention. "Friends, I have just come from meeting with Liethis. I sent for her as soon as we returned to Bargia." He paused and looked at each man at the table as if looking for a sign. No one spoke. All eyes remained on him, silent.

"What she tells me may come to Bargia is never certain. Liethis is always the first to warn us that Earth's sendings can change. Yet, there is that which has already passed that makes me heartsore … and against which I must act. I need your assistance in this. Liethis senses a traitor in our very midst … possibly in this very room." He looked around pointedly again. "She tells me this same man was behind the abduction of my lady's maid. You all know that my father trusted each of you completely. It grieves me to think that I must now beware, lest one of you have turned against Bargia. I can only hope that the traitor is outside this inner council. Yet, Liethis tells me he is very close. She could not identify him but did say that the future of Bargia hangs on our actions." Gaelen paused to search the face of each man again.

"If I am to succeed in holding both this demesne and Catania, I need a council and a court I can trust. I rely on all of you to assist in unmasking this man, so that the threat may be swiftly dealt with. With preparations underway for Summer Festival, activity in the city has increased. This makes it harder to note anything out of the ordinary. But the festivities must go forward as usual. Bargia needs a celebration after the war. We still grieve our losses too keenly. Victory alone is not enough. The only noticeable action I will take is the guard on my lady and her maid. The people will understand this in light of the tales of the attack on us." He rubbed his hand across his eyes and sat down heavily.

Shock held the room in silence for a moment. Then they tumbled over each other declaring their loyalty and erupting in questions. Gaelen let them flow over each other without interruption. Nothing could be gained from his direction. This must play itself out. After what he deemed long enough, Gaelen deliberately left, hoping his absence would allow the men to speak more freely.

He headed immediately for the garden where presumed he would find Marja.

45: A SECRET

Though she understood the reasons for it, Marja chafed at the restrictions of her constant guard and limited mobility. Preparations for Summer Festival proceeded apace, and she wanted desperately to participate. This was her new home, and she its new lady. That meant that she ought to be in charge of planning the decorations in the castle, deciding the menus for the banquet and seeing to the distribution of small tokens to the people. Yet, she could only collect greenery from her garden, plait ribbons into them and hang them about their chambers and open areas within the castle. And all while two guards and other hidden presences dogged her steps and watched her every move. Well, at least she could get to know the kitchen staff and discuss the menus with them. How she longed to take her mare, Keisha, and ride into the countryside, collecting wildflowers and meeting the locals. "Drat, drat and drat again," she muttered under her breath.

Marja felt impatient with having Brensa hover so close. She knew that Brensa, for one, was pleased that their movements were restricted, and that they remained under heavy guard. She had confided that she felt a measure of safety in this small garden. She could relax here just a little. Besides, she told Marja, she enjoyed making flower garlands, a peaceful, creative activity that did not demand too much from her physically while she regained her strength.

Brensa caught Marja's eyes and smiled shyly. "When will you tell him, do you think?" Then she blushed. "Perhaps it is not my place to ask, my lady. Forgive me if I am too forward."

The reminder of her pregnancy made Marja forget her frustrations for a moment, and she smiled kindly at Brensa. "Of course you are forgiven, Brensa. Who else can I speak of this with? You are my only friend here." Then she sobered. "Do you think it is too early? I see the signs, now that you told me what Klast said. I had thought they were caused by the ordeals we experienced. I am overjoyed to stand corrected." She had to grin at her own delight then.

"Oh, my lady, do tell him. Surely he is in need of joyful news, too. These times are difficult for Lord Gaelen as well."

Brensa looked so earnest that Marja laughed. "You are right, Brensa. Lord Gaelen needs good news. I shall tell him when next we find time alone together. He is so pressed, I see little of him."

Brensa's expression brightened, relieved. She lifted the garland in her hands. "The lord's colours blend well with these daisies, do you not agree? The blue of Bargia is so pretty. Much easier to work with than the orange of Catania." Her hand flew to her mouth in dismay at the reminder of what Marja had lost.

"It is all right, Brensa. I miss our old home and our friends." Marja smiled. "But you are right. The blue definitely suits these flowers better than the orange." Her smile turned mischievous. "And it certainly suits Lord Gaelen when he dons his formal dress, do you not agree?"

Brensa gave a small, relieved smile. "Oh yes, my lady. He is most handsome in it."

46: SECRET NO LONGER

Gaelen found Marja in the garden with Brensa, just as he had expected. He strode quickly over to her, and she rewarded him with a warm embrace. He noted that her colour had improved, probably due to relief in having Brensa back. Gaelen turned to Brensa and looked her over. "It is very good to have you among us once more, Brensa, and to see you recovering. I cannot tell you how it grieved me to have you go through such an ordeal. I trust Klast looked after you well?"

At Gaelen's acknowledgement of her presence Brensa seemed to shrink in on herself. Her fingers knotted nervously, and the garland she held crumpled in her tight grip. At the mention of Klast, her head came up, and she looked Gaelen in the eye. "Yes, my lord. He saved me, nursed me when I would have died." As Brensa realized her boldness, her eyes quickly dropped back to her twisting hands.

Gaelen answered kindly, "I am so pleased to have you back safely. Klast is the only one who could have restored you to us, and for that we are most grateful. I owe him a good deal, and not only for your rescue."

Brensa merely nodded, not lifting her head.

Marja joined in. "Brensa," she said softly, "I would like a few moments with Lord Gaelen. Will you be all right alone in our chambers for a while?"

Brensa looked up timidly and nodded. Indicating the garland she asked, "Shall I take these with me?"

"That will be fine, thank you. We shall not be long. If you become frightened alone, you may come back."

"I will be all right, my lady." The words were brave but the tone not so convincing. Brensa gathered up the flowers and left Gaelen and Marja alone.

Marja looked suddenly shy, as though at a loss for words.

This was a side of her that Gaelen had never seen. She had always appeared strong and confident, not like this blushing young maiden. Gaelen looked at her expectantly, waiting for her to speak.

Seeming to suddenly make up her mind, she reached for his hand and placed it on her belly, looking up to meet his eyes.

"Gaelen, I have wonderful news." She smiled expectantly at him and waited for it to sink in.

Gaelen looked at the hand on Marja's belly, then back at her face, a broad smile widening across his own. He reached his arms around her waist and drew her close. "This is indeed wonderful news." He pulled his face back to look at her again, grinning. "Is it a boy or a girl?"

It was Marja's turn to grin. "Yes," she teased.

Gaelen laughed and hugged her tight. "Are you well, my love? Is all as it should be?"

Marja gave a short, derisive snort and laughed. "All is unfortunately as it usually is. I want to sleep all the time, I am grumpy, I want to cry for no reason and I lose my breakfast to the privy every morning." Then she sobered and looked at him again. "But it is good to know now why I feel as I do." Her smile returned. "And that it will soon be better."

She pulled away and looked at Gaelen seriously. "Gaelen, does Klast have the gift of seeing? He told Brensa I was with child when he rescued her. She claims that was how he convinced her I would still want her with me."

Gaelen raised his eyebrows in surprise. "If he does, I know nothing of it ... though he is canny. I sometimes wonder at his ability to judge people's intentions and to find ways out of dangerous situations." He continued thoughtfully. "They say there are men who have a small gift which comes upon them at unexpected times. Perhaps Klast is one of these. I wonder if he is aware of it himself? I wonder if I should speak to him about it ... no, it may be best left as it is."

Marja nodded distractedly. "Gaelen, Summer Festival is in two days. At home in Catania, I would have been riding in the hills, gathering greens and flowers to decorate the castle. I miss that sorely. It makes me homesick. And I need exercise. So does my mare. I want to take her out and acquaint myself with the countryside. I need to breathe, Gaelen. I know you want to keep me safe, especially now, but this confinement is driving me mad. I wish to take Brensa and ride outside the city. If you must increase the guard, then do so, but I truly need to ride."

Before Gaelen had time to answer, another thought popped out. "And we need to find a good midwife. I will want to interview several to find one I trust and who has knowledge and experience. I will not have a surgeon. I will not trust a man with this. What can men know of childbirth? Midwives have borne their own and have seen many births." Marja stopped and looked at him anxiously.

Gaelen decided to deal with the second request first. "I am certain there are excellent midwives who would serve well. There is no need to insist on a surgeon. I tend to mistrust them myself and prefer to go to a healer woman with my ailments. Their knowledge of herbs and medicinals seems more effective." He stopped for a moment, stuck by an idea. "I wonder if Liethis might assist in choosing one."

"Liethis, the seer you sent for?"

"Yes. She arrived early this afternoon. I have already spoken with her. She plans to remain here for Summer Festival. I would like you to meet her. I think you will find her very interesting." He nodded, having made up his mind. "I will have her come to meet you tomorrow ... and perhaps she will be able to say if it is safe for you to ride out."

He regarded her closely as if making up his mind. "Marja, she has given me much to think on. I can only speak of this with you in strictest confidence, but I think it important for you to know. It will help you understand why I keep you under such strong guard. Do not even speak of it to Brensa." He eyed her, waiting for agreement.

Marja nodded slowly, waiting for him to continue. When he did not, she answered, "You may depend on my silence."

"Both Klast and Liethis have informed me that I have a traitor among my most trusted men. Liethis does not know his identity. Klast does because he overheard his name spoken by the men who took Brensa. You need to know his name so that you may be vigilant for your safety, since his first treasonous act was his attempt to remove you. The attack on our party was meant to take you, not Brensa. You probably already know this."

Marja nodded.

Gaelen continued, "Though it will be much more difficult here, I fear he will make another attempt on your life. His identity has given me great cause for concern. I would have trusted him completely had I not the information Klast gave me." Gaelen hesitated, rubbing his hand over his eyes.

Marja placed her hand on his arm in reassurance and waited silently a moment. When Gaelen did not continue she whispered, "Who is it, Gaelen? I swear it will not leave my lips."

Gaelen's answer was barely audible. "It is Sinnath." He shook his head. He still could hardly believe it. "One of my father's oldest and most trusted advisors. I have Klast looking for proof." Gaelen sat down on the garden bench and sighed.

Marja sat beside him and wove her arm through his. "You will overcome this. He is the only one? Liethis does not see any others?" Gaelen shook his head. "Then he will be found out. And now our child will strengthen the union of our peoples. You will succeed … no, we will succeed, all of us together. If he is the only one, it means you have many who stand with you. Look to them."

Gaelen tried his best to give a hopeful smile and squeezed her arm. Then he straightened and rose. "Will you see Liethis then? Tomorrow?"

"Certainly. Do you have time to have tea with me before you leave? Brensa could join us. She is afraid to be alone. I fear I have already left her overlong."

Gaelen hesitated. There was so much that needed to be done. Then he made himself relax. This, too, was important. "Tea would be most welcome."

Marja called to Brensa to have one of the guards send for the tea and invited her to rejoin them in the garden.

Over tea Gaelen admired the women's garlands. "How are the preparations for the Festival going?"

"I have planned the menu with the cook, and the great hall is decorated. These garlands are for our chambers," Marja told him.

During a lull Brensa gathered her courage and inquired of Gaelen, "My lord, has there been word from Catania? Have you heard how Nellis and Mikost fare? Has she delivered her child?"

At Brensa's anxious expression Marja's face fell, and she looked guilty. "Oh, yes, my lord. What news of Catania? I have been remiss. Thank you for reminding me, Brensa."

Gaelen shook his head. "None yet I fear. I expect a messenger soon. When he comes, I will be certain to inquire about your friends. Perhaps he will carry special messages for each of you. Of course, I have sent word to Argost of events here, since we arrived in Bargia."

He gave the women what he hoped was an encouraging smile. "Soon we will have better news. It is too early to speak of the coming child, but I am certain your friends will welcome the announcement when we are able to tell them."

Gaelen turned. "Brensa, I am aware that you already knew of this from Klast. I must demand that you speak of it to no one until I deem it safe."

Brensa nodded. "Of course, my lord, I understand." She looked pleased at being included in this important secret.

Gaelen stood. "Ladies, I regret I must leave you now. There is much that requires my attention." He turned to Marja. "I will send for Liethis. Tomorrow I promise to give you an answer regarding riding out." With that he gave her a quick, worried embrace and left.

47: LIETHIS SEES

Liethis arrived with a single guard as escort. Common belief held that to harm a seer would bring years of darkness and bad luck upon the people. No one wished to test that belief. Liethis thought it to be untrue, that Earth's ways were inscrutable, but she did nothing to dispel the idea. It would be impossible to dissuade people, and the belief did no harm.

Liethis felt drawn to Marja immediately. She warmed to her calm demeanour, her clear, open gaze and welcoming smile.

The guard left her at the gate to the garden. The air was still quite warm for this late in the afternoon, so Marja led them to two small benches facing each other in a shaded corner. They provided comfort without shutting the women inside. The tea and cakes, along with some fresh new cheese she had ordered, arrived right behind Liethis.

Before they sat, Marja held out her hand. "Liethis, I am honoured to meet you. My lord speaks of you as a trusted friend and tells me he relies on your talents. Any friend of my lord is most welcome. It would please me if we should also become friends. Please, will you sit down?"

Liethis took the proffered hand and held it a moment, gathering impressions of this woman who had experienced so much in such a short time. She sensed a mixture of warmth and coolness and a strong core that would not be easily bent. She felt decisiveness, well balanced by compassion. Yes, this woman must be kept safe. Gaelen would rely on her insight and strength in the trials to come.

Liethis smiled warmly at Marja in acknowledgement. "Thank you, my lady. I am confident it shall be so." Then she turned her attention to Brensa.

Brensa had remained behind Marja, as became her position, but Liethis could sense the effort it took Brensa not to blurt out her own questions. Liethis reached around Marja and offered her hand to Brensa, who took it timidly and allowed herself to be drawn forward. As soon as she had, she relaxed noticeably. The sense of calm Liethis sent her put her at ease. The tension left Brensa's shoulders, and she met Liethis' eyes with gratitude.

Liethis could feel turmoil emanating from Brensa. She knew what the girl had gone through and understood her need for reassurance. In spite of the girl's fear, Liethis sensed a small gift of healing in Brensa's hands. This would be useful during Marja's pregnancy, as it would help her give comfort to her lady. In her turn, it would assist in Brensa's own healing process, which Liethis saw would be long and difficult.

As Liethis looked into Brensa's eyes, her foremost question came to her mind. There was a man she felt a connection to … yes, the man who had rescued her. The longing to know what might become of this attraction was so strong that Liethis could almost touch it, as though it were a physical thing. She sighed inwardly. She could not divine the outcome of this connection. Klast, too, had his demons to wrestle. Yet she sensed a thread there, still connecting the two.

Liethis kept Brensa's hand in hers as she spoke. "Brensa, you will heal from the ordeal you have been through. It will not be easy, but you are stronger than you think. Your lady will need you during her pregnancy. You will be a comfort to each other."

Liethis hesitated, still feeling the longing emanating from Brensa around Klast. "Brensa, I cannot be certain where the path leads with regard to Klast. That way is unclear. All I can say is that he cares for you and will never knowingly hurt you. He watches over you."

Brensa sagged with disappointment as she nodded her understanding. Her pain made her thoughts as clear as if she had spoken them aloud. Klast had been candid with Brensa that he could never entertain thoughts of a relationship with a woman. His duties made that impossible … but Liethis said the path was unclear. Did that mean that there might be a way? And Liethis said he cared for her, watched over her even. Brensa knew there was something between them. She felt it. Whenever Klast was near, even though he seemed invisible to others, Brensa always knew where he was. She saw him even when he did his best to avoid her notice. Brensa also knew Liethis' sight was true. How else could she have known what Brensa ached to ask her? Hope. She must hold on to hope.

Liethis suppressed a sigh of sadness and addressed Brensa gently. "The way is still unclear for you. Do not despair."

She turned back to Marja. "My lady, you, too, have been through a difficult time." She glanced back at Brensa to include her. "You will rely greatly on each other in the time to come."

Liethis then gave her full attention to Marja, pleased that she sensed no jealousy after the consideration Brensa had received. "Lady, Lord Gaelen will rely on your wisdom. Others will advise him to act more rashly and swiftly than is prudent. It will rest with you to provide the balance. He will need your strength and your sense of justice."

Then the grave expression left her face, and it became wreathed in a broad smile, "Your son is strong. Keep him safe. He will provide the people with the hope they need to follow Lord Gaelen's rule."

She grew serious again. "He must be kept safe until he is born. I sense danger to yourself and to him. But I have told Lord Gaelen that you need to be seen by the people, so I have suggested he agree to your request for more freedom."

She sensed the next question from Marja. "Your health is not in danger. Riding will be good for you. The menace I sense around you comes from someone close by you, perhaps within the castle itself. Lord Gaelen has agreed to increase your guard so that you may move about Bargia as you wish … under one condition, which I suggested. You must always take Brensa with you. I sense that her presence is linked to your safety."

Marja's elation lit up her face. "Thank you, Liethis. You know what this means to me." Then she stopped as what Liethis had just told her sank in. "A son, lady? You say I carry Gaelen's heir? Are you certain?" She turned to Brensa and gave her a spontaneous hug. "Did you hear, Brensa? An heir! Gaelen will be so pleased." She released Brensa and turned back to Liethis. "Thank you, Liethis. I will take care not to overstep my freedom. Lord Gaelen must have his heir."

Liethis rose to leave. She smiled warmly as she turned to go. "Take care of each other." With that she opened the door and nodded to the guard waiting for her that she was ready to go.

48: A RESCUE

Marja greeted her beloved Keisha with a nose rub and a carrot. She felt lighter and more optimistic than she had since before the invasion of Catania. Even Brensa seemed less fearful as she took the reins of her small mare, Senna. The double guard put the only wrinkle on the day. The weather shone sunny and bright without being overly hot. A kitchen maid had filled their saddlebags with a lunch of fresh dark bread, new cheese, potted meats, cakes and wine. Marja exclaimed in delight when she discovered the inclusion of some honeyed fruits left from last fall's harvest.

The party left by the north gate. This road wound into the low hills that made up the best lands for growing. Green meadows dotted it; small copses of trees showed the bright greens of new leaves. Some still bore pink and white blossoms that promised apples, pears and plums come fall. Fields of grains gave evidence to the richness of the soil. In between, cottages and small steadings nestled.

Once well away from the castle, Marja called to the guards. "I wish to give my mare her head and put on some speed."

They did not like the idea, but Marja insisted. They all galloped down the beaten dirt road until Marja and Brensa were both flushed with colour and covered in fine dust. Marja slowed Keisha and bade the guards find a good place to rest and eat. She had intended to pick flowers and branches to decorate with, but had noticed that preparations were mostly finished and decided just to enjoy a day out.

Marja loved to ride, and this afternoon she could almost believe she was home in Catania again. Except, back home she and Brensa would have ridden out alone. She shook the thought away. One of the guards had spread a blanket under a tree, brought the food out of the bags and moved off at a small distance with the others to eat their more simple meal.

"Brensa, we will never finish all this food. Take the remainder and give it to the guards. They will enjoy it," she instructed.

Brensa hesitated in fear, but at Marja's encouragement she quickly took the bundle over and more quickly returned. Marja even sent over enough of their fruits that each man could enjoy one of the sweet treats. They made their pleasure evident with nods, waves and grins of delight. Such treats were rare among their ranks.

As the sun descended midway to the western horizon, one of the guards approached the women. "It is time to return, my lady. It will be dark soon."

Reluctantly, Marja agreed, knowing he was right. They needed to be home before the sun sank behind the hills. She knew Gaelen had given orders to be notified as soon as they returned. He would be mad with worry if they delayed, and he had enough on his mind without that.

The ride back remained uneventful until their way took them past some narrow alleys that ran between a section of poorer shops selling cheap wine, dry goods and amulets. One of the alleys emitted a cacophony of youthful shouting amid a background of cries of pain, obviously from a small animal. Both Marja and Brensa halted their horses abruptly. One of the guards almost bumped into them. Marja shouldered past the forward guard and entered the narrow alley without thinking, Brensa close behind her. They ignored the shouts of warning from the men who could not get in front of them in the narrow space.

They came upon three lads of about twelve gathered around a young kitten. They had tied a rope around its neck and were poking it with sticks. Its tail was a bloody stump and one of its ears had been cut or torn half off. One of the youths wielded a small knife.

Brensa cried out, and her hands flew to her face.

Marja filled with such moral outrage that she forgot where

and who she was. She jumped off her horse and ran toward the boys with no thought for danger. "Stop that!" she shouted.

A sneer started to cross the face of the one with the knife, but it was soon replaced by fear when four guards filled the alley and two interposed themselves quickly in front of the women. By now, Brensa had also climbed down and stood shaking beside Marja. The miscreants fled out the other end of the alley, leaving the kitten behind. Marja tried to send the guards after them, but the leader shook his head.

"I think that would be unwise, my lady. Better let word spread without reprisals. This sort of behaviour is common among these youth, who have nothing better to do. Save your reputation for more important matters."

Marja opened her mouth to upbraid him for his effrontery, but found her attention drawn back to Brensa and a guard who had his small dagger poised to deal the mercy cut to the mauled kitten. Brensa lunged toward the guard, wailing, "Nooo!" and shoved his hand away. Then she hovered over the kitten protectively, preventing the guard from dispatching it.

He looked at Marja helplessly, "My lady, the poor thing is beyond help. It would be a mercy to kill it, to save it from a slow death."

Marja looked at the kitten and knew he was probably right. She squatted and put her arm around Brensa, saying, "You know it is best for the poor little thing."

Brensa turned to her, tears making tracks down her stricken face. "Please, my lady. I can save her. I know I can."

Seeing Brensa's obvious anguish, Marja suddenly realized what made this so important to her. She needed to rescue this kitten as she herself had been rescued. Marja believed it to be a futile endeavour, and she wished to spare the kitten more misery. Yet, she understood that it was necessary to allow Brensa to try to save it. At the same time, she worried how Brensa would react if the kitten died in spite of her efforts.

Brensa continued to hover over the kitten. She had by now freed it from the rope around its neck. She squatted, examining it where the fur had been chafed off. She looked up at Marja again, hands still on the kitten, which to Marja's amazement made no protest. She pleaded, "Please, my lady, let me try."

Marja sighed. "Very well, Brensa. I fear it is too late, but I see that you are determined. But on one condition. That you can keep it calm enough to get it back to the castle without help from anyone else. I will not subject others to the nasty bites and scratches a cornered animal may inflict in an attempt to escape."

Brensa flashed Marja a look of gratitude. "I can, my lady. I am certain of it." She let go of the kitten and took off her apron. Then she reached back toward it, apron in hand, crooning softly. The small cat bristled at first and spat weakly at the apron, but as Brensa's hands touched her, she stopped spitting and merely eyed her warily. Brensa kept crooning soothingly as she gently wrapped the apron around it, taking care to apply pressure to the still bleeding stump where the tail had been. It mewled weakly when Brensa scooped it up and cradled it to her chest.

Brensa looked at the guards, then turned to Marja and hesitated. But her need to hold the kitten made her speak up in spite of her fear of the men. "I will need help to mount, my lady."

In the aftermath of the fright they had just experienced, the request struck Marja as funny, and she had to choke back a fit of nervous laughter. "Of course. Marrell, will you lift her into her saddle?"

Brensa was so intent on the kitten that she barely reacted to the guard's touch when he obeyed. The party did not speak for the remainder of the ride home, each wrapped in their own thoughts. When they reached the stables, at Marja's nod, Marrell reached Brensa down. She accepted the assistance but flinched at his touch.

49: NO-TAIL

Back in their chambers, Marja watched Brensa set about nursing her tiny patient. She looked on in mild disbelief as the little cat allowed Brensa to bathe its wounds, apply salve and bind its stump. All the while Brensa kept up a low, repetitive crooning. She cleaned the matted fur with deft, gentle motions, something the kitten apparently liked, for as Brensa continued her ministrations it relaxed. It even seemed to cooperate by lying docilely on either side, its head resting calmly on the soft cloth Brensa had spread underneath it.

As Brensa worked, the kitten's colour showed through, a tortoiseshell, having large black spots ringed with greyish brown. It would be very pretty when it dried ... that is, except for the lack of a tail and half an ear. When she had done all she could, Brensa presented her with the bowl of warm milk Marja had ordered.

For a moment Marja's hopeful anticipation fell, as the poor thing seemed to show no interest in drinking. But Brensa lifted it gently and placed the chin into the milk, so she would taste it. She held it up then, and to Marja's amazement, it took a few laps. That seemed enough to satisfy Brensa. She put the little cat back on the cloth she had arranged in a basket, close to the warmth of the hearth. There the kitten curled into a ball and went to sleep.

Brensa met Marja's gaze, and with a proud determined look, declared, "She will live. And she will heal. I know it." Then she smiled, and, with a flicker of humour added, "Maybe she will even become a good mouser for the castle."

Marja smiled back. "Then she ... if she is a she ... will need a name."

"Oh, I am certain she is a she. Yes, I will need to find a strong name for her to match her brave nature." Brensa looked thoughtful for a moment. "On the other hand, perhaps I will call her

No-tail. That way, when she goes about the castle and I am looking for her, everyone will know who I mean. And they will all recognize and remember her. Yes, she will be No-tail." She gave a satisfied nod. No-tail she was.

50: FESTIVAL

At Summer Festival, tradition dictated that the lord provide a feast for the citizens in the great hall of the castle. All were free to come and partake of the bounty that Earth had provided, prepared by the servants in the castle kitchen. Extra help was hired to have everything ready and to keep the flow of sated and often inebriated citizens moving through. The castle filled with a jostling, cheerful crowd. Often Summer Festival provided children with their first taste of sweetmeats and other delicacies they had never dreamed of. Happy chaos was the order of the day. Those who served the food and ale took turns, so that everyone had an opportunity to participate in the celebrations. Even the guards rotated.

New summer greens, cress, early bunching onions, dandelion greens, wood fungi, and early peas were among the delicacies available, made into salads or cooked into main dishes. Most sweets soaked in new wildflower honey with its delicate flavour. Early wild strawberries abounded, both fresh and baked into all manner of breads and treats. Instead of the heavier smoked or dried meats that sustained the people through the winter, meats at this festival had been freshly killed and stewed, roasted on spits, or pan fried in butter. New ale and hard cider flowed in abundance as well as wine in more modest quantities.

Nightfall came late this time of year, and the festivities lasted until well after dark. Few business owners expected any work to be done until after midday the following day. As often as not, they were in no better shape than those they employed, pained heads being the order of the day.

Usually, though Grenth posted extra guards, they seldom proved necessary, other than to make sure those who had too much to drink were efficiently escorted out the door. This year, due to recent events, Gaelen had ordered an additional cadre of soldiers present. The majority of these had orders to keep close to the head table, where Gaelen, Marja and all the local dignitaries sat, greeting those who wished a glimpse of their host's finery.

Klast, disguised as a peasant, stationed himself behind the head table close to Marja. He lounged against the wall with a mug of ale and a plate laden with riches that he hardly tasted. He could tell that only Brensa and Gaelen sensed his presence. Even Marja remained unaware of him. Klast kept his eyes particularly on the movements in and around Marja. This event provided a prime opportunity for a second attempt on her life. The hard part was keeping his mind off Brensa. Her nearness, and his awareness that she knew he was there, made concentration more difficult. Every now and then she would steal a quick glance in his direction. She did not try to meet his eyes, but nothing escaped his attention, so he found these looks distracting.

Gaelen followed his father's example in not using a taster. He shared Lord Bargest's belief that no one ought to die in the place of another. Since there had been no need of one for generations, Klast agreed it would seem out of place were Gaelen to change that tradition now. It would not be wise to alert Gaelen's detractors that he suspected something. But it made Klast's job more critical, and he felt the pressure.

As a new shift of servers appeared, a young woman approached the head table with a fresh jug of hard cider, the drink Marja preferred, in her condition, to the stronger wine. As she filled Marja's cup, Klast noticed a furtive, anxious glance around that seemed out of place. He dove forward, stumbling awkwardly in a semblance of drunkenness, and reached the table just as Marja lifted her goblet to her lips. Klast lunged clumsily into Brensa, shoving her into Marja, and knocking the cup from Marja's hand to the floor. Two dogs, which had been waiting patiently for whatever fell from the table, eagerly began to lap up the sweet drink.

As Klast lurched back upright he managed to whisper the

word "poison" into Brensa's ear between loud, slurred apologies, before the guards grabbed him and escorted him roughly out.

As soon as the guards let him go, he re-entered the hall by a different route and sought out the narrow passageway he had seen the young woman leave by. This rarely used way led from the great hall into another small hallway and directly out a side service entrance of the castle. He hoped to find the woman alive to question her. That hope proved in vain. He located her body in the first passage. Her throat had been neatly cut, and her assailant was gone without a trace. Klast spared a thought of compassion for the poor maid who had played such an unfortunate part and paid for it with her life. Shock still showed on her lifeless face. No doubt she had had no idea it would be she herself who would become the victim. Klast cursed his luck in arriving too late both to get information and to save the girl's life. Taking on a different guise, he hurried back to his post. To his dismay, Brensa noticed him immediately.

Klast noted with relief that the situation appeared under control. Most of the revellers remained ignorant of the clamour at the head table. Gaelen and Marja did their best to draw attention away from the dogs, writhing and foaming at the mouth, death almost upon them. Gaelen had a guard stab them in the heart, to avoid too much blood, and wrap them in their cloaks to remove them.

Brensa assisted Marja to wipe off the spilled drink with exaggerated loudness and apologies to draw away attention. It kept those aware to a merciful few. No doubt, by morning many stories would circulate about what had happened. The truth would be indiscernible from the tales arising from the imaginations of folk who had eaten and drunk too much. Unfortunately, those few sitting at the head table, and those guarding it, were all too aware. Gaelen's plan to keep his knowledge of a plot secret had been compromised. He would no longer be able to feign ignorance. This would make Klast's work much more difficult, as the traitors would take more care to avoid discovery.

When Marja shot Klast a look of disbelief mixed with gratitude, he knew that she had been informed of his involvement. He acknowledged her with the briefest of bows.

He watched Brensa make a worried inspection of the deep pocket she had sewn into her gown. He had heard of the rescue and understood the gesture. No-tail lay curled there, apparently unharmed by Brensa's tumble into Marja. Brensa stroked her with visible relief. Thank Earth the kitten had not tasted the poisoned drink. It would have been hard for Brensa if the kitten did not survive. He saw Marja notice Brensa's attention to the pocket and give her a wan smile of understanding.

No one outside their inner circle yet knew of Marja's pregnancy, so in spite of the events at dinner, she stayed as long as was politely expected. When Klast saw her bend to Gaelen and whisper in his ear, he was ready. Klast knew that Gaelen wished to stay longer, for appearances. As Marja and Brensa made to leave, Gaelen nodded slightly, and Klast surreptitiously followed. When the women had safely reached their destination, with the door barred and the guard back in place, he left in search of clues.

51: ENTER DEATH

The worn, grey wagon, pulled by a swaybacked nag, approached the north gate at a tired plod. On the bench, just big enough for two, a dusty old man held the reins in lax hands, shoulders slumped, chin resting almost on his chest. The wagon's bed held an aging trunk and three dilapidated baskets. A blanket, some twigs for kindling and a few pots, spoons and bowls filled out the cargo. Beside them lay a bundle just over four feet long, tenderly wrapped in another faded blanket and covered with a fine layer of dust.

The guard, Brest, looked at his partner and groaned. "Earth, what now. I was about to lock the gate." His partner grunted understanding.

Dusk dimmed the light, and the gates would be locked for the night. No one else travelled the road outside the city that evening. The air held that expectant pause that comes at the end of a hot midsummer day, when businesses close their doors and tired workers look forward to supper and a quiet span by the hearth before retiring for the night.

"State your name and your business, sir. We are about to close the gate. You travel late." The guard made no effort to hide his annoyance at being bothered at this span. His wife waited at home with a hot stew, and he looked forward to spending some time playing with his infant son before he went to sleep. The lad was his firstborn, strong and happy. Those few moments spent in play each day made the boredom of guard duty bearable.

The old man raised his head and answered slowly. "We come, sir, to attend my daughter, who bears her first child. We be invited to stay with her. We be old now and canna manage our small croft outside the city." Then he shook himself, as though remembering something he had pushed aside. "Alas, my wife willna know her grandchild. She took ill on the way and lies in

188

yon blanket. I beg you, sir, let me enter, that my daughter may bid her mother farewell and that we may bury her." One tear escaped a sunken eye and rolled between the creases in his face to fall on his dusty collar.

Brest hesitated. After all, the woman had been ill. He studied the old man as he decided what to do. The rules said that diseased persons could not be admitted. But this couple was old and the woman already dead. Surely she had just died of age, a flux, maybe, or a cough. The old man seemed well enough.

"What was the nature of her illness, sir? Did she suffer from fits or a fever?" As he asked his questions he stepped up to the wagon and gingerly pulled back a corner of the blanket to confirm the man's account. The old woman looked grey but had surely been dead only a short while. He dropped the blanket back in disgust, then spat on his hands and wiped them hastily on his tunic.

"No sir. She just felt unwell, said 'er eyes hurt and she couldna eat. Then she just went to sleep and dinna wake."

"Very well, then. Enter. Sorry for your loss." He stepped back and made way for the wagon to pass. Then he hurriedly shut and locked the gate. Bidding the lone remaining guard goodnight, he strode home to his wife and child, whistling tunelessly.

52: PLAGUE

A young soldier hurried to Gaelen with a request that he see Liethis in her chamber as soon as possible. Gaelen had not expected her in the city, as he had not sent for her, so he knew this must be urgent. When he knocked on her door he found, to his surprise, that she had not unpacked and looked ready to depart again.

She closed the door swiftly behind him and started pacing back and forth across the floor with obvious agitation. Gaelen's eyes widened in surprise. He had never seen Liethis this way. Respect made him hold his peace until she felt ready to tell him what had made her travel here and ask to see him so urgently. She did not make him wait long.

"Gaelen, I must leave again immediately. The city weeps in pain and mourning. I can barely breathe. A pestilence has entered. It leaves no home untouched. Children weep for their mothers. The gravediggers cannot keep up. Pyres burn those that cannot be buried. Orphans need food and shelter."

Liethis slowed for a moment, looking at Gaelen as she explained. "Children survive this disease best. Adults die more easily. Of those that survive, some are blind. If you can, tell the people to keep away from strong light until they recover. This disease chooses rich and poor equally. No house can be kept safe. It is too late to warn people to leave. That will only spread death beyond the city's walls more quickly. It cannot be stopped."

Gaelen's stomach knotted as he heard Liethis speak.

She resumed pacing as she spoke, then again stopped to look at him.

He whispered his worst fear. "Marja?"

Liethis face softened slightly. "She will be spared." Then she answered his unspoken question. "As will your son, since I see him born and hale."

Gaelen breathed a small sigh of relief. Then concern for his people reasserted itself. "Liethis, you speak as if these things have already happened. But no one has reported any unusual deaths."

Liethis continued walking back and forth, hands clenched white-knuckled at her sides, face pinched. "The seed has entered the city. It will not be long. You must prepare. Now I must leave, for it becomes unbearable. I can tell you no more. The rest is lost amid this pain." She picked up her travel bags and opened the door. She managed a wan smile for Gaelen as she hurried out. Gaelen stood rooted in the room, shocked, as the import of what he had been told sank in.

As soon as he gathered his thoughts he called an emergency meeting of the inner council. This included Janest, Grenth, and, unfortunately, Sinnath. Surely even he could not use this crisis to undermine Bargia further. Gaelen still found it hard to accept that a man who had shown such loyalty to his father could turn traitor.

The council decided it was premature to alert the people. They agreed with Gaelen that it would not do to have a mass exodus from the city. That would only spread the contagion further. Instead, they quietly set up plans for the distribution of emergency food, decided how children left without parents would be cared for, made a list of gravediggers and planned how the army would be deployed to keep order during the panic that would surely ensue.

Gaelen's next action was to go to Marja and share the grim news with her. He knew she would keep it to herself. He needed to share his worries with someone who would not expect complete self-control from him. And he needed to spare her the worry over her own safety and that of their son.

Lastly, Gaelen sent for Klast by the method they had set up. A soldier took Klast this coded message. "I need you to make an arrest. Meet me for information." Gaelen intended to send Klast immediately to Catania to warn Argost. Uncovering Sinnath's betrayal would have to wait.

53: TO CATANIA

Klast's orders made it clear that speed was of the essence. Knowing that hunting and cooking would waste precious time, he packed travel food that needed no preparation and weighed little. Nuts and seeds, dried fruit, hard biscuits, strips of dried salted meat, a wedge of aged cheese and a waterskin; not the most appetizing fare, but Klast had survived on much less and much worse in the past. At least his belly would be full. Though he wasted no time, he packed methodically. As always, his medicinal pouch stayed strapped to his belt and his weapons remained hidden about his body and his clothing.

For his mount he chose an unremarkable roan gelding that had seen hard work. He made sure the tack and saddle were sound but not new. No point inviting attention or theft. Besides food, he carried only two blankets, a rolled up oiled skin against rain, and two changes of clothing of different types, in case he needed more than one disguise. Once ready, he slipped out of the city under cover of darkness through an opening in the wall few knew about. As he left, he had a sense of foreboding, something to do with Brensa. It left him with a feeling of urgency that made it even more important to hurry back. The further he rode from Bargia, the stronger the need to return became.

He recalled a recent conversation with Brensa. He had caught her watching him with silent longing when he had entered the castle in search of clues to Sinnath's plans. He had been surprised that she had noticed him. The way she looked at him made it plain that her feelings ran deep, so he had taken pains to make it clear he would never return those feelings and that he was no good match for her. He had been quite blunt. While she had nodded miserably that she understood, he still had the sense that she wanted more from him. He was aware how unlikely it was that any other man could ever win her trust and that saddened

Klast. She deserved better. He still kept an eye out for her safety and checked on her regularly. It had surprised him just how often he had caught her watching him, when no one else seemed aware of his presence. How did she do that, and what was this strange connection he could not escape? In his solitary moments it gnawed at him.

Klast stayed on the trail as long as it remained dark, then slipped into the woods at first light. He found a small stream, where he watered his mount and hobbled it on the grassy bank to graze while he took a couple of spans rest. Sleep eluded him. His mind kept going over what Gaelen had told him and to the darkness he sensed surrounding Brensa.

As dusk lengthened the shadows between the trees, Klast resumed his trek. He allowed himself to enjoy the quiet that increased as the woods settled for the night. He listened for the scurrying of the night hunters, and the hoot of an owl occasionally breaking the stillness. The weather remained clear and cooled to a crispness at this higher altitude that foretold the first frosts of autumn just a few eightdays away. Through the topmost branches he could spy the occasional star flickering in the indigo of the cloudless sky. The solitude of the journey provided a much needed change from the pace he had kept the past eightdays. Klast's deeply solitary nature required such respite. His progress was swift and uneventful throughout the night.

Dawn found him only spans away from Catania's north gate, the same they had left by less than two moons ago.

Klast chose to enter by this gate, in full view of the people. He wore his "I am not important" look, just in case someone might remember that he had not been there previously and become suspicious. If asked to explain his arrival, he planned to say he had run out of work in the countryside and had come to try his luck finding work rebuilding the city. "Surely a man wi' a strong back and good hands be of use?" This would provide him with a cover and allow movement throughout the city.

54: CRISIS

Bargia seemed to hold its breath for several days. The weather grew hot and still. A miasma rose from the guttered streets, wafting from rotting debris and human waste where flies feasted and deposited their eggs. At the peak of summer, the lack of rainfall left major areas of the city as foul as a midden. The only true respite lay inside the walled gardens of the wealthy. Even so, many of these regularly left for summer homes outside the city, where it stayed cooler, especially the women and children. Husbands had business that needed their attention and travelled back and forth as they could. Their mistresses received much more attention during these days, though they did not always welcome it. The numbers of newborn among them increased in late winter and early spring.

The old man's daughter watched her man bury him alongside his wife five days after he entered the gates. The old man never saw his granddaughter. As the young husband lowered the body into the grave and covered it over, he began to feel chilled, and his eyes hurt in the light. By evening he was delirious with fever. His frantic wife kept wet cloths on his brow and invoked Earth for his recovery. Three days later the fever broke, and the red blisters that had covered his body crusted over. He would recover, though his eyes would never again enjoy the fineness of his wife's needlework or see the lashes framing his daughter's eyes as she laughed into his face. He was one of the lucky ones.

In the area of the city where the soldiers and guards made their homes, the one who had examined the old woman's blanket fell ill. He died in four days, still ignorant of what he had allowed in when he opened the gate. His infant son developed a mild rash and recovered without harm. The babe's mother also raged with fever and was covered in red blisters. She lay raving for three days before her fever broke. Her milk dried up, and a wet-nurse had to be found. That good woman, too, was placed on a pyre ten days later, leaving the poor mother with two babes to find milk and pap for.

The contagion spread like mist, insinuating invisible tendrils into every nook and crevice, silently invading every home and alley, undetectable to all but a seer such as Liethis. Some lesser adepts felt it too but could not interpret what they sensed. It showed no favourites. Rich and poor alike succumbed to its stealthy touch. It did seem to show preference for age; the older the victim, the more likely they would die. Children recovered best, though many would never see again to welcome Earth in Her new spring dress. They would shun bright light, as it always hurt their eyes. Or worse, blindness robbed them of sight altogether.

As Liethis had predicted, the gravediggers, those who still lived, could not keep up. Even mass graves could not prevent the bodies from piling up. Soon the stench of pyres almost masked that from the gutters. Also, as Liethis had predicted, the shelters set up for orphans and invalids overflowed with survivors. It became difficult to find enough able-bodied workers to cook and care for them, as they, too, fell prey to the disease.

Before it was all over, an eightday after the first hard frost, death claimed fully one fourth of the inhabitants of the city. Once the pestilence took full hold, no one had time even to mourn. That would have to wait until some order returned, until shops reopened to feed the citizens, and firewood could be bought once again, until the gates once more opened to wagons filled with goods from the outside.

As soon as it became clear there was contagion in Bargia City, Gaelen ordered the gates closed and declared quarantine. A futile gesture, he knew, as the plague had already travelled into the countryside via the carriages of the wealthy departing for their summer homes and the wagons of merchants and tradesman carrying goods to sell in neighbouring towns and villages. Yet, those who did not understand what he knew expected the measure.

It also gave him some control over what went on within the city. And it avoided the added confusion and panic that always accompanied the mass exodus that would surely have occurred.

Once he ordered the gates closed, all Gaelen could do was oversee the organization of relief efforts and wait and hope that his enemies would not choose this time to attack. Perhaps Sinnath would wait to see if the disease would do his dirty work for him. The irony of that possibility was not lost on him.

55: ARGOST

Klast's first business took him to a respectable but modest looking inn on the outskirts of the city. He needed a bath before meeting with Argost and wanted to take a few spans to sense the mood of the people. His mission here was twofold: to warn Argost of the coming contagion and to take back any relevant information he could gather. He and Gaelen both suspected that Sinnath had connections outside of Bargia and that others might have designs on Catania as well.

As Klast entered the inn, the aroma of fresh mutton and onions made his mouth water and his stomach growl. He decided his bath could wait until he had eaten. A small table stood against one wall, a rough bench bracketing two sides. With his back to the wall, Klast could observe the entire room without inviting undue notice or risking that anyone would ask to join him, as it was still too early to be busy.

"I be wantin' a bowl o' yer stew, sir, and a bath when I be done." Klast made his request to the innkeeper at the counter before he sat down.

"Yer coin first." The innkeeper regarded Klast's dirty, coarse attire with suspicion. "That be costin' three coppers. And if ye be needin' a bed it be four coppers more."

"No bed." Klast handed him the three coins and took his seat. The mutton, when it came, was young, mild and tender, stewed in a rich onion broth. The bowl included boiled dumplings smothered in the same gravy and glazed new beets in a smaller bowl to the side. The dark bread was still warm and crusty. The only disappointment was the ale, which, while chilled, was flat and watery. Klast fell to with gusto as he let his eyes and ears take in what they could.

It soon became apparent he would gather no news here. The locals talked of good prospects for the upcoming harvest, where one might get the best new cheeses and the higher costs of wine, this last an effect of the burning of the warehouses during the invasion. Overall the mood seemed positive, and Klast sensed no unrest that might allow him to make inquiries without appearing too curious.

The inn had no public bath, so Klast took his bath in a private room and allowed himself to enjoy a few moments of leisure before entering further into the heart of the city. The hot water, plentiful soap and clean linen did much to improve his outlook. The innkeeper had made it clear, though, that he must vacate the room within a span or pay the bed rate.

With no leads to follow, he made up his mind to seek out Argost next. After that, he would hire a room in the seedier part of city, where he could be more likely to find some leads. He put thoughts of Brensa and the tug he still felt firmly out of his mind and concentrated on the work ahead. The sooner he finished, the sooner he could return and report back to Gaelen. Only then would he allow himself to ponder this urgency regarding Brensa.

As he neared the central square, Klast spied Mikost and asked him if he knew where Argost might be found.

When Mikost recognized Klast, he asked, "Sir, how fare Lady Marja and Brensa?"

"They were well when I last saw them. How fares Nellis?"

"We have a strong son." Mikost beamed with pride. Then he sobered. "But Nellis misses Lady Marja fiercely. Even the birth of our son is not enough. She is most unhappy. She wishes to go to Bargia, the three of us." Mikost suggested to Klast that his skills might be put to good use in Bargia, perhaps even more effectively than in Catania. Could they possibly travel back to Bargia with Klast, so Nellis could rejoin the service of her lady?

Klast advised him that it was not safe to travel to Bargia at this time but agreed to mention to Argost that Mikost might be needed there before winter made travel impossible.

Klast liked Mikost and knew that Marja would welcome Nellis. Brensa, too, might be cheered by the presence of her friend. Argost might agree to let Mikost go in the fall. Thinking of Brensa reminded him of the pull he still felt. He pushed the thought aside and brought his focus back to his mission.

He located Argost in the main square, conferring with two men. By the costly fabric and detailed embroidery on their tunics, they appeared to be persons of influence. He faded back into the shadows until Argost had finished, then followed him into the castle. Three men and two women waited in line outside the door to the audience chamber to meet with him. It looked like the usual mix, each person with some complaint that required advice, mediation or a decision of law. People came here for an audience when all other avenues had failed. Argost's decisions were binding.

Again Klast waited, taking his place at the end of the line as though one of this afternoon's regular petitioners. As he stood, looking unimportant and bored, he studied those in line and the two guards by the door. Other than one woman anxiously relating her tale about the apparent theft of her breeding ewe, nothing seemed worth anyone's attention. The line moved in an orderly fashion, and the people exited the chamber with apparent satisfaction. Even the woman with the missing ewe huffed importantly as she left.

Klast stepped inside the doorway and watched as Argost checked the notations of the scribe.

When Argost raised his head his eyes lit up in recognition. He turned quickly to the scribe. "Your services will not be required until tomorrow. Thank you."

The scribe looked puzzled for a moment, realizing the room still held a newcomer. When it became apparent the audience was over, he shrugged, picked up his sheets, ink and quill and departed.

Klast barred the door behind him and made sure there were no places for eavesdroppers to hide.

The precaution made Argost chuckle. "I chose this room carefully, my friend. You will find no extra eyes and ears here. Come, speak with me. Tell me the news of Bargia." As he spoke he stood and indicated the chair the scribe had vacated.

Before Klast had a chance to sit, he found his hand and forearm in a warm clasp of welcome.

As Klast took the proffered seat, Argost reached for a goblet from the tray on his desk and filled it with rich, red wine which he handed to Klast, a wide smile creasing his face. "It is good to see you." Then he sobered somewhat. "But if you are here, it must mean that either Lord Gaelen thinks he can spare you or he has urgent business only you can handle." He watched Klast expectantly as he waited for him to swallow a large gulp of wine.

Klast managed a tight smile in return, the expression unfamiliar to his face. Yet Argost's pleasure in seeing him was so genuine he could not help himself. He sensed once more that this man, at least, could be trusted. He had been impressed, too, with the order and sense of quiet normalcy in Catania. This had, no doubt, come about by Argost's diligent work and sound decisions. Gaelen had left Catania in able hands. Klast set down his goblet, forming his thoughts as he did so.

"It is good to see you again, too, Argost ... and to see Catania so obviously recovering and peaceful. Lord Gaelen will be pleased." Then he resumed his serious mien. "You are correct in both your assumptions, Argost. I have urgent news from Gaelen that he did not wish to entrust to another, and he was willing to have me away for a short while. The reasons are dire."

Argost raised his eyebrows in question but said nothing.

"Bargia is under quarantine," Klast began. "Since I have not acquired the disease that plagues Bargia I am confident that I do not carry it into Catania. Otherwise nothing could be so urgent as to bring me among the citizens here. Lord Gaelen wishes you to know how to deal with the disease before it strikes, as it most certainly will. He fears closing the gates in Bargia occurs too late to prevent its spread." Klast went on to share the instructions Liethis had given.

By the time he finished, Argost had gone grey with concern. Together they decided on a plan of action involving food, shelter and containment. Argost's greater worry centred on the question of power in Catania, should his men be decimated by the disease. He himself was already past his prime and needed a plan that would cover the eventuality of his own death, should he succumb. Catania remained stable now, but that would not last if his carefully implemented recovery and governance fell apart due to a lack of trustworthy people or to panic among its citizens. He did not doubt that others existed who waited eagerly to take control.

Their conference lasted until well past dark, neither man giving any thought to hunger. Argost informed Klast he had received intelligence that Lieth, the demesne to the west, had spies in Catania. One had been caught and interrogated. Before his execution, the man had revealed that Lord Wernost of Lieth had an informant in the house of a former aristocrat from Lord Cataniast's court, a certain Wilnor.

"Wilnor owns a large estate well outside the city," Argost explained. "However, without proof of treason, I have decided to wait and keep my ears open. Unless I receive more evidence of treasonous plans or activities, the improving stability and peaceful recovery in Catania should make it difficult for Wilnor to muster the support he needs."

Klast agreed. Argost had heard nothing from Gharn or Handosh but hoped no news meant just that.

Klast heard that recovery in Catania was proceeding even better than Argost had hoped. Most buildings had been repaired at least to the point where they were functional again. Most businesses had reopened, and those people who had lost jobs had found new positions. There appeared to be very little resentment against the presence of the soldiers from Bargia. As long as people could safely carry on with their lives and could look after their families, they cared not who ruled them. The harvest looked promising as well, a great source of relief to both Argost and the people.

Before leaving, Klast mentioned Mikost's request.

Argost confirmed that Mikost had proven an apt informant and had learned valuable skills as a diplomat. He felt reluctant to part with him, but he understood that Nellis suffered from loneliness and missed Marja and Brensa.

"Marja has only Brensa to trust. She would benefit from having another friend." Klast filled Argost in briefly on Brensa's ordeal in the cave.

Argost agreed that Gaelen could make good use of the skills Mikost had acquired. "I will consider sending Mikost to Bargia before winter. But only if I can find a party large enough to make attack from bandits unlikely."

Klast's further probing provided nothing more than Argost had already told him. Things seemed almost too quiet. Klast knew that would change soon, but he had done all he could to prepare Argost for the crisis the plague would bring.

The need to return to Bargia felt more urgent as each day passed. When he could find nothing worth his attention, his thoughts kept turning back to Brensa and the vague sense that she needed him. Two days short of the time he had planned to stay, he met with Argost a last time to receive any new messages, collected his horse and headed back to Bargia by the same way he had arrived, again travelling mostly at night.

56: RED FEVER

Marja took to pacing through the castle several times daily, a worried frown written on her face. Brensa attributed this to anxiety resulting from the attack at Summer Festival. She hurried dutifully after Marja, occasionally suggesting that she rest due to her condition. When the first reports of illness began to drift in, the frequency of Marja's tours increased, along with the depth of the frown lines between her brows. Brensa got her exercise, as did the guards ordered to protect Marja, just trying to keep up. When Brensa questioned her lady, Marja gave distracted, evasive answers or ineffectual murmurs of reassurance. Brensa could get no more out of her. Eventually she gave up and followed her silently about. She even held back her admonishments to Marja about tiring herself.

By this time rumours ran amok about Marja's unconfirmed pregnancy. Many sent knowing looks in the direction of the party as they made their rounds. Some were bold enough to try to corner Brensa and question her, actions the guards quickly intercepted. This was the one situation in which the constant presence of the guards gave Brensa a sense of safety. Normally, having men around still made her uneasy. But now, they prevented her from being constantly accosted by even more frightening individuals and saved her from needing to dissemble about Marja's condition.

Keeping the pregnancy secret soon became moot. Old mothers noted the glow of health in Marja's cheeks and nodded sagely. Others swore they detected a swelling in her belly. Still others claimed they had the gift of seeing and could sense the child growing within her. Nevertheless, Marja and Gaelen kept a stoic silence, refusing to confirm or deny anything. Brensa could do no less.

When people began to fall ill in greater numbers, Brensa finally understood the true reason for her lady's anxiety. She pleaded with her one last time. "My lady, you must not become ill. Think of the child you carry. Please do not put yourself in danger."

Marja remained adamant and ordered Brensa to say no more about it. She confided the second reason for keeping her condition secret. "If others became aware they will behave just like you. They will press me to curtail my work and try to convince me to pamper myself. I have no intentions of doing anything of the kind"

"But, my lady, I—"

"No, Brensa. I must work as I can alongside my people. I must show them that I care for them. I am needed." Marja told her firmly that nothing would stop her from ministering to "her people" as the need arose. Stubbornness can be a strength as well as a weakness, and Brensa knew that Marja could be nothing if not stubborn.

"Besides, I have Liethis' assurance that both myself and my son will be well, so I see no reason to hold back from my duty." The set of Marja's mouth convinced Brensa that she had best keep her silence on the subject and help as she could.

Two eightdays after Summer Festival, just days after the first reports of illness, Brensa had gone to fetch some dried raspberry leaves from the kitchen to make a strengthening tea for Marja. On her way back, a washer woman, arms laden with clean linen, blocked her way in the narrow hall. Brensa could feel the woman's hot breath when she coughed in her face.

"Yer lady'll have folk wonderin' if'n Lord Gaelen be cuckolded, bein' it comes so soon, eh? Did ye see 'er lover, back afore, eh?" Then she winked conspiratorially.

Before the woman could say anything more, the guard outside Marja's door had her by the arms and hustled her away.

Marja noticed Brensa's ghostly face and trembling hands. "Brensa, what is amiss?"

When Brensa told her what had happened, Marja had the guard trace the woman and permanently bar her from the castle.

The first to show signs of illness—sore throat, fever, chills, sore eyes and red rash—were the workers who lived outside the castle and came in daily to fulfill their duties. By the time the first servants and guards started falling ill, rumours of an impending birth were forgotten. A new fear, coming on the heels of the first deaths, eclipsed such gossip.

Mere days after the first outside workers fell ill, reports of cases inside the castle reached Marja. Within an eightday more, it became difficult to find enough people to complete the day-to-day tasks of running the household and looking after those who had contracted the fever. Brensa worked tirelessly beside Marja and kept a worried eye on her. Each day her anxiety increased as she heard the reports Gaelen brought Marja.

The illness raged in the barracks as well. Two of Marja's regular guards fell ill, one dying within days. On learning this, Marja insisted that Gaelen reduce her guard from four to one. Gaelen protested, but was finally convinced by the reminder that Liethis had seen their son born and Marja safe. Brensa had to be content with that as well.

In the end, Gaelen had little choice. Soon, he had to call even the last guard to more pressing duties. All able-bodied adults became involved in caring for the ill, the dying and the children left behind. Others were needed to tend the pyres where the dead burned. The stench of burning bodies permeated the streets. Adults who survived were called back into service as soon as they were able. Food became rationed, cooked mostly in temporary, communal kitchens.

Brensa and Marja made themselves useful in the castle kitchen. Brensa watched the growing respect Marja garnered as she put the skills Cook had taught her to good use. Marja knew what needed to be done and worked tirelessly alongside the others without getting in the way. Nor did she look for preferential treatment. She ate what everyone ate and let herself be directed by the head cook, just like the others. Soon they stopped remarking on it and accepted her as one of the team. Brensa felt proud of her lady, and it spurred her to greater efforts as some of that respect fell on her own shoulders.

But Brensa watched helplessly as Marja grew thin and exhausted. No amount of entreaty would convince Marja that she needed to rest and eat more food for the sake of the babe. Her terse response was always the same. Her people needed her. She and the babe would be fine. At night the two women fell into a leaden sleep for only four or five spans. Marja had given standing orders that they must be wakened at dawn to resume working.

Brensa had immediately sensed when Klast left the city. His absence left her with an added sense of apprehension, and not only because it left Gaelen, Marja and Bargia more vulnerable. Brensa had grown less fearful over time, due in part because she knew that Klast watched out for her. With him gone, the castle seemed more dangerous. His presence always made her feel safer. Now she needed to find courage within her own self. She wondered bleakly if she would ever be able to stop looking over her shoulder.

They saw little of Gaelen during the crisis. His duty lay in keeping relief efforts, funeral pyres and law and order running as smoothly as possible. Brensa's pride grew as the news of his success filtered back to them. The people spotted Gaelen everywhere, it seemed, his clothing dusty, obviously exhausted like everyone else. Here was no pretty lordling, they said, hiding within the protection of the castle. Their new lord risked his health and his safety by working openly with the others. The people noticed and they talked.

"A good man."

"Strong leader, like his sire."

"Not afraid to get his hands dirty."

But the pyres grew higher and more citizens fell ill. With no relief in sight, Brensa wondered how long they could manage.

57: BRENSA SUCCUMBS

A fortnight into the quarantine, Brensa developed a sore throat, and her eyes felt achy. She said nothing to Marja but continued to work beside her. By the next morning, she could no longer hide her symptoms.

"Brensa, you are ill. Why did you not tell me you were unwell? You know how this disease kills. Brensa, I need you. Go to bed at once." She could not hide the panic in her voice. Not Brensa! Oh please, Earth, not Brensa!

Marja ordered her to bed with the window slit covered up. By evening, the telltale spots covered her small frame, and her fever had risen. Her little cat would not leave her side but curled up under Brensa's chin as she shivered under her blankets.

Marja made the difficult choice to stay by her friend's side, despite Brensa's urgings that others needed her more.

"No Brensa. I almost lost you once. I will not leave you."

She entrusted her care to no one else. While Brensa was awake, Marja held back the tears and panic she felt. They only emerged when Brensa slept. Marja resisted the impulse to send word to Gaelen. There was nothing he could do, and he did not need the added worry. She hovered by the bed, pacing or in a chair, afraid to sleep lest Brensa need something. Her isolation and inability to do more left her feeling completely alone and helpless.

When Brensa's fever hit its peak and delirium set in, the name that fell from her lips was not Marja's or her mother's. The name she cried out with increasing desperation was Klast's. Yet, Marja could not even offer her that small comfort. Klast was away, and she had no idea when he might return. It made Marja feel even more impotent. She sensed intuitively that Klast might be the only one who could make Brensa fight to survive and that his voice might be the only one that could ease her suffering even if she did not survive. Marja wrung her hands and paced the floor. Her friend's cries pierced her heart.

Marja finally understood just how deep Brensa's feelings for Klast ran, just how much she trusted him. That realization brought a fleeting pang of jealousy. She dismissed it immediately. She swore that if she ever had the chance to bring the two together again she would do whatever she could. Brensa had never recovered from her earlier ordeal and still followed Marja about with wide, frightened, rabbit eyes and still jumped at shadows. If Klast could make Brensa feel safe, she deserved that … if she only lived long enough.

For four days, Marja did not leave Brensa's side. She ate only what she could force down for the babe's sake and slept in fits and starts in her chair between Brensa's ravings. In all that while, Brensa fell in and out of consciousness, tossing in her delirium and calling out for Klast. Marja could only force small amounts of water into her and try to keep cool wet cloths on her brow.

But Klast did not return.

Brensa lay near death, and Marja could do nothing more.

58: PLAGUE AND TREASON

Klast headed back to Bargia carrying far less information than he had hoped. The first signs that the disease had made its way to Catania were already apparent. Argost had received news of soldiers falling ill. Among the itinerants who had travelled to Catania to assist with the coming harvest, a few had succumbed to a strange fever. Argost prepared for the worst, as he had been instructed by Klast.

At this same time, three men met with Wilnor at his summer estate outside the city. These were Merlost, eldest son of Wernost, Lord of Lieth; Kanin, one of his top spies; and Korff, Wernost's second advisor.

Their guide, Muillon, waited for them in the stables. While the others were feted on roast meats, creamed root vegetables, honey cakes and rare sweetmeats, Muillon dined alone on stew and coarse dark bread sent to him from the kitchen.

The party had been sent to seek out Wilnor with this message: "Lord Wernost has learned Wilnor is not happy with the state of affairs in Catania. He might be persuaded to fall in with Wernost if the wind blew in his favour."

Wernost had designs on Catania and wanted to take advantage of the current unrest he had been led to believe existed there. Sending his heir and his second highest advisor was meant to show good intent. The spy was meant to keep all of them honest. Wernost trusted no one, not even his son, and held the reins of power with iron control.

In return for information that might lead to a takeover of Catania, he had instructed Merlost to hint at a governorship for Wilnor should the campaign succeed. If Wilnor agreed to the terms offered by Wernost, his son had instructions to leave his seal ring as a sign of their pact and to bring a similar token from Wilnor back to Wernost in Lieth.

The four visitors left early next morning for home, secure in the belief that their mission had been a success. Wilnor had agreed to secretly recruit "large numbers of men willing to fight" as well as weapons and have them ready to join those Wernost promised to supply.

Wilnor thought himself a clever man and had formed a contingency plan in case Wernost broke his promise. He had also been in secret communication with Sinnath's man. His messenger had gone back and forth twice already, and Wilnor expected him again within days with news from Sinnath. When he arrived, if all went according to plan, he would send him back again with a coded letter. The contents of this letter would outline the same promise of many men willing to fight to restore Catania to its rightful people of whom Wilnor would, of course, become the new lord with an alliance to Bargia. The plan would have Sinnath dictate to Gaelen the terms of this agreement or be ousted in favour of Sinnath himself. Either way, Wilnor believed he could not lose and congratulated himself on his cunning. His influence with Catania had been tenuous before the invasion due to the Lord Cataniast's madness. These new developments promised more power than he could have achieved under the old rule.

Muillon complained of a sore throat and achy eyes as they left. While the visitors ignored him, Wilnor noticed the fevered look in the man's eyes and felt relieved when they rode out of the gate.

59: THE BEST LAID PLANS

Merlost's party buried Muillon in a shallow grave on the second day of their return journey. By this time, they knew their way home, so they did not concern themselves overly with his loss. It saved them the trouble of killing him later to keep him from selling what he might have learned.

Three days later, only two days travel from their destination, they abandoned Kanin to the crows and wolves, his throat cut. In their haste to outrun the fever, they had not even taken the time to bury him. They left the knife they used to kill him behind, in the mistaken belief that the disease was passed by blood.

Fear gave wings to their flight, and the pair reached the gates of Lieth a half day sooner than expected only to find the people in mourning and the demesne in total chaos. The contagion had entered the city and found it unprepared. Lord Wernost had died, and many more were ill or already dead as well. Those who could afford to hoarded food and barricaded themselves indoors. Bodies lay in rotting heaps outside the walls of the city. No one was available to organize their burial or burning. Orphaned children wandered the streets, starving or stealing what they could to survive. Earth played no favourites.

Those of Wernost's council who still survived turned immediately to Merlost for solutions. Without Wernost to tell them what to do, they were at a loss. His secretiveness and tight control had left the council without the courage or the skills to make the hard decisions. While Merlost welcomed his untimely rise to power, he, too, was unprepared for leadership. Even had he been trained properly to his new position, he still would have been unprepared for the panic and chaos that presented itself. One thing became clear. The campaign to annex Catania would have to wait, at least until order could be restored. Wilnor would receive no assistance from Lieth.

60: KLAST RETURNS

Klast entered Bargia unseen just as dusk lengthened the shadows. The red glow on the horizon was blocked by the wall, and he had to find his opening almost by feel in the dim light. As soon as he emerged into the street he hailed a guard and ordered him to summon Gaelen to a meeting. He gave him the copper ring and proceeded directly to their usual cell, where he paced anxiously. The pull he felt to go to Brensa had become so strong it was all he could do to remain and wait for Gaelen. But dedication to duty prevailed, and he stayed where he was.

Gaelen hurried in within less than a span, holding his hand up to forestall Klast from speaking, and asked, "Is there anything that requires my immediate attention?" When Klast shook his head, Gaelen gave him no time to speak. "Klast, Brensa has fallen ill. She calls out for you."

Klast yanked the door open and was already halfway out when duty caught him. He looked back at Gaelen, his hand still on the latch.

"Go," Gaelen said, gesturing his own urgency for Klast to leave.

Klast needed no second invitation. He charged down the hall, out into the street and raced to Brensa's chamber. When the lone guard at the door tried to prevent him from entering, he knocked him aside with one sweep of his arm and burst in. He showed no recognition of Marja there, and simply roared, "Get out!" as he dropped to his knees beside the bed where Brensa lay.

The force of his outburst sent Marja hurrying to the door. Then, she stopped, hand on the latch.

As Klast glanced at her in distracted irritation, she raised her chin haughtily and declared, with ice in her voice, "Do not forget that I love her, too."

And she left, closing the door behind her.

61: LIVE!

By the time Marja reached the door, Klast had already scooped Brensa up and lowered himself halfway into the waiting chair. He had turned his head as Marja spoke to him. While her statement did not register now, later he would remember it and realize how much Marja had sacrificed to look after Brensa. It brought him to a new level of respect for Marja that recognized her devotion to those she loved.

At this moment, Klast knew only fear for Brensa. She must not die. The man so proud of his self control now found that quality abandoning him. The logic he had relied on so heavily had fled. Wetness covered his cheeks and dripped onto the top of Brensa's head. It did not register. He did not know he was weeping. He had not been able to weep since Rand had held him prisoner. Now, one thought kept repeating. "You must live!"

Soon, without being aware that he did so, he began to rock Brensa like a small child, and the lullaby he had crooned to her in the cave found voice again between gasps for air and gulping tears. Something in him sensed that this might be the only way to reach her, as it had that other time. All of this he did without conscious thought. It came unbidden.

Gradually, Brensa relaxed in his arms and seemed to fall into a more natural sleep. Somehow, at some level, Klast knew she sensed his presence. As her spirit recognized him, her body lost its tension. She sank into Klast's chest like a babe asleep in her mother's arms. Her breathing quieted, and she no longer twitched and flailed in delirium as she had when calling out for him.

As Brensa calmed, Klast found the presence of mind to look about the room for anything he could give her to drink. His eyes fell on a bowl of cooled beef tea, some raspberry leaves to make a strengthening brew and the small brazier that had been placed beside the bed to heat water. With his one free hand, he reheated the broth and carefully helped her to swallow some, spoonful by spoonful. Klast was well aware of the need for liquids to bring down the fever and to sustain her.

Brensa did not regain consciousness as he fed her the nourishing broth but moaned slightly with each swallow, occasionally choking as the liquid slid down her parched throat. In time, she refused any more, and Klast set about boiling water for the tea. To it he added some of the willow bark he always carried in his belt pouch, to bring down her fever. This done, he set it aside to steep at the edge of the brazier. With some satisfaction, he spied a jar of honey. That would take some of the bitterness away from the willow bark and provide a little nourishment. Through all of this, he kept her on his lap and continued to croon the snatch of melody that was all he remembered of that lullaby from long ago.

She slept for several spans. Klast kept his vigil, never allowing his eyes to close lest he miss clues that she might wake, or, Earth forbid, show signs of getting worse. He shrank from that possibility and pushed it from his mind.

During his vigil, a revelation dawned on him, one he had avoided with stubborn determination ever since he had returned Brensa to Marja's care. He loved her. This small slip of a girl had, in spite of the high walls he had built around himself, slipped past his carefully guarded barriers and awakened feelings he had long believed himself incapable of. He could no longer convince himself that he was beyond feeling. The realization shook him deeply. Caring about another opened a man to weakness, a definite liability in a spy.

Slowly, the silence and the warm, lax form of the girl in his arms, so frail and light, soothed his mind just enough that he began to accept this new insight into himself. He could never go back to the stone he had been. Once breached, those walls could not be mended or rebuilt. It occurred to him through his hypnotic lassitude of exhaustion that he no longer wanted to. In spite of the pain, this felt right and good.

Klast had known for some time that Brensa trusted no man but him, that she was in love with him. His aloofness from her had been deliberate, from the belief that this was best for them both. He had already explained to her that he could never have a relationship with a woman. He had nothing to offer a woman … or so he reasoned. Both his own nature and the nature of his work made it so. To think otherwise was pure folly.

It had not occurred to him that Brensa might disagree, that she might prefer the lonely times and the uncertainty around his safety to the life at court she now lived. He only believed that he knew best. There was no point in discussing it.

Now, as he faced the possibility that he might lose her, he could no longer deny that he had been running from himself. And even more, that he no longer wanted to run … or to be alone. The solitude that had for so long seemed his sanctuary now felt more like a prison.

62: EARTH NEEDS THEM

At the same moment that Klast had received permission from Gaelen to go to Brensa, Liethis made ready to return to Bargia. Liethis sensed the plague had run its course. Though it was the last thing she wished to do, she knew she must go to Bargia in order to speak with Klast. If that proved impossible, she needed to give her message to Gaelen, so he could pass it on. The future of Bargia and its neighbours depended on it.

Earth had shown her that there was only one clear way to restore the Balance that the war and ensuing plague had disrupted. She sensed both pain and triumph in the signs. Balance was necessary if the lands and their peoples were to avoid further upheavals.

And somehow this required that Klast and Brensa make peace with each other. Klast must not avoid her any longer. Earth had shown Liethis She needed Brensa for the role she was destined to play. And Brensa needed Klast. Earth had not revealed to Liethis what Klast's and Brensa's roles would be, but she felt a sense of urgency around the sending that she could not deny. Something momentous lay dormant, waiting to waken.

*   *   *

Brensa's fever broke, and she wakened in Klast's embrace. Klast remained in the room for two more days, until she was able to sit up and take some solids.

Only when he reassured her that he would not leave the room until she woke again did she agree to be placed in her bed for more healing sleep.

No-tail resumed her former position, once more tucked firmly under Brensa's chin. She had kept her own vigil, watching

Klast minister to Brensa from a vantage under a table, and seemed relieved to have her place back.

Marja had come in several times after the first crucial day to bring food and check on her friend. By tacit agreement between Marja and Klast, all others were refused entry, even Gaelen.

By this time, Liethis had reached Bargia and taken up residence in her customary chamber. As soon as she had settled, she hurried to meet Gaelen and Marja where she knew she would find them, close to Brensa's chamber.

63: REPRISE

Liethis explained the importance of encouraging the bond between Klast and Brensa. But she told him it would be unwise to rush him, and so they agreed to wait until Klast came to them.

Marja had a maid ready with clean sheets when Klast finally emerged, and sent another for a tub and hot water so that she might bathe Brensa. Brensa managed a weak laugh when No-tail hissed and retreated to a corner at the sight of water being poured into the copper tub.

The tub filled, Marja dismissed the servants, barred the door and assisted Brensa into her bath. Brensa needed to lean heavily on Marja, and they almost fell into the tub together. The near pratfall brought a fit of hysterical giggling from the women and helped break the long tension both had endured since the plague arrived. Marja had to hold Brensa tightly during their fit of laughter, so that she did not slip too deeply into the water, as she was still too weak to hold on herself.

Once Marja had Brensa firmly tucked back in her clean bed she emerged from the chamber, exhausted but still smiling. She sought out Klast, Gaelen and Liethis, still quietly conferring in the lord's chambers, and brought them up to date on Brensa's progress.

At Marja's reassurance that Brensa slept comfortably, Klast remained with the others to continue their discussion. Their discussion finished, they all emerged back into the hall.

When Marja saw Klast sway on his feet she recalled that the man had not slept for days. She watched Gaelen catch Liethis' eye and Liethis nod her head in understanding. Liethis stood nearest to the door to Brensa's chamber. She opened it and gave Klast a small push into the room, indicating the cot next to Brensa's bed with a short nod of her head and an ironic smile. Klast gave Gaelen a questioning look.

Gaelen nodded. "There will be time enough to speak later, my friend. Come to me when you have rested and are able to leave Brensa for a few spans."

Liethis pulled the door firmly shut behind him.

64: CAPTURE

Klast had made a number of inquiries before Gaelen sent him to Catania. Questions such as how he might get information about ridding Bargia of the threat of this new rule, one in which its new lord's woman had too much influence. His probing had produced no results.

On this night, the man of many disguises went out in the same trader's guise he had used in the bath house before the plague.

Those he had tried to make contact with had been very canny and so far had not approached him, despite his efforts to appear available. Now, with the plague all but over, he could renew his efforts.

With his usual skill, he feigned discreetness, clumsily and without true finesse. He wanted to be caught, to find out how he might infiltrate those responsible for carrying out Sinnath's plans.

Again, night had arrived with no success. Klast, exhausted, started in the direction of his small chamber for some food and sleep. Fatigue and discouragement took the edge off his usual vigilance, so he missed the appearance of the five men who converged on him in the short alley until they were on him.

Before he could react, a bag descended over his head, his weapons were swiftly stripped from him and his hands were tied tightly behind his back. He made a sham of struggling, making sure not to appear too skilled. With a show of indignation and fear, he obeyed the order to, "Shut up and go quiet, or we will finish you." While he had not counted on being taken by surprise, the situation fell neatly into his plans.

They half led, half dragged him through several more alleyways, no doubt intending to confuse him. Finally, they shoved him into a building with the smell and chill of a warehouse. Klast's wits, now sharpened by renewed adrenalin, had no trouble keeping track of their movements, so he knew exactly where they had taken him. This building was one of Sinnath's warehouses.

Long years of training had taught him such skills. But his captors must not know that. His survival depended on anonymity and his ability to convince them that, in his assumed identity, they had nothing to fear and possibly an ally to gain. So he stumbled more than necessary, bumping into each man that held him, gleaning information as he did so. One smelled like a heavy drinker, the odour of sour wine penetrating through the scent of barley from the flour bag over his head. The other badly needed a bath. No refinement there. He could also tell they were inexperienced in taking prisoners. Not trained soldiers, then. Good.

The men shoved him roughly down by a pillar set in the floor, trussed him up to it and bound his ankles. They were obviously taking no chances. Confident that he could not escape, they removed the bag from his head. Klast gave himself a moment to adjust to the dimness of the warehouse and looked around. What he observed confirmed his suspicions. This warehouse stored casks of cooking oils and sacks of flour.

Four men sat around on casks, pulled into a semicircle around the pillar Klast sat tied to. The fifth sat on a stool to the side, half hidden in the shadows.

As soon as he spoke, Klast recognized the voice as that of the man from the bath. Klast's opinion of him rose a couple of notches. This was no fool. Not only had he not revealed himself at the bath, he had not met him in the common room afterwards and had made no effort to contact him since. And he had managed to capture Klast and bring him here unseen. Klast knew he would have to proceed very carefully. He needed to gain this man's trust in order to infiltrate the conspirators. Failure likely meant death, not an option he cared to think about. Klast made a show of looking warily about him, straining to see the man in the shadows. He knew enough not to speak first.

"Seems ye be unhappy with the changes in Bargia. Bin mouthin' off about the new lady," said the man in the shadows.

Klast remained silent. He needed more clues before deciding how to respond. He felt carefully behind his back for the familiar feel of the blade he kept hidden in his belt.

He had commissioned the finger-length blade to his exact specifications years ago. It fit neatly between the two leather layers of his belt at the back where he could reach it with his hands tied. Klast had removed the stitching from the belt and had restitched only the outer layer, so that the change remained invisible. In all his scrapes, no one had ever discovered it. The secret had saved his life on more than one occasion. With each new belt he bought he always took out the stitching, placed the blade in between the layers, and stitched up the outside layer to look like it had never been altered.

Yes, he could still feel it. The movement served as much to keep circulation going as to reassure himself he could retrieve it, as his fingers had begun to go numb. The bindings had been pulled expertly tight. The men had relieved him of the dagger in his boot and the larger one visible at his side but had missed this hidden blade. He did not think he would need it, but in the event that they left him tied up alone, it would allow him to free himself.

Shadowman went on. "What be yer name and why be ye so interested in the doings of the lord and his lady? Ye ask a lot o' questions fer a trader."

"Name's Mirral. And what's it to you what I say or think? No harm in sayin' my mind, last I heard. No crime to talk. And who be you, anyway?"

"I be askin' the questions. Best talk so we dinna have to make ye. Could be, if I get the right answers, I might let ye in on a thing or two."

Klast gave a derisive snort and kept still. He didn't want to appear too stupid, but not too clever either.

The next half span had Klast treading a fine line between arrogant self-importance and servility. He tried to convince the leader that he could be trusted and that he also knew enough to be useful if action had to be taken in a pinch. In the end, the leader decided he did not want to make the decision on his own.

"Ye seem t' speak true," Shadowman told Klast, "but just t' be sure we be able t' use a man like you, I be checkin' wi' the boss. I be leavin' ye the light, but I willna untie ye 'til we get back." With that he stood up and motioned the rest to follow him out the door.

"Ye dinna think he needs a guard on 'im?" one of the men asked, looking back from the door.

The leader chuckled. "He isna goin' anywhere. Best no one talks to 'im 'til we get word what to do with 'im." With that he locked the door, and Klast found himself alone.

Within moments, Klast had cut himself free and replaced the small blade back in its hiding place. Then he made careful note of the placement of his dagger and boot knife. They lay on the floor in shadow, next to the stool the leader had sat on. He could not change their position without giving himself away, but wanted to be able to grab them swiftly if needed. He moved them just a little closer, hoping no one would notice since they remained in shadow. While he worked, he looked carefully about and set up an escape plan. He toyed with the idea of leaving but discarded it immediately, shaking his head at his own stupidity. Disappearing would not only prevent him from getting the information he needed but would also give him away.

The lamp they had left burning for him stood a few feet from where he sat, just out of reach of his boots. He drew it closer, so that he could reach it instantly. This warehouse had been kept exceptionally clean. The floors were swept and all bags and casks neatly piled. Klast remedied this by breaking open a bag of flour and laying a trail from the bag to the lamp. He kept it small so that, in the dim light, it was almost unnoticeable. Next, he opened a small clay jug of oil and poured it over the flour trail in a thin stream. These he scuffed together, so that they looked like dirty boot marks left behind by his captors. If blame were to be laid, it would fall on them.

Klast knew the grave risk he took by starting a fire in the warehouse district. If it spread out of control, it spelled disaster for the city. The warehouse buildings were built mostly from wood. Many had small docks at the back, where irrigation streams allowed offloading of the boats that arrived via the river.

But Bargia had also been well-planned for the possibility of fire. By law, each warehouse had to have two full wagon widths of open space around it. This space had to be kept clear at all times. While many traders obeyed this law loosely, and most warehouses had at least some debris piled outside, Sinnath was not one of them. Klast knew Sinnath obeyed the law to the letter. He owned a number of warehouses under his family business, and he always kept them clean and clear. Sometimes being a stickler for tradition and control could be an asset. Klast hoped this warehouse, on this particular day, would not prove the exception and that those adjacent also remained free of debris. He could not risk going outside to check. He did remember that the warehouses on each side of this one also belonged to Sinnath, so he could be reasonably confident about at least these three.

He had some time yet before the men would arrive back, so he used it to stretch arms and legs that had become cold and cramped tied to the post. When he heard the commotion at the door that announced his captors' return, he positioned himself back at the post as though still tied.

65: FIRE!

"'E's back 'ere, sir." That was the voice of the group's leader, whose name Klast still had not been able to confirm. The man was cagey. But Klast thought he went by Markel.

Another piped in with a nervous laugh. "Got 'im tied up good 'n tight."

"Bring that other light. I will want to get a good look at his face when I speak to him. I can tell if a man can be trusted."

That voice clinched Klast's reservation about fire. He knew Sinnath would recognize him, even in poor light, in spite of his disguise. He could not risk that. With a swift kick he knocked over the small oil lamp by his feet and waited just long enough to see the start of the dense black smoke he knew would soon envelop the room. Even as he confirmed that the oil had caught the flame, he had his dagger back in his belt and the boot knife in his hand. He fled to the back in the dark, just ahead of the smoke. It was well that he had planned his escape route. He had kept his eyes closed at the last, while waiting for the group to return, so that they needed no further adjustment to the dark. Even so, the dim light from the fire became so blocked by smoke he soon found himself moving by feel.

Klast just managed to flee behind some barrels, as Sinnath and the others rushed in yelling, "Fire!"

He heard Sinnath shout in fury, "Where is he? You idiots!" before he was forced back by the flames, coughing.

As Klast exited by a small side door and ran through the shadows, he could see that the warehouse already burned beyond saving. A quick glance confirmed that the one next to it had nothing in the way, much to his relief. He watched from a hiding place under an overhang by the door of the next building as the group stumbled out, shouting for buckets and water. No one heard. All Bargia's good citizens lay asleep in their beds.

He watched Sinnath eye the building and the surrounding street. The man's nervousness told him that Sinnath realized the precariousness of his position, out here so late at night when he ought to be in bed. He watched Sinnath stride away quickly, pulling up the hood of his coat to hide his features and keeping to the shadows, as Klast had. Klast let him go and chose different prey. He had seen and heard enough to confirm Sinnath's treachery but knew that his word alone would not be enough to convince the people, possibly not even the other members of the council. He needed more.

As Klast watched the men helplessly trying to put out the fire with water from the canals, he chose his victim. The man who had tied him up seemed too stupid to keep his mouth shut, a bully who most certainly would prove too cowardly to keep silent under pressure. When the man stumbled close to where Klast hid, he wrapped an arm around his throat from behind before he could squawk.

Klast growled softly into his ear as he held his knife in front of the man's eyes. "One sound and that breath will be your last." The warning was more to instill fear than out of need.

The commotion around the fire had by now attracted attention from newcomers, who began to pour out of nearby streets and alleys, buckets in hand.

The man gave a tight nod, which was all he could do given the grip about his neck.

"Let us take a short trip to see Lord Gaelen. I am certain he will have some questions for you." Klast released his grip long enough to slip a rope around his captive's neck, which he tightened just enough to let the man know his breath would be cut off if he pulled on it. Klast had readied the makeshift noose with the rope they had used to tie him to the post.

With the noose firmly in place and no rope left with which to tie the fellow's hands, Klast hissed in his ear, "Place your arms inside your belt, to the sides where I can see them."

When his captive tucked his hands in his belt just to the wrists Klast gave a tug on the rope and growled, "Deeper!" The man gasped and quickly complied, pushing his hands as far as he could reach, so that his elbows sat just above the edge of his belt. Klast hiked the belt up as far as it would go and gave the man a small shove. "Walk."

Klast took him by back ways and narrow alleys, with enough turns both to thoroughly confuse his prisoner and to stay out of sight of curious eyes. Once inside the walls of the castle, Klast grabbed a lamp from its peg on the wall. At the last, they arrived at the same small, windowless cell where Klast had left Brensa those long eightdays ago. Klast shoved the man in, barred the door and removed the noose, all while holding his boot knife ready.

The fellow eyed Klast, and at a nod from him removed his arms from his belt and rubbed them where its edge had pressed into his skin. Klast ordered him to remove his belt and boots. He set them beside the door, dropping the small dagger the prisoner had carried into one. A cursory check of the blade had revealed that it was almost uselessly dull.

Then Klast shoved him to the floor in a corner and thrust a battered bucket into his lap. "That is to piss in. Miss and you'll never please a woman again."

The man's eyes widened in fear as they fell on the knife still held menacingly in Klast's hand. He nodded spastically, his hands moving instinctively to protect his manhood.

Klast grabbed the handle of the lamp he had taken from the hall and turned to leave. To his surprise the prisoner uttered a strangled, "No! Leave the light!"

As Klast turned back to look at him, he recognized the same stark terror he remembered from years ago in Rand's victims. He felt a small pang of sympathy but dismissed it immediately. Fear of the dark would make the traitor more tractable when they returned to question him.

"I need it, I'm afraid," Klast said coolly and shut the door, taking the boots and belt with him. He placed them behind a loose stone in the wall that had been hollowed out for just such a need before he strode off to speak with Gaelen.

He found Gaelen in a rare moment of repose, taking an early tea in the garden with Marja. Brensa sat in the sun doing needle-work, out of earshot but within sight should her lady need her. It was she who noticed Klast first, as she always did. Her eyes went to the gate as the guard opened it to admit him. Her embroidery stilled in her lap, the needle halfway through a stitch. She met his eyes briefly as he entered, then smiled shyly and looked away as he approached Gaelen and Marja.

Gaelen's head came up as Klast spoke.

"My lord, I must speak with you in private immediately. There is a new development with regard to the news you seek."

Marja's eyes narrowed at this, though she said nothing. As Gaelen rose, she sighed in resignation. Gaelen's one shoulder rose with a small shrug of apology.

Klast stopped on the way out to acknowledge Brensa. Her eyes had been boring a hole in his back, and he could feel the longing there. "It is good to see you stronger and well again, Brensa."

His heart gave a painful lurch, as her face fell at his failure to say more. She looked so forlorn. Earth, he was no good at this! He must try harder to be friendly. But how? What else could he say to her? He did not want to lead her on.

Klast knew that his own longing matched hers, but old habit had led him to withdraw from her again. Surely she could under-stand that they could not be together ... could she not? He shook his head in frustration.

Anyway, he expected Gaelen would soon send him away again on another mission. She would have to learn not to count on him. He wondered why that thought gave him no satisfaction.

66: MESSALIA

Messalia was mildly surprised when she found herself wakened by her guard in the middle of the night. This happened only rarely. When it did, the visitor was always important. The man had orders to send all others away until morning. So it piqued her curiosity when the guard told her the identity of her night visitor.

Messalia arrived in the hall to find Sinnath pacing and led him into her private study. Neither spoke a word until both were seated.

Messalia opened. "Tea is on the way Sinnath. I must say I am surprised by your arrival at this early span. I am not accustomed to being roused out of my bed and would not do so for many. Your need must be great, so I will not engage in idle talk. Tell me what has occurred while we wait for the tea."

She leaned back in her chair and regarded Sinnath through lidded eyes, trying not to study his agitation too obviously. There was something going on, and she needed to be on her mettle. She could afford no mistakes. They lived in dangerous times.

Sinnath, for his part, was clearly too worried to notice Messalia's calculated observation of him. She could see that something had shaken him badly and left him off balance. Yet, he still retained enough self-control not to blurt everything.

"Thank you for seeing me, Messalia. I apologize for the early span. I have just come from one of my warehouses, which burns to the ground as we speak. While it does not ruin me, as I have others, nevertheless its loss will be felt." He hesitated, as if not sure how to proceed.

A small knock came at the door, and Messalia rose to admit the servant woman bringing tea. The poor woman had dressed hastily and had left her hair still covered with her nightcap.

Sinnath's gaze fell on the currant bread, butter and honey.

So, he was hungry, Messalia mused. She used the distraction to make a show of pouring and serving tea as she continued to evaluate the situation. His hands shook as he accepted the plate and buttered his bread. She set the teacup on a small table beside his chair and noted that he added far too much honey compared to last time, another symptom of his distress.

She set her own cup and a plate with a small slice of the bread and honey beside her on her writing table and sat down to wait. Before she opened her mouth she wanted more information. Things must be desperate indeed.

Sinnath swallowed a large bite, his Adam's apple bobbing convulsively, and folded his hands together between his knees to control their tremor.

"I was called to the warehouse a few spans ago by a worker of mine. He said he saw a light inside, and he heard voices. Rather than accost the intruders, he came immediately to fetch me. He is not a fighting man, you see, and had no means to arrest anyone."

Messalia smiled to herself as she watched Sinnath examine his thumbs, hands still stuck between his knees. When she did not immediately speak, he raised his head to study her face. He would read nothing there, she knew.

Messalia noted the sweat appearing on his brow. Finally, she took pity. "What is it you wish from me, Sinnath?" She took a sip of her tea, watching his face over the rim of her cup.

Sinnath threw his hands open in a gesture of helpless inquiry. "What does it mean? What does it bode? I need to know what it is safe for me to do. These are unpredictable times for Bargia."

The last was added to cover his realization that he had spoken almost with panic, not thinking clearly. The gesture gave Messalia a small shiver of delight. The man was positively squirming.

"These are indeed unpredictable times for Bargia, as you say, Sinnath. We have had changes in leadership, a new lady, added a demesne under our rule and suffered losses from the plague.

Things have been unsettled and will continue so for some time. This much is apparent. Yet what these things bode for you is hidden to me. My sight has given me nothing about you, particularly." Then, in a soft, soothing tone, she added, "Perhaps, if you can be more specific in your questions, more will come to me." It did not hurt to make a show of compassion.

Sinnath's face almost crumpled. He caught himself but not before Messalia had seen. She smiled into her hand again. He would surely reveal more in his shaken state.

He shifted nervously, as if trying to decide how much he could tell her. He took a deep breath to compose himself. "Messalia, you seem to have a grasp of where Bargia is heading, in general, that is. Can you tell me if we shall experience more unrest, or will things settle down now? More specifically," and here he hesitated, "are the citizens inclined to accept our new lord and his lady, or will they rebel?"

Messalia smiled enigmatically and looked at the ceiling as if trying to gather her thoughts. She was enjoying his discomfiture immensely. Men thought themselves so powerful, but she, Messalia had the power now. Sinnath would find no information here. She thought on how best to answer.

Gaelen's actions during the epidemic had gained him a good deal of respect. His popularity had grown as he had moved among the people, making sure food and shelter were available. Still, some had been unhappy with his decision to close the city gates and declare quarantine, particularly the traders and merchants. Their businesses had suffered. Yet, even they had to admit that it had slowed the spread of the epidemic. Some conceded that it had likely saved the lives of family members living in summer homes or further into the countryside. Now, as life began to return to some semblance of normalcy, widowers, widows and orphans alike felt a debt of gratitude to Gaelen. Their fates could have been much worse without his foresight and leadership. Rebellion seemed an unlikely prospect. Yet she also knew an element of unrest over the new regime still existed. She felt certain Sinnath had had a part in this, even though he had not told her so directly.

Her decision on how to respond to him rested on whether it was more expedient to expose him or to protect him, now that she had him in her grasp. She sighed, deciding to bide a while to see which way the wind blew.

"I am sorry, Sinnath. It appears Earth is loath to give up her secrets. The only thing I can say is that rebellion does not seem imminent, though I do still see unrest. I cannot divine where that will lead." She offered him a weary, apologetic smile and watched his face fall yet again and the hopefulness fade from his eyes. Men could be so easily manipulated, she told herself for the thousandth time.

Messalia stood up to indicate the consultation was over and watched as Sinnath reluctantly followed suit. When the servant came to the summons of the bell, he followed her wordlessly to the door. The guard would lead him back to the hidden exit and lock it behind him. Messalia smiled with satisfaction as she headed back to her bedchamber. He had not even had the presence of mind to thank her. She shook her head slightly. Sinnath was a beaten man. She would do well to distance herself from him.

67: BROKEN DREAM

Brensa's joy at hearing Klast tell her he loved her faded as she watched him withdraw from her again. True, he had thought her delirious when he had murmured those words. But she had heard truth in them, and they had brought her back from death. Now, his behaviour hurt and puzzled her. The few times she had tried to engage him in conversation he had hurriedly made excuses to leave. Brensa knew something must be done about this, but she was unsure how to proceed. Something had to change.

Marja could not help her. Marja understood she loved Klast but believed Klast incapable of returning her feelings. Marja told her she still agreed with Klast's assessment that he was destined for a solitary life with no ties. His work demanded it. Spies did not make good husbands. There was no point in belabouring the issue. So Brensa stopped talking to Marja about Klast.

In her quiet moments, Brensa tried to unravel the mystery of their connection and what it meant for their future. Part of her musings included examining herself. Who had she become since her abduction? Before—what seemed like years ago—she had been a carefree, naïve girl, full of dreams of romance, joining and children. That girl had died. Brensa could hardly remember her at all. So who was she now? What could she truly expect? Certainly, she would never trust any man but Klast. So joining was out of the question. Unless … but Klast had made it very plain that he wanted no part of that life. But what if that changed? After all, he had said he loved her. Could she do the things expected of a wife, even with him? She shuddered at the memories that evoked. Could she overcome her fear enough to make … that … possible? She dared not even name it. Klast would not knowingly hurt her. Of that she was certain. But if they did join together, she did not want to deny him. She could see the cruelty in that. He deserved more.

She stalled on that thought every time, and the tears welled in her eyes. It was the thought that wet her pillow every night as she cried herself to sleep, the one thought she could not get past. If he would only speak with her, perhaps they might find some answers. But he avoided her, and so they seemed at a stalemate that would not break.

Meanwhile, she watched Marja blossom with glowing health and widening girth. Brensa tried to find purpose in that and in the assurance that she would be able to remain close by. This would have to be the child she gave her love to. She would never have one of her own.

68: STRATEGIES

Heads bent together so they would not be overheard, Klast informed Gaelen about the prisoner, Narlost. Gaelen decided not to go directly to interrogate him. This matter need to be handled carefully. The questioning and trial had to convince the council, and the people, that Sinnath had indeed betrayed the House of Bargia. Instead, Gaelen chose to call a meeting with Janest, Grenth, and Kerroll, his top military advisor. He dispatched individual guards to summon each man in confidence. This insured that no one would know Sinnath had not been invited. Such an omission would cause suspicion and lead to talk. Until proof had been established, Gaelen could not afford speculation or gossip.

The two agreed that Klast should not be present during questioning but would wait outside the door, in case he was needed. This would make accusations of a setup less likely. Gaelen wanted to avoid suspicion that Klast had any previous knowledge of Sinnath's actions. Some still did not share Gaelen's trust of Klast, and his presence might be interpreted as proof that Klast had too much influence over him. He was not an official member of the council, and as such should not be privy to their closed-door discussions.

As Janest, Grenth and Kerroll entered the council chamber each one glanced at the man tied to the chair, at first with surprise, then with open curiosity. Yet, they knew enough to keep silent until Gaelen explained. Not until the last member took his seat and Gaelen rose to bar the door did they realize Sinnath remained absent. The locked door could only mean that he had been deliberately left out.

As Gaelen returned to his chair he expected that each had already formed a good idea of why he had convened the meeting.

Kerroll eyed Gaelen expectantly, but both Grenth and Janest

took a sudden interest in their hands, uncomfortable with the unpleasant implications they must soon face. Gaelen could guess what they must be thinking. Surely, there had to be some mistake. Sinnath had served loyally for so many years. They were about to be ordered to betray an old friend.

Gaelen wasted no time. "Thank you for coming. You see that one member is absent and have probably surmised the reason." He indicated the man tied to the chair. "Klast has just apprehended this prisoner at a warehouse, which at this moment still burns to the ground. Earth grant that this is all that burns, and the fire does not spread."

He gave a nod in the direction of the prisoner. "Klast arrested this man at the fire. He is a member of a band involved in treason against us."

Gaelen avoided naming Sinnath, as he wanted to have that information come directly from the prisoner. He needed to know if the man knew Sinnath by name, or if he merely followed Markel, the name the leader went by.

"This traitor will tell us what he knows." The last was said with a coldness Gaelen had never used before. As he spoke he turned to the prisoner. With a low, feral growl he commanded, "Start with your name."

The tone had the desired effect. The man shrank back, the whites of his eyes visible, "Narlost, … m … my lord. Please, I … I know nothing of treason."

Gaelen stopped him on the last word by leaping up and lunging at him, so close they came almost nose to nose. The prisoner would have fallen backward, along with the chair, had the guard behind him not caught it. He squeaked in fear, choking on his last word.

"Silence!" Gaelen roared in the man's face. "Do not take me for a fool. We know what you are and those with you."

Gaelen stood tall then, remaining beside the chair, hands on hips, feet apart. Resuming his former coldness, he continued.

"You will give us the names of all those at the warehouse before the fire started, especially your leader." He waited a few seconds and added, "Now! Or you will wish you had."

He nodded to the guard, who grabbed the man's hair and put a knife to his throat. The prisoner sat as straight as he could to back away from the touch of the blade against his neck, eyes crossed and almost bulging out of their sockets as he tried to see it. Gaelen nodded to the guard, who backed the knife away slightly but still kept hold of the man's hair.

Gaelen had not misread the man. He was a follower and a coward. In moments, they had a list of all the gang members and confirmed the leader's name as Markel.

"We know Markel took a prisoner to question him. Why?"

"He didna trust 'im. He wanted to join us."

"Join you for what purpose?"

The prisoner paled but did not speak.

Gaelen nodded, and the knife went back to his throat, this time drawing a thin line of blood.

"Next will be an eye."

Gaelen stated this so calmly, Narlost had no doubt of its truth. "He was following orders, m … my lord. We were to find a way to …" his voiced died in a choked whisper.

"To what?" At Gaelen's nod the point of the knife poised just in front of his right eye.

"To kill your lady." It emerged as an almost inaudible whisper, and a wet stain spread across the man's breeches.

"Who gave Markel those orders?" The knife held steady.

Narlost looked wildly around the room without moving his head to avoid the knifepoint so close to his eye. Seeing that Sinnath was absent, and none of the others showed any signs of stepping in to help him, he sagged as much as seemed possible with the blade in his face, and, with a beaten look, whispered, "Sinnath."

It was done.

Gaelen returned to his chair and sank back into it, looking at each of his advisors in turn. Grim resignation, residual shock and sorrow registered on each silent face. The evidence could not be denied. He remained silent for several moments as if trying to make up his mind how to proceed.

He turned back to Narlost. "Traitor, your life is forfeit." Then he rose, went to the door and invited Klast in. "Klast, this man has admitted to treason. We have what we need from him. He will be executed, but we need more than this to convict Sinnath. Have you any suggestions? Can this prisoner be of more use to us?" The strategy had been agreed on in their private conference, but Gaelen wanted the others to hear it.

"My lord, the members of his band will have found out by now that he is missing. They will be suspicious. We must arrest all of them before they inform Sinnath. I propose we let them find the prisoner's burnt body in the warehouse. It will lead them to believe he lost his life in the fire, and so buy us time."

"If we kill him first, will his wounds not be visible?"

This, too, had been rehearsed.

"My Lord, may I suggest that he be strangled, so there are no visible wounds? The bruises can be partly covered with burns."

"Good. Do it." Gaelen made it sound like this was an ordinary decision, trying to hide his distaste. He hoped that only Klast would know how difficult this was for him. Nothing escaped Klast, he knew. But he wanted his advisors to see that he had full command. They all watched in silence as Klast approached the traitor. The guard stepped back out of the way, and Klast's large hands reached for the terrified man's neck. As he squeezed, the man bucked and kicked, then twitched and fell still. Klast released his grip and let his hands fall to his sides.

Gaelen was aware how much Klast hated this part of his work, necessary though it was, and sent him an understanding look. Klast had confided more than once that it filled him with self-loathing to kill someone who could not defend himself. Yet, he never hesitated to do his duty. Gaelen felt a stab of sorrow for his friend. He knew Klast would have nightmares tonight, as would he.

"Klast, I rely on you to see that the body is correctly disposed of." He turned to the others. "My friends, you have heard it. Sinnath has turned traitor. But to convict him in a way that no one can question his guilt, we need more. You will speak of this to no one. Go on as if you have learned nothing. In time, we will have what we need. Let us leave now so Klast may be about his business."

He opened the door and left. Gaelen knew they wanted to talk, but his exit and Klast waiting inside gave them no choice but to follow him out. This, too, had been part of the plan.

69: A RUSE

Klast closed and barred the door behind Gaelen and studied the body, deciding the best way to make it look burned but still recognizable. He found what he needed to do now almost as repugnant as killing the man. After a moment he gave a long sigh, untied the body and slung it over his shoulder. He carried it out by the secret passages that only he and Gaelen knew to a cell in the wall at a far corner, where the smell of smoke would not draw attention. There he gathered a small pile of kindling and set it ablaze. He turned the body in several directions to create random burn marks on both skin and clothing. Then he stomped out the fire and rolled the corpse in the ashes. Satisfied, he carried the body to the passage that opened closest to the warehouse and waited for dark.

He could hear by the faint voices coming through that the blaze had not been completely put out yet. This told him that he still had time to deposit the body before the man would be missed. Finally, all the noises ceased. Klast left the passage to confirm the fire was out, and all the people returned to their homes to eat and rest. Thankfully, no other buildings had burned, though he noted scorch marks on the one adjacent.

When he was certain no one would see him, he hoisted the body once more. Being careful not to step on areas that were still hot, he entered the skeleton of the warehouse. He found a spot where the fire had burned, but now had no live embers left, and lay the body face down in the ashes, confident it would be found on the morrow. Then he went in search of a bath and a large jug of wine, not necessarily in that order.

Nightmares plagued Klast, so he slept little in spite of his fatigue. Dawn had him up, dressed and at the stables, preparing for a long ride to clear his head. He looked up in surprise to see Liethis striding purposefully toward him. Something told him this was not a coincidence.

70: RELUCTANT HERO

Liethis smiled at him in greeting as she walked toward him. "I am ready to go home, but before I leave I must speak with you."

Klast's heart sank, but he managed to keep his face impassive. He merely gave a silent nod to show he was listening and waited. He wondered what she could want with him.

Always frank, Liethis got right to the point. "Klast, Earth has shown me an omen. I am not certain why it is so, but there can be no doubt that it is important for the future of Bargia and all of its neighbours. If you ignore what I tell you, I fear it will take Earth a long time to recover from the disruption the plague and the invasion of Catania have left. To heal Her, Balance must be restored, and you have a key role to play."

Klast stood beside her, eyes averted, hands held loosely behind his back, his face wearing an unreadable mask. When Liethis mentioned that his role was crucial, his head rose abruptly, and he looked at her directly for the first time. He dropped his show of indifference, knowing she could see through it.

Liethis smiled kindly. "This surprises you. You have never thought of yourself as anything other than a spy, as someone of no importance."

Klast realized then that he could hide nothing from her and let go of his mask completely.

"Liethis, tell me what I must do to help assure Bargia's future. I will do what I may." Klast hesitated. "But you know I am loyal to Lord Gaelen. Will I be required to betray him? If so, it will go hard for me." He made no attempt to hide his anxiety. "I owe his father my life. Since his death, Lord Gaelen has proven a fair and apt leader. To break his trust may be more than I can do."

"No, Klast, I see no treason in your future. Gaelen's rule is secure for now. If you succeed in this, it will remain so for many years to come. No, what I see concerns your connection to Brensa." She looked steadily at him.

Klast gaped in unfeigned astonishment. What could Brensa have to do with the future of Bargia?

"Klast, I do not fully understand why, but your connection with Brensa must not be severed. It needs to grow stronger. Difficult as it may be, you must foster closer ties with her. I sense that doing so will also ease the pain you both carry, though the way may prove difficult for both of you."

Klast felt both puzzled and agitated. He had thought it best to keep aloof from Brensa, even after realizing that he loved her. He believed he had nothing to offer her.

Liethis continued before he could reply. "I have seen you remove yourself from her since she recovered from her illness. This must stop. She needs you, and I sense that you need her as well. Speak to her. Find out how you may make peace with your feelings for each other. She does not hide her love for you. Do not think you are able to hide your love for her from me, either. Lord Gaelen is aware of it too."

The look she gave him was filled with empathy. "Remember, Gaelen is your friend as well as your lord. Some things are hard to hide from those who care for you. I have informed him of what I am telling you, and he understands its importance."

"I will do what I may, lady, to be sure. But I must think on how." His mind whirled. This revelation was so unexpected that it completely unnerved him.

"You will find the answers you seek." Liethis' voice conveyed her confidence.

Liethis left with assurances that Klast would speak with Brensa and not avoid her further. A deeply troubled Klast watched her go. He could not imagine what, exactly, he was supposed to do.

71: KLAST'S DILEMMA

Liethis' admonition put Klast in turmoil. He could not get around the problems that developing closer ties with Brensa posed. Unanswerable questions kept his head going in circles, and he got no closer to finding answers no matter how much he thought about it. Some of the questions concerned his relationship to Gaelen and how his work would be affected. Others revolved around what his relationship with Brensa would look like. Was he to be her guardian ... her friend ... her ... lover?

Was he supposed to join with her, to take her to wife? That last idea frightened him most ... and led to even more questions. If he and Brensa joined, how would they solve the problem of Brensa's fear? Brensa had been so damaged that he believed she might never be able to lie with him without terror or pain. Hurting her by insisting was out of the question. She trusted him. Nothing would incite him to break that fragile trust.

Could they live together as brother and sister? How would he manage that? He could no longer deny he desired her. Would they grow to hate each other? Liethis had been so vague about the nature of their destiny that he had few clues to go on. The more he wrestled with the problem the more rattled he became.

In the end, he decided talking to Brensa might be the best way to find some answers. He had been such a solitary person for so long that the idea of consulting another, especially a woman, was alien to him. So before approaching Brensa he went to Gaelen for advice. Since Gaelen had been told of the problem, and since he owed him first loyalty, that seemed a good place to start. He sent a message requesting that Gaelen meet him in their usual spot.

Klast lit the lone tallow candle in the cell where he waited and paced, head down, hands clenched at his sides. Sitting was out of the question. The two rickety chairs remained close to the table, undisturbed. He looked up, startled, when Gaelen appeared at the door.

"My friend, it is good to see you again." Gaelen smiled warmly. "My lady sends her regards, as does Brensa."

Gaelen sat down on one of the chairs but did not bid Klast to do so. He opened directly, "I understand that Liethis paid you a visit before she left?"

It was more statement than question. Klast understood the intention. Gaelen was letting him know he anticipated the reason for the meeting.

"Am I correct in thinking this is what you wish to speak to me about?"

Klast struggled for the right words. "Indeed, my lord. I find myself in a most difficult situation." Then, as if Gaelen had been part of that conversation, he added, "Although Liethis assured me it would not interfere with my allegiance to you."

"That is good to hear. I know you well enough to understand how hard that would go for you." He caught Klast's eyes and added, "Your loyalty is not in question, my friend. How may I help you?"

Klast took a deep breath, collecting the courage to proceed. "My lord, it appears I must foster closer ties to Brensa. Until now, I had believed it best for us both if I remained away from her and discouraged her affections for me." He glanced at Gaelen for a reaction, but he could read nothing but interest there.

Klast plunged on. "I deemed it both dangerous and unwise to let any tie between us become known, for her safety. And I believed it unjust to expect that she should concern herself with my own safety, when my duties take me away from Bargia."

"Perhaps I can ease you on that level at least, Klast. I had planned to speak with you after we had resolved our business with Sinnath, but perhaps this is a good time to do so." Gaelen stopped, looking at Klast directly. "Understand that what I offer is a proposal only, not an order. But perhaps it will make your decision regarding Brensa easier."

"My lord?" Klast grasped at the momentary reprieve.

"Yes, for now Bargia seems out of danger from attack from outside its borders for the foreseeable future. This is partly as a result of the losses our neighbours suffered from the illness that weakened us as well. Too many of the guards that I relied on since my father's death have also died. This leaves me with few I can trust to guard my person and none with your special skills."

Klast stood, alert … waiting.

Gaelen paused again, as if reluctant to continue. "I know that you have preferred a solitary life with no true place to call home, but I have need of your services more here in Bargia than outside its borders. I ask you to consider staying here, as head of my personal guard, with possible excursions as need arises." He paused again and added, "My friend, I cannot order you to do this. It is a request only."

Klast looked at Gaelen, eyebrows raised.

Gaelen quirked a smile. "It seems I have managed to surprise you, my friend." He laughed. "I had not thought that possible."

Gaelen sobered again. "Of course, the change will not take place until we have Sinnath unmasked."

Klast did not respond, digesting this turn of events.

Gaelen added, "Now that you may have an added reason to stay in Bargia, I hope this eases your dilemma."

Klast recovered his tongue and stammered, "My lord! I must think carefully on this. It does offer possibilities. But as you say, I am unused to living among others. Questions arise!" He resumed his pacing.

After some time he stood still and looked at Gaelen. An unwelcome realisation suddenly hit him.

"My lord, will it be necessary to take up permanent residence in the city? You know me well. If you command it, I will obey, but this would be most difficult for me." He grew even more serious. "I do see that this would benefit Brensa."

He sat down suddenly, placed his elbows on the table and lowered his forehead onto his palms.

"Klast, my friend," Gaelen spoke quietly, leaning toward him. "I know your need for solitude well. Without a good dose of it, and frequently, you will be of little use to me or anyone else. I cannot ask that of you. I will promise you a good deal of time in more solitary duties. It will not be necessary to spend overmuch time at court." He stopped a moment, as though a new thought struck him. "I think Brensa, too, would welcome less time at court. She still has not recovered her former carefree disposition and jumps at every noise and shadow."

Klast shook his head slowly. "My lord, will you give me leave to consider this?"

"Certainly. I do not require your answer immediately. But do not leave it overlong."

Klast stood to go. Then, recalling what he had come for, he turned back to face Gaelen. "My lord, it seems I must speak with Brensa in order to find the answers I seek. How may I request a private audience with her? Preferably away from court, where we may speak without interruption. Do you think Lady Marja will release her for an afternoon?"

"I am certain that she will do so, and gladly. You two have much to discuss." Then he gave Klast a teasing look. "I think you will find my lady inclined to look favourably on any request you might make, since you have, once again, saved her dearest friend." He gave a wry chuckle. "I am confident she does not hold your ordering her out of Brensa's chamber against you any longer."

Klast's sudden dismay about this reminder of his breach in protocol brought another laugh from Gaelen. "She is not angry, my friend. Go. She understands better than you know." With that, he stood to go and held the door, waving Klast out of the room ahead of him.

In his turmoil, Klast did not even hear the door close.

72: THE TALK

As Gaelen had predicted, Marja readily gave permission for Brensa to leave with Klast for a few spans. She assured Brensa she wanted a nap and had no need of her for a while.

Klast led Brensa through a maze of passages to a small, enclosed courtyard in the oldest part of the castle.

"No one knows of this place," he explained, "not even Lord Gaelen. I come here when I need to think."

Klast used the courtyard when he wanted to make sure no one interrupted him. It made a good refuge. He found its stone walls, too high to let in enough sun for a garden, comforting.

A few tufts of brown grass and a stubborn patch of goldenrod gave the only signs of life. The ground was a dusty, cobblestone square. No benches lined its perimeter. Many years ago it had been used as a refuge where the lady and her maids could get some air if the city was under siege. Now it stood forgotten and neglected. Klast wondered what Brensa thought of his rough sanctuary.

She waited to one side, looking around, but showed no inclination to speak.

Klast withdrew a bundle from behind a loose stone. It consisted of an old horse blanket with a crock of wine rolled up in it and two poor clay mugs. He spread the blanket, poured wine, sniffed it, and curled his nose in disgust. It had gone sour.

"Had I planned this better, there might have been cakes and fresh ale. As it is, I fear this wine is no longer drinkable. Forgive me." He indicated the blanket. "Please sit. We have much to speak of."

Brensa did as she was bidden, but instead of joining her, Klast began pacing as he had done with Gaelen. After a moment's silence he started. "Brensa."

Brensa spoke at the same instant. "Klast."

They both stopped short and Klast barked a short uncomfortable laugh.

Brensa smiled shyly as their eyes met. "You start, Klast, since you asked to meet."

Klast agreed with a short nod. "Brensa, you know me to be a man of few words. I do not know how to make pretty speeches. Allow me to finish what needs to be said before you speak. There is much, and I do not wish to forget anything important." He looked to Brensa for agreement. She merely nodded, clearly puzzled and anxious.

He continued. "Liethis came to me before she left Bargia. She tells me that there is a connection between us that needs to be made stronger. She says this is important for Earth, in order to restore the Balance lost to the plague." He looked at Brensa to see if she understood. She nodded again, open interest on her face.

He spread his hands wide, a puzzled frown creasing his brows. "I cannot see why we have been chosen. Of what import can we be? I do not understand it."

She nodded again, eyebrows raised slightly in question, but remained silent, waiting for Klast to elaborate.

"To answer the obvious question," Klast went on, "no, Liethis does not know how or why this is so."

Brensa looked disappointed but still held her tongue.

"Brensa, until now, I have tried to discourage your affections for me, believing this to be in your best interest. Liethis tells me I am mistaken. It seems we must seek out each other's company." He spread his hands again, palms up, unable to understand, unable to hide his frustration, hoping she would not take it amiss. Earth, but he was no good at this!

Brensa brightened slightly, hope lighting her eyes.

Klast gave an almost imperceptible shake of his head and resumed pacing. How should he proceed? What should he say that would not lead her astray? Best be blunt, not give her false hope.

He stopped and faced her again. "I am not like ordinary men." His pacing resumed. "I cannot offer you a home in the city, near the court, as you deserve. I need solitude, time away from people. I am not accustomed to spending more time than necessary in the company of others. And I am much older than you."

A sudden thought brought him up short. He stopped in mid-stride and spun toward her. "I have told you I have never lain with a woman." He knew this sounded angry, almost as an accusation that he needed to defend himself against, but it popped out that way, and now he could not take it back. What must she think?

Brensa merely nodded again to show she remembered. Klast could see her confusion. It mirrored his own. He could not face the questions in her eyes, so began pacing again, hands clasped behind his back.

"Lord Gaelen has offered me a position as head of his personal guard. This means I will not be sent away so often on more dangerous missions. I will remain in Bargia." He glanced at her over his shoulder to see if she could tell where this was leading.

"We must decide what we shall do." Klast whirled back and looked at her intently to make sure she was listening. She nodded, rapt, eyes never leaving his face. At least she did not look hurt. Maybe he did not sound as angry as he thought. Or perhaps she understood how hard this was for him.

"Here are the two ways I see. We can continue as we are but act as friends. You will stay with Lady Marja, and I in my quarters."

He hesitated, watched her face fall, then admitted, "I do not think this will satisfy what Liethis sees." He felt embarrassed at this new realization. Why had he not understood that before now?

He shook himself and made himself relax his posture, though his pacing continued. "I could find a place for us to live together … but it must be outside the city. We could live as brother and sister. That might present its own problems, which we will need to discuss … or …" He stopped, took a deep breath and forged on. "We could be joined and try to live as husband and wife … I do not know if this is possible for you," he added hastily.

There. He had said it. He stopped abruptly and turned to face her. "I am finished. Now I will try to answer your questions." He waited, feet firmly apart, hands behind his back, expectant and alert. It was her turn now. He understood how overwhelmed she must be, just as he had been. She looked at him for what seemed like a long time, her expression going through changes faster than he could read.

Finally she spoke.

"Klast, please sit. I know you are waiting for me to speak, but this is all most unexpected. I do not know where to begin. I have so many questions, and now you also wish a decision from me."

Klast felt chagrined and immediately sat across from her cross-legged. "Forgive me. I have had more time to think on these things. Of course you will need time to make your decision. Please ask what you wish. Then I will return you to your quarters and wait upon your reply when you are ready. You will wish to discuss this with Lady Marja as well, I expect."

He watched Brensa square her shoulders in determination, though she could not hide her anxiety. "Klast, are you truly willing to honour each of the offers you have presented? Can you live with each of them?" Then she took a deep breath and went on before he could stop her. "Do you love me still?"

Klast was caught off guard. He blurted, "Still? You know that I love you? How?"

Brensa gave a trembling smile. "When I was ill you whispered it. You thought I would not hear … but …is it still so?"

Klast sagged. He looked at the ground, then raised his head to meet her eyes again. He felt as if he had been caught in a fault of character. But he made no attempt to dissemble and answered softly, "I did not think you heard. Yes, it is so. I cannot deny it.

How, I do not know, but you have captured my heart. I did not think such a thing possible for me." His failure to understand himself better made him feel lost.

Brensa's face lit up, and she blushed, her eyes bright with hope. She was so transparent. It made Klast uncomfortable. He sat up straighter and put his closed mask back in place. He watched Brensa's brightness fade and regretted his awkwardness.

"Klast, I think you already know that I love you. And that you are the only man I trust completely. Not even Lord Gaelen can ask that of me."

Klast acknowledged that with a slow inclination of his head, eyes never leaving her, knowing there was more to come.

Her voice shook as she continued. Klast admired her courage as she took a deep breath. "You know what happened to me. Klast, before I can make a decision about sharing a dwelling, I must know. If I cannot share your bed can you truly be content to treat me as sister only?"

Klast tried to hide the conflict he felt. He had made a promise. He must honour it. But he suspected she would know. "Brensa, I have made you that offer. I can and will honour it. Since I have never lain with a woman I can continue without it." But he knew his tone lacked conviction.

Brensa studied his face for a long moment. "Klast, I need time to think about what all this means for us. As to living outside the city, that is what I wish also. I no longer feel safe among so many people. Lady Marja has done her best to help me recover, but I fear I will never again be comfortable with court life." She paused and looked at him shyly. "Truth be told, I dream of a small cottage, with a hearth of my own and a garden, far away from court."

She gave an ironic laugh, breaking the tension. "But in my dreams I already know how to cook. I fear if it were so I may starve before I learn to feed myself ... us." The last word came out in a whisper, and she studied her hands, fingers twisting.

Now it was Klast's turn to laugh, a rich sound that surprised even himself. "You need have no to fear there on my behalf. Some of what I have had to eat in the past made dogs turn up their noses. And I can teach you the few things I learned in my travels. I am satisfied with very little."

Then he sobered again. "But you are accustomed to court food." It hung between them like a question as he waited for her to continue.

Brensa smiled at that. "You fed me well enough when you rescued me. I am sure you will be an apt teacher. Perhaps neither of us would starve after all." The ice had been broken, and the air felt lighter. Klast smiled back, a new warmth suffusing his chest.

After a short, more comfortable silence, Brensa spoke once more.

"Klast, you have just offered me my heart's dearest wish, that we should spend our lives together. Yet, I need time to think before I answer. I do not wish to act only for myself. What we decide must also be best for you. To do otherwise would be selfish of me. I have much to think on. It helps to know that we have the blessing of both Lord Gaelen and Liethis. But there is more to consider. I am Lady Marja's friend, and her child is due in a few moons. I do not wish to leave her alone after she has been so good to me." She paused again, her face growing anxious. "Do we have some time, do you think? Before we must decide?"

Klast relaxed, relieved. "Some time, I think, yes. Liethis did not know exactly what is expected of us. We may proceed carefully, I think. If we are so important to Earth, surely She will give us time to sort out what it is She requires from us."

"Good. Then I am ready to go back. I need to think. When shall we speak again?"

"You may send word when you are ready, and I will come to you." Klast stood, ready to go. When Brensa stood as well, he rolled up the blanket and returned it and the mugs to their cubbyhole behind the stone. He tucked the crock under his arm after he emptied it against the wall. Then, looking back at Brensa to see if she followed, he led the way out of the courtyard.

When they had reached the small hidden door that led into the main halls, Brensa spoke up once more. "Klast?" He turned, eyebrows cocked in question. "Will you kiss me?"

Klast started in surprise. This was not what he expected. "Do you not think it best to wait until we know what is to come?"

Brensa hesitated only for a second. "No. I need to know …" She could not finish, shocked at her own temerity.

Klast felt suddenly awkward, but in spite of her obvious embarrassment, he could tell this was important to her. After a moment's hesitation he set the crock on the ground, reached toward her, put one hand awkwardly around her waist and drew her closer, watching her upturned face. Slowly she let him take her hand in his other one. Then he bent to her face and brushed his lips on hers. Brensa kept her eyes closed and held still. He tightened his grip and kissed her again, more firmly, fighting to control the stirring he felt. When he raised his head and loosened his hold, Brensa opened her eyes, smiled tenderly at him and rested her head on his chest. They stood that way for only a moment, until Brensa gently withdrew and raised her head to look at him, suddenly shy.

"Thank you," she whispered and stood back, waiting for him to unlock the door. "I will send to you when I am ready to speak with you again." With that, she slipped through the door and stepped quickly into the hall.

Klast closed the door behind her. Earth, now she knew! He returned to his sanctuary to think, leaving the crock forgotten on the ground.

73: SEND FOR MIKOST

Gaelen knew better than to pry. Marja burned with curiosity, but when they talked about it in their chamber that night, Gaelen convinced her to let it lie. He explained what Liethis had told him. But there was no hurry, and he felt confident the pair would make the best decision. Gaelen firmly believed that Klast and Brensa were meant to at least share a dwelling and that they would be good for each other. Marja was inclined to agree but expressed her misgivings about how Brensa would adapt to living with someone so dour and uncommunicative.

It relieved Gaelen that Marja had abandoned her belief that Klast could not be trusted. But she told him that she felt Brensa needed affection as well as trust, and she could not see Klast giving that to her. He was too closed, too secretive. So she fretted for her friend but agreed to wait for Brensa to come to her when she felt ready.

Marja also shared her concerns over what would happen should Brensa decide to leave her position as her lady's maid. "There are a few young women who could fill the position, but it is not the same. Brensa and I have been close for so long."

Gaelen knew it would be lonely for Marja if Brensa left, especially with no one to share her excitement over the impending birth or the care of their new son. At the same time, he agreed that Brensa no longer seemed comfortable with court life.

"She used to be so carefree. Now she starts at the slightest noise or shadow ... mostly with men, but even with groups of women. She has not made friends here." Marja sighed. "Even you make her nervous. The only person she relaxes with is me, and even then, she has a wariness about her."

Gaelen knew Klast well enough to simply wait for word of his decision. Meanwhile, the problem of unmasking Sinnath and bringing him to justice still needed to be resolved. Gaelen understood that even if Klast accepted the position as head of his personal guard, he would need much time away from court. If Klast declined the offer and requested to be completely released from his duties, Gaelen was prepared to do so. Klast had earned the right to be free. But he would be sorely missed.

It was one of the reasons he sent a message to Argost requesting the transfer for Mikost. That, and the realisation that Marja would need a trusted friend with her when Brensa left, as he knew she probably would. Marja would be overjoyed to be reunited with Nellis. He smiled to himself at the image of Nellis and Marja swapping motherhood stories as they cared for their sons together. He had a moment of concern for their safety on the journey, then decided that such thoughts served no purpose. He could do nothing more to insure their safe arrival. Argost would certainly do all he could to put them into good hands.

74: A GIFT

Movement of men and goods between the demesnes had resumed and soon approached their normal volume. Businessmen and traders alike were anxious to see life return to a profitable state. Many took it on faith that travelling would be safe in wake of the devastation the plague had left. Messengers travelled more frequently, too, carrying information between Catania and Bargia.

Soon after Argost received Gaelen's request he learned of a family of traders in salt, linen, jewels and scented oils bound for Bargia. This party was large, composed of an extended family. The head of the family, a certain Corrin, always employed three trained guards. Argost checked their reputation and sent a request to meet with him. Satisfied with what he learned, he offered Corrin a generous sum to see to the safe delivery of Mikost and his wife and child.

Four days later, Argost watched a delighted Nellis and son, Borless, settle themselves on a narrow two-seater wagon bound for Bargia, their meagre belongings piled behind them. In return for their passage, Mikost agreed to add his skills to those of the guards. Nellis accepted duties looking after the younger children, leaving the other women free to cook and make camp.

Before they left, Argost called the couple into his meeting room, where Cook waited for them. He watched, smiling behind his hand, as Cook handed Nellis a small scroll of rolled leather. Nellis put it in a pouch at her waist with great care. The letter contained detailed instructions for the making of the honey cakes Marja loved so well.

Cook could not write, so she had approached Argost. Swearing him very solemnly to secrecy, she had told him what to put down. Cook had never before been persuaded to divulge her recipe, though many had asked, including Marja. That she did so now showed how much Cook missed her lady. The recipe included a letter, also dictated to a smiling Argost, amused by such secrecy between women over such a trifle. In it, Cook told Marja that she must share the recipe with no one and that she and only she must make the cakes with her own hands. It almost made Argost laugh out loud to think that Cook would tell his lord's lady what to do. But he remembered the way Cook had run out to say goodbye when Gaelen took Marja away. He knew Marja would welcome the letter and understand the love behind it.

Cook was a widow and childless. She immersed herself in her work and reigned in the kitchen with efficient authority and effusive enthusiasm. Argost had encountered her on several occasions and found her to be cooperative and pleasant. Now, as he was reminded of her devotion to Lady Marja, he looked at her with fresh eyes. He saw a plump woman who obviously liked to eat as well as to cook. Her skin was still smooth despite her middle years, and her thick brown hair, worn in a severe bun and usually covered with a linen bonnet, was liberally streaked with grey. A handsome woman, he thought. He wondered what she would see if she looked him over. He was well past his prime but still straight backed and strong.

Argost had immersed himself in service for the last twelve years since his young wife had died giving birth to their first child, a stillborn daughter. His chest still contracted whenever he remembered the pale face of his dying wife, as she whispered goodbye, tears flowing at the news that their daughter had not breathed. Now, as his duties eased and Catania seemed to settle into a routine, he had time to think about what his future might hold. He decided to visit the kitchen more often to find out which way the wind blew. Who knew? Perhaps they might find some comfort together in their old age.

75: TO BARGIA

The party followed the same route Gaelen had taken when he brought his bride home to Bargia. Argost had informed the trader of the dangers from possible thugs using the cave, but Corrin had already known about them. Traders had to make it their business to know and to be prepared.

This late in summer, the tall pines had left a thick carpet of needles on the path, which dampened the clopping of the horses' hooves and the squeaking of the wheels on the carts and wagons. The muted sounds lent an air of magic that affected the entire party. Even the children grew less boisterous.

The sun sent dappled patterns of light dancing through the dimness to the forest floor, and at night only a few stars could be seen through the tree canopy. The air remained still and cool under the trees, and a peaceful calm settled over the travellers. They enjoyed the respite, knowing it would last only a few days.

On the fifth day they neared the area where Gaelen's group had been attacked. Nellis watched apprehensively as Corrin sent Mikost and two of the other guards out to scout for trouble. A third was ordered to check the cave.

Corrin decided to take special precautions based on Argost's warnings. He found a small bare spot where others had set up camp before. There he gathered his wagons in a circle with the horses tied loosely on the inside. His family also stayed inside the circle, eating a cold meal and ready to jump into action at a moment's notice. Even the women had long knives to hand and had been trained in their use. Mothers kept children close and hushed them when they cried.

At dusk, the men returned one by one. Nellis could not contain her relief at seeing Mikost and set upon him with a huge hug.

The other guards had no attachments, so merely shook their

heads, grinning at such a display. They took their places in front of the main wagon to speak with Corrin and get some food. When Mikost joined them, red-faced, he had to put up with some good natured ribbing.

The last to return was the man sent to the cave. He reported no evidence of recent occupation or activity. With all reports in, Corrin relaxed and ordered a fire for a hot supper. After dinner some of the men took out flutes and a drum. Women donned colourful shawls, and children followed the adults in weaving patterns about the fire, as they took turns dancing, playing and singing. Even though they revelled well into the night, everyone was up and ready to leave again at dawn, tired but happy.

In two days they would enter the gate at Bargia, and the bartering would begin. Nellis enjoyed the excited talk among the women about the new baubles they would buy and the sweets they would give the children. Two young, single women giggled about the conquests they would make. Nellis had not shared the company of women much since Marja and Brensa had left. Now she remembered how much she missed it. She had so much she wanted to tell them.

76: CONSPIRACIES

The lone trader, just one of the many that came and went in increasing numbers now that quarantine had been lifted, entered by the north gate. His wares, mostly root vegetables such as fresh carrots, turnips, onions and some edible gourds, lay in the back of his rickety wagon, pulled by a swaybacked nag. They passed inspection without incident.

Once inside, Ornan led his mare on foot to the trading area and went about his declared business. Only when all his goods had been sold did he seek a room at the Cock and Pheasant, an inn at the edge of the area where Sinnath kept his mistress. There he ordered lamb stew, ale and dark bread from the innkeeper's wife, Norlain, a narrow faced, lean woman with suspicious eyes and a strident voice.

With her customers her manner was all business. She made it clear that she would brook no rowdy behaviour. Ornan decided she did this mostly to protect her young, comely daughter, also serving clients, from being accosted by lonely men in search of female companionship. The sour looks the daughter sent her mother from time to time made it equally clear that she might have enjoyed some of their advances. He wondered what his chances might be.

"What can I get ye, sir?" Norlain asked.

"Lamb stew, please, mistress."

Ornan's request was a code she had been advised to wait for.

Norlain leaned closer. "Lamb stew is not on the menu this time of year, sir, lambing season being over." She lowered her voice to a conspiratorial undertone. "Will mutton do?"

Ornan felt relieved that she appeared to know what was expected of her. If he asked for fowl, instead, she had been told to send her son with a message. The son, a young lad of only eight, would deliver it to an agreed upon address. That was all she knew. That, and the fact that her cooperation paid handsomely.

"Mutton is not to my taste, mistress. Do ye have any fowl, perchance?"

Norlain gave him and oily, knowing smile. "Indeed, the roast fowl is very tasty. I will have my son bring it at once."

"Very good. And I have a message to be delivered to a certain address. Is the boy of an age to deliver it? There is coin in it for him if he brings back a reply."

"Indeed, sir. I will have him take it right off." She almost bowed but caught herself. Ornan noticed the slip. He hoped she would not give him away.

When the lad arrived with his meal, Ornan gave him a large silver ring in a small, worn, leather pouch, and advised him to keep it hidden inside his breeches. He made sure the lad knew the address and told him there was a good reward for a swift reply. The boy nodded quickly and ran off.

The ring was worth a good deal, and Ornan hoped his information that these people could be trusted would prove accurate. The lad could as easily sell the ring as deliver it. The promise of a reward had been an added incentive against that.

*   *   *

Haslin, Norlain's husband and owner of the inn, looked up from his work to see her sidle into the kitchen. She informed him about their visitor and the errand he had sent their son on. He gave a small, disinterested nod and advised her to return to her work.

Once alone in the kitchen again, however, he reached far under the table where he had been cutting the remaining roast fowl and found the lump he had hidden there. This lump, no more than a small sac of stale herbs in an ordinary looking leather pouch, had been there for three eightdays. Norlain knew nothing of its existence.

Haslin, unbeknownst to her, had also had a visitor, one who had heard rumours that the inn served as a meeting place for persons unhappy with Gaelen's joining to Marja. Haslin had been taken into confidence by the visitor, and knew from the visitor what Norlain was up to.

She had not informed her husband. Greed and secrecy ran deep with the couple.

The visitor, who went by the name Bethin, had promised Haslin a generous sum if he would inform him, via the herbs, when a message had been sent. Haslin had readily agreed and had made this his own secret. It gave him a sense of satisfaction to have something on his wife.

Now, Haslin dispatched his stable hand to the designated spot with the herb bundle. He knew Bethin would not be there, but he had left instructions to place the bundle behind a loose stone in the wall, next to the door. Haslin hoped that Bethin would receive his message and act on it before their visitor left. This was a dangerous, double-edged game he played.

77: INDECISION

Brensa returned to her chambers both highly elated and deeply troubled after her talk with Klast. He had just offered her what she desired most. But she wondered if it could ever be turned into reality, even with his willingness. The kiss had told her what she needed to find out. But it put the offer of living as brother and sister already out of the question. In spite of his awkwardness, and the extreme care he had taken, she had sensed his desire. She could not ask him to spend his life under the same roof and deny him. She would have to find the courage to share his bed or remain in her present position at court. To do otherwise would be unjust, and the tensions it would cause could even cost her his affection. If only she had someone she could talk to. But she had no one. Not even Marja could possibly understand the conflict and fear she felt. She had to solve this problem alone.

After many tears that left her pillow sodden, she admitted to herself that what she truly wanted was to be properly joined with Klast, to share that life in all the ways it implied, even his bed. The kiss had not only told her that Klast desired her. But she now realized that she wanted his touch and his affection too, in spite of her fear.

Once the tears had spent themselves, she calmed sufficiently to sort out the important questions. Could she trust Klast enough that she would not panic when he showed he wanted her? Did she have the courage to try? Would Klast proceed slowly enough, have enough patience, so that they could eventually complete their union?

A thought struck her that made her go cold. Had her body been damaged in such a way that either the coupling or the bearing of children would not be possible? How could she find out? When the panic of that question faded, and she was able to think about it more clearly, an idea came to her. It might provide the answer to at least part of the problem. Marja expected a visit from the midwife next morning. She would ask Marja if she might have the midwife examine her, too, to see if Lotha saw anything that would prevent her from sharing a man's bed.

Marja would know where this was leading, of course, but Brensa would have to swallow her embarrassment. At least this was one piece of the puzzle she could solve. With that decision made she fell into an exhausted sleep. She did not wake until Marja knocked on her door, and the sun shining through the window slit told her morning had already passed the halfway point.

Marja's voice came through the door full of concern. "Brensa? Are you all right? Please open the door and let me see you."

Brensa jumped up, chagrined that she had slept so late, grabbed a robe and flew to the door. "One moment, my lady, forgive me." She did not even have time to think about the scene that would greet Marja when she entered: the wet pillow, her dishevelled hair, puffy eyes and her face still mottled from last night's tears. What must Marja think of her, to have given her yesterday away from her duties, and now still be kept waiting for Brensa to attend her?

"Oh, Brensa, whatever is wrong? What happened?" Indignation crept into Marja's voice. "What did Klast say to you?" She put her arm around Brensa's narrow shoulders, led her to the bed and sat beside her. "Tell me what happened."

Brensa hurried to defend Klast. "Oh no, my lady. Klast has not said anything to upset me." She briefly told Marja what Klast had offered her, leaving out the part about brother and sister, since she had already decided against that option.

"But, my lady, I do not know what to do!" And she blurted out her fears about her ability to consummate their eventual joining. Marja listened with such sympathy it gave Brensa the courage to ask if she might have the midwife examine her. Marja agreed it was a good idea.

Since the midwife was expected momentarily, Brensa agreed to get dressed. Marja assured her she would bring Lotha to her once her own examination had been completed. Brensa nodded, feeling apprehensive. It was all happening so quickly. But it had to be done, so she dressed, brushed and braided her hair, straightened her chamber and tried to drink some of the tea Marja sent. She found she could not swallow any of the bread and honey.

The wait seemed endless. Waves of nausea assailed her as she contemplated the woman's hands and eyes on her ... on those parts she had allowed no one to see, other than the two baths Marja had given her when she had been too weak to protest. Not since Klast had tended her after ... but she was determined to go through with it. Only if she knew that her womb had healed could she even think of sharing Klast's bed. And if she could not do that ... well ... then she could not dwell with him.

Questions ran in circles. Would Lotha be disgusted by her, by what had happened? Would she blame Brensa? Would she be gentle or rough? Would she understand Brensa's fear? No tears flowed any more. Terror prevented even that release.

78: WHAT NOW?

Klast wrestled with his own demons. After he had returned Brensa to the main castle, he went back to the private courtyard to think, knowing no one would look for him there, not even Gaelen. He desperately needed to be alone. Once there, he again spread the blanket he had hidden and made himself sit.

The kiss Brensa had required of him had sent him reeling. How had she done it? She had already breached walls he had built so carefully in order to survive. Now the rest came tumbling down. The strongest men had not been able to penetrate them with their cleverest or cruellest strategies. But this mere slip of a girl had completely unarmed him with the request for a single kiss.

He knew that he could no longer be merely her brother. He wanted to be her lover. And somehow, he understood that this was exactly what she had meant to discover. A thousand words could not change what she had learned from him. And, he realized, this was probably what Liethis meant should happen. Though he had to admit that he hoped it was so only because it was what he himself wanted. Liethis had made it plain that she had not really known what Earth's sending meant. Klast ran his hands roughly through his hair in a vain attempt to clear his mind. He might as well have stood on his head for all the good it did.

Now that he had admitted to himself what he wanted, he felt helpless. What if Brensa did not share his wish or was afraid to pursue it? He had offered her the choice. She had the right to ask it of him. He had given his word so could not back down now. If he did, it would surely break the fragile trust they had built. And that could, most certainly, not have been what Liethis meant should happen. So he must keep his word, if Brensa asked it of him. And he would. But how? She would know eventually if she did not already … she did know already! Oh Earth! What could he do?

He took some deep breaths, as he had taught himself to do many years ago and somehow only now remembered. It stilled him enough to reach one conclusion. He must woo her. He must help her overcome her fear sufficiently, that she would allow him to lie with her. Or tell her she must stay at court, just be friends. No! That could not be what Earth destined for them. He ran his hands through his hair again.

So he must woo her. How? He had never lain with a woman, let alone tried to get one to return his desire. He had heard tales, it was true, of what happened in the bedchamber. He knew what to do, physically at least. But this was different. The tales of conquests and lovemaking he had heard had come either from bragging soldiers or from ladies of pleasure trying to lure him. Such bawdy behaviour would terrify Brensa. Impossible! So what could he do? He knew it would require patience, and he had plenty of that. But every time he pictured himself above Brensa, his desire plain before her sight, all he could see was her screaming in terror and fighting to get away from him. What would it take to convince her he would not hurt her?

The answer, when it came to him, was filled with such irony that he laughed in spite of himself. Who better to teach him how to please a woman than one of the ladies of pleasure, the very sort of woman he had avoided all his life? He had chosen to remain celibate, believing that too many secrets were given up in the bedchamber. Too often, women came, or were sent, to men for just that purpose.

Klast had met many ladies of pleasure in his travels. Some had filled him with pity or disgust. These were not the kind who could help him now. He eliminated them immediately. No, the woman who could tell him what he needed to know had to have both discretion and refinement.

Not all women who lived by their bodies were loose, stupid

or down on their luck. There were a few who chose the profession because they liked men, who could afford to be selective about their clients and had the connections, wealth and freedom to show for it. Joining would have made them servants of their husbands, a state which they found unacceptable. These independents chose freedom over the security of a loveless joining. They could not be found in brothels but lived alone, or in twos, at select, high-class inns. The owners of the inns afforded them protection in return for keeping certain clients satisfied. The women paid for their own rooms. The food and drink with which they entertained were, for the most part, purchased at the inn. The payments they received for their services were their own, and they were free to leave if they wished. The arrangements suited both innkeeper and lady.

In one such establishment, the Lucky Stallion, Klast had become acquainted with a woman who worked her profession there. Klast knew Simna liked him. She had tried more than once to lure him into her bed. She had even once offered herself at no charge, but Klast had never taken her up on her invitations. He had made it plain that he was not interested. He had explained to her, once he came to understand that she would be discreet, why he eschewed the company of women, at least in the bedchamber.

Since the food at the inn was to his liking, and his business had taken him there on several occasions over the years, a sort of friendship, or understanding, had developed between the two. The last years, whenever Klast had come for supper or on other business, Simna had shared a meal and conversation with him in the main room. She had proven her discretion, and Klast had grown to trust her. It was of Simna that Klast now thought in his search for tutelage.

His decision made, Klast replaced the worn blanket in its hole and left in search of his bed. On his way to his rooms he stopped by a doorway, and making sure no one spotted him, removed a stone and felt behind it. There he retrieved a small leather sac filled with cooking herbs. When he found the bundle, he gave a grim smile of satisfaction. At last he had a breakthrough. Perhaps now he could find the proof he needed to convict Sinnath. Duty came first. Sleep and Simna would have to wait.

79: EVIDENCE

Klast put off his sleep, donned his Bethin disguise and proceeded to the inn to speak with Haslin. Dawn just showed its first glow of red behind the buildings, hinting at rain to come, when Klast entered the inn and sat at his usual corner table.

He ordered the not so usual breakfast of porridge with a fried egg on top and brewed chicory, a bitter drink made from the roasted, dried roots of that plant. Klast liked its bitterness sometimes, when he needed to sharpen his mind.

Norlain protested that the porridge was not quite ready, so Klast advised her he would wait for it. The odd breakfast request was a code Haslin would recognize. Norlain would merely think it strange.

Shortly after Norlain disappeared into the kitchen, Haslin came out to Klast to apologize for not having porridge ready. Klast knew Haslin had told Norlain to stay behind in the kitchen so they would not be disturbed. Haslin had the mug of hot brew with him as he approached Klast's table.

"What do you have for me?" Klast demanded.

Haslin shifted from one foot to the other. "A man received a message, sir, delivered by my son. Paid him well, too." He jerked his head in the direction of the stairs. "Top room at the right."

"And the address he got it from?"

Haslin licked his lips, now clearly nervous. "Second house on the left, past the bakery, the one three streets over in the good part of city." He looked ready to run. "Sir, my wife will become suspicious."

"Go. I will send your payment when I see the message and verify the address. Do not allow your guest to leave. I suspect he will sleep late, so that should not cause difficulty."

Haslin heaved a sigh of relief and hurried back to the kitchen. Norlain soon reappeared, scowling. She stalked out with his bowl and plunked it in front of him without a word. Her attitude had not changed. *So,* thought Klast, *Haslin is keeping his word. She does not suspect.*

Klast ate hurriedly, left coin for his breakfast and went in search of guards. They frequented another inn a street away, which had friendlier young maids. Removing his old tunic along with his sly demeanour to reveal his true identity, he strode hurriedly over to find them. His memory served him well. A half dozen soldiers shared porridge, ale and flirtations at a table in the centre of the main room. Two recognized him immediately and hailed him to join them. Klast knew they did not like him particularly, but it was politic to be friendly with the lord's man. No matter. As long as they did their duty.

Klast went directly to one of the guards who had hailed him. He gave him and a second man he did not recognize orders to arrest the guest at Haslin's inn and place him in the dungeon away from others. They were not to question him or give him a reason for his arrest. He ordered the other guard who had recognized him to accompany the first two and to stand guard outside the man's room to make sure no one went in or out until Klast returned to inspect it. He took the remaining three with him and headed for the address Haslin had given him.

Klast knew the house well. Sinnath had kept his mistress here until she died of the fever. Sinnath's wife had refused to take in his son by the woman. Now the boy was looked after at the house by another woman, who had lost her husband. This woman also had a child, a year younger than Sinnath's son. Klast suspected the new woman offered Sinnath more than housekeeping and childcare. The arrangement no doubt suited them both. No matter. That was not what he was after.

Sinnath had already left when they arrived. Undeterred, Klast posted one man at each of the two doors and set the last one to hold the woman and children in the kitchen. The woman was plainly frightened and perplexed. She shrank back from the door, pushing the two curious boys behind her skirts. Klast surmised she knew nothing of what Sinnath had been up to and did not bother to question her. He only asked if Sinnath had received a message from a young lad the evening before and where Sinnath usually wrote his correspondence and received visitors. He started his search there.

The chamber where Sinnath conducted his business held a table where he kept his correspondence. It bore the traits of a man organized to the point of compulsion. The room was clearly out of bounds to the children. Everything had a place and kept its place. Klast went straight to the ornately carved writing table in the centre. It had a foreign design. Eastern, Klast decided, perhaps from the demesne of Karlin, rare except in the homes of certain aristocrats. He found no letters on top and pulled out each of the three drawers. Here, too, he found nothing of interest until he turned the smallest one upside down. There, affixed to the bottom with bee's wax, sat a flat sac of stiffened folded linen. Inside, he found three pieces of scraped leather with writing on them, in two different hands. Each showed that the wax from the broken seals had been removed, leaving only the stain of their colour, so that the identity of the sender could not be traced. Klast's reading skills were only rudimentary, but he recognized Lord Gaelen's name and the words *woman, dead* and *poison* in the one with the odd hand and red wax. He knew the orange colour of the stain on the other two to be that used by aristocrats in Catania.

Klast carefully peeled off the sac, placed it and its contents in his belt pouch and searched the rest of the room, finding nothing more. He hoped it was enough. He gave the rest of the house a cursory search and concluded there was nothing more of interest to be found. Then he left the three puzzled guards with orders that the woman and children were not to leave the house, and no one was to be allowed to speak with them or enter the building.

Klast needed to find Sinnath before the traitor found out

what had happened. And he needed to search Haslin's guest's room as soon as possible. He hoped the guards he had left could be trusted. He felt confident about the two who had recognized him at the inn, but knew nothing of the others and had no time to find out more.

As he left the house, Klast considered the best way to arrest Sinnath without creating a public spectacle. Such attention could alert Sinnath's supporters and cause speculation among the rest. Both must be avoided.

80: HASLIN'S REVENGE

When the three guards burst into the inn Norlain froze, and her face went ashen. Then, as many fearful persons do when they think themselves found out, she went on the offensive.

"Stop! What is the meaning of this?" she shouted, striding after them as they approached the room Klast had indicated. "I will not have my good guests disturbed!"

She might as well have ordered the sky to fall.

While one guard stood aside, the first two burst through the door and hauled the groggy trader out of bed and onto his feet. Ornan had slept with his clothes on. Norlain gawked through the open door as they relieved him of his only dagger and checked his boots, where they found another blade.

Ament, the first guard, commanded, "Put on your boots. You are coming with us." He also sliced a pouch from his captive's waist and threw it on the bed.

"What is the meaning of this?" Ornan sputtered in indignation. "I am a peaceful trader. You must have the wrong man."

"No questions. You will find out later," Ament growled, nodding to the second soldier to tie the prisoner's wrists and hobble his ankles, while he held him. Without another word, amid ongoing protestations, the two each took an arm and marched him down the stairs, out the door, and down the street to a cell in the dungeons.

All Norlain could do was wring her hands and watch.

The third guard, Gresh, closed the door behind them and stood in front of it, alert, sword ready.

Norlain fled into the kitchen, where Haslin had remained the entire time. She found him calmly preparing stew for the evening meal. She shrilled at him. "Haslin, what is happening? Do something!"

He merely shrugged, looked at her, and said, "But my dear,

I already have. Surely you can see that?" and went back to his carrots.

This only agitated Norlain further. "I see nothing of the sort." Her voice rose to a shriek. "We are undone! We shall go to prison!" Then she stopped and looked at him, suspicion dawning as he continued calmly chopping carrots. "What have you done?"

"Assured our survival and the goodwill of our lord. What else would you have had me do?"

He turned and gave her a sardonic smile. "I suggest, my dear, that you be quiet before you give yourself away. I have been granted safety for us both, but only if you do not implicate yourself. Then I cannot protect you. Your own mouth will send you to prison." He hesitated a long moment and added, "Or shall I tell the guards what you have been up to?"

Norlain paled again and took a step back from him. "No. You would not," she whispered fiercely. After a pause she eyed him carefully and asked, "Would you?"

"No," he answered mildly as he scooped the carrots into the pot, "not unless I need to." Then he smiled at her knowingly again. "I will not need to, will I? Now, do you have no work to do?"

Norlain knew she was beaten. She said nothing. Her shoulders sagged as she retreated back to the main room.

81: LOTHA

"Do you wish someone present when I examine you, my dear?" the midwife asked when she emerged from Marja's chamber.

"Oh, no! Please, I cannot let anyone see!" Brensa hurriedly showed the midwife into her own chamber.

Brensa's distress was even more acute than Marja had prepared Lotha for. The midwife understood immediately that Brensa had suffered some severe trauma. It was written clearly in her hunched posture and in the way her eyes darted about the room, afraid to meet hers, filled with both fear and shame. She had seen such in her work before and had no trouble recognizing the signs. *Poor girl,* she thought as she closed the door behind Brensa.

"My child, you need not fear. I think I know somewhat of what you have endured. Men can be brutes."

Brensa's eyes widened even further in shock. Had someone told her? "Do you have the seer's gift?"

Lotha shook her head. "But I am right, am I not? You have been ill-used?" At Brensa's tight affirmation she nodded briskly. "I have seen such before. What you tell me or show me will not surprise me. But before we begin, perhaps you will permit me to brew you a calming tea, and you may tell me why you have chosen to see me at this time. Do you suspect you are with child?"

"No, no! Not that! But ..."

Lotha put water on the brazier to boil and began to rummage in the basket she carried with her everywhere for the right herbs for tea. She avoided looking at Brensa, hoping the girl would find the courage to go on. She made a show of looking for something and muttering to herself to give Brensa time.

Brensa stammered on. "Something happened in the spring and now ..."

"Ah, here it is," Lotha announced. As she straightened up she gave Brensa a delighted smile, as though this were the most ordinary conversation in the world. As Lotha hoped it would, the kindness in her smile reached Brensa so that she relaxed slightly. Lotha turned to her tea again. As she filled the pot with herbs, she went on. "So you were ill-used in the spring. I would very much like to hear just what happened. It will help me understand what it is I need to look for."

Brensa stammered out her story, snatches at a time between shamed silences, while Lotha bustled about and inserted the occasional "tsk," and "terrible," with an attitude that suggested she understood but was not too surprised or disturbed by any of it. All in a day's work, so to speak. Nothing new here. Not really so serious and shameful as all that. None of this was spoken, but Brensa heard the message just the same and gradually calmed.

Lotha handed Brensa a mug of tea and poured one for herself. She sat down next to her on the bed, patted her hand and said, "Now, my child, what is it you wish from me today?"

The practiced, motherly gesture disarmed Brensa, as it was intended to do. She hung her head, tears spilling into her lap, as she whispered, "I need to know if I can ... you know ... without pain ... and bear children?" She ventured a sideways glance to see Lotha's reaction.

Lotha merely nodded at the floor. She knew from long practice that Brensa would reveal more if she did not make eye contact. "I see. Tell me, are your moon times normal like before?"

Out of the corner of her eye Lotha saw Brensa give a timid nod.

"Yes." The whisper could barely be heard.

"Good. That is a good sign."

Lotha turned to look at Brensa's face as she went on. "I will need to look at you under your gown. Will you permit me to do that? I will be gentle and do no more than necessary. And there is nothing you can show me that I have not seen before."

Fear returned to Brensa's eyes but also determination. She met Lotha's gaze, gave an affirmative jerk, and looked quickly away again. Lotha could see the effort it took the girl not to back down.

Lotha patted her hand again. "That is very brave of you." Taking the now empty mug from Brensa's rigid hand she set it alongside her own on the small table by the bed. "Now, Brensa, will you lie down for me?"

Brensa obeyed stiffly, legs pressed tightly together, ankles crossed. Lotha took no apparent notice. Still muttering small soothing murmurs, she simply untied Brensa's sandals, slipped them off gently, one by one, and set them under the bed. "There, that is better."

She looked up briefly at Brensa's face. "Such dainty feet, my dear," and went back to her work. Massaging them lightly, she added, "The stockings will need to come down, too. I wish to see if there are scars on your legs as well."

She moved Brensa's skirts halfway up her thighs. Receiving no protest, she tugged slowly at Brensa's linen summer stockings until they sat around her ankles. All the while, she continued her soft patter. Brensa's legs no longer pressed convulsively together. Lotha suppressed a grim shake of her head. What had happened to this one had been terrible indeed. With deft hands, she continued to stroke Brensa's feet and ankles, gradually working up to the calves.

When Brensa showed signs of relaxing further, Lotha stopped to watch her face, leaving one hand resting on Brensa's leg. "Are you ready to let me see, child?" Brensa hesitated a moment, then nodded, eyes widening again in fear.

"And will you let me touch you and check deep inside?"

Brensa nodded again, this time turning her head away, shutting her eyes tight. She lay with fists balled tightly at her sides, unbidden tears once again sliding onto her pillow.

"You are very brave, Brensa. I can see what this costs you. You must have a very good reason for asking this."

Brensa did not turn back but nodded mutely. When Lotha

raised Brensa's skirts to her waist, she instructed her gently to spread her knees and raise them slightly, so she could examine her. Brensa complied without turning her face back or unclenching her fists. Before inserting her fingers to check inside, Lotha applied a soothing balm. Even so, Brensa tensed with discomfort.

Lotha shook her head sadly as she noted this. If the girl wished to bear a child it would take a special man indeed to make it happen. Such men were more rare than queen bees.

At last, she removed her fingers, pulled Brensa's skirt back down and helped her sit up. Lotha remained silent a long time.

Knowing Brensa watched her closely, though Lotha's back was turned, she poured more tea and laced it liberally with honey. What could she say to this girl? In truth, she thought it unlikely that Brensa could ever permit a man to enter her. Yet the girl seemed so desperate for hope.

Finally she turned back to Brensa and handed her the second mug of tea. "Brensa, I can tell you there is no reason your body should be unable to couple with a man or to have a child. But…"

Lotha watched hope rise in Brensa's face. Now it fell again in dismay. Lotha sighed deeply as she sought the right words.

Shaking her head again she went on. "Brensa, it is not your body that will bring pain when you wish to lie with a man but your mind. Your body is not seriously damaged. The scars you bear are no worse than many women carry after childbirth. These will not prevent you."

Lotha paused, still searching for the right words. "But what you have experienced in the cave has made you so fearful that you may not be able to allow any man to enter your womb. Your body may close up, and the pain you would feel if he tried to insist would be too great."

Lotha shook her head again, looking at her hands. "My child, the one who wishes to lie with you will need your complete trust first. And have more patience than I have ever seen in a man. I do not know if such a man exists." She finally lifted her eyes to meet Brensa's and saw, to her surprise, a glimmer of hope there. She had expected despair and fear. Understanding dawned. "You think you know such a man."

Brensa nodded timorously. Her tears had stopped and only their dried tracks remained upon her puffed cheeks. "It is Klast, the man who rescued me."

"Ah, I see." She thought for a moment. "Yes, he might be the only one you would trust. I do not know this man, Brensa. But even the kindest and most trustworthy may not have the patience and understanding this would take. In order for a man to enter you without pain, you must feel no fear. It is much to ask of any man to wait as long as you may need."

Lotha watched the flicker of hope die in Brensa's eyes and wished she had chosen an easier way to earn a living. This poor girl had seen so much pain, and now she had to deliver more. She sighed again, more deeply that before, and looked at Brensa once more. "My child, I must tend to my other duties. Do you have any more questions before I go?"

"I trust Klast," Brensa ventured, as though to convince herself. "You think it impossible for me to … to master my fear?"

Not wishing to hurt the girl further, Lotha gave a noncommittal shrug. "I know not, child. You are brave. I certainly see that. Perhaps, if your man is very patient …" She let the sentence trail off.

Brensa nodded dejectedly, and with sagging shoulders, went to the door to open it. Lotha took her basket and at the door turned to Brensa a last time. "Earth may hold hope for you. I wish it may be so."

82: A DECISION

Messalia watched the now silent prisoner being marched past her house between the two uniformed guards and made the decision to turn what she suspected into an opportunity to further her influence. If she guessed correctly, it could prove profitable. If she had it wrong, she still would not lose.

A short while later her serving man hastened in the direction of the castle with a message for Lord Gaelen. Would he grant Messalia an audience? She had information of a delicate nature that could affect the security of Bargia.

Once certain her man had gone, Messalia dressed in her most serious gown, put on understated jewellery and set her best cloak to hand by the door. Then, confident that Gaelen would see her as soon as possible, she had her housekeeper bring tea. She went through her correspondence once more to make sure she had not left anything incriminating unburned. She was always scrupulously careful, but this situation was so crucial, she could afford no chances that she had missed something.

While she made ready she hummed to herself, a victory tune usually sung at banquets after battle. She liked its lively melody. And, though this was not a battle in the usual sense, it subtly spoke to her feeling of power and that she could expect another coup. Intrigue and danger always energized her. Others' secrets invariably afforded her an advantage.

83: TRAITOR!

It did not take long to find Sinnath. As Klast had surmised, he had gone back to check on the progress of the warehouse. Rebuilding had started almost immediately after the cleanup from the fire, and little remained to remind anyone that it had burned. All the debris had been cleared, and the stone that could be reused sat in a heap to one side. Half of it already marked three walls of the perimeter, in preparation for the wooden framework of the walls and beams for the roof. The rest would soon complete the foundation.

Sinnath stood to one side speaking with a craftsman who gesticulated angrily as he pointed at the workers. It appeared all was not proceeding as well as Sinnath expected. He looked angry as well, though he showed better control.

Klast remained in the shadow of another building, where he could observe unseen, as he determined how to arrest Sinnath. He wondered if a ruse would induce Sinnath to accompany him to the castle without arousing his suspicions. It would be best if it appeared that they merely walked together to a meeting of the council. But if Sinnath became suspicious, Klast had no one to assist him, and things could become difficult. Sinnath might have his own men nearby, though Klast had seen nothing that suggested such. Klast knew he could take the man by himself, but if Sinnath called out for help, there were many who still honoured him as an elder council member and might come to his rescue. Klast, on the other hand, had no such reputation. So much of his energy had been spent on maintaining anonymity that to the people he looked like just another citizen.

Klast watched Sinnath scan the area carefully again and relax. Apparently he still had confidence in his immunity. The plant of the burned body had worked. Sinnath had mentioned the fire, and the discovery of the body, to the other council members as though it had been caused by a gang of careless thieves.

Klast decided to tail him until he could find backup before he tried his ruse. If the guards stayed out of sight it might still work. He watched Sinnath finish with the overseer and stride briskly off in the direction of the castle. Perhaps Earth would side with Klast this time. He almost snorted derisively at the idea. When had Earth ever given him good luck? He made his own destiny. Luck could never be counted on.

Klast spotted two guards on patrol, just as Sinnath turned into a side street and entered a shop that sold building tools. Keeping one eye on the door to make sure Sinnath did not reappear, he beckoned the two and called them to the corner out of sight of the shop. One of them recognized him, so he had no trouble establishing his authority.

"You," he ordered the first, "go to the barracks and bring back six soldiers to assist me. Make sure they are well armed and well trained. Not raw recruits. I need skilled men." He turned to the second. "You stay behind the corner and watch for my signal. If I leave, follow me. Keep an eye open for the others. Make certain all of you remain hidden."

The first nodded briskly and ran to obey. The other positioned himself behind Klast and prepared to wait, standing alert and ready. Klast knew the men probably welcomed the break in routine.

He hoped that the new guards would spot them and get out of sight before Sinnath exited the shop. If he had to follow Sinnath, the others might be unable to find them quickly enough. Or worse yet, Sinnath could catch sight of them, suspect something and go on the offensive.

It occurred to Klast that his ruse might work better if he sent the young guard to invite Sinnath to the meeting. Sinnath knew that Klast was Gaelen's man and no errand boy. Gaelen would not send him with an invitation to a council meeting. He would send a lesser guard to fetch him. So when Sinnath emerged from the shop and Klast's backup had not arrived, he made the risky decision to send the guard with the invitation instead of going himself. Then, if something went amiss, Klast could fall in to assist.

Sinnath strode confidently into a side street in the direction of an inn where he frequently took his midday meal. Klast hid behind a low wall to one side of the next building and motioned the guard to approach Sinnath. He nodded and moved forward.

Klast could tell by the studied familiarity in his manner that Sinnath sensed something was amiss. Sinnath looked casually about him as the guard spoke, as if making sure no one was around, as if planning something.

Klast cursed his luck. He watched Sinnath answer affably while the young guard fidgeted with his tunic. With each step and each attempt at easy conversation the guard's nervousness became more apparent. They turned a corner into an empty, seldom used alley that provided a shortcut. Before Klast could react he saw Sinnath ease slightly behind the guard, swiftly draw his dagger, and slit the man's throat.

Klast was upon Sinnath before the guard reached the ground.

Sinnath shouted, "Guards! To me!" With a dead body as evidence he no longer needed stealth or subterfuge. He threw his dagger down and drew his sword all in one fluid motion. Though no longer young, Sinnath was still lean and fit. He had not lost his fighting skills.

"Give up, traitor!" Klast hoped the direct accusation would put Sinnath off balance just enough that he could take the advantage.

Sinnath was too experienced to fall for the gambit. "Guards!" he yelled again, "take this assassin!" To Klast he said in a feral undertone, "You will not kill me. You need me alive."

Klast was the better fighter. But he knew Sinnath was right. Gaelen needed a trial, not a dead body.

Sinnath had no such compunctions. He fought to kill.

Klast fought defensively, making sure he did not injure Sinnath. This put Klast at a disadvantage. He just avoided a touching blow to Sinnath's shoulder. The awkward feint allowed Sinnath to slice a nasty cut into Klast's sword arm.

The touch spurred Sinnath to attack with greater vigour. "You are a dead man, Klast."

Klast was forced to match him, thrust for thrust. He was losing blood from the cut and tiring. If backup did not arrive soon, Sinnath would have the upper hand.

Klast heard running footsteps. Thinking these were from the soldiers he had sent for gave him a surge of renewed energy. The sense of relief shattered immediately when two guards appeared, swords drawn. They took one look at the situation and recognised Sinnath.

Sinnath sent a triumphant grin in Klast's direction as he shouted, "Kill this assassin," and fell back to make room for the two fresh fighters.

Klast's heart sank. He did not know how long he could hold out. He needed those soldiers! Now!

He caught a glimpse of Sinnath wiping his sword, leaning against the wall, a look of cold satisfaction on his face. As Klast parried another thrust, he saw Sinnath disappear around the corner. *I have lost him,* he thought. His fight became desperate now, to save himself. He would be no use to Gaelen dead. Gaelen needed him. He was the only one who could back up the evidence against Sinnath.

Just as he thought he could find no more strength to swing his sword, his backup arrived. They soon made it plain to the first two who Klast was and why they had been sent for. But by then, Sinnath was nowhere in sight.

"Find him," panted Klast. He tore the sleeve off his tunic and tied it around the cut on his arm to staunch the bleeding. He had no time to give it further attention. "You two, follow him down that alley. If you find him, keep him in sight but do not try to take him. He must be arrested unharmed."

Klast looked at a third man. "You, find Grenth and alert him. Tell him Sinnath must be found and arrested. He will know what to do." Klast thought furiously as he looked at the five remaining. "You, find Lord Gaelen. Here, take this ring. He will know what it means." His thoughts were for Lady Marja. The ring signified grave danger. He hoped Gaelen would understand and increase the guard on her. Who knew what Sinnath would do now that he had been discovered? He held onto the ring for a moment to allow himself time to think, then added, "Tell Lord Gaelen that we will meet at the Cock and Pheasant as soon as I am able."

He faced the last four. "Come with me to Sinnath's mistress' house. He must not be allowed to enter it. He may try to take hostages there." Without waiting to see if the men obeyed he ran ahead of them in the direction of the house. He did not think it likely Sinnath would return there, but he wanted to make sure his guards got back-up in case they were needed. As he ran he tried to put himself in Sinnath's shoes. What would the man do now? Where would he go?

84: CAUGHT!

Sinnath missed the arrival of the six new guards. But he knew that his next moves must be quick and decisive if he had any hope of salvaging his position. His first thought had been to go to the castle and see if he could take Marja hostage. But he realized that such a move would only prove his guilt. His only hope lay in convincing the rest of the council, friends all, to side with him against Klast. He was aware of the discomfort some still felt around Klast and hoped to persuade them that Klast could not be trusted, that he had been spreading rumours to discredit Sinnath, that the attack which had resulted in Brensa's capture was a random act by brigands. It might work, if he got to them soon enough, if they were not already suspicious of him, if no one had been told he was suspect, if, if, if ... It was a long shot, but also his only chance.

He hurried to his home. From there he would have his wife tell anyone who came to see him that he was not at home, that she did not know where he was. He would send messages with two of the men he employed to guard his home, and whom he trusted, to the other members of the council, asking them to meet secretly.

Of course, wording the message had to be perfect. They must agree to see him without Gaelen's knowledge. As he made his way home, taking care that no one saw him, he went over his message: "We have a traitor in our midst, just as Gaelen suspected. I have evidence you will wish to hear. Lord Gaelen will not wish to believe it. We must be certain before we confront him. We must show unity...." Yes, that ought to work. He smiled at his own cleverness. This would get rid of Klast for good. He looked about, saw no one, and slipped through a back door in the wall surrounding his home. He nodded to the guard there.

"Daresh, fetch Failest and meet me in my private

chamber immediately. The safety of Bargia is in peril. We must act quickly."

The stunned guard hurried to do as he was bid.

*   *   *

What Sinnath did not count on was the arrival of an entire cadre of twenty soldiers, led by Grenth. He posted ten around the perimeter of the wall, with orders to let no one leave.

Grenth took the remaining men and scaled the wall by a ladder they had brought. Once inside, he commandeered a small chamber, where he had two guards hold all who happened to cross their path, including Sinnath's wife, Marlis, who sputtered indignantly to no avail. The party worked quietly and efficiently, so all who entered their view were taken by surprise.

All, that is, except the lone man outside Sinnath's private chamber. As soon as he saw the intruders he shouted a warning to Sinnath. They silenced him with a swift dagger across his throat.

When they burst into Sinnath's room they were met by three drawn swords.

Sinnath recognized Grenth immediately and realized that he was beaten. "Put down your weapons, men. We are too late."

His guards gaped in disbelief, but when they saw that Sinnath had laid his sword on the table and backed away, they hesitated only long enough to be disarmed and held between Grenth's men.

Aside from the man at the door, no blood had been shed. Sinnath and his two guards were marched away in manacles, and the rest of the household put under house arrest.

Still arrogant and proud, Sinnath held his head high and eyes straight ahead, as they marched him to the dungeon.

Grenth sent one guard in search of Gaelen and another for Klast.

85: STRATEGIES

Gaelen dodged a feint from his sparring partner outside the barracks at weapons practice. Now that the demesne had resumed its normal pace, he could afford some time to rebuild his fighting skills. He enjoyed the hard exercise and found that it cleared his mind as well as hardened his body and honed his reflexes. He immediately spotted the lone guard arriving as the man came into his line of vision. The man stood respectfully to the side, waiting for Gaelen to tell him he might approach. Gaelen gave his sparring partner the signal to desist and waved the guard over.

As soon as Gaelen saw the ring and heard what had happened, he sent four soldiers to guard Marja with orders to tell her to wait in their chambers until his return.

Gaelen left immediately for the inn with one of the guards. He sent the other back to Klast, both to let Klast know his message had been safely received and to provide more backup if he needed it.

Gaelen arrived at the Cock and Pheasant to find Klast's last guard standing outside the prisoner's room. He ordered ale, fresh bread and cheese from Norlain. He also sent some to the guard upstairs and received a grateful salute of thanks. Then he settled down to wait.

Norlain hastened to the kitchen and did not appear again. Instead, Haslin came out to look after their illustrious guest, trying to hide his nervousness behind effusive affability.

Gaelen wondered at the man's uneasiness and Norlain's rapid exit. He hoped Klast would not be long, in the event that he had been set up. Two common guards were not many to protect him if Haslin had his own plans, especially if those guards belonged to Sinnath's group.

Normally, Gaelen travelled with two of his elite guard. But with things quiet in Bargia and still much to do and few able bodies to do it, he had lost the habit of that precaution. As the wait stretched out, he squirmed at his oversight.

Gaelen hailed Klast's arrival with relief. Only later, over a private goblet of wine in their secret meeting room, would he admit the reason.

At Gaelen's invitation, Klast sat down. Gaelen beckoned to Haslin to bring more ale and food. The ale was fresh, the dark rye bread still steamed and the sheep's cheese was better than most. Gaelen watched Klast wolf it down and wondered how long it had been since he had eaten.

In between mouthfuls Klast brought him up to date. Halfway through the tale, Klast stopped and apologized to Gaelen for his ill manners.

Gaelen only laughed, clapped him on the shoulder and ordered him to finish his meal. He had more than earned it.

Gaelen had waited almost three spans before Klast finally arrived. Klast explained that he had returned to Sinnath's mistress' house to see to the safety of the woman and children. He had feared Sinnath might be desperate enough to try to take siege of the house. Faced with an enraged Sinnath, the guards might have given in to his authority, in spite of Klast's orders.

On hearing that Klast had sent Grenth to Sinnath's home, Gaelen nodded. "Grenth will know what to do. He has been prepared for this possibility." Gaelen shook his head at this turn of events. Though he had known this was coming, it still saddened him to know that Sinnath had persisted in his treason.

"Once I posted the additional guards and gave them further orders to keep Sinnath out, I came here straightaway," Klast went on. "Now we need whatever evidence we may find upstairs. Without it Sinnath may yet sway the council."

"Possibly, though I think the council will be wary." Gaelen ordered more ale, and the two put their heads together. They agreed that even if nothing could be found in Ornan's room to incriminate Sinnath, the right pressure would induce their prisoner to talk. With Ornan's information, the evidence from Sinnath's desk and the statement from Markel's man, they would have enough to bring Sinnath to trial.

Gaelen decided to interrogate the trader himself, with Klast as witness. Meanwhile, Sinnath must be kept isolated and would not receive an audience until he could be brought before the whole advisory council. That confrontation would take place only after all the evidence had been assembled and presented to them in an organized fashion. Not until the council had seen and heard all they had uncovered would Sinnath be given the opportunity to speak. Nothing must be left to chance.

Their consultation finished, they went to search the prisoner's room. They found only the ring in its pouch. But with the lad's word that it was the same one he had taken to Sinnath's house, it would serve as further evidence.

"Your son might be needed as a witness. You and your family must remain in Bargia until we tell you otherwise," Gaelen told Haslin.

"As you wish, my lord." Haslin seemed unperturbed by the news. Gaelen now understood this was because Klast had kept his promise not to expose Norlain.

The two men left together and headed back to the castle. Klast insisted on accompanying Gaelen in the absence of the elite guard. Now that matters had heated up, Gaelen could see the wisdom in this and did not protest. But when Klast told him he would check on their prisoner, Gaelen held up his hand to forestall him.

"My friend, the prisoner will be there on the morrow. I see that you are exhausted. Tend to your arm. Then get some sleep. You will think more clearly for it. I wish to hear what he has to say, but before we speak with him I want to examine the correspondence you found under Sinnath's table. It may help us in our interrogation." He waved off Klast's feeble attempt at protest and bade him goodnight.

Klast acquiesced with a weary bow. "As you wish, my lord."

Gaelen shook his head at Klast's back with a wry smile. The man never forgot his place. Would he ever relax? Gaelen turned back to the castle and went in search of Marja.

86: NO USE

Brensa emerged from her chamber late the next morning. She had remained there all the previous day and refused to open her door or take food. Finally, Marja had simply let her be. Now Brensa read the unspoken questions on Marja's face. But Marja surprised her by not asking them right away. Instead she busied herself with making tea. She said nothing until it had steeped.

"Brensa, please have tea with me and eat something. Whatever has happened, we will weather it together. Come. Sit. Tell me what happened. It can help, I know." Marja indicated the large chair beside her and went to the brazier to pour the raspberry and camomile tea that sat there keeping hot. She turned to Brensa as she poured. "Shall I add honey?" Not waiting for an answer she stirred in a liberal dose.

Accustomed as she was to obeying Marja, there seemed nothing for it but that Brensa must sit and accept the tea, so she nodded bleakly and sank into the chair. In a way, she was grateful that Marja had taken charge. She felt unable even to decide what to eat at the moment. So she watched dully as Marja took a platter and arranged a small slice of fresh, buttered spelt bread, a wedge of pale sheep's cheese and two new plums on it. When Marja put it into her hands and instructed her to eat, she complied more out of the lack of energy to refuse than the desire for food. Still, when the tea and food settled in her stomach, she began to feel a little better.

Brensa knew her reprieve would not last. Marja waited and watched her for several moments, sipping on her own tea and nibbling on some bread and honey. She poured a second cup for Brensa, laced it again with honey and, seeing that Brensa's plate was mostly empty, finally decided to press her more directly.

"Brensa, you must tell me what Lotha said. Is something seriously wrong with you? We will not leave this room until I know what ails you. I cannot watch you suffer so in silence."

After another long pause, Brensa flashed Marja an accusing look. "How can I speak my heart's desire when I know you dislike Klast so? You barely tolerate him."

Marja's eyes widened in surprise. "Brensa, I will be forever grateful to Klast for twice saving your life. It is true, I cannot love him as you do, but I know him to be a good and true man, loyal to Lord Gaelen. If I could help bring the two of you together I would. Please, speak what is in your heart that saddens you so."

On hearing this, Brensa felt tears prick her eyes and threaten to spill down her cheeks. She held them in check by sheer force of will. Brensa had not truly opened up since her experience in the cave in spite of Marja's attempts to get her to talk. She had believed that Marja would never understand and that she still disapproved of Klast.

Marja opened her hands in supplication. "Brensa, I love you and want you to find contentment. I have missed you sorely. While you have been here in body, I have not truly had you with me since coming to Bargia. I have tried, but you have not trusted me. Please trust me now. Tell me what I may do."

Brensa stared, incredulous. "You want me to be with him?"

"If it is what you wish. You love him. I have known that for a long time." Marja knelt by Brensa's chair. The words came out so softly, and Brensa saw such concern in her friend's face that she burst into tears. Marja squeezed beside her into the large chair and pulled her close, rocking her silently. Finally, Brensa broke the silence.

"But I cannot!" she wailed.

"Why can you not? Has he said so?"

"No, he wants me. He has offered to join with me. But I cannot give him what a wife gives a man." Brensa's head dropped in dejection.

"Did Lotha say you must not? Are you so damaged?"

"No," Brensa whispered, turning away, "my body is whole."

"Then what is it that prevents you from accepting?"

"He will grow to hate me. I am too afraid to lie with any man, even him. I have not the courage." Brensa no longer even tried to hold back her sobs.

Marja remained silent. Finally, she ventured, "Brensa, if we truly desire it, anything is possible ... even this."

After a moment she added in a decisive tone, "You must speak of this to Klast. Perhaps he will help you find a solution. He is resourceful and," her voice gained confidence as she spoke, "his love for you will inspire patience. I do know him to be a patient man."

Brensa's sobs subsided. Marja gave her another quick hug and pulled back to meet her eyes. "Yes, that is what you must do. It will be hard, but just as you have done with me, you must find the courage to speak to Klast."

Marja spoke this with such confidence and determination that some of it reached Brensa, and she began to think more clearly. She refused to meet Marja's eyes for a moment. Then she nodded in resignation. "You are right. I must, though I do not know how." She met Marja's eyes again. "Oh my lady, I hope I can find the strength."

87: REQUEST FOR AN AUDIENCE

Gaelen spotted Messalia's man, Sorliss, waiting for him at the entrance to the castle, anxiously shifting from foot to foot. Sorliss hurried over to speak with him. The guards accompanying Gaelen intercepted him with swords drawn, demanding to know his business.

"I have a message for you, Lord Gaelen, from Messalia."

When it became apparent that he meant no harm, Gaelen waved the guards away. "What message have you?"

"She respectfully requests an audience with you. She says to tell you she has important information concerning the security of Bargia that she believes you will wish to hear as soon as possible."

"I see." Gaelen thought a moment. Then, aware of the position Messalia enjoyed, answered, "Tell her she may come to the council chamber at one span past dawn. Advise her that I will have a scribe and some of my advisors there as well. We will wish to record what she has to tell us."

Gaelen planned to have all the members but Sinnath there, partly to impress upon Messalia that he had too much to do to meet with her alone, and partly to make her get to the point. If her information proved no more than speculation or hearsay, she would embarrass herself and understand that she had no influence with him or the council.

Sorliss bowed deeply. "Thank you, my lord. I will inform her." He stood to the side and waited respectfully while Gaelen turned and entered the castle.

Once inside, Gaelen sent a separate guard to inform each of his council members, swearing them all to secrecy, and one to find Klast to make sure he would be there as well. He was taking a risk in calling this meeting, but if Messalia had information about Sinnath, all of them needed to hear it ... before he informed them of Sinnath's arrest. Until now, only Grenth knew of it. He also called on one of his spies to watch Messalia's house and movements. Something about this did not sit right with him; he mistrusted it. He knew Messalia was no true seer. Liethis had confirmed that suspicion long ago. He wondered if the rest of the council understood it, too, or if any actually trusted her. Until now, it had not been important.

As Gaelen turned toward the stairs to his chambers he spotted Marja waiting on the bottom step. She had come down to greet him and accompany him to supper. A surge of pride squared his tired shoulders, and he beamed at her. She was so beautiful, now that she had recovered after losing weight during the plague. She bloomed with health, and her growing bulge had become obvious. A son, my heir, he thought, his smile widening as she approached.

"You look tired, my love," she murmured as she embraced him. "It is late, but I have kept a platter hot on the brazier for you. I think it will not be over dry yet. You have made do with cold meals too long. Come."

Gaelen kept his arm loosely about her waist as they ascended the stairs together. "We have Sinnath," he murmured, rubbing his eyes and pinching the bridge of his nose.

88: A SHOWDOWN

Messalia understood the warning in Gaelen's response. That he wanted to meet with the council meant he did not trust her. Or that he considered her so important that he wanted them all to hear her story. Or he wanted everyone to hear her, so she could incriminate herself and be immediately arrested. Or … she could think of a few more possibilities but eliminated them as preposterous. Unless she had already been betrayed, she saw no possibility that Gaelen could be aware of what she wished to reveal. Or … Sinnath was a member of that council. If he were there he would know that she meant to expose him. If not, then Gaelen already suspected him. She had no idea which way it would go. An error in judgment or a slip of the tongue could be her undoing, and she might well find herself swinging at the end of a rope in the public square or with her head in a basket. If she had had it to do over again she would have waited. Too late to change her mind now.

So she stayed awake the rest of the night, going over every possible scenario and developing a strategy for each. Feeling as well prepared as possible, she put on one of her best, but most sober, daytime gowns, dressed her hair in a conservative braid, wound at the nape of her neck, encased it in a pearled net and dabbed on a hint of berry juice to hide the paleness of her cheeks from lack of sleep. Then she stepped into her waiting carriage. She arrived at the door of the council chamber at precisely the appointed time to find the door closed and Klast guarding it.

She noticed that Klast looked in both directions to make sure no one saw them before he opened the door and bade her enter. He followed her in and barred the door. Messalia quickly scanned the room. Noting that Sinnath was absent, she was relieved to eliminate at least two of the scenarios she had prepared.

Gaelen indicated an empty chair at the table with a goblet of wine already poured. "Messalia. We are pleased to have you meet with us. Please sit and be comfortable."

Messalia observed that all the men also had wine in front of them, but she hesitated to drink. She had not lived this long through carelessness. Who knew what the wine contained? However, when Gaelen took a draft from his goblet, she had no choice but to follow unless she wished to appear suspect. She suppressed a sigh of relief when nothing happened. She decided that Gaelen had nothing to gain from poisoning her, and she ought to enjoy the rest of the excellent wine.

She had seen Klast take up a position beside the door in the practised stance that rendered him of no apparent consequence. But she took no further notice of him. Instead, her attention went to Gaelen, who began without preamble.

"Your messenger tells me that you have important information for me. I have asked my council members to attend, in the event that further discussion is required. Unfortunately, Sinnath could not be located last night. I have sent a messenger again this morning to see if he can be found and invited to join us."

Messalia's eyes narrowed ever so slightly at Gaelen's explanation of Sinnath's absence. She was not sure what it boded, but she sat just a bit straighter and put her best face on it. "My lord. As you are aware, I receive information that others are not able to see. My work as a seer puts me in contact with many persons who seek my advice." She halted momentarily, trying to ascertain Gaelen's reaction. He gave none.

"We are all aware of your reputation."

Her eyes darted from member to member, but they, too, remained inscrutable. She decided there was nothing for it but to be blunt.

"My lord. In recent times I have received two visits from Sinnath. He was most interested in hearing predictions with regard to your lady and how Bargia would be affected by her presence. He also wanted to know if our people would accept your lady, and what would happen should she disappear … and if I saw rebellion in Bargia's future." Her observation around the room gave no indication that this was news. They gave no clues she might use.

"You will need to be more clear, Messalia. Have you any knowledge of why he would be interested in these things? We need something more than questions." This last came from Grenth. The directness of his approach unsettled her. She forced herself to relax into her chair.

"Sir, he was most circumspect in his inquiries. But as a seer," she decided to be bold, emphasizing the word *seer*, "I sense things that are not said. I have built my reputation on the accuracy of my interpretations and my predictions." She took a deep breath. This needed to be said before Sinnath arrived, if he arrived. "I have reason to believe that he is plotting to rid Bargia of the Lady Marja, my lord." Then she hastily added, "Though I cannot prove this."

Gaelen nodded. "I see. Have you anything more?"

"No, my lord. I just thought it my duty to inform you of this. It may be helpful to you and to Bargia. I am your loyal citizen." She watched for his reaction. His face still showed nothing. Earth, but he was good for one so young and inexperienced. She would not wish to contest him in a game of Bluff.

Gaelen nodded again. "Loyalty is always appreciated. Thank you, Messalia. We will discuss this. If you have anything later that can be verified, we will be interested to hear it." Gaelen stood. The audience was clearly over. Messalia allowed herself a small sigh of relief and stood to leave.

Once out the door, she quickened her steps to make sure she was well away before Sinnath might arrive. As she approached her carriage she glanced around. Still no sign of him. Good. When she had taken her seat and had ridden well away, she let out a huge sigh. She still had no idea what to make of the meeting, and the uncustomary loss of control unsettled her greatly. She would need to be even more careful for a while. Gaelen and the council were not the gullible men she normally dealt with. On the ride back she went over all that had been said and, deciding she had said nothing to incriminate herself, allowed herself a small smile. Yes, she would wait, and watch, and she would survive, as she always had. She leaned back more comfortably with a satisfied smirk.

89: SUSPICION

When Klast had barred the door firmly behind Messalia, Gaelen invited him to take her chair and pour himself wine. "You observed her from the side, my friend. What do you make of her?"

Klast made a derisive sound. "She cannot be trusted, my lord. She seeks to protect herself." Then he added, "And she has given us nothing. A clever woman. But she is afraid. Of that I am certain."

The others around the table nodded thoughtfully in agreement. Janest ventured, "She knows more than she has told us. What do you think it is?"

"I do not know, but she will bear watching," Grenth spoke up.

Gaelen looked around the room. "Friends, we have more." He turned to Klast with a grim smile. "Klast has uncovered another piece of the plot."

Gaelen pulled out the correspondence and the ring. He held up the ring first. "This ring was found in the possession of a man from Catania who now rests in the dungeon. He has not yet been interrogated. But Klast has information that Sinnath has been in correspondence with a Catanian from the old court and that they plot the overthrow of Bargia. When the prisoner tells us what he knows, we hope to confirm this.

"And," Gaelen held up the messages taken from Sinnath's desk, "these also confirm that Sinnath is plotting treason against Bargia." He ran his hands across his eyes and pinched the bridge of his nose in the familiar gesture, then added sombrely, "And we have Sinnath. He was arrested early last evening. Now we must prove his guilt to the people."

The room seemed to hold its breath a moment in stunned silence. Then it erupted as Janest and Kerroll both spoke at once, their questions tumbling over one another. Gaelen met Grenth's eyes, and they waited for quiet.

Gaelen held up his hand for attention. "Friends, when we received this evidence last night we thought it best not to give Sinnath the opportunity to gather support. He awaits us in a cell far from any others. His guards have orders to admit no one but Klast and myself and to stay far enough from the cell that he cannot speak with them." He sat down, placing the items on the table. "Let us examine the evidence. Then I will decide how to proceed with his trial."

Gaelen looked at each man in turn. "I need not tell you this must not be spoken of outside of this chamber."

90: INTERROGATION

As Gaelen and Klast had planned they met unseen, except by the guards, outside the cell where the prisoner from the inn was kept. They had agreed to find out if he knew anything useful before proceeding with the prosecution of Sinnath.

Gaelen had gained a great deal of respect among the people as a result of his leadership and work during the plague. But Sinnath's history as a trusted advisor to his father stood in the way of convincing the people that he had turned traitor. Some would remember that Gaelen was the second son, not the one destined to rule, that he lacked the experience of age and still, in some opinions, remained untried. And he had wed a daughter of the enemy, a decision considered impulsive and dangerous by some of the older traditionalists. Unless treason could be proven beyond a doubt, some might side with Sinnath and plunge Bargia into civil war. Gaelen knew how disastrous that would prove. He had lost too many men between the invasion of Catania and the plague to fight such a war and be confident of victory. Some would take it as a sign that Earth did not approve of Gaelen. There were others, such as Messalia, who would be only too ready to use the chaos to their own advantage. And Bargia would be the ultimate loser. No, the evidence against Sinnath must be irrefutable.

When Klast spotted Gaelen approaching, he unhooded the lamp he had lit and unbarred the door. Gaelen motioned Klast to precede him in.

The prisoner leapt up wildly, arms shielding his eyes, blinded by the sudden light. "Who be there?" he cried out.

Klast set the lamp to one side on the floor and stood between it and the man, who by now had sunk back onto the stone bench that, with one ratty blanket, served as his bed.

"I am the nightmare you had last night, and this is the man who will decide your fate." Klast made his voice cold and menacing. Gaelen stood back in the shadows, arms crossed, feet well apart, giving the impression of great size and immovability.

The man shrank away further until the wall pressed against his back. His hands clutched the edge of the bench, white-knuckled.

Ornan had not been trained as a soldier. He carried only one dagger as a rule, which had become dull from using it to cut rope and meat. As a messenger/trader such skills had not been necessary. Lone, poor traders generally travelled safely, as they carried nothing of value to thieves. Courage and cunning were other qualities lacking in this man. He knew how to follow orders, not make decisions. He had not been required to think for himself. Now he sat paralysed with terror.

Gaelen spoke from his place in the shadows.

"You will not speak unless spoken to. You will answer all questions. If your answers are useful you may live a little longer. If not ... I'll leave you alone with my man here. I am sure he can find a slow and painful way to rid Bargia of you. He is most skilled in such things. I do not think you will be missed."

Klast gave a low-throated snarl that made the man start to whimper.

"P ... please."

"Quiet!" Gaelen spoke to Klast then, his voice cold. "If he speaks other than to answer, break his fingers ... one at a time, mind." Klast jerked a nod.

"Your name?"

"Ornan," he answered, his voice strangled with fear.

"Who sent you?"

Ornan hesitated until Klast started coolly forward. "Wilnor," he stammered.

"What were your orders?"

He hesitated again until Klast made to reach for his hand.

"To deliver a message and bring back the answer." He leaned

forward slightly, opened his mouth as though to continue, took one look at Klast and sank back again.

"Tell all of it. Leave nothing unsaid. My man will know if you try to hide something." Gaelen let a note of sinister satisfaction creep into his voice. "Earth has given him a special gift."

Ornan's tale came out in halting pieces. It proved much more involved than expected. Wilnor had fled Catania City to his estate in the country when the demesne had been overthrown. When it became clear that Wilnor could not influence Argost, he contacted Lord Wernost of Lieth. He made him an offer of assistance if that man wished to take over Catania. In return Wernost was to make Wilnor governor. When the plague killed Wernost that plan had been postponed, and now Wilnor schemed with Sinnath instead.

Ornan had been Wilnor's man since well before the invasion. His duties had taken him to various places within Catania for years, while Wilnor still had Cataniast's ear. But Wilnor, a cunning conspirator, needed more ways to increase his power. So when a man arrived spreading hints of a plot to overthrow Gaelen and take Bargia, he befriended him. Ornan had acted as Wilnor's go-between, both in Bargia and in Lieth.

"We must see to it that Merlost of Lieth understands it would be unwise to entertain thoughts of challenge to Bargia or Catania," Gaelen declared. Klast grunted assent, not taking his eyes off their prisoner.

Ornan had travelled to Bargia with messages twice, but this was his first visit to the inn. Norlain's greed had made her an easy mark. One of Sinnath's men had prepared her for the coded message. She had offered her son as delivery boy. Ornan had an address, but not the name of the man who planned the takeover.

It seemed Sinnath had remained most circumspect. He had sent the ring and the address to be used for correspondence via his own man. Ornan could not read and did not know what the correspondence contained. Wilnor also had not revealed the details of their plans to him. Ornan did divulge that Wilnor had concentrated his efforts on Sinnath after the death of the lord of Lieth from the plague. The ring had come back the last time with only the verbal message to wait for further instructions. He did not know who owned the ring. Norlain also did not know it, he said. He had asked her. He had not had time to discover who owned the address.

When Gaelen had no more questions he looked at Klast. "Let him rot here for now. We may have use for him later."

Klast nodded silently, picked up the lamp and followed Gaelen out the door, barring and locking it again. They waited until well out of earshot before they spoke.

"It is fortunate that we have the letters from Sinnath's desk. Without those Ornan is of little use," Gaelen said.

Klast nodded slowly. "You know that I do not wish to involve the boy. I have given my word to Haslin that I will do what I can to keep him and Norlain safe, but I fear it may be necessary to have the lad tell his tale." He shook his head. "I am loath to break my word."

"I agree. We may yet avoid it, at least in public. You do agree that a public trial is necessary." It was more statement than question.

"Indeed. The people must see clearly that Sinnath has turned traitor. Anything less leaves you open to conspiracy, even rebellion." Klast grew silent for a moment, and asked, "How do you propose to handle Sinnath himself?"

"I think we leave him alone, with no access to information or visitors. When we have all our other evidence in order, we will set it before the council. We will include Ornan and perhaps the boy. Then, with all of this already arranged in the council chamber, we bring Sinnath in and confront him with it. He will see his guilt laid out, as will the other members of the council. You will be present as well, of course."

"A good plan I think. But we must keep him hidden and unaware until we are ready. If any news reaches him he will use it to plan his defence."

"Agreed. No one but Grenth knows where he is held since you changed his cell. Only you shall bring him food and drink until this is over. I trust no one else."

"As you wish, my lord. I have hand picked the guards. I believe they can be trusted. They do not know who we hold there. The door has no window, and sounds cannot penetrate the walls. They have been posted well down the hall, as you have seen."

Gaelen gave a small distracted nod, frown lines creasing his forehead. Then he gave his head a quick jerk as if to clear it, turned to Klast as they approached the door to the exit and said, "Now, my friend, my orders are to go and get some food and sleep. I know there has been little of such for you these last days. I need you alert." The last came with a slight smile and twinkle of the eye.

Klast nodded his understanding, and they exited into a back hall and went their separate ways. But instead of heading for his room to sleep off his exhaustion, Klast decided he still had time to visit Simna.

91: SIMNA

So much had happened the last days that Klast had had no time to spare for the situation with Brensa. He had eaten nothing since early morning. A good meal would revive him. So he entered the Lucky Stallion as the moon climbed high and the stars told him it was not too late to find Simna available. He hoped she was not entertaining another client. With luck the last one would already have left. He knew from past visits to the inn that she often sat with a goblet of wine and a late meal before she retired to her private chamber to sleep. This chamber she kept for herself alone. She had another, richly appointed, where she entertained her clients.

It seemed Earth conspired in his favour. This evening, he found Simna sitting quietly in her favourite corner, just finishing her drink. The main room was empty of other clients. When Klast entered, the sound of the door brought a fleeting annoyance to her face. He watched her expression change to one of genuine pleasure as she recognized him.

"Klast! What brings you to seek a lady's company at this late span?" She turned to the kitchen and called out, "Mearin, bring more wine and some of our good cheese and cold fowl for my friend."

The innkeeper stuck his head out, nodded brusquely and disappeared to do her bidding. He grumbled just loud enough for the words to reach them about needing his bed and having baking to do before dawn.

Klast gave Simna a weary smile and sat down gratefully at her table.

Simna had reached that stage when most women had born a child or four and begun to wear the badges of age. Simna, however, had weathered the years remarkably well. Approaching thirty, her figure had filled to maturity, and her expensive gown showed her full breasts to advantage. She still had a slim waist, and her skirt draped the curves of her hips enticingly where she sat at the end of her bench, open to view. She had arranged her hair in a loose braid, wound about her head to enhance the softness of her cheeks. Her lips showed just a hint of red stain from the berry juice she used. Yet somehow she managed to combine all of this with an air of dignity that belied her profession.

Very early on, Simna had mastered the art of seduction while still maintaining control over the men who sought her favours. Only twice had she miscalculated and been left with bruises from men who needed to inflict pain in order to be aroused. They had appeared so charming before they entered the bedchamber that she had been fooled. But only twice. Simna now immediately recognized their subtle signals and avoided engaging such men. And the two who had abused her had found themselves barred from at least five of the better establishments. Her ability to read people well was a trait she shared with Klast and one of the reasons he admired and trusted her.

Klast was aware of the code that existed among the ladies of pleasure. When one woman found out that a man had certain tastes, word passed around. Such men soon found it difficult to engage any woman on whom they could inflict their rage or hatred. On rare occasions, when a woman had been badly injured or maimed, the man who had inflicted her wounds ended up dead in a gutter in another part of the city, stabbed through the heart or with his throat cut from behind. Their assassins were never apprehended. No one mourned their loss.

Klast had met Simna several years earlier when business had brought him to the Lucky Stallion. Simna had come to see that Klast did not desire a woman in that way. Over time and many shared meals, they had formed an understanding that resembled friendship, though Klast would not have recognized it as such. Klast trusted her not to ask unwelcome questions, and she welcomed the company of a man who merely wanted conversation.

Now, Klast could see her assessing him with mild curiosity. No doubt she could already tell that this occasion was different.

As they waited for the food and wine Simna kept silent, but Klast could tell that her interest was piqued. Klast was grateful that she knew him well enough not to pry. She knew he would tell her what he wanted in his own time. Simna had learned patience over the years. Theirs was a comfortable bond with no unwelcome expectations.

They waited for the food to sate his hunger and the wine to ease a little of the tension in his shoulders. Simna leaned, relaxed, into the back of the bench, letting go the airs and postures she employed to call attention to herself. When he finally looked up to meet her gaze she quirked a brow in encouragement.

He cleared his throat. "Simna, I have a strange request to make of you."

Simna could not help herself. Her eyes danced, and she put a lilting flirt into her voice, though her relaxed position did not change. This was teasing, not seduction.

"Why Klast, are you finally here to succumb to my charms and let me take you to my chamber? You won't be disappointed." Her laugh was rich and throaty, her face alight with mischief.

Klast, too weary and nervous for banter, just shook his head and continued. "No, Simna, I need your wisdom and your help with a delicate situation." He hesitated, then plunged on. "It concerns a young woman."

She looked at him in mock surprise, having intuited where this was leading. "Klast, I do believe you have fallen in love. I had not thought to ever see you subject to the wiles of a woman."

Klast shook his head again. "No wiles, Simna, quite the contrary." He told her very briefly how he had met Brensa and fallen in love with her. Simna listened without interrupting, nodding occasionally. As Klast told of Brensa's rape and rescue she grew serious, and her face took on a deep compassion and understanding. Simna well understood the harm some men could do.

At last he came to his reason for seeking Simna out. "Simna, I need to learn how to woo her, to help her relax and to desire me, so that I do not frighten her or hurt her. I must not cause her more pain. I would rather live without her."

He put his elbows on the table and rested his forehead on his palms, his hair clenched roughly in his fingers. "Simna, though I have just said so, I cannot live without her. She fills my thoughts and my dreams. I must find a way to help her find contentment … no, for us to find it together, or we shall both live in need and misery."

He looked up at Simna, making no attempt to hide his feelings. "Simna, I have not the skills to court her. I do not know where to begin. You know how I have shunned such things." He held her eyes a moment then let his head fall back into his hands.

Simna sat still for several moments as she observed him. Klast knew she was considering what he had revealed. He did not rush her.

When she finally spoke her voice was soft and solemn. "Klast, I am sure you already know that what you seek will require all the patience even you can muster. I do not wish to dishearten you, but I must warn you that it may not even be possible … though I do not I think it is without hope. If she loves you, as you say, and has courage, she may overcome her fear. Am I correct in understanding that you will do whatever it is in your power to do?"

Klast calmed somewhat. "You are."

"Then I must tell you that you cannot learn how to please a woman by speech alone. To learn what you need, I must show you. For that you must come with me to my chamber."

Seeing Klast blush deep red and begin to shake his head in protest, she added, "I will not require you to betray your lady. You will need to see me and to touch me, but I can teach you much without bedding me. It is the only way."

At first Klast sagged, then he drew himself up and squared his shoulders. "Then let us begin," he declared grimly, as though he had just agreed to some distasteful task that had to be tackled.

This made Simna laugh again, lightening the mood. "I trust you will not find it so onerous as all that. Come." She stood and led the way. Instead of going to the chamber where Simna usually took her clients, she led him into her private bedchamber. No man had ever been admitted there. "I think this will suit better, my friend."

Klast understood the rare privilege and felt honoured. This would be the gift of a friend, not a business transaction.

Simna's chamber was simple. It held a large bed covered in blankets of muted colours. The window wore the same fabric. Against the wall, opposite the foot of the bed, stood a chest, also decorated with a cover of the same cloth. A small round table stood in the corner along the window wall. It held a wash bowl, ewer and a dish with a sliver of scented soap. In the opposite corner sat a second, square table with a small chair in front of it. On top lay a hairbrush, the silvered disc she used as a mirror and a small jar of the kind that held the berry juice women used to enhance their colour. She had left the walls bare. The effect was of serenity and order. Klast took it all in and decided that it suited her.

"Klast, I will not require you to remove your clothes. But, in order to teach you what arouses and pleases a woman, I will need to remove mine." Then she smiled. "But not all at once."

When Klast indicated that he was ready, she took his hands and showed him how to hold her and kiss her.

For the next couple of spans Simna directed Klast in where and how to touch her, showed him how to gauge signs of arousal and how to increase these. Though both were aware that Klast was aroused, they tacitly agreed to ignore it.

Finally, satisfied that Klast had learned how to court her, Simna disengaged and looked Klast in the eye. "The rest may be harder. Brensa will, no doubt, be more frightened by certain postures that remind her of her rape. You will need to avoid these as much as possible, at first. But there are ways of coupling that are very different from how she remembers it. They may allow her to relax enough for you to enter her. And she may not permit light or be willing to undress at first."

Klast nodded cautiously. He had heard enough bragging among the soldiers at the barracks and in other situations to know a man might enter a woman many different ways. But their talk had always centred around the men's prowess and how the women were unable to resist their advances and had lustily participated with them. This was not the way it would be with Brensa.

Simna proceeded to show Klast several positions which would allow Brensa freedom of movement, in the event she needed to break away: on their sides, both facing and spooning, and with the woman sitting facing the man while on his lap.

Both of them continued to ignore the arousal they felt, neither willing to break the trust between them. Klast was aware that Simna was also aroused, now that she had taught him the signs. When she had shown him all she could, Simna pulled away and took a robe from a peg on the wall. Pulling it around her and tying the sash, she sat on the side of the bed. She eyed Klast sideways, as he sat up and regained control.

Simna lightly rested her hand on his knee. "Ah, Klast, I hope she deserves you. You are an apt student. She will have a gentle lover." She removed her hand and gave a small sigh. "Had we met years ago, even I might have been persuaded into joining by a man such as you." Then she stood up, a signal that it was time for Klast to leave. She added one last admonition. "But you must be patient. She will need it. It will take all the skill you can muster to win her." With that she opened the door.

Klast stood and started to leave, then turned back. "Simna," he began hesitantly.

She put up her hand to stop him. "I know my friend. You are welcome. There is no need for words."

Klast sent her a grateful look and left, hearing the door shut firmly behind him.

92: HAPPY REUNION

Corrin's band entered the city without incident and headed for the open area set aside for traders, a large grassed space with several tall trees. The ground had been levelled here years ago, making it ideal for setting up camp. A well stood at the centre, with buckets hanging from pegs on a post. At the far end, behind a row of cedars, ditches used as latrines had been dug. These were turned over regularly, the dirt from the new ditches used to cover the old ones. The field was well populated at this time of year, though not as crowded as other years, after the plague had reduced the flow of goods. Corrin found a good spot close to the well and, once the wagons had been unloaded, Nellis and Mikost thanked him and his family and set off for the castle.

"Mikost, do you have the seal of introduction Argost gave you?" Nellis asked.

"Right here." Mikost grinned as he patted the leather sac at his belt.

Nellis smiled back in relief. She let her gaze rove as they walked. Bargia looked very different from Catania, and her head bobbed back and forth trying to take it all in. She carried baby Borless in her arms so Mikost could keep his hands free in case he needed to defend them, though the precaution proved unnecessary. They had left their belongings behind with Corrin, until they could be certain where they would stay and where Mikost could stable his horse. No one accosted them until they reached the main entrance to the castle, although they had spotted several pairs of guards or soldiers patrolling the streets.

The sinking sun showed the first hints of red on the horizon as they approached the castle gate. Here, two well-seasoned guards stopped them to demand their business. Nellis felt a shiver of fear as Mikost showed them the seal, but the guard showed no signs of suspicion. The first guard instructed a younger one, eating his supper in the stall behind them, to inform Gaelen and verify the seal.

The young soldier came back in short order with an escort. Mikost took Borless over as they followed him. Nellis' knees shook with anticipation. She had to be told twice to keep up because she could not stop looking about, trying to take everything in. Bargia's colours, blue and yellow, hung everywhere in banners and pennants. They made the castle seem light and airy. The great hall looked huge, much bigger than the one in Catania. She guessed it could probably host a dinner for twice as many people. Servants, guards and others bustled about on their business. It all gave her an impression of optimism and efficiency. Nellis sensed none of the suspicion that she had experienced at Cataniast's court. This seemed a much happier place. She liked it right off.

The guard escorting them spoke to Mikost. "I have sent a messenger to Lady Marja to tell her of your arrival." Just at that moment, Nellis spied Marja entering the great hall from the stair on the left.

"My lady!" she shrieked and hurtled herself across the room to meet her, alarming the two guards posted in the hall.

They all reached the same spot together, Marja running almost as fast as Nellis. She laughingly waved off the guards, one of whom had already drawn his sword.

"Nellis! What do you here?" she asked as she hugged her friend. Then she spotted Mikost with Borless and hurried to greet them. But she kept Nellis' hand gripped tightly in her own, taking her with her.

Marja reached for Borless, but he, not familiar with her and upset by all the commotion, would have none of it and set up a loud wailing.

Mikost looked embarrassed and started to reprimand the poor babe, but both Nellis and Marja stopped him, Nellis with an angry, "Mikost, he is afraid. He does not know better."

And Marja with a laughing, "Oh Earth, I have much to learn about babes," as she pulled back and patted her now considerable bulge.

Brensa had entered the hall closely behind Marja, but once Nellis laid eyes on her lady she had looked no further. Now Nellis spotted Brensa standing shyly to one side.

Nellis started to reach for Brensa. Then, just as suddenly, she froze. Her face lost its exuberance and filled with concern. She recovered quickly and went to give Brensa a hug.

Brensa had caught the shock Nellis had been unable to hide. She pre-empted her with, "I am fine Nellis. I am only still recovering from the illness that has taken so many."

For the time being Nellis had to be satisfied with that explanation.

After a few moments more fussing and exclaiming over each other, Marja exclaimed, "Earth, I am forgetting my manners!" She sent the young guard who had escorted them in search of Gaelen. Then she ordered a private supper brought to their chambers, so Nellis could feed and change Borless and they could all catch up.

Gaelen joined them about a span later, admitting he was tired and hungry. "But I am pleased my surprise worked so well. I had a hard time keeping the secret from you," he said as he grinned at Marja.

They spent the remainder of the evening together in high spirits, swapping stories and cooing over Borless. Wine flowed freely, and food disappeared in quantity. Only Brensa remained subdued, though even she had plenty of smiles for Borless.

Gaelen had sent to the camp for their belongings and given directions for the stabling of Mikost's horse so that they did not have to leave again that night. Maids set up chambers for them across the hall and found a cradle for Borless. Long into the night, after the castle had quieted and all but the guards had gone to find their cots, the weary but contented group split up and headed for their beds.

93: MIKOST

Gaelen met privately with Klast about the role Mikost should be given. He suggested Klast might mentor him.

"I think you will find Mikost an apt student," Klast said. "But my concern is that his loyalty to his wife and child may prevent him from taking the risks that are necessary in the work of an informant."

"True, my friend," Gaelen countered, "but I have others I can send on the more secret and dangerous missions. I want to keep Mikost close to home for Marja's sake as much as his own. After almost losing Brensa, she would never forgive me if Mikost lost his life in my service … though I believe you may be wrong about his willingness to do his duty. But his damaged arm means he will never have the weapons skill needed. And it will make it hard to keep his identity secret in any case."

"So what do you propose, my lord?"

"I need someone who can get inside Messalia's circle. We both know she is no true seer. But she knows a great deal and has influence. She bears watching. Do you think Mikost has the skill to do so without making her suspicious? Since Mikost is new here, she will not yet know him."

"Messalia is clever. It will not do to pretend he does not have connections to court. But as you say, Mikost is new to Bargia. And he is young." Klast thought for a moment. "Young men, new to a demesne, could be very ambitious. They would want to know how best to advance themselves. Perhaps Mikost might consult her on his future within the court. Drop some names later. Give her a few interesting bits of information … Yes, I think I can instruct him on this. He must appear slightly overeager and inexperienced. But he needs to offer her some things she will wish to know. What can we start with?"

Gaelen looked disturbed for a moment, then nodded in

reluctant agreement. "Yes, she is too clever to be content with trifles. But let us proceed slowly. We may decide as we go. The first few times she will realize he is too new at court to know much. Perhaps her questions to him will give us the clues."

"Perhaps it is not too soon, now that she is so near her time, to give away that your lady bears a son, an heir." Klast gave Gaelen a wry smile. "But it will unfortunately dry up the gamblers' wagering."

Gaelen barked a laugh. Since Marja's condition had become obvious, the gamblers had changed from "Is she?" to "What is it?" Now they would have to find another question. "Yes, I suppose there is no longer any harm in it, with Marja so close to her lying in." The thought brought a far-away smile to his face. Klast noticed how much younger he looked when he forgot his cares for a moment.

Gaelen straightened, the meeting over. "Well, my friend, I shall leave Mikost to you then."

94: A PACT

The two letters found in Sinnath's desk confirmed that he had been conspiring with Wilnor. The two men had an agreement that Sinnath would rule Bargia and Wilnor would govern Catania. Wilnor had promised more than a hundred soldiers led by his own captain. It turned out Klast knew of this man and doubted very much he could lead effectively. He was a soldier in name only and had a reputation for cruelty but no skill. If the hundred men proved no better, Wilnor's chances of victory were laughable. Sinnath, however, did not know this.

The other letter was from an old, wealthy merchant by the name of Biernal, who had left Bargia for his summer dwelling shortly after Gaelen brought Marja home. He and Sinnath had known each other many years and were of the same bent. He, too, agreed to gather a small army to attack Gaelen. When he and Klast had decoded his message, Gaelen sent a cadre of soldiers to arrest him and bring him to trial. Biernal had not expected this. Ill prepared, he had been found unprotected, abed with pain in his joints. He now rested on a cold, stone bench in a cell in the dungeon, where his joints, no doubt, pained him more.

Gaelen called a meeting with his council for the private trial the next morning. A guard had been sent to fetch the Haslin's son. Gaelen had convinced Klast that bringing the lad to the hearing with the council was necessary. The evidence, the boy, and the prisoner, Ornan, would all be assembled in the council chamber before they brought Sinnath in. He would then be confronted with the totality of his guilt without the opportunity to pick at each piece separately.

When all council members had viewed the letters, been presented with the prisoner's information and heard the boy's story, Gaelen had Klast bring Sinnath in. To avoid speculation by anyone else, he had instructed Klast to bring him through the secret passages that led to the hall beside the council chamber. Guards posted at each end prevented anyone from observing their arrival.

Sinnath looked a sorry sight, unshaven, his usually immaculate clothing dirty and dishevelled. It made it hard for him to carry off the air of confidence and power he typically bore. Yet, in spite of his appearance, he still managed to stand straight, head held high, and to maintain his dignity. That changed when he scanned the room. He took in the table where the letters and ring lay, the prisoner tied to the chair and the frightened young lad sitting on another. His eyes met the grim faces of the council members, and lastly, of Gaelen, standing inscrutable at the head of the table. Gaelen had chosen to wear full formal dress. His torque of power sat around his neck.

Gaelen saw Sinnath's face fall slightly when he noticed that no chair had been reserved for him.

Klast marched Sinnath slowly along the table, so he would get a clear view of what it held. Then he made him stand at the opposite end from Gaelen, who had by now sat down, flanked by the prisoner and the boy. Klast returned to the door, both to observe and to be ready for action in the event this was needed. He left Sinnath's wrists tied.

In the heavy silence that ensued, Gaelen allowed Sinnath a few moments to take stock. He watched, as Sinnath looked at each member, trying to gauge their reactions. Grenth met his eyes evenly with an implacable look. Janest avoided his attempt to meet his eyes by taking a sudden interest in his hands. Then Sinnath started slightly. In the shadows in the darkest corner of the room stood Liethis. Gaelen had sent for her, though once again she had anticipated his need and her escort had met her just outside the gates of the city.

The slight sag of the shoulders and the flicker in the eyes told Gaelen that Sinnath recognized his defeat. Sinnath had seen many years as the consummate diplomat and had learned to keep his feelings well hidden, even under pressure, but his reaction was unmistakeable.

Finally, Gaelen cleared his throat and began. "Sinnath, you have been brought here today to face the charge of treason. You see that the evidence before you leaves no doubt as to your guilt. What have you to say?"

Trained to think on his feet, Sinnath straightened and met Gaelen's eyes without flinching. "As you say, my lord, the evidence cannot be denied. To say that I regret the path I have taken, though true, will convince no one. Nor will saying so mitigate the sentence I must face. My lord, I have only one request. I wish a short, private audience with you, before you pronounce sentence."

He did not break from Gaelen's gaze. Gaelen read only regret and concern there.

Gaelen thought for a moment. He looked at Klast, who gave him a short nod. With a bleak smile, Gaelen said, "Sinnath, do not think for a moment that I would leave myself open to attack by meeting with you unprotected. Yet, in view of your loyalty to my father, I will hear what you wish to tell me. But only with Klast present." He regarded Sinnath for a moment, then added, "And Liethis will know if you speak true, whether she is in the room or not."

"Thank you, my lord. That is acceptable." Sinnath inclined his head and shoulders in a small bow.

Gaelen nodded to Klast, who once more took Sinnath by the arms and guided him to a narrow door behind a tapestry. Gaelen opened it, and the three passed into a small, dark cell containing a dusty table and two old chairs, dry and cracked from long disuse. Gaelen lit the tallow candle that stood on the table and sat down, motioning Sinnath to do the same. Klast stood by Gaelen's side, ready to defend him, and to observe.

"Very well, I am listening. Speak."

Sinnath let his shoulders droop, all pride gone from his

demeanour. "My lord. I will not defend myself. My guilt is plain, my life forfeit. This all began at a time when I believed you unwise and too young to rule. Your choice of lady, from the house of the enemy, went against traditional strategies for gaining dominance over a conquered people. Now these past moons have shown me that I have erred. If I could take back the decision I made, I would do so gladly. Alas, it is too late. Such a path, once taken, cannot readily be reversed."

Sinnath stopped and sighed heavily. "My lord, I have only one concern for the future. I know I face execution. That will not change. But I have a son by my mistress. She died of the plague. He is my only child, only seven years old, and innocent of any wrongdoing. My wife will have nothing to do with him. In any case, she will, if tradition holds, be exiled or possibly executed."

His face filled with sorrow. "My lord, I beg you, as a boon for my years of service to your father, I beg you not to condemn my son for my crime. He is a fine boy. Please foster him with a good family. He knows nothing of my actions against you. I have faith that he will grow into a loyal subject."

Sinnath finally lost control. A single tear slid down his cheek, as he held Gaelen's steady gaze with sad resignation. "My lord, I know I have no right to ask this, but I beg it for his sake."

Gaelen had not expected this. It took him by surprise. The usual sentence for treason, besides the death of the traitor, was the confiscation of all his possessions into the coffers of the ruling house and the imprisonment or exile of his remaining family members. Wives could be sent to a secure retreat if no evidence of collusion could be found against them. Children were exiled along with lesser family. But this child had no family. He had not been legitimized.

The room remained silent, while Gaelen pondered this development. Perhaps the impending birth of his own son softened his position. Perhaps the time had come for change, and Gaelen had become Earth's instrument.

When he finally spoke, he allowed some of the sorrow he felt to show. "Sinnath, I have a proposal for you. You do understand that your trial and execution must be a public one. The people need to be clearly convinced of your guilt and must see that treason will not be tolerated. So, in return for your public declaration of guilt, I will foster your son with a trusted soldier in my military. I will also spare him your public beheading. He will be placed in the care of one of my lady's women until the trial is over and your body cleared away. He will be given military training, and his progress will be closely followed."

Gaelen paused. "Your wife, of course, must be present to witness your execution. Your open and clear public admission of treason will benefit Bargia by preventing bloodshed by those who might otherwise believe you innocent. Do you agree?"

At the word *proposal* Sinnath had tensed. Now his shoulders relaxed. "I do, my lord. I am most grateful. This will spare my son much humiliation and grief."

"Then let us return to the council chamber, so I may pronounce sentence." Gaelen stood. Klast held Sinnath's arms once more, while Gaelen opened the door and blew out the candle. They returned to their original positions.

Gaelen dismissed Haslin's son to a guard, who would escort him back to the inn, and called in another guard to return Ornan to his cell. Then he turned to Liethis. "Liethis, does what has transpired sense true?"

Liethis nodded, her face tight. Gaelen knew the pain such conflict caused her. If he had been able to spare her this, he would have, but he needed her there to confirm that Sinnath told the truth. "It does, my lord. I sense no deception in him. Only regret."

Gaelen nodded decisively. "Then let this be finished."

He outlined the agreement made with Sinnath. Then he pronounced sentence. Sinnath would give his declaration in the central square on a platform. There he would be publicly beheaded with his wife and household present. All his goods and properties would revert to the House of Bargia. Sinnath's wife would be exiled to a secure retreat, where she would spend the rest of her life safely locked away, powerless but comfortable, with no correspondence or visitors allowed. Gaelen gave Klast the task of finding an appropriate fostering for the boy.

Once finished, he looked around the room. "Does anyone have questions or objections?" No one responded. "Then let it be so. This trial is ended. Do not discuss what has passed here. I do not wish to give the people time to speculate. The public execution will be announced only one day ahead."

He turned to Klast. "Return the traitor to his cell." At Klast's short bow Gaelen stood, turned on his heel and abruptly left the chamber.

95: BEGINNINGS

Klast found a small cabin in a glade at the edge of the forest, outside the city. The trees kept it hidden from casual observers. It had been left derelict, abandoned by its previous inhabitants some years past. Shrubs and wild roses had almost obscured the walls and roof from view and completely covered the two tiny windows. The door faced the overgrown rut that passed for a path.

In back stood a shed just big enough for one horse and, in winter, one cow. Now it sheltered only Klast's dappled grey. In the back half, the rafters had been roughly planked in, so that hay and grain could be kept dry in the mow. In the front, a skeleton of aged timbers held a few coloured strands of fading wool from which bunches of dusty, dried herbs still hung. The roof of the shed let slivers of sunlight through, where holes had developed in the thatch. Klast had plans to rethatch it before winter, but for now his attentions were spent on the cabin.

They had talked again and agreed that the only real choice would be to join as husband and wife. This had to be what Liethis had sensed that Earth intended. Klast had assured Brensa that he could be as patient as she needed him to. He had brought Brensa here just a few days before, and she had fallen in love with the place. The roses were in full bloom, and their scent and colour had brightened her spirits.

"Is it too small?' he asked. "Too run down? Too far from the city? Too much work? Too lonely?"

"No, no, no, no, and no!" she exclaimed after each concerned question. "Oh, it is perfect! The garden will grow here in the back! See! Beans, turnips and carrots here, gourds and herbs here and there a row of orange nasturtiums, for colour." Her eyes danced with excitement. It warmed Klast to see her so, and some of her optimism rubbed off on him.

"The windows only need new oiled leather to let in some light. And we have two rooms, just right for privacy in case we have visitors. Do you not think yellow will make a fine colour for blankets and curtains? And No-tail already loves it here. Look at her exploring through the grass!"

Klast looked in the direction she pointed, just in time to see No-tail leap above the grass and pounce on an unsuspecting mouse. It made him smile. It occurred to him that it no longer felt strange to smile. He smiled much more now.

Brensa flitted exuberantly from cabin to garden to shed and back. She crowed over a patch of Black-eyed Susans, just beginning to show the promise of their golden yellow crowns though a profusion of unopened buds. Her face darkened only momentarily when she spied the hearth. She turned to him with a solemn promise to learn to cook on it. He gave a shake of his head and declared that whatever she made was bound to be better fare than he had eaten on many occasions, and she immediately resumed her elated inspection.

It was the first time since he had rescued her that Klast saw hints of the spark in her eyes that had made her so well-liked before. Errant curls had escaped from the braid that bounced over her back and framed her elfin face. Klast watched her with a contentment he had not known himself capable of. Nor could he help but be infected by her enthusiasm and return her delighted smiles with shy ones of his own. It all felt dangerously delicious. The wish that had flickered with a tiny flame when Brensa had survived the fever now burned bright with possibility.

They stayed only a short while this first time. When they had eaten the cold food Brensa had packed, he lifted her back in front of him on his horse, with No-tail once more tucked into the pocket she made for her in all her gowns. They wound their way back to the castle so they would reach it before dark. Brensa still tired quickly, and it would be some time yet before her strength returned to normal. Until then, he planned to make the cabin habitable and clear the spot she had indicated for her garden. At her insistence, he promised not to touch the roses. She loved the way they grew wild over the cottage and wanted to see to their care herself.

They spoke little on the ride back. The feel of her relaxed body against his filled Klast with a tenderness he had never known before. It pleased him that she had embraced the solitude of the croft he had found. He could never live in the city. He needed the extreme isolation to restore himself. It also afforded a measure of safety, mostly hidden and unknown. Yet, it was not so far that Brensa could not visit the city whenever she wished or when he was called away by his duties. She need never be truly alone there.

Klast had been especially pleased when Brensa had declared that at the cabin she did not feel the need to look over her shoulder all the time. She could relax there. That eased any worries he had over their isolation.

By the time they entered the gate into the city, the sun had already sunk low on the horizon. Dusk fell earlier so late into the summer. Outside the city, the wheat had been harvested with the help of some of the guards and the many itinerants who wandered into Bargia by ones and twos. Most of these had lost family to the plague and sought new beginnings. The stooks of wheat caught the late afternoon sun and reflected a golden sheen. Maize, too, had lost its summer green, its leaves darkened with brown edges. Along the stalks ears filled and ripened, promising a good yield in another moon if the rains held off.

Slanted shafts of light scintillated on the fine dust that hung in the still air. Babes sitting waiting for their suppers swiped at the sparkles in delight. Beside the small cottages that dotted the valley grew rows of beans, heavy with drying pods that rattled with seed in the wind. Some had already been picked, shelled, winnowed and stored in cool, dark crocks for winter soups. Plums hung purple on weighted boughs, and apples showed their first blush of red. These and other signs of recovery lent a growing air of optimism. As Earth showed Her resilience, so did the people mirror it.

96: INTERLUDE

Klast spent as much time as could be spared from his duties to Gaelen making the cabin habitable. True to his promise, he did not touch the wild roses that covered the two small windows. But, under Brensa's watchful eye, he trimmed the ones hanging in the way of the door. The roof received fresh sod, which he chose over thatch because it would keep the cottage warmer in winter and cooler in summer. He also made the small shed snug and dry for the horse and eventual cow, and added a few lengths to it to accommodate Brensa's mare.

On the afternoons when Brensa could come with him, she spent her time sorting out the garden. Some perennial sage and oregano still grew there but had become entangled with weeds and grasses. They worked quietly, each engrossed in their own activity, content in being together. When Brensa found she did not have the strength to clear a particularly stubborn patch, she would call Klast to her rescue. Occasionally, he grumbled about having his own work to do. Then he would watch her struggle, ruefully shake his head and do as she asked.

Though Brensa still had her small mare, they both preferred to ride the short distance together on Klast's gelding. Klast used those precious interludes to slowly woo her, holding her close, stealing kisses, and occasionally stroking her neck and shoulders. As she relaxed and began to respond to his overtures, his hope that he would eventually be able to bed her increased. "Patience," he admonished himself silently, over and over.

Brensa's hands grew dry and rough from pulling and digging, but she displayed them as though they were badges of honour. "I never was made for fancy needlework anyway." She gave a rare laugh, her face alight with optimism, as she showed them to Marja and Nellis. The sound warmed Klast. He was glad to see

Brensa regain colour and even put back some of the weight she had never regained after her ordeal in the cave.

Since Marja's son was due around winter solstice, Klast and Brensa agreed that it would be best to wait until spring to move into the cabin. Travel would be difficult once the snow fell, and Klast believed that Brensa would feel too isolated and have too little to do in winter. Brensa argued that this was not so but conceded that she wanted to learn a thing or two about cooking. Winter would be a good time to do that, as she could not garden yet.

Klast gave Brensa some basic lessons in preparing what they gathered, along with the rabbits and game he hunted. Those, along with deer and an occasional boar, would supplement the milk and eggs from the cow and hens promised to them.

But he would not be able to relax until the trial was over and he and Gaelen saw what the mood of the people would be.

97: PREPARATION

Klast rounded up the remaining members of Sinnath's gang, while Gaelen ordered the platform built for the public execution. Interrogation of Markel, the leader, and his followers uncovered no new information. The others, including Sinnath himself, had provided all they needed.

Gaelen wanted the trial and execution to proceed with haste. Harvest Festival was approaching, and he knew the people needed that celebration unmarred by strife, after the long summer of disease and death.

Marlis, Sinnath's wife, was held under house arrest, with no visitors and only one attendant, pending her seclusion at the women's retreat. That move would not take place until after the public trial, where she must be present to witness her husband's execution.

Klast knew that neither Gaelen nor his remaining advisors looked forward to that spectacle. To her immense relief, Marja was excused, due to her condition. Because of the high rank Sinnath had held, they expected the trial would attract some of his supporters as well as the usual crowd of curious onlookers. Gaelen planned a strong military presence to avert any unrest. Klast would stay close to his dais, in case Gaelen needed protection.

As well, there would be those who came to jeer and those who had a thirst for such bloody scenes. Not since before Gaelen's birth had a trial of this importance taken place. Only Marja and Klast knew how keenly he wished it were not necessary now. To all others he kept up the impression of solid strength. As lord, it would fall to him to give the public order for execution and watch it carried out. At least he would not be expected to order the traitors' heads displayed on stakes. That gory sight was reserved for treason during an active state of war. These men's bodies would simply be buried in an unmarked location outside the city, along with their heads, and hopefully soon forgotten.

98: EXECUTION

On the day of the execution, people began to drift into the public square by ones, twos and in small groups, jostling for position and staking out claims for the best view. A special platform stood to the side for the wealthy and influential. This had a canopy over it, in the event of rain or too much sun, and had been set with chairs. Many who expected to fill those chairs would be present only because they considered it their duty. Sinnath had been friend and colleague to them. This execution gave them no pleasure.

A separate, smaller dais, also covered, had been erected on the opposite side. Here, Gaelen would preside over the trial and executions. Sinnath's speech would take place under guard, at the centre front of the main platform. His neck would be the first on the block, followed immediately by the others, watching and awaiting their turn. These would wait, standing at the back of the main platform, heavily guarded and tied to posts.

It seemed Earth mourned along with Gaelen and his party. A steady drizzle soaked the square. Those on the side platform were grateful for the canopies that kept them dry. The chill rain helped keep the mood of the crowd sober, dampening the raucous behaviour that could accompany such occasions.

Liethis had requested to be excused, as she experienced excruciating pain around such events. But Gaelen explained that the people would accept the verdict more readily if she gave a statement about its healing effect on Earth and the future of Bargia. She had reluctantly deferred to his wishes. They agreed that she would not appear until after the beheadings, give a few brief words of a positive nature and have her horse ready to leave the city immediately after.

Liethis' message would be a true seeing. She had told Gaelen that Earth had shown her the trial was coming and that it was a

necessary event for restoring Her Balance. The death of the traitors would serve to balance the birth of the coming heir. Knowing
this did not make it any easier, or Liethis' pain any less. Gaelen
knew she would not be able to take food for days afterward.

At midday, Gaelen ascended his platform and stood at the
rail. He nodded acknowledgement to those seated on the other
side, then raised his hands to still the crowd as he made ready to
speak.

"Good people of Bargia. It is with a heavy heart that I must
today bring to trial for treason one of my lord father's most
trusted advisors. Yet, we have undeniable proof that Sinnath is
guilty of that blackest of crimes against Bargia." Gaelen briefly
described the evidence against Sinnath, then concluded, "Now
you will hear the traitor's guilt from his own mouth. Guards,
bring the prisoner, Sinnath, forward."

Sinnath, ankles shackled, hobbled to the rail between two
guards, who remained standing beside him as he prepared to
speak. He wore the grey sack tunic reserved for those awaiting
execution. He had been permitted to shave and bathe, albeit
under the watchful eyes of guards, lest he decide to take his own
life. Gaelen had suggested these concessions in order to avoid the
impression that Sinnath acted under duress. His feet were bare,
as was his head.

"Sinnath, you stand convicted of treason against Bargia and
your lord. What have you to say?" Gaelen's voice rang out strong
and firm, and he looked steadily at Sinnath. No one saw the
effort this took, except possibly Klast.

Though his ankles were hobbled, his wrists bound, and two
guards closely flanked his sides, Sinnath held his head erect and
stood with a dignity that belied the fate he faced. He waited a
moment for the murmuring of the crowd to still and began in
a strong, calm voice that carried to the farthest corners of the
square.

"Good people. I stand before you a man guilty of the most

grievous crime against Bargia and our lord. You have heard the evidence against me. I tell you, all of it is true. I offer no excuses, no lies. When Lord Gaelen came into power, I mistakenly believed him too young and inexperienced to rule. This made me blind to the advantages of the changes he proposed, not the least of which was to take to wife the daughter of the enemy. That choice flew in the face of all tradition. And I am a man of tradition. So I conspired with others, both inside and outside Bargia, to remove the threat I believed this joining would bring. I see clearly, now, that I was wrong. Lord Gaelen and Lady Marja have both served Bargia ably and nobly."

Sinnath cleared his throat as his voice broke. Regaining his composure he continued. "If any of you have any doubts where I now stand, hear this. Bargia has a lord, stronger and abler than any before him, even his beloved father, Lord Bargest. Lord Gaelen's choice of lady has resulted in greater stability than any victory over a conquered people has brought in history. The Lady Marja has shown her care for the people of Bargia throughout the plague that cost so many lives. And this, while carrying an heir; this, in spite of danger to herself and that son. Both our lord and lady serve the people tirelessly. I say to you again. I was wrong. I confess my guilt in the hope that doing so will prevent further treason and bloodshed. I go willingly to my death. It is meet and fit. I beg those who followed me to desist from any further treason on my behalf."

Sinnath turned and knelt, facing Gaelen. "My lord, I am grateful for this opportunity to speak. May your reign be long and prosperous and your lady be delivered of a healthy son and heir. Forgive me." Then he bowed his head and waited.

The crowd had not expected this. They stood in stunned and awkward silence. None of the usual responses seemed to fit.

Gaelen wasted no time, not wanting to give the crowd a chance to begin its hubbub. "People, you have heard Sinnath's confession to treason. When sentence has been carried out, return to your homes with his plea for allegiance to Bargia in your hearts, that we may look forward to a new prosperity and peace."

He turned to the platform where Sinnath knelt, his head still bowed. "Sinnath, by your own confession, and by the evidence presented, you are guilty of treason. The sentence for treason is death. Your wife, Lady Marlis, will spend the rest of her life in seclusion at Wemblin, with the women keepers there. She will be permitted no visitors or correspondence. All your goods are forfeit to Bargia. Your bastard son will be fostered with a man I trust, raised to love Bargia and to defend her, if necessary, when he comes of age."

Sinnath raised his head and shot Gaelen a look of profound gratitude at this public declaration of his promise.

"Now," regret crept into Gaelen's voice, though it remained strong and all could clearly hear, "you will place your neck on the block and have it severed from your body. The same will follow for those with you. Let all know the punishment for treason. Let it be done."

The two guards helped Sinnath to his feet, led him to the block and lowered him so that his neck rested on it. Sinnath did not hesitate. Later, all would admire his courage. The axe-man raised his weapon high above his head and looked to Gaelen for his signal. At Gaelen's nod he swung with all his strength. The axe curved in a wide arc and bit into its first target. The crowd gasped in unison as they watched the head roll into the waiting basket and Sinnath's blood spurt past in great gouts and dwindle to nothing. Waiting soldiers quickly removed the body and replaced the basket containing his head with a fresh one.

The remaining prisoners followed Sinnath's fate in quick succession. The stunned crowd remained mostly silent. As soon as all the heads and bodies had been collected onto the waiting wagon, they were taken out of the city to an undisclosed burial place. Though rumours abounded, no one ever knew for certain where the bodies lay buried.

Gaelen raised his arms for quiet again as soon as the last corpse had been removed. He called Liethis to the dais, and she quietly took her place behind him. He moved aside to make room for her before he spoke again.

"My people. You have seen justice carried out today. Now hear the seer Liethis. You know her as true seer to my court. Hear her message from Earth." He stepped back a pace and indicated to Liethis to take his place.

Liethis' face was chalk pale, and she clenched the rail with white knuckles, barely able to hold herself up. She clung on with sheer determination and took a deep breath to steady herself.

With the exhaling of that breath, Gaelen saw Earth channel strength into her. She spoke as Liethis, yet not Liethis, her voice somehow more melodious and richer. The sound carried to the far corners of the square, though Liethis spoke in a moderate tone.

"Good people of Bargia. You have witnessed a cleansing. The stain of treason is removed. Soon another, more joyful event awaits you, the birth of a son to your lord and lady, a strong heir. Bargia enters a new cycle of hope and prosperity. Prepare for the Harvest Festival with joy and confidence." The channel left her, and Liethis sagged, once more ready to drop. She stepped unsteadily back from the rail and let herself be assisted from the dais. Gaelen stepped up quickly to distract the people from her weakness.

"You have heard the seer, Liethis. Earth begins a new cycle which will bring an heir, good harvest and a bright future. Let us look forward to these joyful events."

With that he spun abruptly on his heel, left the dais, and strode swiftly away from the scene. He indicated to Klast, standing inconspicuously to one side, to follow.

99: FESTIVAL

The day of Harvest Festival glittered at dawn with a thick layer of hoar frost on the trees and bushes. The people, accustomed to rising with first light, exclaimed over the sparkle it added to the garlands of red and gold leaves and herbs, the decorative sheaves of yellow barley and spelt and the tall stalks of maize tied to lintels and set by doorways. A coating of crystal limned even the rooflines of homes and sheds. Bargians, young and old, regarded it as a good omen. By midday, the frost had given in to the sun, which shone bright and warm and chased it into the sky in gauzy filaments of haze.

On this special day, all able hands set to making final preparations for the festivities. In the city, the cold almost masked the stench of the middens and the run-off trenches along the sides of the streets. As fires and ovens brought their wares to peak perfection, the aromas of cooking, baking, and roasting chased the last vestiges of unpleasantness away.

Around the outer edge of the square, great spits had been set over fires, where older children took shifts turning whole boar, late lambs and haunches of venison. Between these, smaller vendors set up stands where sweets could be found: honeyed fruits, nut cakes, fruited buns, and all manner of breads, new cheeses, and smoked meats.

Bakers in the city set up tables to the side of the square, in preparation for the gifts from their ovens. On them they lay cloths of snowy linen, with stones on each corner to prevent the wind from blowing them away, until the breads would hold them in place.

In the very centre of the square stood a huge platform, one corner covered with an oiled linen canopy. Musicians would perform under it later, and dancers would throng the platform. Those unable to find room on top would spill out onto the cobblestones below. Tonight, rich and poor alike would vie for space there, all differences of wealth or position forgotten for this one event. Even Marja and Gaelen were expected to join in for at least one dance.

This evening would be the one time in the year when artisans and shopkeepers would offer samples of their wares, free to all to eat at the Festival. Of course, this also provided a forum for enticing future customers. The better their products, the more patronage they stood to garner for the rest of the year.

By late afternoon, hawkers could be heard calling out to potential tasters in mock competition with each other.

"Here, try the finest honey cakes in Bargia! None better in all the One Isle!"

"Best cheese this side of the river! Chosen by Lord Gaelen himself!"

"Taste the wines that grace the tables of the castle!"

"Buy your sweetheart a shiny bauble. You will win her heart forever!"

A merry cacophony of sound filled the air, interspersed by the tinkling of bells, low thrumming on small drums and snatches of bawdy songs and gay ditties sung by roving minstrels.

In the trader's field, travellers with carts and tents sold charms or brightly coloured scarves, hawked to young maids or to their sweethearts. Soothsayers made predictions of prosperity and love for all who entered their tents with coin in hand. Travellers set up tents in which all manner of strange sights could be seen for a small fee: a two-headed chicken, a man who could contort himself into wondrous shapes, a bearded woman. Small stages offered puppet shows and mime.

The feasting, music and dancing of Harvest Festival, the last important holiday before the hard winter, offered the people an opportunity to visit, to mingle, to make new acquaintances and renew old friendships. Many romances began here, often the result of a gift of one of the trader's scarves or a bauble given to a chosen maiden. Harvest was the traditional time for joinings, when men and women agreed to bond their lives together. No surprise, then, that many babes were born nine or ten moons later.

As the first rosy glow of dusk appeared on the horizon, Lord Gaelen and Lady Marja walked out, arm in arm, and made a progress around the square, greeting subjects and accepting tokens of goodwill and wishes for the healthy arrival of the babe. Many women considered it good luck to touch Marja's distended belly, hoping their own births, or those of their children, would benefit. Marja, though near her time and becoming uncomfortable, bore this with admirable grace. Gaelen kept his arm securely around her waist, ready to defend her. Klast hovered close behind, invisible among the revellers. Two guards walked to each side and in front and behind, at a discreet distance, their presence underplayed. This was a calculated risk Gaelen had to take, and fortunately greater security was not necessary today.

When their processional around the square had finished, Gaelen led Marja to the nearest table, where a waiting servant handed him two huge platters. He passed one to Marja, and together they made another round of the square, taking bits from each stand, careful not to show preference for one over the other. With their plates heaped high, they ascended the small covered platform erected to one side and sat in the two chairs set out for them behind a rough table covered in blue linen. There pewter goblets filled with wine, or cider in Marja's case, awaited them.

Not until a broadly grinning Gaelen had placed the first bite in Marja's mouth, and Marja followed with one in his, did the people raise a great whoop of cheer and begin to fill their own stomachs. The festival had officially begun. The din of happy talk, competing music, and the rumblings of the jostling crowd made speech between Gaelen and Marja impossible, so they contented themselves with indulgent grins and tired smiles.

After the musicians had eaten their fill, the first climbed the platform, took their place under the canopy and began the more lively dance tunes that would tire the children out. Soon, sated and exhausted, they would fall asleep in parents' laps or on blankets to the side of the square. As darkness descended and stars peeked brightly over the scene, the feast grew more sedate. People found quiet spots to sit and listen to the ballads, lays and heroic songs that the musicians offered after dark. Then, in ones, twos and family groups, they melted into the darkness and headed for bed or to private trysts.

Many heads would suffer in the morning from too much ale and wine, but the work of the harvest had been mostly finished, and no one expected to rise with the dawn. Bakers would not bake, butchers would offer only cooked meats left over from the feast and shops would remain closed until after midday. Customers would be too tired to shop anyway.

100: A WARNING

As winter solstice drew near, Marja kept more and more to the castle and to her chambers. She complained of discomfort, and when she spent time on her feet, her back ached. She began to experience random cramps, which Lotha assured her were normal so near her time. Gaelen felt relieved that with the birth so near, Lotha kept close to the castle so she could be available at a moment's notice. Her apprentice took on the burden of her other patients in the interim.

Lotha told them she did have one worry, however. "The babe has taken the upside-down, breech position. I hope the child will turn, but time is running short. It appears unlikely."

While breech births often ended happily, it was not ideal for a first born.

When she expressed this concern to Marja, Gaelen became apprehensive. Liethis had foretold a healthy son and that Marja would survive. But Gaelen knew that such things sometimes changed, so he sent for Liethis to ask her advice. Too much hung on this birth to leave things to chance. If something still remained unresolved it needed to be taken care of now.

When the escort came for Liethis she met him waiting at her door, her horse already saddled and her bag strapped on. As usual, she wore the traditional, unbleached white of a seer, this time in warm wools for winter. Since the weather remained dry, the oiled skins that would keep out the wind and rain remained in her bag.

A guard informed Gaelen as soon as Liethis arrived, and he made his way hurriedly to his chambers. She would come as soon as she had brought her bags to her room, the guard told him. They reached the chambers at the same time.

At Liethis' suggestion, Marja sent Brensa to fetch Lotha as well, though Liethis reassured them that this was only to keep her completely informed. While the two waited for the others to return, Marja had tea and a cold meal brought. The women engaged in general talk around Marja's state of discomfort and the preparations of the nursery for the new heir.

"I have already chosen a wet nurse," Marja said, "against the event that I may be unable to nurse the child myself, though I dearly wish to."

They all tacitly agreed to avoid the true purpose of Liethis' presence until the others had arrived and been served tea. Brensa and Nellis rounded out the party.

While custom dictated that men should not be present on such occasions, no one ventured to suggest that Gaelen did not belong in this discussion. He took his customary chair as naturally as though this were a casual social visit.

As soon as everyone had taken their places, Liethis cleared her throat slightly to get their attention. Then, as was her wont, she got right to the point. "My Lord Gaelen, Lady Marja, friends. You wish to know what I see with regard to the birth of the coming heir. My vision has not changed. I still sense that Lady Marja will deliver a strong, healthy son and that she will survive the birth."

She smiled her understanding when a series of shoulders relaxed and held breaths released. Then she grew serious again. "But the birth will not be an easy one. My lady, you must rest until then to conserve your strength. Your labour will be long and strenuous."

Liethis looked at Lotha. "I know that the child is breech. You will need all your skill to bring him forth. Do not wander far. Once the birth starts you will be needed."

She turned to Marja. "I am pleased that you have a wet nurse at hand. For the first days you will have little strength to feed the child, though I believe this will be temporary, for I have seen him at your breast."

Everyone gasped, as Liethis suddenly froze, then glared at Lotha with eyes that held an eerie power.

"You must not pull at the child. He will find his own time. Do not let fear make you haste."

The trance left her, and she found herself facing a group whose expressions bore signs of shock. Trembling with weakness, she sank back into her chair.

Liethis looked around at each in turn before speaking again, resting her gaze on Marja.

"The danger that has been shown me is not to the son you bear, my lady, but to yourself. I suddenly saw much blood, and it blinded my vision." Turning once more to Lotha, she reiterated her warning. "Heed this, Lotha. I do not know why, but it is most important. Do not pull the child forth."

Lotha looked as though she had been struck.

Liethis sensed her thoughts and added, "Lotha, I know that you have helped babes and mothers when they have been breech. You know your skills well. This time is different. Do not forget."

Not until Lotha nodded obedience, did Liethis let go her gaze.

The chamber remained in stunned silence for several moments, until Gaelen found his voice. "Lotha, have you all you need? Will you require anyone with you aside from Nellis and Brensa, now that you have heard Liethis' words?" His worry showed clearly, in spite of his firm voice and his attempt to appear normal. This warning had not been what he had expected, and it had shaken him.

"No, my lord, but I will make sure I have more than the usual herbs and that the kitchen is made ready with hot water and linens." Lotha's face had gone chalk white, and her voice shook. She gripped the seat of her chair tightly.

Bone weary, as such sendings always left her, Liethis excused herself and left to rest in her room, assuring Gaelen that she would not leave the city until they had spoken again.

101: AN HEIR

Lotha took up residence in the room set aside for the nursery and slept on the bed prepared for the wet nurse, who agreed to give it up and sleep on a temporary cot, pending the birth. She busied herself with gathering more herbals and teas, with making sure the kitchen had their instructions and with keeping a close eye on Marja. In between she took time to answer questions, when her apprentice came for advice.

Two days later, on the night of winter solstice, Gaelen found himself wakened by Marja shaking him. Marja had been fitful, so his sleep had already been broken several times.

He heard Marja say, "My waters have broken. Get Lotha."

Marja seemed so calm that it took a moment for this to penetrate his still groggy mind. With a start, he realized the birth had begun. Suddenly completely alert, Gaelen vaulted out of bed and ran to fetch Lotha.

The hubbub brought Brensa and Nellis out as well, and the three women banded together to firmly shoo Gaelen out of the room and bar the door. This was women's work. Men had no place here.

Gaelen had never felt so helpless. He went to the kitchen for some tea and food but found himself too tense to eat. His pacing put him in the way of the early bakers and wore out his welcome there as well. They made it plain that he was keeping them from their duties. At first, he thought he might go for a ride, but it struck him that something might happen, and Marja might need him. He could not leave the castle. Without knowing how he got there, he found himself pacing the halls outside their chambers, where Marja laboured to deliver their son. If the floor had not been made of stone, he would surely have worn a path into it.

For several spans, until well past dawn, he heard nothing but murmurs through the door. This lulled him enough that he realized how hungry he was, and he returned to the kitchen, this time able to eat ... and to stay out of the way. He watched as servants took platters of food and kettles of hot water to the birthing room. Everyone seemed calm and efficient ... so why could he not be? He shook his head in exasperation and returned to his vigil outside the chamber, finally falling into the chair that stood in the hall.

*   *   *

Behind the barred door, which opened only to admit food and supplies, an atmosphere of expectant calm reigned. Lotha gave quiet orders to Brensa and Nellis from time to time, but those two mostly sat with their needlework and kept up a stream of small talk to distract Marja. Lotha urged Marja to drink quantities of raspberry leaf tea to strengthen her womb. She kept track of Marja's spasms and determined that things were proceeding normally. The hard work looked yet some time away.

In between sitting to drink her tea and taking small amounts of bread and honey for strength, Lotha had Marja walk about the room, explaining that it would help the babe descend. When Marja began to gasp and hold herself rigid as the pain of her contractions increased, Lotha stroked her belly and soothingly murmured instructions, helping her relax her breathing. She told her not to clench her teeth, as that made the contractions somehow more painful.

Lotha had arranged the birthing stool on a low platform, to raise it up and make it easier for her to help the babe out. Normally this would not be necessary, but with the child in breech position, she wanted the best angle possible. Her own low stool sat ready in front of it.

By late afternoon, nerves began to fray. When Nellis' son began to scream for his mother through the nursery door, Lotha ordered her to have the nurse take the child out of earshot until they were finished. Mother and child had never been apart for more than a few spans, so this arrangement pleased neither. Nellis fought back tears as Borless' howling faded down the hall.

When Marja's pains came closer together and she could no longer hide her agitation, Lotha added camomile to the tea to calm her. She ordered Brensa and Nellis to drink it, too. Their worry could no longer be masked with idle chatter, and Lotha needed them calm, in case she needed help.

As dusk fell, Lotha could tell that Marja had retreated into herself and that her pains came one upon the other with little rest in between. She had her lie on the bed to check her progress and found her fully opened. Now the hard work would begin. No more teas or food, except, perhaps, a spoonful of honey now and then to keep up her strength. She kept her hands on Marja's belly for the next few spasms, and when she could feel that Marja had begun to push, helped her to the birthing stool. Her shift was lifted above her belly to give Lotha a clear view.

With only candles and firelight illuminating the room, amid grunts of effort, two tiny feet peeked out between Marja's thighs. Now came the crucial period, and Lotha began to sweat in spite of her long years of experience.

Liethis' words rang in her ears. "Do not pull on the babe!" But long practice in calming women through births helped her keep up the soothing words and touches that hid her anxiety from the others. Soon the legs were through, and the body began to emerge. Lotha hoped that one arm and shoulder would appear before the other. That hope proved in vain. Marja continued to push with all her strength, but for several moments, no progress could be seen. Lotha told Marja to try to hold back through the next spasm. Then she gently inserted two fingers into the canal to check the position of the child. She found what she expected. Both arms were overhead beside the babe's ears. Instructing Marja to hold off once more, she tried to ease one arm down so that the first shoulder could pass. It took two tries before she succeeded. As the elbow slid down Marja screamed, and Lotha felt her tear.

Gaelen heard the scream and pounded on the door to let him in. Brensa had already risen halfway out of her seat to obey, but at a shake of the head from Lotha, she reluctantly lowered herself back down. Lotha turned her attention resolutely back to Marja. The pounding stopped. Gaelen had given up.

Lotha knew time was important now. Marja needed to push the babe out so the damage could be checked and the bleeding staunched. And the cord needed to be loosened around the child's neck. When the only part remaining to emerge was the babe's head, Lotha would normally have pulled at the same time that Marja pushed. It was all she could do to hold back. She must not disobey Liethis' warning.

Marja had grown very weak by now, and she had not much strength left with which to push. Yet the head was the largest part, and she would need to find enough strength to finish her work. So Lotha had Brensa and Nellis each take one arm and coached them to shout at Marja to push as each new pain came on. Lotha told Marja to yell or scream if she felt the urge, knowing that this helped the canal to relax. All this noise was intended to encourage Marja to forget about Gaelen and decorum. Now Marja was any woman, not a lady.

The chamber seemed suspended in time. After several more pushes, amid loud urging from Nellis and Brensa, Marja gave a final, rending scream, and the babe slipped into Lotha's waiting hands.

A quick check told Lotha that the boy looked strong and healthy. His breathing became regular, and he grasped her finger when she placed it in his hand. She tied off the cord, cut it, held the boy up for an anxious Marja to see, and handed him to Nellis to bathe and wrap. As soon as the afterbirth slipped out, she had Brensa help her get Marja back to the bed, where she carefully examined her womb. The tearing did not appear as bad as she had feared and would heal in time.

When she found Marja bleeding more heavily than she ought, she told an astonished Brensa to fetch the wet nurse's babe. As soon as the infant was brought in, she put him to Marja's breast, where he began to suck lustily.

At the same time, Lotha kneaded Marja's belly. As she did so, she explained that these things often helped to slow down bleeding from the womb. She did not know why, just that this was so. When the bleeding finally slowed, she turned her attention to the tearing. Satisfied that her initial assessment had been correct, she rummaged in her basket for a salve of honey mixed with goldenseal, which she lathered liberally onto the tear and around the opening to the womb.

Now all she could do was hope the fever that took so many new mothers' lives would not set in. She wanted to brew some willow bark tea, for pain and fever, but decided against it, as it sometimes increased bleeding. Instead she contented herself with more raspberry leaf and camomile.

As soon as Nellis and Brensa had Marja bathed and resting as comfortably as possible, Lotha unbarred and opened the door, and Nellis presented Gaelen with his son.

Gaelen stood in the doorway a moment, wearing the bewildered expression Lotha had seen many times on the faces of new fathers. She stood aside as he hesitantly accepted his son from Nellis' arms. He hurried over to Marja's side, where she greeted him with a wan smile. He sat on the edge of the bed, a worried look still in his eyes, as he questioned her silently.

"We are both well, my love," Marja assured him. She asked him to lay their son beside her so they could examine him together. "He is perfect, is he not? I think he has your chin."

Gaelen nodded with obvious relief. "Yes. But he has your hair, I think, and my mother's nose."

The exchange made Lotha laugh. She had seen this so many

times. "You will see new resemblances each day," she chuckled. "Now then, when you have taken a few moments together, I must ask you to leave again Lord Gaelen. Lady Marja needs rest. Her labour has been difficult, and she has lost a good deal of blood. If her milk is to come in, she needs to build her strength back up."

She paused a moment, then added, "And I need some time with Lady Marja to help the babe take the breast. Sometimes both mother and child need a little help with this." She beamed again. "Soon you may wish you were not so near, when the child demands to be fed in the night." Then, as an afterthought, she agreed, "But he is indeed a beautiful lad, strong and healthy. Please allow me to be the first to congratulate you both on a new heir, my lord, my lady."

Before Gaelen stood to leave, he placed a tender kiss on Marja's forehead. Then, rising, he turned to the group and announced, "His name is Lionn, after my brother, who never had the opportunity to sire an heir." With a last proud though still worried glance at Marja, he left.

102: A NEW HOME

Klast and Brensa moved into the cottage shortly after the first strong spring thaw. Snow had all but disappeared, remaining in dirty patches only on the north sides of hills and at the bottoms of trees in the copses. Crofters checked fields almost daily, eager to start spring seeding and planting. Brensa was no less eager to begin working in her garden.

Throughout the winter, Klast had still managed to make several visits to the cabin to complete repairs. He had built a platform which would serve as their bed, made a rough table, and bought two stools to sit on. An old wooden chair with arms and a back had been left behind in the cottage when the previous inhabitants had abandoned it.

As a special gift to Brensa, Klast commissioned a rocker with a low seat and no arms, the type women sat in to knit, do needle work, and nurse infants. Together they had chosen a large cauldron for boiling water for baths and laundry, two smaller kettles for cooking and other items necessary to set up a home.

Marja had given Brensa a large wooden chest as soon as Brensa had announced that she and Klast wished to join.

Actually Brensa had requested leave from Marja to do so. Maids belonged to their ladies and were not free to make such decisions on their own.

Brensa had told Klast that Marja had been delighted at the news and had hugged her tightly across her bulging belly. But she had not been able to hide her relief when Brensa had told her the move would not take place until spring and that she would remain for the birth of the babe. Neither had known, at the time, that Nellis would soon join them.

Klast and Marja had learned a grudging respect for each other. He felt relieved that their conflict would no longer stand in the way of Brensa's friendship with Marja.

As a joining gift, Marja had filled the chest with a featherbed, down pillows, several linen sheets and two warm, colourful quilts. She also included some fine crockery and bronze plates, good quality knives and spoons and several wooden spoons and bowls. Brensa's kitchen would be well stocked. Now she only needed to learn how to use all these items. The very idea made Marja and Nellis roll their eyes at her whenever Brensa mentioned cooking. She took the ribbing with good humour.

Gaelen gifted the couple with a milk cow. Nellis and Mikost gave the pair nine laying hens and one proprietary rooster. These also induced their share of jokes about cooking and animal husbandry. With the addition of their two horses, the shed would be full, indeed, come winter.

As the first thaws of spring uncovered them, Klast showed Brensa how to recognize and collect new cress by the edge of the ponds and river banks. He taught her how to find the early fiddlehead greens, so prized after a winter without fresh vegetables. As summer progressed he would teach her where to find wild leeks, onions and garlic. Mushrooms would remain Klast's duty.

"It would not do for us to die from a poisoned stew." He gave Brensa a wry grin, as she caught the joke and laughed with him.

For the first ten days they spent together, Klast made no attempt to bed her. Instead, he put his efforts into helping her relax enough to fall asleep with her head on his shoulder: stroking her hair, kissing her face, head and neck, and gradually caressing her in more intimate places.

By the end of that period, Brensa began responding by reaching up to stroke his face, resting her arm across his chest, and squeezing him back when he hugged her. He did his best to make sure she never felt his arousal.

To Klast's great surprise, their first attempt came at Brensa's suggestion. In spite of his efforts to hide his desire, he had known she sensed his frustration.

As they talked about it, she shyly agreed it might be best if he tried to enter her from behind, in a spooning embrace so she would not see, thinking it might help her control her fear. Alas, she was mistaken. As soon as she felt him try to slide between her thighs, she panicked, leapt out of bed, and pressed her back against the wall, gasping short pants of fear. It took Klast several moments to calm her and coax her back into bed, where he soothed her by holding her close and crooning the old lullaby he had sung in the cave.

Their second attempt proved only moderately less disastrous. Brensa told him she might not be so frightened if she could see Klast's face, holding in her mind the love she knew she would see there. While she did not leap away this time, his fumbling with her nightshift made them both feel awkward. When he finally made the attempt to enter her, she froze and squeezed her legs tightly together. Klast desisted instantly. He comforted her by insisting that this showed progress, and he told her again and again that he could wait as long as she needed.

103: BRENSA

Meanwhile, their woodpile stacked up much more swiftly than necessary. The morning after their second attempt, Brensa walked around the cabin and stood watching Klast unobserved, as he chopped wood. She knew from the single-minded purpose and force he put into each stroke of the axe that he was using this to release some of his frustration. Even with the last frost still on the fields, he had stripped to the waist, and sweat sheened his bare back. She watched the corded muscles ripple in his arms and roll across his strong shoulders, remembering the feel of that skin under her fingers, and the gentleness of those great hands upon her body.

Sadly, she turned and went back into the cabin. She knew deep inside that she desired him, too. But as soon as she became aware of his hardness, it flooded her with the memory of those others and the searing, burning pain they had inflicted. Tears of frustration pricked her eyes, as she despaired of overcoming those memories. She sat on the side of the bed and thought intensely on the problem, unaware of the sounds of the axe falling and the cracking of the wood as it split.

Brensa tallied up what she knew to be true. Both Nellis and Marja had told her that they never experienced pain when their husbands entered them. Both they and the midwife had told her this was how it ought to be, how most women experienced it. The midwife had explained that the only cause for her pain lay in the fear which made her tighten against it. She had certainly been in immense fear when those beasts had attacked her. But knowing a thing did not help her to overcome it.

She let her thoughts travel to Klast, a man who could, if he chose, kill her with one hand, effortlessly. Yet those hands which had dispatched so many had shown her only the utmost tenderness, even in the cave when he needed to clean her wounds and she had been a stranger. She let her memory recall the touch of those hands caressing her, the look of love in his eyes as he did so and his expression whenever she caught him watching her at her work. She recalled the desire she had felt when he stroked her back under her shift in bed, how his kisses around her neck gave her shivers. He would never hurt her. Never. She knew this just as truly as she knew her own love for him. *Oh, Klast,* she wept, silent tears making tracks down her cheeks. *What are we to do?*

She decided, with grim determination, that tonight they must try again. This time she must not prevent him from entering her. But how? The fear came upon her so suddenly. She decided that tonight she would stoke up the fire in the hearth, to make sure they were very warm and would not need the blankets, and that she could keep his face in view by its light. As well, she planned to set the tallow lamp on a chair beside the bed for even more light. She promised herself she would not allow her eyes to close, that she would concentrate so hard on his face, on the love she knew she would see there, that there would be no room for thoughts of those others. She would focus on the love in his touch, the softness of the skin on his back, the tenderness of his kisses. She would hold in her mind the truth that he would never inflict pain on her. Had he not proven himself over and over again? Had he not shown her? She would keep herself so immersed in these, that no other thoughts would be able to divert her from them. It must work. It just had to.

So deep was her concentration that she did not notice when the fall of the axe ceased. As she came out of her trance, she saw Klast watching her intently from the doorway with a surprised, questioning expression.

When she became aware of him he closed the door, looked at her a moment and asked, "What is amiss? You weep and did not hear me come in."

Brensa rose and embraced him, resting her head on his chest.

They stood that way for a moment. Then she raised her earnest face to his. "Klast, I have a plan."

She smiled bravely up at him and proceeded to explain her idea for how light would help her keep her thoughts with him. He tried to hush her by assuring her he would be patient and she need not press herself, but she would not hear it. "No, Klast, I must try. I cannot continue seeing you so thwarted. I truly want to do this for you … for us."

Klast gave her a long, searching look as he fingered an errant curl back into place behind her ear. Then, satisfied that she would not be swayed from her purpose, murmured, "Very well," kissed her lightly and let her go, changing the subject.

"Brensa, I have business with Lord Gaelen tomorrow. Perhaps you would like to see Lady Marja and Nellis? The shed is ready, and we could bring your mare back with us."

Brensa brightened. "That sounds fine. It will be good to see the children again, too." She smiled in anticipation.

Klast nodded agreement and left the cabin again.

104: KLAST

The patch where Brensa wished to plant her vegetables had dried enough to turn over. After that it would be hers to do with as she wished. Klast shook his head again at the thought of Brensa gardening without any experience. He reached for the spade, wondering absently if one of the gardeners in the city might be able to offer her some advice, since he also knew little of gardening.

As the dark loam gave under the pressure of the spade, and the worms he uncovered hastened to find new hiding places, he thought about how he might do things differently tonight. How could he help Brensa avoid the tension that prevented them from completing their union?

He knew how desperately she wished to please him. He sensed, too, that she desired him, at least until that moment when her fear set in. He went over all the tricks that Simna had taught him, those which had shown promise, and those he had not yet tried. By the time Brensa called him to supper, such as it was, a plan had shaped in his mind. He hoped to Earth it would work.

That night as they prepared to retire, Brensa set the chair with the lamp by the bed, while Klast built up the fire to burn bright. We will roast, he told himself, suppressing a shake of his head. Once more, he fervently hoped all would end well.

To Brensa he said, "I have yet another way we may try. Come. Let me show you." And he drew her to him in a standing embrace. He saw Brensa's surprise when he did not lie down. Instead he sat on the edge of the bed and had her straddle his lap. Resting her on his knees, he watched the question in her eyes, as he caressed first one calf and then the other before placing them to either side around his waist. As he did so, her shift stretched a bit across her knees, its remaining length puddling in her lap. She remained calm as she watched him fumble with the

364

fabric. He could not stop his hands from trembling slightly as he freed her shift, and, profoundly relieved when she did not flinch, reached underneath the back. There, with feather-light touches, he stroked her lower back with one hand, while gradually working his other underneath one buttock, until her full weight rested on it. They remained in that position for some time while his free hand and his mouth found all the places he had learned she liked to be touched.

When Brensa got over her surprise, her hands began caressing his face and back, exploring the muscles beneath his damp skin.

Slowly, Klast drew her toward him. As he did so he lifted her with his one hand, until she rested against his chest, her eyes level with his, knees bent, heels on the bed behind him. As promised, she kept her eyes on his face. For a second, she seemed overwhelmed and squeezed them shut. Klast sensed it was not fear. Her eyes had shone liquid before they shut, and he had seen his face mirrored in them. True to her vow, she reopened them and fixed them again on his face.

Klast had unrivalled strength in his arms, and Brensa was only a small woman, but after several moments her weight had his arm quivering with the effort of holding her up. Sheer determination kept him from moving too quickly. When Brensa seemed ready, he began to lower her onto himself as he teased his member inside, watching her face for signs of distress. All the while he kept up the kisses and the stroking with his free hand. When he felt himself halfway, unable to hold her up any longer, he lowered her further until she rested against his groin.

Brensa's mouth formed a small, "Oh," of surprise when she realized what had happened. He felt her tense slightly and watched the play of emotions cross her face: surprise, flicker of fear, joy and surprise again.

"There is no pain," came the tremulous whisper, a hint of incredulity in it.

He acknowledged this only with a simple, quiet, "No."

Then he rewarded her with a tender smile, pulled her gently against him, and held her close. She wrapped her arms around his back and hugged him tightly in return. They stayed that way for a long moment, neither moving. Klast began to rock her against him, almost imperceptibly at first, then with more purpose. It was not much movement, but Klast had waited so long, and built up so much need, it was enough. At the last, he gave a spasmodic groan and clutched her to him. Then, as he hugged her tight, one ragged word escaped him.

"Brensa."

That one word carried all the longing, pain, and fulfilment he had held back for so long. Brensa, understanding, clasped him with all her strength, her eyes welling with unshed tears of relief and elation. They held each other thus, in silent communion. How long, neither had any idea.

*   *   *

For the rest of her life, Brensa would recall that moment with perfect clarity. Though she had, by now, shut her eyes, she sensed the room filling with a rose and gold light that could not be attributed to the fire. It seemed alive and bathed them in approval. Earth ... showing them Her pleasure. Later on, whenever the fear from bad memories threatened to creep in, she would bring back that memory of Earth's glow, and it would calm her again.

They rested like that, unmoving, until Brensa felt him slip from her, and Earth withdrew Her light, leaving the room, once more, as it had been. Klast leaned her slightly away from him and studied her face. In his, she saw the mirror of her own joy.

"It worked," Brensa breathed, "and it did not hurt."

"Yes, my love," he answered. It was the only time he would ever use an endearment. It was not his way. He always used his eyes to show her his feelings. And she could read those as no other could. That was as it should be.

105: DESTINY FULFILLED

Klast woke early into the night, as was his habit, unable to sleep. He eased himself from the bed, taking care not to wake Brensa, and moved to the rocker beside it. He watched her soft breathing, still amazed that they would find themselves together. As his gaze lingered over her sleeping form, he sent his mind back and searched it for memories of his own mother. The only one he could dredge up was the sound of a soft, slightly husky voice, crooning the same lullaby that had come to him unbidden when he had needed to comfort Brensa in the cave and again when she had been near death from the fever. He had a vague idea that his mother had dark hair but could not be sure it was a real memory. He did recall people telling him, as a child, that he resembled his mother. Yet he could never reconcile the hard-bitten soldier that looked back at him from a still pool or a polished silver disc with such an image.

Brensa had asked him about his parents, and he had explained to her that he had stopped trying to think of them many years ago. It seemed a useless, even harmful exercise that brought only pain. It always carried with it a self-loathing from his belief that he had been somehow responsible for his father's death, that he had not done enough to save him.

Brensa had done her best to convince him that the best parts of him had come from those years, that as a child, he could have done nothing to save his father. She had even suggested that his choice of occupation might have been a way of punishing himself. He had rejected that idea at the time. Now he felt moved to look at it again and wondered if she might be at least partly right.

Thinking about their new life that lay ahead, he sensed that he needed to remember the things he had spent so much effort trying to forget. The lullaby played in his mind, and he allowed it to repeat softly on his breath, making sure it did not waken Brensa. A new sensation of peace settled over him, stronger with each line, as he let himself remember the voice that had soothed him with it, so many years ago.

He watched Brensa's breathing deepen. She seemed to relax as though she could hear, though she showed no sign of waking. The room still held the heat from their fire and she had pushed the blanket off, so he could see the slow rise and fall of her chest, in rhythm with her breathing. She was so small, yet so strong. His throat tightened at the thought of her courage last evening.

After some moments, a bright spot of light appeared and seemed to grow from inside Brensa's belly just below her navel. He sensed it spread, and two filaments, as fine a spider silk, reach out, one connecting to Brensa's heart and one stretching to touch his own. Klast held himself stock still, hardly daring to breathe. Soon the glow took the form of the tiny figure of a child, all of light. He could see her clearly, in spite of her diminutive size. Her eyes found his. She smiled at him, and sent him a deep look, filled with understanding and love. In his head, Klast clearly heard the tiny being say, "I am Liannis." For a long moment they hung suspended in time. Then the vision faded, and the room was, once again, shadowed only in moonlight.

Brensa stirred and found him watching, still rapt with wonder. She waited until he became aware of her, and asked softly, "Klast, what is it?"

He met her eyes, awe still written on his face. "Our daughter just greeted us. She will be a powerful seer. She told me her name. It is Liannis." He reached over and pulled her onto his lap. "Brensa, she showed herself to me. She knows she has been brought forth with love. She told me it will be well." And he heard the truth in his own words.

*   *   *

Half a day's ride away, Liethis woke from a dreamless sleep, and understood. Earth had regained Her Balance. Destiny had been fulfilled and the old cycle completed. A new cycle had begun.

EPILOGUE

Eleven-year-old Liannis sat on the sod roof of her parents' cottage in her nightshift, stroking No-tail's soft fur and gazing into the night sky. She loved to sit here to think but chose to do so only after she was sure her parents slept soundly below. They did not approve, fearing she might fall off and be injured. Liannis knew better. At times like this, No-tail usually followed her and took advantage of a warm nest in the hammock made by her skirt as Liannis sat cross-legged.

As a small child, Liannis had spent many happy days at court playing with Lionn and Borless, but as she grew older, the press of her growing sight made it harder and harder to be among so many people. Like Liethis, the sendings she received began to overwhelm her. At first, Gaelen and Marja had been reluctant to have their son and heir come to the cottage, fearing for Lionn's safety away from the guards. But Liannis knew he would be come to no harm. She told them, with full confidence, that nothing would happen to him as long as he was with her.

Liethis had convinced Gaelen and Marja that Liannis had true sight. So Gaelen had relented. From that time on, the two boys had visited with her often, under the watchful eyes of Klast and Brensa. They had occasionally accompanied her in her night vigils.

Liannis had not returned to court again. It caused her too much pain.

Tonight, Liannis kept her vigil alone. She considered what her future would hold. When she reached her twelfth birthday, she understood she would start spending the winter months with Liethis, as her apprentice. Liethis had already told her parents that Liannis would grow into a much more powerful seer than she was. But the girl needed other skills that would help her use her gift to its full potential; how to dampen the press of sendings that would drive her mad if she could not, how to deal with persons of influence diplomatically and how to handle unwelcome questions from those whose problems were too small for Earth to bother with.

Liannis did not look forward to leaving her peaceful home, but she understood its necessity. At least the summers would still be spent here. She smiled, as she sensed her father reach for her mother and lay his sleeping arm across her waist. Earth had given her very special parents. She knew they would never have another child. Seers were always only daughters. Earth never burdened a seer with siblings. Seers matured too quickly and felt the emotions of those around them too keenly to thrive in larger families. They needed a serene environment in which their gift could grow without constraint.

She dreamily pulled a blade of grass from the sod to chew. As she put it between her lips, her eyes beheld a streak of blue light falling to Earth from between the stars. A sending. Liannis sensed this clearly. But what kind of sending, a good one or a bad one? And this one had not come from Earth, but from the sky. She wondered about that for a moment. Then, with a maturity that belied her age, she understood she would learn the answer when Earth chose to show her. Gently removing the little cat from her lap, she climbed down and returned to her bed.

GLOSSARY:

Span; period of approximately an hour

Eightday; just as it sounds, eight days, meant to replace our week

Join; marry or wed

Demesne; a region ruled by a lord

Stook; a pyramid shape made by stacking sheaves of wheat, grain end up, against each other as part of the harvesting process

Balance; a state of equilibrium sought by Earth, as goddess, and the people; always in flux due to the symbiosis between Earth and people and actions of people; results in peace and prosperity when temporarily achieved

LaVergne, TN USA
04 October 2009
159835LV00002B/92/P